The Postmistress

Sarah Blake

VIKING
an imprint of
PENGUIN BOOKS

VIKING

Published by the Penguin Group
Penguin Books Ltd, 80 Strand, London WC2R ORL, England
Penguin Group (USA) Inc., 375 Hudson Street, New York, New York 10014, USA
Penguin Group (Canada), 90 Eglinton Avenue East, Suite 700, Toronto, Ontario, Canada M4P 2Y3
(a division of Pearson Penguin Canada Inc.)
Penguin Ireland, 25 St Stephen's Green, Dublin 2, Ireland (a division of Penguin Books Ltd)
Penguin Group (Australia), 250 Camberwell Road,
Camberwell, Victoria 3124, Australia (a division of Pearson Australia Group Pty Ltd)
Penguin Books India Pvt Ltd, 11 Community Centre,
Panchsheel Park, New Delhi – 110 017, India
Penguin Group (NZ), 67 Apollo Drive, Rosedale, North Shore 0632, New Zealand
(a division of Pearson New Zealand Ltd)
Penguin Books (South Africa) (Pty) Ltd, 24 Sturdee Avenue,
Rosebank, Johannesburg 2196, South Africa

Penguin Books Ltd, Registered Offices: 80 Strand, London WC2R ORL, England

www.penguin.com

First published in the United States of America by Amy Einhorn Books, a member of Penguin Group Inc. (USA) 2010
First published in Great Britain by Viking 2010

001

Copyright © Sarah Blake, 2010

The moral right of the author has been asserted

This is a work of fiction. Names, characters, places and incidents are
either the product of the author's imagination or are used fictitiously, and any
resemblance to actual persons, living or dead, or to actual events or locales is entirely coincidental.

While the author has made every effort to provide accurate telephone numbers and internet addresses
at the time of publication, neither the publisher nor the author assumes any responsibility for errors
or for changes that occur after publication. Further, the publisher does not have any control
over and does not assume any responsibility for author or third-party websites or their content.

Printed in Great Britain by Clays Ltd, St Ives plc

A CIP catalogue record for this book is available from the British Library

ISBN: 978-0-670-92347-2

www.greenpenguin.co.uk

MIX
Paper from
responsible sources
FSC® C018179

Penguin Books is committed to a sustainable
future for our business, our readers and our planet.
This book is made from Forest Stewardship
Council™ certified paper.

ALWAYS LEARNING   **PEARSON**

For Josh, always

War happens to people, one by one. That is really all I have to say, and it seems to me I have been saying it forever.

—MARTHA GELLHORN, *The Face of War*

The Postmistress

T HERE WERE YEARS after it happened, after I'd returned from the town and come back here to the busy blank of the city, when some comment would be tossed off about the Second World War and how it had gone—some idiotic remark about clarity and purpose—and I'd resist the urge to stub out my cigarette and bring the dinner party to a satisfying halt. But these days so many wars are being carried on in full view of all of us, and there is so much talk of pattern and intent (as if a war can be conducted like music), well, last night I couldn't help myself.

"What would you think of a postmistress who chose not to deliver the mail?" I asked.

"Don't tell me any more," a woman from the far end of the table cried in delight, shining and laughing between the candles. "I'm hooked already."

I watched the question take hold. Mail, actual letters written by hand, being pocketed undelivered. What a lark! Anything might happen. Marriages might founder. Or not take place! Candlelight glanced off the silverware into eyes widening with the thought of such a trick. Around the table the possibilities unfurled. A man might escape the bill collector's note. The letter assuring a young man of his first job might never arrive, forcing him to look elsewhere.

"And be perfectly happy," suggested one of the older men, smiling at the irony of it.

"And would she tell anyone about it?"

"Oh no," the woman across from me decided quickly. "That would spoil the pleasure."

"Oh, so she did it for pleasure?" Her companion gave her bare shoulder a little tap.

"No. Pleasure is too small a theme," the host pronounced. "She must be a believer of some sort. A scientist of a kind. Someone who planned to watch the machinery grind down. A saboteur." He smiled across the candles at his wife. "It's a great story."

"In fact," I put in drily, "she wasn't any of those things."

Then came the quiet.

"Hold on," said one of the men. "This is true?"

"Perfectly true."

"Then it's monstrous," the first woman piped up. "If it's real, then it's horrible, and—"

"Illegal," the host reached over and filled her glass. "When was this?"

"Nineteen forty-one."

"*Then?*" Now the host was shocked. I nodded. Somehow this had deepened the question. These days, errancy cannot go long undetected. Someone can pick up the phone and call. There are e-mails and faxes. But *then*. When a letter was often the sole carrier of news. The thought of a postmaster tampering with one's letters home, or out to the boys. It wasn't at all in keeping with our idea of the times.

"It's the war story I never filed."

"Because it would have been too much for us?" The host tried to laugh it off.

"It was too much for me," I answered.

The lark had ended. The host rose abruptly to uncork another bottle. The woman down at the other end of the table studied me, still unconvinced that I could be telling her the truth. Writers. They are not to be trusted with our hearts.

Never mind, I thought. I am old. And tired of the terrible clarity of the young. And all of you are young these days.

Long ago, I believed that, given a choice, people would turn to good as they would to the light. I believed that reporting—honest, unflinching pictures of the truth—could be a beacon to lead us to demand that wrongs be righted, injustices punished, and the weak and the innocent cared for. I must have believed, when I started out, that the shoulder of public opinion could be put up against the door of public indifference and would, when given the proper direction, shove it wide with the power of wanting to stand on the side of angels.

But I have covered far too many wars—reporting how they were seeded, nourished, and let sprout—to believe in angels anymore, or, for that matter, in a single beam of truth to shine into the dark. Every story—love or war—is a story about looking left when we should have been looking right.

Or so it seems to me.

Here is the war story I never filed. I began it at the end of the forties, when I could see quite clearly, and charged myself with getting it right, getting it sharper, all this while. What I knew at the time is pieced together here with the parts I couldn't have known, but imagine to be true.

And the girl I was—Frankie Bard, radio gal—lives on these pages as someone I knew, once.

—*Frances Bard, Washington, D.C.*

Fall

1940

IT BEGAN, as it often does, with a woman putting her ducks in a row. It had occurred to Iris a few weeks back—at the height of summer when tourists jammed the post office with their oiled bodies and their scattered, childish vacation glee—that if what she thought were going to happen was going to, she ought to be prepared. She ought, really oughtn't she, to be ready to show Harry that though she was forty, as old as the century, he would be the first. The very first. And she had always put more stock in words set down on a clean white piece of paper than any sort of talk. Talk was—

"Right," said the doctor, turning away to wash his hands.

Iris supposed she was meant to get up and get dressed while his back was turned, but she had not had the foresight to wear a skirt, thinking instead that her blue dress was the thing for this appointment, and no matter how thorough a man Dr. Broad was, he'd have turned around from the sink long before she'd gotten it over her head, and then where would they be? The leather banquette on which she lay was comfortably firm and smelled like the chairs in the reading room at the public library. No, she would stay put. She slid her gaze from the ceiling over to the little sink at which the doctor stood, rubbing his hands beneath the gurgle. He was certainly thorough. Well, there must be all sorts of muck down there anyone would want to wash their hands of. And as the next step was the certificate, she'd be the first to insist that nothing chancy landed on that page by accident.

He straightened, turned off the taps, and flicked his fingers against the back basin before taking up the towel beside him. "Are you decent, Miss James?" He directed the question to the wall in front of him.

"Not in the least."

"Right," he said again, "I'll see you in my office."

"For the certificate."

Nearly to the door, he paused with his hand outstretched, glancing down at her. She gave him her post office smile, the one she used behind her window, meant to invite cooperation.

"Yes," he said, and he grasped hold of the handle, pushing it smartly down and pulling open the door. She waited until she heard the latch click softly after him before she rose, holding one hand to the loosened pins in her hair and the other around her front. She felt a bit as she did in the mornings, unbound by bra or girdle, herself come loose. All fine in the security of her own bedroom, but here she was in the middle of Boston, in one of the discreet buildings fronting the Public Gardens, after lunch on a Thursday in September. On the other side of the door, the steady rhythm of a typewriter clattered through the quiet. The tiles were cool under her feet and she reached first for her underthings, leaning against the banquette as she drew one stocking on, then the next, snapping the garters firmly. Hanging from the back of the chair, the cups of her brassiere pointed straight out into the room—like headlights. She smiled, pulling the bra on, and for the third time that afternoon, she thought of Harry Vale.

A single rap at the door. "I'm ready when you are, Miss James."

"I'll be right in," she called back.

Everything had been genial. Everything had been perfectly nice. The doctor's office was the sort to glory in—thick green curtains pulled back from high windows, just skimming a rich gray carpet. The secretary in the outer nook, typing away. The hush of order as she had taken Iris's coat and slipped it onto the wooden hanger. And the doctor, just right, too. How he'd opened the door and held out his warm hand to her, half as greeting, half as a hand up from where she sat waiting. And he'd led her through into his office, signaling the chair in front of his great oak desk as he continued around it to his own position. He'd even pressed his fingertips together under his chin, his serious eyes upon her as she placed her pocketbook upon her lap. They'd spoken briefly of Mrs. Alsop, exchanging pleasantries about the woman from whom Miss James had acquired Dr. Broad's name, just as if they'd all been acquaintances bumped into in the lobby of a traveler's hotel. The doctor had listened and smiled, asking Iris if she got to Boston often.

It had all cracked slightly, with her request. Not audibly, but noticeably enough for Iris to recognize that the doctor was going to need some prodding: that the capacious room notwithstanding, Dr. Broad lacked imagination. He was happy to examine her, he told her, leaning back in his chair. But why the piece of paper?

"I would have thought every man might like to have such a thing?" she suggested.

Dr. Broad cleared his throat.

"Perhaps that's a bit familiar of me," she concluded aloud, watching the man across the desk from her inch his hands along the arms of his chair, making as if to rise.

"Why don't we begin?" He smiled and did rise, bringing the interview to a halt.

So she had not had a chance to answer the question fully. And opening the door between the examining room and his office, she could see, by the studied lifting of his head from what occupied him at his desk, that she'd not be given another chance. He was very busy. She was just one of many women he tended to.

"Please," he said, "have a seat."

"Everything's in order?"

"You're perfect," he answered.

"Good."

His eyes remaining on the paper before him, he took it up and handed it across the desktop to her. "Will that do?"

She reached and took the page in her hand and looked down.

This is to certify that
Miss Iris James
was examined on 21 September 1940
and found to be
Intact.

She had been right. There'd been no skimping on the paper. Dr. Broad's stationery was beautifully creamy, nearly linen. And though he'd obviously had little enthusiasm for the project, he'd written it all out wonderfully. She thought he might have won a handwriting prize in school.

"It's perfect," she smiled up at him. "Thank you."

"Glad to help," he said, and graciously stood behind his desk as she rose and moved to the door.

For several moments he remained standing, listening to her there on the other side of the door, asking for her coat from Miss Prentiss, and then for the quickest bus route from here to South Station. Their voices were light and agreeable, the lilt and tone of which he usually managed to ignore while working inside. Then the outer door opened and shut, and, after a pause, Miss Prentiss resumed her typing. He walked over to one of the two windows facing down into the Public Gardens.

He almost missed her. She had emerged so quickly from his building that she was across the street and around the corner pillars of the Gardens, walking swiftly away from him up the outer walk. She carried herself like someone under review, shoulders thrown back, her head pulled up. "What a queer character," he mused. He followed her the fifty-odd feet she remained in sight, until eventually she was swallowed up by the city and the distance. He turned back around to his desk. "I thought every man should want such a thing," she had said right there.

AND BOMBS WERE FALLING on Coventry, London, and Kent. Sleek metal pellets shaped like the blunt-tipped ends of pencils aimed down upon hedgerow and thatch. What was a hedgerow? Where was Coventry? In History and Geography, Hitler's army marched upon the school maps of Europe, while next door in English, the voices recited from singsong memory—*I will arise and go now, and go to Innisfree, And a small cabin build there, of clay and wattles made.* Bombers flew above the wattles, over an England filled with the songs of linnets and thrush. There were things being broken we had no American names for. There was war. What did it mean, War? Stretched out upon the pages of *Life*, the children of Coventry stared up into an inquisitive camera. We could see them. They looked unafraid there in the ditch dug for safety. Their hands spread-eagled against the dirt walls for balance, the two girls still in skirts. There was a boy with no expression. He looked back at us straight, and the collar of his jacket was fastened by a safety pin. He was already there, in the war.

Where our boys were not going. The president had promised. He spoke bluntly, as if he were one of the people, but he wasn't, thank God. Nobody thought so. When he said the boys would not fight in foreign wars, we believed him, though we had listened to the names of the French towns falling the way people listen to the names of medicine before they are taken ill themselves.

Now the talk was of a German invasion. Would England stand? Their tanks and trucks, their guns, hulked useless on the other side of the Channel where they'd left them at Dunkirk. But when we were told the Brits had dragged cannons out of the British Museum, wheeling them down to the Thames, we nodded. Bombs had crashed down on London now for sixteen nights. Buses were stopped in the street. Babies hurled from their beds, we were told. Still, in the morning, one by one, Londoners crept back out into the light and we cheered them. England would stand. Nobody knew the ending. Buchenwald was as yet only a town in Germany, where sunlight splattered the trees. Auschwitz. Bergen-Belsen. Simply foreign names. It was the end of summer and the lights were still on.

IN SOUTH STATION, Iris made her way toward the train for Buzzard's Bay, amusing herself by watching the transfer of mailbags into the freight cars at the back. It happened rarely that she traveled with the mail, but it gave her exquisite pleasure to take a seat in the foremost car, the very front seat if she could manage it. All these letters, all these words scratched out one to the other, spinning their way toward someone. Someone waiting. Someone writing. That was the point of it all, keeping the pure chutes clear, so that anybody's letter—finding its way to the post office, into the canvas sacks, the many-hued envelopes jostling and nestling, shuffling with all the others—could journey forward, joining all the other paper thoughts sent out minute by minute to vanquish—

Time.

The stationmaster announced the departure of the Buffalo Express and she gazed up at the clock and watched the hand stitch one second to the next. In another minute her train would be called, and she'd join the crowd boarding, pulled back into the shape of her name and of her person. She'd be Iris James, again. Postmaster of Franklin, Massachusetts.

Where Harry was. And the new place in her chest that seemed to have been made by him—that flipped and moved when she caught sight of him on the street, or in line behind others at the post office—bounded. A year ago, he'd just been Harry Vale, the town mechanic, nice enough, good for a spare tire and a chat. And then, one day, he wasn't. He was something else. For he had walked into Alden's Market not too long ago and come slowly up behind her so that when she turned around, a can of creamed corn in one hand and plain in the other, there was nothing to do but raise them both to him, offering a choice. He looked at her and then down at the cans, seeming to consider the two very carefully. Finally, he put his thick hand out and pointed to the plain. She nodded. He'd have to tip his head up to kiss her, Iris found herself thinking.

She'd never imagined it would come to her, but here it was—Harry Vale had looked at her with the look that signaled something's on. And he had done it in plain sight. Never mind Beth Alden watching at the counter. Never mind the heat bolting from the canned goods at the back of the store. She patted her pocketbook. Was it odd what she had done? Well, so what if it was. What she had said to the doctor was God's own truth—any man would want to know he was the first, she was sure of it—and she could give Harry the paper, beautiful and clean as a white dress at the end of an aisle, which she was too old for, and anyway white was her least becoming color.

At Nauset, Iris descended the Boston train and walked the four blocks through the central town on the Cape to find the bus out to Franklin. Mr. Flores sat in the shade cast by the bus and pushed himself up onto his feet, ambling forward. She had reapplied her lipstick and combed her hair as the train had pulled into the station, which was a good thing because he was staring.

"Hello, Miss James. Good trip down?"

"Yes, thanks." She looked him straight back in the eyes, daring him to ask her anything more.

He nodded and pointed her toward the bus's open door. Iris pulled herself up the three short stairs and into the bus. There was a foreign couple, a couple of stray women sitting alone, and an assortment of men clustered around Flores's seat at the front of the bus. Iris nodded and made her way toward the back, past a young woman with her head in a thick book, the curve of her neck laid bare as her hair swept forward.

She did not look up, and she didn't stir as Iris passed her by to find a seat three rows back.

Iris reached into her skirt pocket for her cigarettes, shook out a Lucky, and considered the head and shoulders of the little child-woman reading in front of her. A runaway, thought the postmaster, though she was quite well dressed in a sensible blue suit, her brown hair cut short and feathering along the straight edge of her collar. In any case, she was the sort who needed tending, the small-breasted women who tip their faces up to men, smiling delightedly as babies. At last the little creature turned slightly, as if to meet Iris's gaze, aware of her attention, and gave a noncommittal smile—a mechanical response like a hand put out to ward off the sun. Iris nodded, companionably, exhaling smoke. It's all right— she addressed the woman's back, now turned away again—I won't bite. The bus bounced a little as Mr. Flores climbed up behind the wheel and swung himself into his seat, and the engine roared to life, shaking the floor under Iris's feet.

VRONSKY WAS *making love to Anna.*

Emma read the sentence again, distracted by the pillar of a woman behind her. Did Tolstoy really mean making love? She couldn't think so. Having sex? It would be so bald written on the page like that. Surely they can't have been making love here and there like this in the nineteenth century. It must refer to something else, something more benign. She flushed, a little guiltily. Not that having sex wasn't benign—of course it was, it led to babies, after all. Though the things that she and Will had begun to do in the dark had nothing whatsoever to do with babies. But Anna and Vronsky? They had been constrained, wasn't that the idea? Perhaps it was the translation. She flipped to the cover of the book and read the name beneath Tolstoy's—Constance Garnett. Emma thought she understood. Vronsky had whispered something loving to Anna, or soothed Anna lovingly, or something like that, and

Miss Garnett had used other words instead, painting what ought to be a pink scene—scarlet. Probably a spinster; the pathetic type who reads passion into the twist of a shut umbrella. Like that woman in the back of the bus.

She pushed her bottom back a bit against the seat on the bus so that she sat up straighter, the doctor's new wife in a very attractive travel suit with a matching scarf thrown around her shoulders. She stared out the window. Since she had said to Will Fitch two weeks ago—hurriedly, afraid to look up at him, Yes. Yes, I will. I do—something firm and satisfying and entirely new had entered into the frequent chaos of her mind. As though Edward R. Murrow's voice, that brave, impassioned masculine voice, full of its own urgency and volume, had laid down the track upon which she now hummed. Clarity ran upon that track, and purpose.

Pamet. Then Dillworth. Finally Drake. Closing her eyes, Emma recited the names of the towns she knew only through Will's letters, in which the geography of her new land was mapped by the various ailments of the people he treated. Heart disease. Bursitis. A pair of twins delivered in Drake, which was a miracle, wrote Will, given that the mother had neither the time nor the means to get off the Cape quick enough—

"Is your Bobby turning twenty, twenty-one?" The man's voice in front of her broke in.

"Twenty-one."

"They won't send 'em over there. Get them trained up, okay. Hell, have them build a few bridges! But they won't send 'em."

The second man didn't answer right away and stared out the window. Emma found herself watching the strict profile of his nose and chin as if for some sign. The trees flashed past. "Sure they will," he said, turning back to his companion.

It served her right. Emma sat back, annoyed at herself for listening in. She had heard it this morning and tried to forget it, had forgotten it in fact, but now here it was again. The draft had passed in Congress, and all men of serviceable age were to report to the draft boards that had sprung up in every town, little and large, like mushrooms after a rain. Not that it would matter to her, she protested to the slight reflection of her hands on her lap in the window. Will wouldn't go. He had said as much. (Though not definitively, she corrected, scrupulously honest even in her worry.) He shouldn't go, she amended. He certainly had cause to plead hardship. He was the last in line of the Fitches. He was the sole doctor for miles—and she had just married him.

Anyway, he couldn't leave her. There was a central fact to everyone's life, she thought, a fact from which all else stemmed. Hers was that she had been utterly alone in the world—until she met Will. She had lost her mother and father and brother in the epidemic in 1918. They had died in a fever dream, and she had lived; and now, it had been so long, they might have never lived at all. There was a house on a hill, far from the sea, where she had been born. And a town she remembered full of the flappings of flags, which she realized now was her memory of the tents they all lay in, out in the field, because the hospital was gorged with the sick. The memory she might have had of her mother was blotted out by a nurse's face, wrapped in a mask, bending over her in her cot, checking to see if she breathed.

Now it would start, this next part. The orphaned girl with the serious eyes and the mole at the base of her throat was now the doctor's wife, with a husband, a house, and a town. Marrying Will had pulled her through the dim gray curtain of unaccented time. The time spent in a shared room at the top of a boardinghouse, her stockings drying on the ladder-back chair. She was going home. She tried a smile in the window glass. Home. To Will.

Emma slid the Federal Writer's Project guidebook on Cape Cod out from her satchel, turning to its section on Franklin: *The bait at the end of the sandy hook sticking fifty-odd miles into the Atlantic, the town of Franklin*

waves slyly back at the shore. The first thing one loses there is a sense of direc-
tion. Ringed by the yellow-white sand dunes and water on all sides, North
and South seem to switch points on the compass, and the sky is no help. It is
a place swollen by fish and the smell of fish, of cod oil, of the broken spars of
whale bones and masts spat back from the sea onto the broad swath of beaches
behind the town. Pilgrims of one sort or another have always come: first the
Puritans, then the Portuguese whalers, and then at the turn of the last century
artists arrived, wrapping their scarves on the tops of old dories and painting
them; and policemen's daughters who have come down from Boston mixed
with the parti-colored crowds, saying wasn't it fun, wasn't it something how
the Mediterranean sons of fishermen walked arm and arm with the Yankee
gold while the bright lights of the summer theaters glow out into the dark—
Christ! She flipped the book shut and stuffed it back. It was as purple as
the Garnett.

Mr. Flores hunched low over the wheel, peering into the slanting
light, and Emma felt the road spinning her closer and closer in. The
stark white houses of Woodling passed one after another. Through the
Tralpee forest they went, the squat beechwood flinging away on either
side, until at last the bus reached the crest of the hill before Franklin.
And as the bus stuttered at the top in the beat before descending, she sat
up straight wishing—suddenly, unaccountably—that the line between
her and this town would snap. Mr. Flores's fist paused above the gear-
shift. The dunes spread wide around them.

For a brief instant, Emma felt they might fly. The sky through the
broad front window called. And she nearly stood up in her seat, imagining herself able to continue straight, the road falling away as the bus
rode forward into the illimitable air. But the gears caught, and the
bus shuddered down through the high hills of sand. Down they rode
until the tarmac pulled free of the dunes and curved toward the sea, jog-
ging alongside the gray harbor into town.

The bus churtled past the stark lines of the shingled roofs triangling into the September evening. The flag snapped in the wind above the steep pitch of the post office, and the bus slowed to a crawl as Mr. Flores negotiated the narrow street shared now with people walking, hallooing to the bus, on bicycles spinning alongside. The town unfolding outside the window, she put her hand out upon the seat in front of her, a flush rising in the hollow of her throat. She had prided herself on how quickly she would get the names of all the townspeople, showing off her knowledge to Will, whom she imagined would return every night as if to a theater of her making, delighting to find himself in his familiar town, revealed and illumined now by his Emma's perceptions. Emma meant to be an asset to him in this way. He would be the best doctor because his probes need not be blind.

But the flesh was a different matter. Arriving, as she had, straight into the center of the town, the slightness of her imagination struck her full force. For here they all were already. Two women in conversation on the corner broke off to stare as the bus pulled to its stop. The town was not waiting to start up with her arrival. The town was clearly already itself without her. The door swung open and she smelled the sea in the air. She sat still in her seat for a moment, collecting her gloves, marshaling the courage to find Will in the crowd, certain he was just there on the other side of the bus waiting with that impatient, exacting smile of his. The woman from the back of the bus brushed past, causing Emma to look up, and then she made out Will's head above the line of some others coming toward the bus, his long body tipped forward. One felt that he had much on his mind, and much to do. He had caught sight of her through the glass and he waved. She waved back and the scarf slipped off her shoulders as she bolted up now, she was that happy, and through the empty bus toward the door.

"Hiya." His head came around the open door and he was up the stairs just as she arrived at them and he reached for her and pulled her directly into his arms. She raised her mouth to his and the warm familiar lips pressed hers, softly at first and then more deeply as he gathered her even closer so she could feel the whole hard length of him against her skirt. Though they were right out in public, she closed her eyes and moved into the grotto of their kiss where it was dark and cool, her lips opening under his, and then with a happy moan she pulled herself away from his lips, back out into the light.

"Hiya." She smiled up at him breathless, a little prick of pride rising at the sight of him right there before her. How *had* she managed it? She had sat beside him in restaurants, on buses, walked next to him on the streets of Cambridge, the familiar length of his stride a comfort, almost like knowledge. They knew each other this way. He had shepherded her around, his arm under hers, his hand at the small of her back propelling her into smoky rooms, and back out again. They had talked and laughed. They had even quarreled. And then, suddenly one afternoon in the spring, he had asked her to marry him. It was crazy, mad—but that was part of the story, wasn't it?—Dr. Lowenstein had written to take him into the practice and he had stuffed the telegram in his pocket and gone down on his knees right there in the Back Bay post office. And she looked down at him and began nodding before he had opened his mouth. They had arrived at the pact like children. It was the next step, the only step, the serious one. As if, joining hands, they had closed their eyes and jumped, without even holding their breath.

He leaned down to read the title of the book in her hand, still holding tight to her as he did. Her scarf had slipped off her shoulders and the long triangle of her bare skin gave off a bright heat like summer grass. "Like it?" he asked.

"Could they have been making love in the nineteenth century?" She pulled her gaze away, offering up the last thing, least important, that had rested on the shelf of her mind.

"I don't see how we'd all have gotten here if they hadn't."

"No, no. Look." She opened the book right there on the top step of the bus and rippled through the pages, sharply aware of his eyes on her shoulders and arms. They had kissed. They had touched each other through layers of silk and wool. Through jackets and trousers and blouses and skirts, but his eyes might as well have been hands now, her skin prickling and flushing as he put his foot on the stair next to hers and his jacket slid open. "There," she pointed.

He looked down and read, *"Vronksy was making love—"*

"It's so naked," she said and then blushed, "to say it like that."

He pressed against her. "Like what?"

"On the page. Wouldn't the readers have been shocked? I am."

"You are not," he whispered.

"I am," she giggled, leaning her shoulder into his. "I really am. A modern reader."

"It meant something else. Everyone understood."

"Sex?"

"Courting," he answered, his smile lighting up the impossible inches between them.

"Oh," she sighed happily. "Well, you would know."

"Come on," he put his hand under her elbow to draw her down the stairs. "Let's go home."

Through the open door, a suitcase sailed off the busman's hook, flying for a moment in the air until it crashed down and split, cracking open upon the sidewalk neat as a tapped egg.

"Oh!" cried Emma.

Will stopped where he was at the door of the bus, staring down at the voluptuous explosion of what must be Em's underthings cascading over the popped sides of the case. They were numerous, silky, and a twilit blue, tossed and flung in a delirious striptease, showing themselves like sirens. He squeezed Emma's hand tucked in his behind his back.

"No one saw," he said to her. "I'll step around and help Flores. That'll give you a minute."

Emma nodded, letting go of his hand, and slipped off the last of the bus stairs onto the pavement. She had to fight the urge to fling herself onto the smashed case and cover the strewn clothing with her body, but that woman from the bus was leaning against the railing on the pavement, watching.

"Shall I help you pick up?" she asked.

To her own surprise, Emma found herself nodding. The two of them kneeled down without another word to gather the stockings, the soft bras, and the slight blue panties from the ground. The woman was so quiet and so careful with Emma's things that the bride's throat closed over with tears.

"It's only clothing," the other woman said quietly. "It doesn't mean anything."

"I know," Emma whispered back.

"Then don't let him see you cry. He'll think you are ashamed."

Emma's hand hovered over a nightie and she flushed up. What did this woman know about Will or about what he would think? She tossed the thing into her case.

"I'm not ashamed in the slightest."

Iris heard the warning in the girl's voice and glanced across the suitcase at her. "Fine," she answered. And then, as an afterthought, she added, "I'm Iris James."

Emma looked into the woman's square but not unpleasant face framed by dark red hair pulled back on either side like curtains. "Hello," she answered.

"And who might you be?"

Emma threw the last of the things in the suitcase and closed the lid. "Emma Trask," she answered, and then blushed—"I mean, Fitch."

"Nuts," said Iris with a disarming smile. "The doctor's bride. And here I had pegged you as a runaway."

It was the first time Emma had laughed in days. And she would always remember that bubble of her laughter overtaking her there on the sidewalk at Miss James's feet, her things disarranged, the green slant of the trees behind Miss James's head, and the evening sun warm on her own back. Will came around from the side of the bus and reached out his hands to pull her up to him. It would all be all right, she decided there and then. And she had laughed out loud again, falling into the circle of Will's arm.

"Thank you," he smiled down at Iris. "You've been a great help."

"You're very welcome, Dr. Fitch," Iris answered.

"Let's go home," he said to Emma.

"All right." She smiled. And he grabbed her suitcase with his free hand, never letting her loose from his side. Several paces away, Emma turned her head in the crook of Will's arm and saw Miss James waiting out the stream of cars before slipping in and crossing the road.

"Who's that?"

"Postmaster James." He wanted to kiss Emma right there again on the street, but picked up his pace instead.

"Hey," she protested, laughing, but she skipped along beside him, not taking in anything at all of her new town except the dank smell of the sea, and the heavy air, and the *thunk thunk* of the waves against the seawall to her left. Straight through the thick of town and out toward the older, quieter part where the steep-angled houses softened as the afternoon wore down. Anyone watching—and everyone was, Emma knew it, it was a small town, after all, and she had to be the topic of most dinner tables, why not? she was young and fairly attractive and he was their doctor!—anyone watching would probably notice how easily the two fell into step as if they'd been walking together for years already. Anyone would have commented on that, and the lamps lighting up inside the houses they passed seemed to Emma a silent strain, like a low murmur beneath the chat, of approval and attention. She straightened herself a little in reply.

Perhaps this was why, when Will reached slightly ahead of her and pushed open a gate, looking down proudly, she hesitated. Here she was, at last. She glanced up at the house, which looked just like all the others along the way—steep-angled roofs and grayed shingles, a wide front porch and a door the color of the shingles, unpainted. They walked slowly toward it, and when they reached the porch steps, Will put his hand under Emma's elbow. Someone was speaking inside the house, a woman, and as Emma rose up the steps toward the screen door, the urgency in the voice drew her in, as though the house were talking. "For Christ's sake," Will muttered as he pulled open the door. "I left the radio on."

She walked toward the voice. Down the hall she could see through to the kitchen where Will had put beach roses in a jam jar against the window to welcome her. The evening sun splintered through the water and the flowers hung there like pink stars. *At the back of the pub, there's a scoreboard*, the woman on the radio said. *And tonight, it reads RAF 30, Luftwaffe 20. Although it has been a bad night for the British, it's been worse*—she paused—*for the people of Berlin. RAF 30, Luftwaffe 20. There it stands, the score that London keeps each night the Battle con*—

Will reached to turn it off. "No"—Emma pushed gently against his hand—"no, who is that?"

"Who is what?" She was tinier than he remembered—he could wrap his arms around her and nearly hug himself, too—and he pulled her in to him and felt her heart just there against him, waiting. That was how it felt just then. Embedded in that whole sweet length—breasts and small belly and hips—her heart waited against his as they pressed together in the sweetening dark, listening to the woman carrying the war toward them, so urgently Will couldn't stand it, he couldn't stand there waiting anymore, and just as the woman on the radio slowed to say "*This is London, Good ni*—," he did, at last, snap it off.

"OH, FOR CHRIST'S SAKE." Frankie Bard leaned back against the chair in the broadcast studio and closed her eyes. "That came off too high, didn't it?"

Murrow was silent. She opened her eyes.

"Too high and too fast." She grimaced, agreeing with what he hadn't said.

"You'll get it." He stood up and reached for his hat. "Your type always does—"

She looked up in time to catch the grin. "My type?"

He leaned toward the studio door. "Mix a martini neat as she can shoot a bear—isn't that right?"

"That's right." Frankie stood. "But New York won't like it."

He jerked open the studio door. "Hell with New York. You did fine."

But New York wouldn't like it one bit. They'd had this same trouble with Betty Wason, in Norway. The door swung slowly closed behind him. A woman's voice ought not to be telling America about men fighting. It was too high, too thin. It got too excited. For Christ's *sake*. Frankie bent and flicked off the microphone. Mr. Paley's right-hand man refused even to hire women in the CBS top office as secretaries. Hospital junkets, daily life, that sort of thing—the kinds of thing you might hear in the shops—but *for God's sake* women shouldn't be reporting the war. Men were over there dying in the skies above London. She pushed the pages of her script together into a neat pile, switched off the light in the studio, and reached for the door. Women really ought to marry and settle down and have babies. Women ought not to walk bareheaded under the German bombs looking for vivid word pictures to paint for the people back home.

So there, she chuckled, and rounded the third set of stairs, climbing her way back up from the underground studio to the street level. She pushed open the heavy back door of Broadcasting House into the blacked-out city waiting for the night's sirens.

When the bombs started at teatime on the seventh of September, there had been nothing to distinguish that moment as the beginning—there was no way to know what was coming, or why or for how long. War dropped down and settled. Four hundred people died in the first minute of the Blitz. Fourteen hundred were left blown up and bleeding that first night, and now seventeen nights later there was no way to know who was still alive—every night new numbers, and you don't say, Murrow instructed Frankie, "the streets are rivers of blood. Say that the little policeman you usually say hello to every morning is not there today."

The new moon had risen over the smoking rooftops, and for a moment one could remember the sky without the bombers and the bright rocketing lines of antiaircraft fire over the chimney pots and the distant medieval spires of Westminster Abbey.

She walked briskly along the shuttered house fronts noting with a reporter's eye tiny slits of light escaping from some of them. Beyond prayer, beyond chance, for some people lay the simple reward of staying put. Come what may. The moon glinted on the chrome bumpers of the taxis. From the big public shelter along the north side of the street she heard someone singing "Body and Soul," and the man's voice in the gray quiet of the moonlit street made it all human. Frankie smiled. War weather.

There was a pattern to the night attacks, the high uneven drone of the Luftwaffe planes rising like a deadly song to a crescendo around midnight. The searchlight shot straight up into the blackness where, singly or in pairs, the German planes flew like shuttlecocks up and back down the river—a relentless rhythm. The incendiaries dropped first, firebombing the darkened city, forcing it alight and ablaze, cutting open a pathway for the others to follow. Those came down screaming, or whistling, the heaviest ones roaring like an express train through a tunnel. Worst of all were the parachute bombs that floated gently, silently down to kill. Frankie turned off Oxford Circus onto the Wilmot Road and began the walk home. Two fire trucks streamed through the emptied streets, racing with their shrouded headlights like blind sirens to the fires. There was heaven, there were the shelters underground, and then here on the street—between the gunners and the gunned—was Middle Earth. In Middle Earth at night, everything was turned upside down in a brilliant kaleidoscope of dizzy bright death set against the black silhouette of London.

A month ago, before the bombs had begun in earnest, Murrow had pulled off a broadcast from five points around London, bringing home the sounds of the bombarded city at night. Frankie had stood with him, watching him poised at the mouth of the bomb shelter down in the crypt of St. Martin's-in-the-Fields, moving the microphone cable out of the way of the Londoners as they descended, a courteous escort underground. There had been no way to know whether the Germans would bomb that night, but Murrow concentrated on the steady beat of the people walking in the dark, walking home or down into the shelter, their footsteps sounding like ghosts shod with steel shoes, he said. And when the air raid started, the long swooning climb up the octave in the sky, Murrow's tense, excited voice narrated the incoming drone of the Luftwaffe, here they come, you can hear them now, and Frankie had felt untouchable then, immortal, holding the microphone up to the night. Here and now. Do you hear this? She wanted to add her voice to Murrow's, wanted her voice to find the ear of the listeners on the other end of the cable. In that moment, through the air, the Germans plowed straight into an American living room and Frankie was holding the curtain back so they could hear it better, and it was a dare. I dare you, she thought now, to look away.

2.

A ND WHERE WERE WE LOOKING? Over there. As September passed into October and the bombs worsened, the children of London had been put on buses and trains, and thousands more on ships across the Atlantic. The songs that broke your heart warbled on the airwaves before and after the nighttime news.

> *My sister and I recall the day*
> *We left our friends and we sailed away*
> *And we think of the ones who had to stay—*
> *But we don't talk about that*

We listened to Murrow and Shirer and Sevareid. *This is London*, Murrow paused before launching into last night's broadcast. *"Tonight, having been thrown against the wall by blasts—which feels like nothing so much as being hit with a feather-covered board—and having lost our third office— which looks like some crazy giant had been operating an eggbeater in its interior—I naturally conclude that the bombing has been heavy."*

Frankie smiled remembering his grin, the weird exhilaration of danger seen and passed by. Not all of them had Murrow's calm. Though he had covered the fall of France and was no stranger to the war, after three months of the Blitz, Eric Sevareid was heading back to the States. Trying to walk to Broadcasting House to make the night's broadcast, he'd whispered, "I can't stand it—when the shrieking starts no matter how sternly I lecture myself, I do the last fifty yards at a dead run."

"Come on then." A man ahead of Frankie on the street leaned against the high brick wall behind him, pulling his girl into his lips.

Easy and laughing, the girl wrapped her arms around the man's neck and pressed herself on him *as though they had all the time in the world and were completely alone*, Frankie began to write in her head. The light was going in the autumn afternoon and the twilight sounds, the endings, lowered all around her in the dark and chill. Across the street in the tiny public garden, a child roared in outrage, "That's mine, Charlie!" *It is regular life with the lid pried off*—she turned down the street—*and the lid in peacetime is the kettle on to boil, nothing ahead but bedtime, children in their bath, and the supper dishes on the lip of the sink for later.*

She crossed the High Street, heading toward Argyll Road. *It is evening in the upstairs world, the hour before the time to go underground, the last hour of light. Though it is a chilly October evening, everyone is out in it. Good night. Good night, God bless. The bells no longer ring in the churches.* Fifty nights into the bombing, the Germans could be counted on to come, and—though this would never get by the censor—the truth was, the regularity of the bombs, the consistent appearance of the Luftwaffe, was losing the Germans their battle. Because Londoners had realized they could go on. One could plan around the night. At the corner, Mr. Fainsley pulled in his cart and shuttered his plate-glass window—can't help it, the grocer had shrugged the night before—can't help closing up the way I always have, though they both knew the window and the shop might be gone in the morning. Can't help it, she'd heard over and over for the past six weeks with the same wry grin, can't help going on the way I always do.

One could stand on a corner and see a long row of untouched houses, their white fronts perfectly sharp against the autumn sky—all England in a block—then turn the next corner to find nothing but flat waste and fire, the exhausted faces of the women carrying cheap cardboard suitcases and handing their children up into the refugee buses waiting at the square. Each night of the Blitz, the war passed over London like the Old Testament angel, block by block: touching here, turning from there, and Frankie followed, wanting to get it down, wanting to get at the heart of it.

She rolled her eyes. *The heart of it* would have been redlined without a pause by Max Prescott, her editor at the *New York Trib*. It? What's *it*, Frankie? he would have asked. What's the story? Where's the story in *it*? Be the gal who hooks the throat of the world. Not the lip, for God's sake. The throat. Okay, Boss, she'd say, smiling at the image she'd called to mind.

A woman heading into the Liverpool Street shelter, carrying her baby and—improbably—the baby's heavy wooden cradle, looked backward over her shoulder at Frankie as she descended into the dark. Frankie stopped short. Many people went down into the shelters like this, before the sirens sounded, to get a good spot—a corner spot—an elderly woman had explained to Frankie last week, is what you're after. The woman with her baby looked back at Frankie standing there on the pavement, long enough for Frankie to see the dull blond hair tied back with a black ribbon, and the collar of her sweater sagging slightly where she had lost weight.

And not for the first time, Frankie wished she could return to this spot in the morning to make sure the woman and her baby were rising back up into the day, just to know they had slept and woken and would carry on. Just to know the next part.

The danger all around meant that everyone—Frankie jammed her shoulder against the front door of number 8 Argyll Road—might be living their last days. Everyone's—she turned her head toward the street as she pushed on the door—might be a heartbreaking story.

"Say, Miss!"

She relaxed her shoulder and straightened up. The boy from the end of the block stood in her walk. "Hello, Billy. What's cooking?"

He shifted his weight, impatiently, with the wary attention of a six-year-old. "My mum says all Americans have chocolate—but it's a secret, she says. And we aren't to ask."

Frankie nodded. "So you thought you'd get to the bottom of it?"

"That's right." He stared back at her.

She wished she had some chocolate to give him. "It is a secret," Frankie agreed. "Because I haven't heard anything about it. And I'm in the know."

He nodded. He knew all about her and the other lady upstairs. From his mum. They were reporters. Come over here to tell all the Americans about what's what.

"Does that mean *you* don't have any, then?" he asked, disappointed.

Frankie leaned toward him and put her finger to her lips, a conspirator. "I'll get on the job," she said to him, "I promise. If there's a secret, I'll find it out. Right?"

"Right," he breathed, and turned and ran.

She leaned back into the door to shove it open. His father was in the RAF, gone since the summer. His mother—the door gave—couldn't have been more than twenty-three.

"Harriet?" she called, closing the door to the flat behind her.

"In the bath," her flatmate shouted.

"Get out, quick. I've got news," Frankie called down the hall, hanging her key on the hook by the door. She unwound her scarf and shoved it into her hat, glad to find Harriet home. One of the stringers for the AP, Harriet Mendelsohn had been in Europe since 1938, and she was good for a laugh or a chat at all hours. She was older than Frankie and deadly earnest about the need for war reporters, people who were hopeful, and indignant, truth seekers.

"It's not enough to stay home and be a good man. Hurt no one, tell no lies. It's not enough," she had said as she clicked her glass against

Frankie's the day Frankie took the room in her flat. "It's not dirty—but it's dead."

There was a letter from Frankie's mother on the sideboard. She picked it up and slit the envelope open, walking along the tiny passageway into the front room where Harriet had already pulled the blackout curtains on the windows. Frankie flicked on the light by the door and read her letter still on her feet, leaning against the doorjamb. Her mother's tiny scrawl conveyed all the ordinary news of the house on Washington Square in the past week, and though Frankie loved the familiar slant of her handwriting, her mother was a meticulous accountant of meals eaten, thoughts had, conversations overheard, and she offered all parts of her day as evenly as a mare clopping along a familiar route. Nothing need be hurried, nothing would be missed. And nothing was missed, Frankie would groan to herself, though she read every last word, grudgingly aware that her mother had been a journalist without a paper, or an editor—for years. *I woke on Tuesday to a decidedly dreary day and the only cure for it was two eggs on toast followed by a long walk to the Library. Mrs. Taylor sends her. . . .*

"Hullo." Harriet had come up behind her.

Frankie wheeled, still reading the letter in her hand. "Hello."

"You in or out this evening?"

"Out." *Good night, dear—*. Frankie folded the letter, smiling, and slid it back into its envelope, turning to glance at Harriet. "Guess what Murrow tossed me."

Harriet narrowed her eyes against the thrill in Frankie's voice. "Tell me, cowboy."

"A story on the Gunner's Battery over there by the hospital."

Harriet whistled.

"It seems I am not, after all"—Frankie raised her eyebrows—"just a blonde in a skirt. So there."

Harriet chuckled. From the minute Harriet had first laid eyes on her, Frankie called to mind prairies and Indians and men on the loose.

"How about some scrambled eggs and toast before you go to the boys and the guns?" she said drily, but she was smiling as she moved past Frankie into the tiny kitchenette. "You read Steinkopf's report from Warsaw?" she called, reaching into the icebox for the eggs.

"No." Frankie appeared in the doorway.

"They've built a concrete wall around a hundred blocks of the city."

"How do you mean?'

"A wall, eight feet tall, so tight and smooth, he said, a cat couldn't climb it."

"Around the ghetto?"

Harriet nodded.

"Where was this?"

"Just now, it's on the wires."

"At least they're in their own houses."

"For now," Harriet answered without turning around.

Frankie watched the slant of the older woman's shoulders. Like a seamstress, Harriet Mendelsohn had gathered scraps of news about what was happening to Jews as the Nazis swept country after country into their pile, and she had been doing it since the Nazis had taken Poland the year before. She wrote of the thousands of Jews from Warsaw and other Polish cities seeking refuge in Latvia and Lithuania who were turned away at the borders. The suicides in Warsaw, the expulsions, the mass arrests: what she heard she typed up and sent out on the wires. It was Harriet who'd first reported Hitler's proposal to the Reichstag in 1939 that Germany establish a Jewish reservation within the Polish state, modeled—Hitler had assured his audience—after an American Indian reservation. When Harriet sewed the scraps together, it seemed as if the Nazis were trying to set the Jews moving, set them on the run, set them off—above all else, get them out of Germany.

But was it organized? That was the question. And was it credible? That was the worry. There had been so many sensational and fake atrocity stories written about Germany during the First War, much of the press was chary of a story about deliberate, ominous action against the Jews now. That hadn't seemed possible until the beginning of this year when the Vatican confirmed that the Nazis were moving Jews—from Austria, Czechoslovakia, and all parts of Poland—into ghettos. But were they being gathered for a reason? the *Times* of London had gently wondered aloud, a couple of weeks ago. Yes, Harriet had begun to believe, they were. The story here was a story about some kind of organized assault. And Harriet parsed scraps and lines of Nazi policy otherwise buried in large speeches to tell that story, though it beggared belief. She had cousins in Poland, and when their letters appeared on the front hall sideboard, along with their news came the unmistakable relief that they were still there in their house, on their street. Still there.

For now, Frankie poured two whiskeys and put one on the sill beside Harriet. For now. For now. Those were the words that built the dread. And how to write that story? Murrow's three questions, which formed the basis for every broadcast—*What is happening? How does it affect Americans? What does the Common Man say*—didn't cohere in the face of this one. The scraps added up to a terrible time for the Jews, any man at home could see. Terrible, it was terrible. But war was terrible. God knows, War was hell. And what were we supposed to do about it?

Pay attention—Frankie tipped her glass against Harriet's—*and then write like hell*. She took her drink and threw herself into the curve of the white club chair in the front room. A Smithy, class of '32, she had returned to New York after graduation, presenting herself, to her mother's bewilderment, at Max Prescott's office at the *Trib* the following morning. He had taken one look at the impatient, coltish flash of female in front of him, and directed her back out the door to bring him what she found. Her satchel swinging off her hip, she walked without knowing what she looked for, down West Fourth Street into the chaos and maw of Broadway and farther east, toward the tenements hulking along the river. She walked, and found to her bemusement she could go anywhere with a notebook. Not only that, but people would talk to her. People were suckers for a listening ear. And so she collected the scraps she saw or heard and wrote them down. After six months, Prescott had set aside two column inches—without a byline—for her "City Pulse."

Right through the end of Hoover and out the other side into the New Deal and the great broad teeth of Mrs. Roosevelt, Frankie covered the city, uptown and down, in satin heels and loafers, *Summa cum*, as her mother insisted on introducing her, proudly, hopefully, even still, to a prospective husband. *Summa cum lucky*, Frankie would mutter, watching, reveling in taking something she had seen and turning it until it was torqued tight. Not snapped. Not with the air rushed out of it. But tight and telling. Telling something about living. About life.

Until the evening last spring when she had let herself into her house and heard William Shirer coming through from Berlin on the radio that very minute, and Frankie sank down on the stairs and leaned against the banister, listening to his voice. Thin and reedy, pained, it was not at all like Murrow's mahogany tones. But for these minutes he was speaking, all of the unseen world was carried in his breath, in his careful, calm measures across distance and time. Here was the world in a voice: what was happening *now*. There in the effort he made to keep his voice under control, in his broad unaccented pronunciation of the words, *Führer* and *Herr*, a Midwestern disgust slipped right by the censor. In this voice lay more than the story, more than the words. Within two weeks, she'd booked herself on the SS *Trieste* and come over with nothing whatsoever to recommend her into radio but a letter from Prescott, her typewriter, and her smile.

When she saw the "studio," however, not much bigger than a closet, equipped with a battered table and chair and a single light shining on the microphone set in the middle of the table, heavy and blunt as a murder weapon, she nearly laughed at how humble it all was. And how uncertain. You sat at the table, listening on the headphones for New York to say *Come in, London*, and then you flicked the switch on the side of the mike and spoke. If the weather cooperated, your voice was relayed, like a distance runner, through the British air, from the vacuum tubes through to the wires and cables and on to the transmitters, somehow emerging beneath the click and stutter of three thousand miles back out into the air, into America. Or, all of the points along the way could fall through at any time, and your voice would simply vanish into the airwaves.

She typed Murrow's scripts. She filled the water glasses and set them beside the microphone. She found the people Murrow needed to speak to, and brought them to him for interviews. And she did what she had always done: she walked and she listened. She walked London without a map, turning down streets toward the sound of voices in pubs and in the still-bright lights of theaters and dance halls. Hitler marched on Paris. The British pulled back to Dunkirk. Civil Defense passed out gas masks to the city. The children were sent to the country. And in the shops and waiting in line for the buses, she listened to the Londoners making flesh of these facts. "What does the grocer have to say today?" Murrow had asked her one day early on, and without thinking she'd replied, "Well, he says the sheep won't make it to mutton if the bombs keep up like last night." Murrow had chuckled. Two nights later, she was on the air with him, and *What does the grocer say, Miss Bard?* had been a hit with New York, becoming Frankie's beat. The milkman's struggle to keep glass bottles; the pair of men's shoes left unmolested on its plinth in the bombed-out window of a shop, *for two entire weeks,* Frankie noted, as necessary in their perfect peace as the king. With shoes like this still standing, England stands. For the past six months, Frankie had roamed and gathered these scraps of life. But tonight would be a brand-new game. It was a single piece, on men in battle, and it would be all hers.

At nine o'clock, Frankie let herself out the door and back onto the street, casting a reflexive glance upward to check the blackout curtains in her windows before heading west toward the Antiaircraft Gunnery station. When the bombing first started, the guns on the ground were left silent, the War Office betting that the RAF could better blow the

Luftwaffe out of the skies. But it made everyone in the city loopy, like sitting ducks, remarked Mrs. Preston from two doors down to Frankie, us down here while the planes buzz and bomb us up above. After a month, the order was given to let the antiaircraft guns fire away—sending ten 28-pound shells a minute, soaring twenty-five thousand feet into the air—though what they aimed at God alone knew. Because the men—huddled under their blankets, the four uncovered guns each aimed at a different quadrant of the sky—waiting for the drone of the German bombers, only knew the cold.

Around the four AA guns at 165 Battery in Kensington Gardens sheep's meadow, a command post with two spotters glided in slow arcs on the reclining seats, their night glasses trained at the sky.

"You can't stay here, love." One of the spotters spoke, his eye on the telescope.

Frankie reached into her satchel for her press documents and handed them up to the other spotter who had taken his eye off the sky and held out a hand.

"You'll get hurt." He thrust it back at her.

"As will you, if I do," she commented.

He grunted and went back to the sky.

She turned and faced the gunners. Nine of them, she saw, and young as they come, sitting ready and waiting.

"What are the chances of hitting anything tonight?" She settled herself next to one of the guns.

"Slim as my wife's waist," a man across the circle of guns sighed.

"Shut up about your wife, will you?"

Frankie smiled at that man. "Where's your wife, soldier?"

"Kent."

Safe, in other words. Out there in England where the distant fires of London were the new moon in the otherwise pitch-black country sky.

"Take post!" one of the spotters cried, and the men around Frankie ripped off their blankets and took their stations—gun layer, fuse setter, gun elevator, rammer, breech man, ammunition carrier. "Ready," the man from Kent shouted. "Ready, sir!"

The men around her were tense and quiet. She flicked on her flashlight and glanced down at her watch, noting the time and the sound of waiting all around her. Men breathing, a couple of coughs. A quiet with eyes and ears. An animal quiet.

Off her left shoulder, to the east, came the old, familiar, uneven drone of the first of the German planes. Fly straight, you buggers, whispered one of the men, his hand on the gun, fly straight so we can get a shot at you. Frankie put her helmet on and pressed hard against the battery wall.

Boom. The first shell shot out of one of the guns, roaring toward the sky at a plane no one could see, but whose sound the spotters tried to read as they started yelling coordinates. The first shell was followed right away by another, and the windows of the houses around the park buckled in the dim light and popped. Shattering glass silvered down into the street. Now the shells slammed again and again into the sky above, and the shrapnel from the guns clattered down on the rooftops, like clog dancers without a song. Murrow had considered sending a recording truck over here with her, but even if she could have heard the sound man's voice at that moment urging her, *Come in, Frankie, come in,* it was too wild, too loud, and there would have been nothing to say but *it's wild.* "Fuck you," the soldier beside Frankie grunted, his cheek against the trigger, *Fuck you, fuck you,* like a prayer he hurled up and blasted. Blasted again and again upward into nothing, and Frankie wanted to grab something and hurl it up, too; and the fact that every shot could be traced back to them, every shot could draw the attention of a pilot high above them, who could flick his thumb and rain down death so fast they'd never hear it coming, didn't matter—now, despite the cold of the October night, the men were sweating, the shells roaring out in answer to the spotters' shouts, stripped to their shirtsleeves and going at their guns like drummers. *Come on, come on, come on,* the gunners bellowed, drawing fire, and the lights blazed green and bright electric blue and the cordite burned down the back of their throats. *Come on, come on, you fuckers*—they slammed the shells into the guns, deadly hopeful stevedores, again and again and again until one of the spotters called the halt.

Some of the men simply sunk down on the ground beneath their guns where they had been standing. Frankie's legs were shaking. It was over. They hadn't been hit. The sudden quiet, the release from the explosions, was deafening.

"Christ, you're brave," she said into the exhausted silence.

"Just the job, Miss," someone joked from the dark.

One of the other men snorted, "Shut up, Jack."

"You are, though." She was close to tears and wanted to laugh out loud at the same time.

A draft of night air hit her, and the sound of bombs falling now, farther along to the west. A thick gust of smoke crossed as the wind shifted off the river carrying the stink of the explosions. Around her, some of the men seemed actually to have fallen asleep. There was no veil, no protective curtain where it happened out of sight, "over there." This was the shock. This had always been the shock, and it seemed to Frankie the most important thing for people to know. Over here, there was nothing between you and the war. She picked up her satchel and stole away, quietly as from a nursery, elated and exhausted, her mind racing forward already into what she would say on the air.

That was it, wasn't it? The nothing between. That scant air between the couple kissing this evening: their bodies leaning against each other before going underground was the same air between the gunners and the bombs, and it was the same air that carried her voice across the sea, on sound waves, to people listening in their chairs at home. A newspaper story had to be cast in lead, the words had to be bound and trussed, printed onto paper, folded, and delivered to boys who'd stand on corners saying *Extra Extra,* the story held in a hand, the story bound. In radio, the story flew into the air, from lips to ear—like a secret finding its immediate spot in the dark lodges of the brain—the dome of the sky collapsing space, and the world become a great whispering gallery for us all.

A terrific explosion banged overhead and then the bright torch of an incendiary streaked straight down from the sky. Frankie stopped where she was and began to count, as if she were counting the miles between thunder and lightning. The underside of the silver barrage balloons sailing above the city reflected the flames, carrying their color sideways across the dark. Boom, came an answer. Safe. She didn't know when she had started the counting, but she'd forgotten how not to anymore. It had been about a mile ahead of her, somewhere near Parliament, she guessed. She walked forward, waiting for her eyes to adjust back to the dark. Just ahead of her the line of white paint the Civil Defense had painted on the pavement to guide people along the unlit streets came to an abrupt stop, then rose three feet in the air where they had painted the circles around the trunk of a tree.

"Mind where you're going!" someone said right beside her.

"Sorry," she called after the dark shape hurrying past.

It took her over an hour to make her way back to Broadcasting House. The thick fog of smoke clogged her lungs and she pulled her collar up around her ears, walking forward through the crash and blaze. There were cars lined up outside of bomb sites, orderly as taxis lined up after the theater let out, and a woman in a canteen truck pouring tea. Black and red and the blue blaze of the weird night light caught the sheen of an auto's hood passing swiftly under a bomber's moon.

"You look like hell," Murrow observed as she hung her coat on top of his on the back of the studio door.

"Well, thank you, Mr. Murrow," Frankie replied tartly, sliding into the chair.

"What have you got?"

She grinned up at him. "It's mad, Ed. These boys firing round after round into the sky—you can't see anything, and after a while the noise and the guns and the slam bam, boom, over and over—well, you start to ride it," she said, "like skiing, down down down into the white, mindless, given up to it." She stopped. Tom had given the fist with five fingers through the glass behind Murrow's head.

"We'll play the opening bit," Murrow told her, "and then you simply come in and tell it, tell it all just like you were starting to—and with that coil in your voice, Frankie. Keep that."

She nodded and when Tom gave the signal and the light went on and Ed looked at her and started the chat that led into the story, she smiled and answered, and then he, too, fell away and she closed her eyes as she always did and simply began to say what she had to to her mother— imagining her sitting beside the jet-black box in the front room at number 14 Washington Square—about the men and the cold and the noise and the great surge toward fighting—that was it, wasn't it?—how your blood roared up into the moon with the shells and how different it was from sitting in a shelter underground.

"Put yourself in the place of any of these men," she said as she slowed to her ending. *"Not a one of them wants to be the one who gets it. Still, there comes a wild, intoxicating rush where you take your heart in your hands and hurl yourself right into the teeth of the danger, to forget the danger. So be it, you think, it's all up to God"*—she smiled—*"and some men. Over here, you close your eyes, do your job, and fling yourself toward it—whatever it may be."*

JESUS, Harry Vale turned all the way around in his chair in Franklin, Massachusetts, to look at the wireless.

"This is Frankie Bard, in London. Good ni—"

Harry snapped off her voice and sat there, without moving. Throttled in the gal's voice he heard the rush forward toward the end, the leap that you take into the middle of danger when all you can do is look straight at it, because whatever is coming will come. Harry had forgotten how that felt. Hell, he had heard her *smiling*, though it was past one o'clock in the morning in London, and eight o'clock here. He stood up without thinking, and switched the light off in his sitting room, pulling his jacket off the back of the chair. There, in the new dark of the room that stretched above the shop of his garage, he stood and listened.

The foghorn moaned on Long Point. Harry zippered his jacket and made his way down the dim lit upstairs hall.

He passed the tiny bedroom he had given Otto Schelling in the spring, and saw that the German man had fallen asleep again with the light on, fully clothed. Sleeping like that, his thin blond hair fallen away from his cheeks and onto the pillow, he looked like a child. On the day Flores had brought him down on the bus from Nauset, the man had stood for a long while on the pavement where the bus let off, and it had been cold that afternoon, never mind that it was April. Clear and cold enough to scare the tulips back down for another month. And long after the bus pulled away, through the café window Harry had watched Otto, still on the spot, utterly stalled, as though he had run out of gas. Exhausted and lost, the man stood there, it seemed to Harry, as if waiting for the world to stop spinning.

It had been queer, Flores said later. The Kraut just arriving like that out of the blue and staying.

Harry shrugged.

"Why is he *here*, Harry? That's all I'm saying."

"He may be a Jew," Harry answered.

Harry pulled the door closed on Otto, passing along the hallway and down the stairs, out the door at the bottom into the night. No one was out tonight, the town dark save for the three streetlamps put in to great fanfare last year, punctuating the three blocks of the center of town. To his right lay the green, the town hall, and across the street from them, the post office. To his left, and vanishing into the dark, the road climbed up the hill and away. It was the radio hour up and down the street, the hour before bed. Harry shook a cigarette out of his pocket and lit it, his eye on a pair of headlights moving slowly toward him from the houses on the other side of town. The lights shone along the wooden fences and then, for an instant, lit up the whitewashed flagpole on the post office, rising high above the town like a ghost finger pointing in the night. Harry frowned. With lights on it like that, the flagpole clearly marked the town's center. He ought to speak to Iris about lopping off the top, he thought, lifting his hand in a wave to the car. Honking as he passed, the doctor's face flared briefly in the reflected light of the gas station sign, and then it was darkness behind him, darkness pulling the two red taillights away with him up the hill.

Iris. Harry grinned stupidly. He could almost hear her—*you want to cut off my flagpole, Mr. Vale?* He nodded, still smiling, but it wasn't a joke. Across the road lay the swath of harbor beach. Past the gray sand it was black. And past that—in the space of eighteen months, Hitler had snatched Austria, Czechoslovakia, Poland, and France, and whether he would cross the twenty-one miles of the Channel, marching triumphant up the Dover Road to London, remained to be seen. Harry stared across that vast dark and tossed his cigarette into the gutter. He turned in the direction Dr. Fitch had driven, but it was pitch-black, the red lights long gone—the town hidden again in darkness. And then Harry turned and stared back out across the water, where the war was waiting for all of them.

3.

A T THE REAR of the post office, the wind whipped straight off the water into the high-ceilinged sorting room, and Iris found herself stiff with cold after a couple of hours of work. An inlander, she was used to winter snow, but the wind blasting unchecked across the Atlantic found its way inside and gripped hard at anything it could. She drew the school map out from its mailer and unrolled it on the table. The green, demarcated world before the war spread out.

There was France and Germany. Austria. England. Poland. Letters printed in straight lines in the comforting typeface of school, the world ordered as neatly as the men now were. Since the draft had begun in October, each man's number pulled by hand from the War Department's glass fishbowl and recorded, the roads and rails were full of American boys being sent all over the country, leaning over books and maps in their olive drab, sprawled in the too tight seats moving from Ohio to Omaha. Tennessee. Georgia. The Carolinas. From town the two Snow brothers would go first, then a Wilcox, a Duarte, and a Boggs. Johnny Cripps and Dr. Fitch had numbers so high, it was as good as if they hadn't been called. They'd never be needed now.

But Iris James had ordered a map nonetheless. And now Florence Cripps, owner of the largest B&B in town, stopped right where she was in the doorway of the post office lobby and put her pocketbook down on the floor. Large and handsome with blond frizzed hair in a good silk dress, Mrs. Cripps stood like a striped tent without an occasion, studying the scene before her. Full attention must be paid. For here was Franklin's most public official, stepped away from her window and standing on a stool, carefully tacking up a large school map of the world, blithely covering the faces of the Most Wanted.

"Iris! What are you doing?"

"Putting up a map," replied the postmaster, giving a good solid bang upon the last tack with a hammer.

"But—Iris," Mrs. Cripps said reasonably, wishing only to point a gentle finger, certainly not to wag. "What if one should come through *here*"—she advanced upon Iris—"then we're lost. We'll never know the criminal element in our midst."

Iris stepped off her stool and unlocked the door in the heavy oak partition between the lobby and the sorting room at the back of the post office. "In all your life, Florence, have you ever seen one of the men in these drawings?"

Mrs. Cripps took every question seriously, and as Miss James was a federal official, she gave the question still more of its due. But no, she shook her head, she couldn't say as she ever had.

"There you go then. You've been fine until now. Should be so again."

"But a map, Iris? We hardly need to know where we are."

Iris turned around. "If we are going to war, then we'd better know where the boys are going."

"Our boys are *not* going." Mrs. Cripps did not like how easily the woman had said "the boys." They weren't hers to speak of like that. "The president has promised," continued Florence. "And Churchill has said he doesn't need our boys to be sent, *not this year, nor next*"—she recited the prime minister's ringing words—"*nor any other*. He said that."

Iris shrugged. "They'll have to."

"Oh, and why's that?"

Iris stuck her pencil behind her ear. "The British aren't enough, Florence. They never have been. What've you got?"

Rankled, Mrs. Cripps handed over her single letter. Iris took it through with her, and reappeared behind the window, throwing Florence's letter upon the scales.

When word got out that an unmarried woman was coming to take old Postmaster Snow's job a year ago, it must be said there were doubts. Mrs. Cripps had made sure she was standing at her sink watching out the kitchen window when the bus with the new postmaster drove into town. Right away the woman's neat figure and the black beret pinned on top of her straight red hair signaled trouble ahead. Attention would have to be paid.

"She'll do the trick, I'd say," Johnny Cripps drawled at his mother's elbow.

"It doesn't matter to me what she does, as long as she stays at the job," Mrs. Cripps returned. "Though it's still a mystery how the United States government sees fit to hire an aging single woman in such a position of influence, when there are plenty of men around unable to find work right now."

Mother and son watched the new postmaster follow Flores, the bus driver, along the sidewalk to the bottom of the post office stairs where he set down her three suitcases, touched the soft brim of his hat, and left her. They watched her take off her beret and slowly stuff it in the pocket of her greatcoat. Still she didn't move, she seemed rapt instead in a long consideration of the solid brick building before her. And then, just before pushing open the gate, the new postmaster had turned and taken a good long look at the town.

"Well!" Mrs. Cripps burst out. "She won't find anyone around here to marry!"

"She may not be looking."

"Everyone is looking." Mrs. Cripps smiled at her son a little dangerously. "Even if they don't think it."

Like a stone tossed into a flock of birds, talk startled swiftly into flight whenever the new postmaster was mentioned. Miss James was easy on the eyes, though no one agreed as to how. Tall and slim, she wore the Postal Department's standard-issue navy blue cardigan buttoned at the neck, so it swung over her shoulders like a light cape, leaving her freckled arms to move freely in and out with the deliberate care of a page boy, or a squire.

That image, of course, disregarded the postmaster's lips, painted a good bold red, which alarmed some, until the temperature of those lips could be fully taken by the married women in town. Within days, however, it was clear they were nothing to worry over—no more sinister than a channel marker at the mouth of a well-run harbor.

No, it became clear to them that Miss Iris James's motives were best understood by looking around at the Franklin post office. As in any of their houses, the spirit of the woman had insinuated itself firmly there. Inside the lobby, the wastepaper basket was emptied regularly, and the pads of money order application blanks were stacked firmly upon the wall desk. The black-and-white government posters never had a chance to flap untidily in the breeze, pinned as they were on all four corners directly into the big bulletin board hung to the side of the postmaster's window. Not once on Miss James's watch did wadded-up envelopes, torn scraps of letters, or ripped catalogs lie on the floor below the tiers of gun-metal lockboxes, as they did in some towns down Cape. One entered, as one did every day, and was immediately met with a sense of calm born out of rigid adherence to an unwavering routine.

"I just think you ought to be more careful, Iris," Mrs. Cripps sniffed now. "There's that German man around, as you well know. The other night I was coming home and there was his light shining straight through the window above Harry's Garage—no curtains at all, you understand? It could be seen plain as day on the water, shining straight through like that. And then he snapped it off. What do you make of *that*?"

"He was probably going to bed." Iris tossed the envelope into the sack.

"Yes." Florence inclined her head. "Well, that's what I thought, but then, I hadn't walked much farther when it went back on again."

Iris didn't answer.

"It may have been a sign, Iris. He might be a part of a German invasion, their advance man on the ground." Florence drew the phrase out, impressed with herself.

"He has a wife over there," Iris said evenly as she could. "In a refugee camp. In France."

"So he says."

"Yes," Iris flashed back.

"I read all about those camps," Florence sniffed. "There's no need to tell me. But why is she there in the first place? She must have done something to get herself in there—at the very least stuck her neck out somehow."

"I expect there was something wrong with her papers."

"Exactly." Florence nodded, a little triumphant. "That's exactly my point. You've got to be careful. You've got to watch out, watch yourself. It's horrible, but honestly, the French have had a hard enough time without all these people, Jews and what have you, displaced by the war, flooding in from all over Europe, masses of people suddenly to deal with, as if they hadn't enough already. First the Germans, now this, and *she* may not be, but some of them *are* dangerous, you can be sure of it—"

"It's been very hard on the man, I think," Iris broke in to shut the woman up. Otto Schelling came in every day with a letter addressed, *Frau Anna Schelling, Gurs Ilot K 20, France*; and on Thursdays, he'd add to it a postal order she'd fill out in the amount of five dollars, earned working over at Harry's Garage. Deep set and dark blue, his eyes regarded her from a long way off as she asked the necessary questions—*How are you? Same amount as last week?*—taking the single dollar bills he pushed across, writing him a receipt. He wrote a letter every day. And he had never yet gotten a letter back. Every afternoon, he turned around and walked back out as quietly as he had come in, with the exhaustion of a man who hurled himself against the wall of each passing day, and would do so again and again, until the wall broke.

"We all have to be careful, Iris." Florence was determined to be mild. "That's all I am pointing out."

"Careful about what?" The doors had opened on Marnie Niles sailing in. "I thought I'd find you in here, Florence," she declared, satisfied.

Mrs. Cripps raised her eyebrows at Iris, punctuating the end of their conversation before she turned around to Marnie. But her attention was caught by the sight of Emma Fitch's head wrapped in a yellow scarf bound who knows where, crossing the frame of the open door.

"Isn't she the tiniest thing?"

"Yes, yes she is." Marnie had to agree.

All three women followed Emma out of sight. Iris quite liked "the little bride," as everyone in town seemed to think of her. She dove in and out of conversations gamely, offering commentary on what her husband thought, what her husband was determined to try—playing the doctor's wife straight up.

"Do you need anything?" Iris asked Marnie Niles who shook her head. Iris nodded and retreated to the back room where the pile of unsorted morning mail lay thick upon the table. Most of the town did not venture in until after eleven or so, when suddenly she'd look up from the sorting table in the back and find the lobby nearly full, as though someone had called a meeting. The women in the lobby kept on a running patter, to which Iris only half-listened.

"It's unfathomable."

"Unfathomable and unforgivable."

"That's a bit harsh, Marnie."

"No, dear, it is unforgivable for a man to marry a weak woman!"

"But I imagine he likes taking care of her. Perhaps that makes him feel stronger?"

"A man takes better care of a woman when she doesn't depend upon him," Marnie sniffed. "Will Fitch'll have his hands full, now that he's gone and chosen a tiny slip of a city girl—and from away."

Marnie's voice trailed off as Iris returned to the front window with letters in need of canceling.

"Of course she's from away," Florence retorted. "Who would have married Will after what his father did?"

Iris glanced up. What had his father done?

"Do you remember after it all, how he'd stand at the end of the garden dressed head to toe in khaki looking like the summer people's help, his neck and shoulders bowed, staring into the bank of roses?"

"What was he going to do?"

"He ought to have left town," Mrs. Cripps replied crisply. "Anybody with any shame would have, instead of sticking around. Think of the Aldens and the Dales. They lost everything. Everything. And there he was still with his roses."

"Still," Marnie reflected, thrusting her hand into her mailbox and sliding out with a single envelope. "It was hard on Mary."

"Always is hardest on the wives." Mrs. Cripps nodded darkly. "We all might as well be Indian brides."

"For pity's sake, Florence!" Marnie burst out laughing. "You ought to stop taking *National Geographic*!" And her laughter fluttered behind like ribbons long after the door closed.

Seeing Mrs. Cripps intended to stay put, Iris went right on feeding the mail into the canceling machine. The envelopes skimmed under the lip of the machine, *November 18, 12 pm. Franklin. November 18, 12 pm. Franklin, November 18, November 18, November 18.* The letters sped out the other side, Iris giving the crank a good shove. The last envelope had stuck and she had to give it a yank to pull it out the finishing end of the machine.

"I suppose it's the power," Mrs. Cripps commented quietly to Iris, evidently finishing some discussion with herself, "that one loves about a job like this."

Iris gave Mrs. Cripps the briefest of glances.

"After all, just look at what passes through your hands."

Iris could feel herself going red. This woman! And something was off with the machine. The next envelope was sticking in exactly the same place. Yanking it out, she saw with annoyance that the date had smudged. *18? November 19?* Iris held it closer. No, it really was off. It could easily be saying that today was the nineteenth.

"What's the trouble?" Mrs. Cripps asked solicitously.

"The date." Iris put down the envelope. She'd have to write a note to Midge Barnes, the postal inspector down in Nauset. Damn.

"Does it matter, really?" said Mrs. Cripps, sticking like a burr. She had never seen the postmaster bothered before. "One day or the next, the mail will get there all the same, isn't that right?"

Iris had made the mistake of hoping the glitch had ended, but now a third envelope had gone through and hovered somewhere between November 18 and November 19. "Yes, it does matter, Mrs. Cripps," burst out Iris. "It matters very much."

The machine looked the same as always. She stared at it, irritated. Its blue body lay there dully, as if she had done something wrong. She knew that was silly, but this kind of random inexplicable happening drove her around the bend. She could countenance that milk had a shelf life, that human beings trip and fall down, that perfectly clear skies might suddenly cloud and rain—but she refused to accept these things happening without some reason. Someone had left the door ajar on the icebox, someone else had not been looking where he went. But the canceling machine.

The lobby doors swung open, and Florence turned around to see who it was. A big smile spread across her face. "Hello, Harry," she said, luxuriously. "Miss James is having some problem with her machine."

Iris rolled her eyes.

"Oh?" said Harry. "What's wrong?"

Mrs. Cripps decided that she had quite a lot to tell Marnie Niles. Harry's hair was combed, for starters. And as he crossed the lobby, she could tell without looking that the temperature had risen slightly behind the window. Oh, she smiled to herself, I will be right in the end about this one. She turned back to Iris and patted the counter between them. "Good-bye, Miss James. I have work to do. Good luck with that," she pointed.

Harry set down the mug he was carrying and looked at the canceling machine. "You having some trouble with that?"

"Yes," answered Iris, flushing, acutely aware that it was just the two of them suddenly, alone in the post office. "It's sticking on me."

"Let's have a look."

Iris pushed the small machine across to Harry. He picked it up in his hands and shook it. It didn't make a sound. Then he put it down very gently and reached for a screwdriver in his pocket, looking up at Iris for her okay. She nodded.

"What do you suppose happened?"

"Beats me," he answered with the cheerfulness of someone who's been around machines all his life. "Things break."

How was it possible that he wouldn't know—or that he wasn't bothered by not knowing? Iris watched as he carefully loosened the four brass screws that held the front in place. The inside of the machine resembled the gears of a clock and the tiny hammers with the dates, little bells. He leaned down and blew into the belly of the machine, pulled back and looked, then blew again. Iris watched his fingers. There had been nothing said between them, nothing at all but this kind of steady attention. He was in every day for his mail, and though at first she had thought she ought to signal somehow that she was ready, she realized this slow unstated comfort between them was some kind of movement—the beginning of the dance. Without paying much attention, he replaced the plate and screwed it down quickly. "There," he said, pushing it back toward Iris. "See if that does anything."

She slid a clean piece of paper into the canceling slot and turned the knob. Out it slipped onto the ledge in front of Harry. "*November 18, 1940,*" he said.

"Wonderful," Iris heard herself saying. "Thank you, Mr. Vale."

"Harry."

She looked up.

"Harry," he said to her quietly. "It's Harry." She flushed and looked down.

He cleared his throat. "Say, listen."

She opened the stamp drawer, her heart thudding.

"I've been meaning to ask you something."

The stamps lay in fresh sheets in perfect order before her.

"Any chance you'd think about lowering your flagpole out there?"

Oh. She glanced back up, disappointed. He was one town official speaking to another. That was all. "Why?"

"Well"—he hesitated—"it seems to me it's sticking straight up, just begging for attention."

Iris had to smile, despite herself. "Is that how it seems?"

"If the Germans get within sight of town, they're going to plot a course straight in off that pole."

He was quite serious.

"I'd have to speak to the post office inspector," Iris said and shut the drawer.

"Fair enough." He dipped his head, but made no move to leave.

He had only come in to ask about the flagpole, Iris told herself, a little hotly. Why else would he still be standing there at her window? Best to serve him and be done with it.

"Need a box for that, Harry?"

He went a little pale and glanced down at the mug on the counter between them.

"A box?"

"Yes," she answered. He was very pale, indeed. "To mail," she added.

"I—"

She pointed at the mug. "Shall I measure it?"

And she pulled the tape measure off her waist, to take its height and width. "Just a small box will do you," she decided, and disappeared behind the sorting boxes into the back of the mailroom where the parcel supplies were kept.

"I brought some tissue, too. A nice mug like this needs care."

"Right." He leaned his elbows upon the counter. Deftly she folded the thick cardboard along the creases and pulled the sides up into the shape of a box. She fluffed the tissue paper up and carefully settled the mug into that nest. He seemed fixed upon her hands, which only made her work the faster to get them out of the way. At last, the box was sealed up tight.

She looked up at him. "Where to?"

"You," he said.

Iris blinked and reached for the sleeve of her cardigan slipping off her shoulder. "I beg your pardon?"

Harry put his hands on either side of the box and slid it forward toward the postmaster. "It's for you."

Iris regarded Harry for several seconds. Then she smiled very slowly. "Shall I open it?"

He grinned then, and leaned his elbows upon the counter. "Go ahead."

Carefully, she slit the tape covering the opening with the blade of the scissors hanging from the window and slid her finger in to pop up the top. The mug lay snug in there and she peeled off the paper she had just wrapped it in, aware of Harry watching her, helpless and in a kind of thrall.

"It's grand," she pronounced, setting the blue ceramic mug between them. "Thank you."

"I thought you probably like your coffee."

She smiled at him. "I do."

"Good." He patted the counter in lieu of good-bye, turned around without another word, and headed for the door. She flushed and looked down. He passed through the door without closing it, and a small breeze reached where she stood.

4.

A STEADY, COLD RAIN blew more and more people into the crowded Savoy Hotel bar, bringing the smell of damp wool and hot bodies with them. One hundred and twenty-one nights they'd all lived through, one hundred and twenty-one, night after night, and the people who remained, the people who climbed back up into the light every morning, could be forgiven the extravagant gestures, the brave huzzahs, the fists in the air. Though the bombers might come in the next hour or two, and everyone knew it, no one was going down into the funk holes just now. London was out in the streets. For now, people hurried along calling out to each other even on this miserable wet night, strangers calling—*Good night! Good night*—sending voices into the streets, not sirens, not whistles, not bombs.

Frankie sat at a table at the back of the bar, between Jim Dowell, an AP reporter just returned from Paris, Harriet, and Dusty Pankhurst, another one of Murrow's boys. There was nothing to report tonight but the lack of bombs. Not that there could have been anyway, Frankie thought, watching the scene in the room in front of her—the newsroom was in here.

"Who dat?" Pankhurst tipped his head idly in the direction of a trio of women just arrived on the threshold, shaking out their umbrellas and laughing, sending a bright heat into the crowded room.

Dowell turned to look. "More glamour girl reporters," he drawled, turning back to the table, "come over to be where the action is."

"Present company excepted, of course." Pankhurst was magnanimous.

"We're not glamorous?"

"You're not girls," Pankhurst parried.

"In that sense," Dowell finished with a smile at Harriet.

Frankie's eyes flicked to Harriet, who stuck out her lip but didn't say anything. Up until recently, only a handful of women survived in the European press corps, but more and more women were pushing their way into serious wartime reporting, coming over with assignments to write about French hemlines and simply staying, sending back copy on bombs and breadlines instead.

"Matter of fact"—Dowell exhaled, looking around the room— "seems the number of war tourists has hit a record high in here."

"It's wet outside, Jim, that's all," retorted Harriet.

"In any case, plenty of Americans don't want to enter the war." Dowell continued the point he'd started before the girls appeared in the door. "Over eighty percent plenty."

"Never mind." Pankhurst waved the point away. Round-faced and sweating and impossible to overestimate—he played the goof so well, people had the habit of telling him more than they thought they had— "never mind that. The vote to reelect Roosevelt ended up being a vote to fight."

"And the Germans are putting all their pegs in place now," Dowell agreed. "Way I heard it over there, Admiral Dönitz plans on having his subs in Boston Harbor this time next year."

"Crap," Pankhurst answered. "The Krauts have got the upper hand right where they are. Why would they waste it? You see how fast they shot down thirty-seven ships last month in the Bay of Biscay? They'll be spread too thin if they try and make war crossings."

"Shut up," Dowell said amiably, "and listen to your elders. I sat in the sailors' bar last week in Lorient and heard them—bluffing, sure, but you listen underneath the talk and it sounds like there's a U-boat being fitted up to make the shot all the way across."

"God, your lot gets away with murder." Harriet stubbed out her cigarette.

"Our lot?" Dowell quizzed.

"Men," she pronounced.

"Ha." Dowell pressed his shoulder against hers, and Frankie saw the two of them were on again. There'd be the three of them at breakfast in the flat tomorrow. "Because we're better at getting the goods?"

Harriet pushed his face away, lightly. "Because the sailors aren't measuring the precise angle at which your breasts are sailing above the table."

Frankie sputtered.

"You can be invisible, you can be a walking tape machine," Harriet sighed. "And you can bury that sailor's chat in your smile, while you file it for later."

"I know that smile." Dowell grinned. "See, here it is." And he smiled blandly, without any light in his eyes. "The censor's special."

"The story beneath the story," Pankhurst agreed.

Frankie nodded. Bill Shirer wrote ten minutes of script for five minutes of airtime, and Murrow often finished every broadcast in a cold sweat, having orchestrated the news so that it went under the wire, his mind ahead of the censor's, bending and swaying to the imagined cut. Early on, she'd learned what she could say she saw—a full moon could be described as a bomber's moon—and how to seed the story without telling the Germans, who were listening, what they heard. It was a dare—a dance up to the line. It was the performance of what is, what isn't.

"I'll bet I could get something through from over there," Frankie mused.

"I'll bet you could, Beauty."

"Shut up," she lobbed at Jim. "I'm serious."

"That's two of us, then." He smiled back.

She tipped her glass against Dowell's and finished her drink, watching the sweep of Harriet's hair as she leaned forward into his hand cupping the match, her gold sweater soft against Jim's jacket, the way she held her head to the side while she asked and answered, peppering him with questions about France. Though they were never going to be one of the boys, Frankie rather liked this no-man's-land where she and Harriet reported from. She was a woman, sure. But this talk—the frank and curious talk of reporters, the drug of getting in there, getting it down, *getting* it—skeined between all of them, man or woman.

"You really think the Krauts will launch an attack on the States?" Frankie returned to Dowell's point.

Dowell drained the last of his whiskey sour. "I'm just telling you what I heard. Dimes to dollars, Dönitz's boys will surface in New York Harbor one of these nights, do nothing, and come home smiling—an ace in the hole. And then a pack of them will follow"—he squinted into his empty glass—"by end of summer, 'forty-one."

"Is that a bet?"

"Bet." Dowell nodded. "That's a bet."

"Sure they will," Pankhurst snorted. "Hey, Reggie," he called to the bartender, holding up Dowell's glass. "The dreamer needs another."

At a table in the center of the room, Frankie watched one of the men lean over to his companion and say something in her ear. The girl tipped toward him, listening. Then she smiled. Frankie looked down and sipped her scotch. When she looked back up, a good-looking man sitting on one of the stools at the bar held her eye.

"I'll tell you what to place your bets on," Harriet said quietly. "Whether immigration quotas back home are ever going to get lifted."

"For the German refugees?"

Harriet nodded. "Twenty-seven thousand three hundred and seventy spots. That's what we've got to offer. Twenty-seven thousand three hundred and seventy. What in the hell kind of number is that? And so far it won't budge—hasn't budged in two years—though there are floods of people waiting on visas. Stuck waiting for pieces of paper."

"There's the worry of spies," Pankhurst observed.

"You know and I know these refugees are not Nazi spies," Harriet retorted. "And though we are still reporting them as 'refugees'—people washed out of their homes by the tide of war, and that kind of crap—they are Jews. Being moved. Being deported. Being given twenty minutes from the time a knock comes on the door until they are herded down the street. Twenty minutes to pack whatever they can grab. Told to get out. Get out of Germany. Of Austria. Europe. And the United States won't allow you in unless you can prove you have means. So they're stuck. And no matter how I phrase it—the indifference of bureaucracy, the refugee crisis—the stories don't make it onto the front page. What's happening to the Jews is getting buried in the middle of the newspapers. It's being cast as a secondary story, that's all."

"Someone ought to go over there and prove that. Paint the picture of the people who are trying to get out of Germany. Follow a family. Then it might be clear that it's no accident the refugees are Jews. That's the story to get," said Pankhurst.

Harriet shook her head. "Can't be done. It's already too dark to tell—there was a woman I met last week in the Marylebone refugee center who was separated from her husband at the border between Spain and France because of a clerical error. One *n* too few on her visa. And though she had her passport, which showed her proper name, and their marriage certificate, they held her for twenty hours before releasing her. And he had gone on. And all she knows is he was bound for Lisbon and from there to America. *America*, she said to me, as if somehow I'd know how to find him. They are utterly lost to each other, see? There is no hand to put the two together. She's not where he thinks she is, and all she can say, over and over to whoever comes into the center: *You are from America? America?* It's too grim. You might as well say God has dropped out of heaven. He's gone. There's the fucking story."

"Christ!" Frankie said. Reckless and itchy, she flicked at her glass with her fingernail. She shifted in her seat, wanting to stand up, wanting to move. "Christ almighty, I want to make some noise."

"Say there, Beauty, don't you ever have any fun?"

The man who had been watching her from the bar had leaned down between her and Pankhurst. He was fine-featured and dark, his accent upper-crust, Oxbridge. His eyes rested lightly on her face.

"All the time," she tossed back at him.

"Ha!" Pankhurst slapped Dowell.

"Then come and dance." The man reached in and held out his hand, and Frankie, looking up at him, took it.

Following him down through the room, toward the dancers, she looked back over her shoulder and saw Dowell and Harriet stand up also, and Pankhurst raise his glass to them in a toast. The noise in the hotel bar dialed up, the orchestra swinging into "In the Mood," sending gusts of chatter into the air. Outside in the cold dark, the city waited, but in here, for now, it was light and there was the chance of laughter and the gay tip of a light wave cresting, and the man was leading her onto the dance floor, easily, so easily Frankie felt the shiver starting along her spine where he lay his hand, and she smiled against his jacket. Easy and familiar, the hours in front of them stretched surely ahead, because of the way he held her and the way her body slid into the curve of his hand. And she gave herself up to what would come like a present, a present about to be opened slowly and with complete attention. The music shifted down a notch, slowing, or he was slowing against a beat, a counterpoint to draw her more cleanly in. It had been months since she had been held like this, and tonight she felt as though she'd ridden to the top of a crest and could slow slightly, and look out, look back. He was very close to her and his lips were so wide, and Frankie smelled the scotch on his breath. All the bombs and the noise had drawn back for a time, and in this moment in between, just right now, the world pushed back and there could be a single complete hour; so when the music stopped, and when he closed the last two inches between them, she opened her mouth under his and he groaned.

They walked outside into the night, still kissing, and Frankie stumbled against him, and it was so dark outside but there was the smell of burning wood, the burning wood of the city—as if, her mind teased, and she kept her eyes shut—as if they kissed in front of a fire and he'd taken her shoes off and stroked her feet, and they were on a couch and there was snow. It had stopped raining. Her back was flat up against the rough brick of the pub wall and she opened her eyes to watch him kiss her again, and when he did, she kissed him, hard. Over the ridge of his shoulder, people passed in the dark, passed in the street, and as he lifted her up and she sunk down on him, she moaned out loud, and anyone passing, anyone looking, as some did, it happened so often, couples coupling under the bombs, in the shelters, though there were children, weren't there, down there; but down there it was dark and it was deep and we were returned to the cave and the fire and the glint of life in each other's eyes, never mind the sigh escaping, the unmistakable *oh oh oh*—it was all right, we were only human.

Someone laughed on the street. Someone laughed and Frankie leaned her head back against the wall, her heart racing. Gently, he held her up as he slid out of her and, keeping one hand around her waist, so sweetly, so dearly, zipped himself back into his trousers with the other.

"Christ," she sighed and felt him lean against her again, and kissed him back.

They were wrapped like this, resting, standing up drowsily with their lips against each other's, when the first sirens whined, distant but unmistakable, to the west. He straightened and she opened her eyes.

"That sounds like it's Hammersmith," he said.

A second bank of sirens wailed up, this one much closer.

"Can I walk you somewhere?"

"No," she smiled back at him. "No thanks."

His smile to her was sweet and very deep, and he touched his fingers to her chin. A barrage balloon crossed swiftly overhead and tinted the top of the wall behind his head. "So long, then," he said.

"See you," she called after him, and pushed off the wall to start in the direction of her flat.

She got no farther than half a block before what sounded like a freight train roared past her and she had enough time to flatten herself against the wall when the bomb hit with a force that knocked her into the air and then slammed her down onto the pavement. Another shriek in the air and another, the bombs falling so nearby, it felt like the air was shaking. She stayed where she was on the ground, too stunned to move or cry out. Dust rained down around her and then someone cried out across the street. And someone else, and then it was human noise around her. A little way away a siren sounded. Christ, she sobbed. She tried to push herself up, but she was shaking so hard she had to lie down again. It felt like her heart would bolt from her throat. She lay there and time crept back and handed her the last few moments, then the last hour, and the man's hands on her and his lips—she didn't even know his name—and wondered if he was walking, where he was walking now.

Someone shrieked. She pushed herself up to sitting, and then, reaching for her satchel, which had blown off the pavement into the street, she pulled herself all the way up onto her feet and started walking. The shrieking wouldn't stop and for the first time in these months, she wanted to break into a flat run and had to force herself to slow down in the dark. It was so dark tonight. Where were the bombs now? She crept a little way forward along the street. Please—her feet moved—please, please let me get to the end of the street. Let me cross it and get to the next street. Let me get home, she pleaded. There were four blocks between here and her building.

She stumbled even before the sound hit, the pop of windows a prelude to the boom of the smashed walls that would follow. *Boom*, the sound so big it rocked in the pit of her stomach and for a moment seemed to grab hold of her heart and beat for it also. *Boom*. The shrapnel clattered on the roofs. Directly ahead, three or four blocks off, another shell burst and Frankie dove for the railing of the basement stairs to the building she stood next to. Then a third shell burst overhead and she pushed herself all the way down the stairs and the door opened at her back and she was pulled inside. And she was safe, she was told. Safe. Underground for the first time in all the months she'd been in London. She stumbled down the stairs into a sea of hands that pulled her forward, *there you go, love, mind out, there you go*, until she reached an eddy and sank down against a wall, catching her breath. And at first, that's all she could hear, people like her breathing. Slowly, her eyes adjusted to the dark and she made out what looked like a family beside her fast asleep in a row, the father around the mother around the child, their blanketed form ranging away into the dark like a granite boulder sloping to the sea. Beyond them, she could hear breathing but couldn't make out how many sleepers there were, or even the size of the shelter she'd landed in.

It had gone very quiet up above. Too quiet. As though the bombs were looking for them. Around her, those who were not sleeping stared at the ceiling. She'd heard that Murrow refused to ever go into a bomb shelter, sure he'd lose his nerve. There was no such thing as safety in numbers, everyone knew it. Still, the feeling ran strong, in the dark while the bombs fell down, if you looked up and found someone else's face— if you heard human voices—somehow the whimpering, which could erupt as laughter hovering just inside your mouth and threatening to spill out, stalled. Come what may, down here, you were all in it together. The quiet twined around them. Frankie's heart started to pound with that horrible excitement, as it used to do, waiting in a dark closet playing Sardines, waiting to be found.

A storm of gunfire shook the windows as the AA guns in the Thames battery started up again, cracking the eerie quiet, as though they'd waved. She leaned her head back against the wall and closed her eyes.

She must have dozed, because when she opened her eyes it seemed to have grown lighter, or at least the dark had grown dimmer, though she still couldn't make out the time on her watch. Dimly lit lanterns hung every thirty feet or so, stringing small pockets of light across the shelter. She patted her skirt for her matches, but the box was empty. Idly she followed the lumpen line of sleeping bodies, counting them in her head one by one until she arrived at the opposite wall.

The father beside her jolted in his sleep and then sat straight up, pulling the blanket off his wife and child. *Christ,* he said to no one. He was staring straight ahead of him as if the dream he had just left continued on there in the near dark. *Christ,* he muttered again and looked swiftly over at Frankie. She nodded amiably, not sure whether he was awake. He nodded back at her and it worked like a hand on the string of a kite, hand over hand, pulling him into wakefulness. *Oh,* he sighed, *where were we?* But he didn't want an answer: the blanket had slipped off his wife and he turned away from Frankie to cover her. In the dim light, Frankie saw the woman's arm reach up and pull her husband to her.

The all clear sounded around five o'clock, though it was still pitch-black outside, and cold. One by one people woke. The family beside her stirred and pushed themselves up off the ground, the blankets falling around them.

"Hello." A hand tugged on her skirt.

She looked over. Billy, the boy from the end of her block, was kneeling beside her. She pushed herself upright, tucking her hair behind her ears.

"Hello," he said again.

"Hi." She smiled, glad to see him.

He had lowered himself beside her and was sitting cross-legged, but rocking slightly from side to side as though he were on gliders. Frankie wondered if he'd been hurt. She came up on her knees.

"You okay?"

His round eyes took her in, but he didn't answer.

"Are you by yourself?" She glanced around. "Where's your mum?"

"She went to get Gran," he said quickly. "She said, stay till I get there."

"Last night?"

He nodded.

"Maybe she's in here, then." Frankie pushed herself up to standing, trying to look over the heads of the crowd.

"She can't be here yet." He shook his head. "She would have called for me."

Frankie looked down at him quickly. "Of course she would have," she agreed. "Shall I walk you home?"

He shook his head. "Mum wouldn't like it."

"I'll stay here then, until she comes."

The child's relief flickered over his little body, but the face he turned up to Frankie showed nothing. She smiled down at him. He stared back at her and then dropped his gaze.

"So, Billy," Frankie said, "I don't believe we've been properly introduced, have we?"

He glanced up.

"I'm Frankie Bard." She put out her hand.

"Very pleased to meet you," Billy answered smartly. Frankie grinned.

"And how old are you, Billy? I've been guessing around six."

"Just seven," he pronounced proudly. "I only just turned it last week."

"Well then, happy birthday."

"Six days late." He was firm.

"Happy birthday six days late," Frankie repeated, smiling.

Slowly the sleepers made their way out, until the large underground room had nearly cleared. Frankie glanced down at Billy who was staring at the bright opening where the winter morning crept down the stone stairs into the basement. He was up on his knees now, and his agitation had grown.

"Do you need to pee?"

He shook his head.

"Come on," she said. "I'll walk you home."

He hesitated and then he stood up. "I do need the loo," he admitted stiffly.

"*I looked down at him and realized that the boy was my neighbor. He and his mother lived just up the street. I looked around the shelter. And where is Mummy? I asked, holding the child's hand comfortably in mine. Mummy went back to get Gran, he answered. So I said, Come on then, and took him home.*

"*But when we turned the corner at the end of the street, smoke was rising in blankets into the absurd blue sky, and the boy broke free and ran ahead of me. The bomb had cut an angled path down our block, shearing off all the roofs, but leaving front stoops and doorways, even first-story windows intact at the end of the block. My heart hammering, I followed the boy, staring at the bombed-out face of my own flat. The windows were smashed, and I could see all the way through to what used to be our kitchen. I stared up, hoping against hope to see the face of my flatmate, Harriet Mendelsohn, staring down. But there was nothing. The boy had run up the steps of his own smashed house two doors down, and stopped on the threshold. Mum! he called*"—Frankie's voice broke there on the word *Mum*. And Murrow, sitting right beside her, put his hand on her arm. She shook her head—"*to his house. He'd come home. Mum? he called again with the faith any child calls out to his house, never mind the bombs. His mother would always come down the stairs when he called; any minute she would come, or come around the corner from the kitchen into the hallway. Mummy! Now he was asking. Now he was knowing. From the sidewalk, I heard the shift in the boy's voice, though his small back was still straight in the open doorway.*"

Frankie put both hands on the base of the microphone and closed her eyes, forcing her voice to keep steady, forcing the imaginary ball in her head to stay floating, stay up, to carry the story forward, though tears were sliding through her shut lids.

Billy! A woman brushed past me on the walkway, and Billy turned around.

Have you got Mum?

Oh, Billy, the woman said very softly.

And then the boy crumbled in the doorway where he stood, the familiar voice cutting the string that had held him upright.

Frankie's hands were holding so tight to the microphone that it had gone hot against her palms. She took a breath and went in for the end.

This is how a war knocks down the regular, steady life we set up against the wolf at the door. Because the wolf is not hunger, it is accident—the horrid, fatal mistake of turning left to go to the nearer tube station, rather than right to take the long way around. There is the sense one gets walking around London at night, of a God grown sleepy, tired of holding the whole vast world in His gaze, tired of making sense—so that shards of glass dagger babies in their beds, boys come home to empty houses, and the woman and the man who had just lain down to sleep are crushed.

Harriet Mendelsohn of the Associated Press died last night in the bombs. She had been covering the war in Europe for two years. If a journalist goes down, tradition has it that others of us in the press corps step in to file their story. And the story of the boy coming home is a story she would have written, only better, far better than I. I tell it to you tonight because Harriet can't.

This is Frankie Bard, in London. Good night.

IN THE QUIET after that voice stopped, Emma found herself stuck at the sink with a cigarette halfway to her lips, remembering being five and standing on the doorstep of her great-aunts' house, staring at the door, waiting to meet them after her parents had died. And it hit Emma for the first time that the voice on the other end of the radio was a woman, a woman like herself, only over there. And she wondered what the radio gal had done in the seconds right after the boy had slid to his knees. She wondered whether Frankie had stood there on the outside of the gate, or whether she had been shushed away by the neighbor. She wondered when she found out her friend had died. All there was was the story she had told, not what happened around the edges. What happened after? What happened next? Where was the little boy now?

"Will?" Her voice trembled.

He held out his hand and Emma crept quietly into the clasp of his arm and sank down on his lap in the kitchen chair.

"It's going on over there, right now. I mean right now." She leaned against his shoulder. "That boy, who's with him? I wish we could do something."

"I'm sure he's safe."

She was flooded with a picture of the last time she had seen her own mother, asleep in the hospital bed, her face turned on the pillow facing the door. *Go on*, the nurse had whispered through the gauze mask, *wave good-bye*. And the little girl she was then had understood there would be no help. The grown-up world had departed and left her standing, waving, all alone. She shuddered.

That she was warm and against him and that her cheek rested in his neck steadied the rocking world in his own head. The picture of the boy staring at his smashed house was so clear. But the picture of the woman on the radio watching the boy, watching helplessly—that got him. And the voice of that gal on the radio stirred him, called to him like a siren. Called him, though he didn't know toward what. He pulled Emma in tighter and lay his head on top of hers.

"We ought to do something," she murmured.

"What?" He could feel her heart beating against the arm he'd wrapped across her chest.

"The boy," she said into his chest. He tightened his hold and leaned his forehead against her back and they were quiet like that for a long while together. Life seemed to her like a city hotel with many floors. She did not like to think of all the hallways she'd never seen, nor all the hall-ways that she might have walked along if she had gotten off at a differ-ent floor. She didn't like to think that there was more than one hallway than the one she was in—one in which she hadn't met Will. One in which his eyes weren't on her, watching her, smiling back at what she did.

"If I'd stayed in my rooms last year as I meant to, and not gone to the doctors' Christmas party, we'd never have met."

"No," he whispered into her hair. "I'd have found you."

The front doorbell rang long and hard.

"Dr. Fitch?" someone called from outside the front door. In three strides Will was up and down the hall to the door to find Maggie's eldest boy on the porch, stamping his feet in the cold. He'd run out without a sweater.

"Ma says would you please come." He was excited and proud about giving the news.

"Tell your ma and dad I'll be right over." Will smiled down at him and the boy nodded and turned out of the porch light and ran back down the road to home.

"Don't wait supper for me," Will called to Emma, reaching for his bag and opening it to check again that everything was there.

"Oh, I'll have something by." She had come out into the hall.

"I may be all night," he said gently, pulling her to him and kissing the top of her head.

"All right," she said and then pulled away to look up at him. "I sup-pose this is what I've married, isn't it?"

She was so small just then in the half-light of the hall. But she lifted her face up to be kissed again and he kissed her. "Are you all right?" Will asked, quite low.

She nodded, flushing. "Of course, darling."

"What will you do?"

Emma lifted the latch. "I don't know," she said a little brightly. "It's still early. Maybe I'll walk into town."

"Good," he answered. "That's good." He leaned down, grazing the top of her head with his lips, but she stepped back and looked up at him a little desperately, as if she were going to say something. Just now with her chin tipped up toward him, all he wanted was to kiss her, kiss her as he was used to doing, long and deep and with no thought of what was ahead.

He put his hands on her two shoulders and tipped his forehead down to touch hers. She smiled. She could feel his breath along the ridge of her chin. It was him. His body here. This was all. This was all, ever, that was needed. "Go along, now," she whispered.

He squeezed her shoulders and let her go. "I'll see you later."

He turned at the end of the garden and saw her, still in the doorway, her dark hair uncombed. "Will," she called, clutching her sweater to her neck with one hand and waving with the other. His heart fell out of its casing and he started walking back to the house, toward her in the doorway.

"Don't!" she laughed. "I don't know why I called out."

He stopped.

"Go on," she said, embarrassed by her longing. "I'll see you later."

She was being silly. And when he turned a little ways along down the street and gave her a wave, she tipped her head to the side and stuck out her chin, as gay and brave as Deborah Kerr.

She followed the sharp cutout of his hat above the tall hedge until it was out of sight, replaced by the empty November air. She stood at the front door feeling the cold and hearing what might have been the echo of his footsteps on the frozen sidewalk and looked out at the blank swatch of sky. She looked down at her wristwatch and then back up at the empty view out the front door. There were hours to be gotten through.

She turned back into the little front room, sank into the one comfy chair, and kicked the door closed on the rest of the house.

She had always thought that having a house would be a source of great strength, like a trunkful of memories one never unlocked. Her own family's house had been sold along with all its contents, except for some photographs and the child's christening set of silver and her mother's little seed-pearl wedding ring, which hung loosely off the third finger on Emma's right hand. She had wondered sometimes where the things had ended up. She didn't begrudge her great-aunts' decision—she had lived off the proceeds, as they reminded her, after all—but sometimes she wondered whether she might feel less lonely, somehow less anonymous, if, when she woke in the morning, she opened her eyes and saw the same bureau her father had, for instance. Or, even less grand, used the kettle her mother used to boil water for their junket.

But here—she sighed—out there and upstairs, there was nothing of hers. She felt for the first time in her life the danger of other people's things—how they might erase her if she weren't careful. A sob caught at the bottom of her throat. It was that report on the boy in the Blitz; she leaned toward the coffee table to get her cigarette case. The report had reminded her of being little, that was all. She lit the cigarette and drew in a deep, long drag.

5.

THE WINTER AFTERNOON had set in and it was near dark, though the last of the sky hung indigo above the water splashing against the spars of the old pier. Maggie and Jim Tom lived in one of the fish houses right along the harbor's edge, built by the fishermen before the pier to stow their tackle and gear. They were steep-angled tiny boxes, like a child's drawing of a house, and without windows except for the big double doors in front, which slid aside to let out the spars and gaffs, the heavy lines and mast for the jib. Jim Tom and Maggie had moved into the Winthrop fish house in the days right after their wedding, and Jim had cut out windows, put down flooring in the sail loft, and promised they'd be in their own house after five years of fishing. That had been ten years ago. Never mind, Maggie laughed at him—and she didn't mind. She'd look up and see Jim Tom steaming in around Land's End after a long haul, and watch him heading straight for her.

Will could see the angle of the Winthrop fish house ahead, and could just make out the lamp that was burning by Maggie's bed; but still feeling the warmth of Emma's body in his, even as he was already outside and long past that moment, he stopped and looked back. The roofline of his house and that of the Nileses beside it bulwarked the oncoming night. Ought he to let Dr. Lowenstein know Maggie had gone into labor? Her labors are hard and long, the old doctor had said to Will the last time he had been in town, and this one will be her fifth in as many years. The porch light went on at Will's house. He felt sharp sudden joy. No, no need to call. He was the doctor now. He turned his back on his own house and started again toward the Winthrops, letting his doctor's bag swing in his hand. Jim Tom opened the door before Will could knock, and Will looked up to see if there was any hint of worry in his face.

But Jim Tom had been through this four times before, and he had, Will saw, entering the single big downstairs room, put on a large pot to boil hot water and prepared a basin. There was also a teakettle steaming. The house was calm, but ready. Up there, Jim Tom nodded in response to Will's glance.

"I'll wash up here, shall I?" He turned on the tap above the kitchen sink and ran the water over his hands several times, finding the soap tucked into the exposed board of the wall in front of him.

"And where are your boys?"

"Mother's."

Will nodded and climbed the open stairs. Halfway up, Maggie began to groan in the grip of a contraction. He took the stairs two at a time and followed the sound into a room that had been made into the sail loft by placing two armoires next to each other as a partition. On this side, the stacked-up gear of generations of Winthrop boats, sails tackle, riggings, and masts lay in orderly stacks. On the other side of the armoires there lay a bed pulled up to a window, freshly made, it looked like, the sheets pulled tight.

Maggie was creeping along the wall, one hand on her side, bent over and gasping, but when Will went forward to her, she waved him away. Her breaths came in rapid sighs and she walked in time to them. At the end of the wall, she stopped and straightened and turned around, walking back along the wall in the other direction.

"Shit," she gasped out, leaning her head against the wall.

"Shit is right," Will agreed.

Maggie nodded, her face contorted briefly. She gave a deep groan and he watched her shoulders relax. She sank onto the end of the bed, a little pale, Will thought.

"Whew," she said.

"How long have you been contracting like that?" He moved around the bed and picked up her wrist for her pulse. Brisk. Her forehead was moist and her hair was damp against her temples.

"Off and on about four hours."

"Pretty strong?" He counted her pulse against the hand of the bed-side clock whose comfortable ticking sounded out into the room.

"Strong and long." She nodded.

"Strong as that one?"

"And forever. That's how all my babies are. Tommy, the littlest, took two days to come."

Will helped her sit back against the pillows piled up on the bed, shook down the thermometer, and slid it in her mouth. "Well, let's hope number five comes a bit quicker for you."

Maggie shrugged, her mouth closed over the thermometer. It had started; they were both in the chute. Come what may, there was only one direction to go in now.

"Let's check how far along you are." Will pushed her knees gently up and open; he slid his fingers up the vagina to the cervix where he could feel the head, but not the bag.

"When did your bag break, Maggie?"

"Has it?" She frowned. "I don't know. Day before yesterday? There was something then, though I wasn't sure what it was, there was so little of the junk—and I didn't have any cramps at all."

He pulled his hand out and with it there was a slight unfamiliar odor, something he didn't remember smelling at the births he'd attended before. He washed his hands in the bowl of warm water Jim Tom had brought up and left by the bed; he toweled them dry, frowning. Then he turned and slid the thermometer from Maggie's mouth and saw that her temperature was slightly elevated. He sat down on the side of the bed.

"Okay," he exhaled, pushing a faint wisp of worry away.

"Oh." She pushed herself off the bed, needing to walk at the start of another contraction. Will helped her onto her feet and waited through the next one with her, all the time watching how she breathed. When it had eased, she focused back on him. "How far along am I?"

"Six centimeters or so. You've got a ways to go still. But you're doing swell."

She smiled weakly, rising to sit on the side of the bed, holding her hand out to Will. He pulled her to her feet and they started walking again, first to the opposite side of the room, then back.

THE GULLS ROSE up suddenly off the pylons on the pier, the swift beating of their wings like hands shuffling cards, and Iris followed them as they wheeled into the sky outside the window. She crossed the wooden floor of the lobby, unlocked the front doors, and the blast of a northerly wind hit her. Quick as she could, she reached out and uncleated the line on the flagpole and the flag came sliding on its tether down the pole into her hands.

"Evening," a voice said from below.

She jumped and clutched the cloth to her chest as though he had caught her at something secret. "Oh, hello," she called over her shoulder, shivering. She should have put on her coat, she realized.

"Want help with that?"

She shook her head, releasing the flag from the metal clips on the line, and turned around. Harry Vale had one foot up on the bottom stair and one hand loosely on the railing. He smiled and she smiled back, embarrassed to be standing above him this way. It had the effect of making him appear very small.

"I've been using your mug." She let her eyes down to look at his hand on the railing, the flag still crumbled into a ball in her arms.

"Good." He nodded. But his attention drifted to the pole above her head. "Just the top three feet," he nudged, smiling. "Would you give me the top three feet? Just to get it below the roofline."

She cleated the line and rested her hand on the painted wood, not quite sure what she wanted to say. It had become something like a joke between them, a running patter, though it wasn't a joke and she knew it. "I haven't heard from the post office inspector," she said.

He lowered his gaze to her face. "It doesn't worry you?"

She flushed. "We can't allow ourselves to take things into our own hands like that."

"Why not?" He slid his hand along the ridge of the gate.

With a small, efficient stab, the question pricked her. They were at odds, she realized, unhappily.

"Never mind," he said gently. "Good night."

"Good night," she answered and he ambled off. That hadn't gone at all the way she wanted.

She crossed the lobby with the flag in her arms and pushed through the door into the back part of the post office, shutting it firmly behind her. One couldn't behave as though the post office was just another building, its flagpole just another piece of wood. It represented something. Order. And here at the very heart of the system, she let out her breath, carefully. Back here the open mailboxes stretched floor to ceiling, ready for her to fill. The broad wooden sorting table was cleared for the morning's mail. If there was a place on earth in which God walked, it was the workroom of any post office in the United States of America. Here was the thick chaos of humanity rendered into order. Here was a box for each and every family in the town. Letters, bills, newspapers, catalogs, packages might be sent forth from anywhere in the world, shipped and steamed across water and land, withstanding winds and time, to journey ever forward toward this single, small, and well-marked destination.

Here was no Babel. Here, the tangled lines of people's lives unknotted, and the separate tones of voices set down upon a page were let to breach the distance. Hand over hand the thoughts were passed. And *hers* was the hand at the end.

Still. Harry's gentle wave as he walked away took some of the pleasure out of it all. She climbed up onto the chair beside the sorting table, holding the flag above her shoulders so it did not touch the floor, and shook it out like a bedsheet, holding a corner in each hand. The certificate in its envelope lay perfectly safe up the hill in her cottage, among her nightgowns in the bureau drawer. It had lain there all these weeks since she'd gone into Boston, and every day he'd come into the post office and she could feel the tie between them tightening, sighing as it tightened, and she didn't have the faintest idea what to do next.

The vision of her mother standing in the passage on the way to her parents' bedroom flashed before her. Thin-framed but gone to fat, her mother's body hung like too many coats thrown over a hanger. She was thick and mealy, but Iris had caught her laughing in response to something coming from her father in the bedroom that Iris couldn't hear, turning her girlish. Iris appeared in her nightie at the end of the hall and her mother had turned, concerned, but still headed for the bedroom— her whole attention in there. In one hand she held a rubber pouch, like a hot water bottle, with a long tube snaking out of it and over her mother's arm. In the other hand, Iris saw she held the glass bottle of vinegar from the pantry. "Iris," her mother said, "you're dreaming, dear. Go back to bed." And Iris had.

How did the next part work? She couldn't imagine it. She couldn't think past the looking and the smiling to a moment like that with a douche in one's hand, without any pretense what for. A woman standing like that, wide open. Like an announcement.

She folded the flag in half, then half again, then held it against her chest, smoothing it flat. Still holding to one corner, she let the other drop against the flat length, so that it made a triangle. And then again, she let the triangle fold against itself into a second triangle. This way and that she folded the flag until it was fully collected into a single triangle of cloth into which she tucked the ends.

The moon was rising as she latched the post office gate and stepped back into the matter-of-fact world where her bicycle leaned against the side of the building at the bottom of the post office steps. A fog was coming in and the foghorn sang its steady single note. Across the green, the light inside Alden's Market shone fiercely down on the people inside. She could see Florence Cripps from here. And another woman. Leaning over the counter to talk to Beth, the grocer's daughter. They looked like figures in a painting, stuck onto the light.

She glanced up at the naked flagpole, then stared in the direction where Harry had disappeared, and flushed. She would go to the movies, she decided. She would not get her habitual chop at the café, she wasn't hungry. She would not go back up the hill to her cottage.

INSIDE THE FISH HOUSE, nothing had changed much, either in the frequency or intensity of Maggie's contractions. The clock beside her bed kept time like a supporter, the minutes passing as Maggie walked and slept. She had been right; she was in for a protracted labor. Will watched her as she breathed. When Will checked her again, the cervix was no wider. She fell again into a doze and Will went downstairs in search of coffee.

"How's everything?" Jim Tom turned from the sink.

"Coming along," said Will. "You want to come up?"

"I'd just as soon wait down here, thanks." Jim Tom glanced at him. "How many babies have you caught there, Will?"

"Fifteen. No, sixteen," Will answered abruptly.

Jim Tom nodded. "Then you ought to know how mean the ladies can get at the end."

Will looked at him, quizzically.

"No?" Jim Tom smiled. "Well, maybe the Boston ladies hold their tongue."

Above them, Maggie started to groan again. Will stopped and looked at his watch, timing the contraction. It lasted roughly the same amount of time as the others, though this one sounded lower than before, and maybe a bit more desperate to Will's ear.

Will looked at Jim Tom. "Does that help her, do you think?"

"What?"

"Making that noise."

Jim Tom stuck out his chin. "You bet," he said.

Will nodded and made for the stairs. As he climbed, he could hear Maggie panting and he climbed a little faster. When he rounded the corner into the room, she was kneeling on the bed with her back to him, holding on to the headboard, her head down between her outstretched arms. He waited until she'd finished and then stepped in. She turned around and he saw that she was growing tired. Her eyes showed her weariness. And this worried him. "How are you holding up there, Maggie?" he said quietly. She nodded and exhaled. "Good," she said.

He drew the fetoscope out of his bag to make an initial assessment of the baby's heartbeat, and the sound, regular and steady, felt like a hand reached out to him from the other side, a greeting.

"He's right there, waiting," Will reassured Maggie. She nodded, blowing against the grip of the next contraction, and as Will watched her face, he had such a profound longing for Emma, for her quiet eyes on his, for her calm—yes, she was his calm—that he stood up and paced to the end of the room without thinking. He wanted to tell her again, firmly—he'd have found her.

When he'd first stumbled upon her at the hospital Christmas party two years ago, she had been staring out the grand windows draped for the season in holly and velvet with her back to the party. The doctors and nurses coming off duty entered with the cold air clinging to them, their bright voices bowling hard and tight into the cloudy good cheer of partygoers on their way out. She hadn't moved for several minutes, and her absorption made all else in that room tiny. On a private dare, he wandered toward her. If she turned before he got there, he'd get a glance at her but not need to engage her. If she remained staring like that, her back to him, he'd offer her a drink.

But she stepped back from the window without turning, bumping into him. For an instant he felt her body light against him and smelled lemon in her hair. She leapt away from him and turned, her face gone pink. "I'm sorry!"

"I'm not." He grinned and held out his hand. "Will Fitch."

"Yes." She took it, shook it, and quickly dropped it.

"Having fun?"

She looked directly at him then, with a slight smile on her lips. "No," she answered. "Not at all."

"Why not?"

"It's Christmas," she said.

"I see," he said, noticing the tender line of her chin tipped as she watched him. He hadn't the faintest idea what to say next.

"We're not for Christmas?" he groped.

She smiled more broadly now, though still a little shy. "No."

"Why's that? If you don't mind my asking."

She didn't answer. He leaned against the wall beside her. After a minute or so he realized she wasn't going to answer. He slid his gaze sideways. "I guess you do mind my asking."

She looked straight at him. "I don't know you."

He straightened up quickly. "True enough. I'm sorry."

She turned away from him and faced the room. "I'm not very good at small talk. Can I have a drink?"

Will was suddenly, painfully happy. "What'll it be?"

"Bourbon," she answered quickly, "and water."

He nodded and made his way through the thick crowd toward the bar at the end of the room. Johnny Lambert was standing in the alcove there, surrounded by two or three other residents. He was telling a story and the circle around him had leaned in slightly to hear. There was a beat and then the group erupted, one of the men slapping Johnny on the back as if keeping time to his laughter, and the sound broke over the rest of the crowd carrying the delicious joke, the thick, hot gaiety gathering everyone in. For a moment the room seemed to collect on the wave of the laughter sent forth by Johnny, whose grace and talent was to treat the world like a ball he spun on one long finger.

Will had seen it the moment he'd arrived at Harvard eight years ago. Johnny's grace was repeated in the easy tilt of the Boston boys as they sat taking notes, their notebooks pushed away from them, the slow scrawl of their pencils across the white pads like some long, lean jazz, some foreign inscrutable music playing just beyond Will's own ear. Hunnewell. Cabot. Phipps. Sure, they worked. They even worked hard. But it was without heat or worry; the prizes given to them at the end of the year were casually taken, and lightly worn. Those boys were finer than the challenges Harvard tossed them. Unimpeachably fine.

Whereas he was Fitch. Sure, the name meant enough to get him into the right house in his sophomore year, enough to warrant the right amount of interest when he was introduced. But then, in the next breath—Franklin? At the end of Cape Cod? Do people live all the way out there? Thought the whole place shut up tight after Labor Day.

Ha, ha, he'd grin. Ha, ha. You'd be surprised. Three or four hundred of us are left there after you all flee. Is that right, the other would drawl, interest waning. Will Fitch from Franklin. He was a curio, an exotic. Not dismissable, but not someone to contend with either. All the years he was in Cambridge, he was Fitch—from Franklin. Which was nowhere to begin from.

The wash of Johnny's joke had sped all the way out. Someone suggested another round, and Johnny nodded without looking up, his hand cupped around the darting flame of his lighter. Any minute he'd turn and see Will standing there alone and talking to no one, a fool in the middle of a party.

Suddenly what to do next had been simple. It was clear. Will turned back around and headed straight for the window, afraid she'd have disappeared. But he picked her out, still standing there. Waiting for him, he realized with a thrill.

"Hullo," he said, coming to stand in front of her.

"No more drinks?"

"No," he smiled. "There are. But there are too many people. Let's go have a drink somewhere else."

She looked up again at him. "I'm Emma Trask." She offered him her hand.

"All right," he said, taking it in his. His long fingers touched the inner place in her wrist where her pulse beat and he felt it race forward, as though he'd got hold of her heart. He tucked her hand under his arm and led her out of the party.

WILL TURNED around to Maggie. "Let's check again," he said softly. He piled up two pillows at the end of her bed, and placed her feet upon them. She opened her eyes and watched his face as he slipped his fingers inside her once more, feeling for the baby's head. He smiled at her, relieved. The cervix was nearly completely dilated and the head was ready to pass into the bony pelvis.

"You're closer," he said, comfortingly, and reached to take her pulse.

As soon as his fingers found the spot on her wrist, he knew it was wrong. He held on to her for another full minute, counting the beats again to be sure. It was definitely accelerated. Her pulse had been quick before. Now it was racing. The earlier worry he had dismissed charged forward. There had been that smell. Her temperature was up. And now her pulse was rapid and irregular. He glanced at her, worried for the first time that these were signs pointing toward sepsis.

She closed her eyes again and groaned, low and dark as the throttle of a cow, the sound seeming to seep up from the ground beneath his feet. *Ohh*, the groaning note widened and grew around the room. He had attended sixteen births and even performed two cesarean sections, but those women had never been this loud. There had been nurses in the hospital and there had been ether and the babies had slid out like seals. He had never delivered a baby by himself before. And somehow, here in the tiny upstairs room of the fish house, it was as though this was his first birth, the first time he'd understood how far below the training women take you, down into the thick of it, into the dark blood stew where life begins. *Ohhh, ohhh, ohhh*—the groans battered him. A scream, the high relief of a scream—like a whistle or a piece of music—that he could manage, but this low deep repetition took him down far underground. Her eyes were shut tight as if she were trying to remember something or make her way forward somewhere, while her mouth kept opening on the crest of the contraction, bellowing the pain.

Dimly, through the floorboards, Will heard the older children returning home; hearing them, Maggie smiled weakly.

"They ought to go back with their grandmother," Will said more harshly than he meant.

"They don't sleep if they can't sleep in their beds," she murmured.

"But—"

"They've heard it before," she sighed.

The next groan started forward again, thick and deep. Will stood up from the bed abruptly. There ought to be more light in the room. In the hospital, scenes like this were reassuringly lit, there was never a question of not knowing where you'd put your things, where you might need to go to get hot water or towels. Light counteracted the horror Maggie was in the grip of, light. He strode over to the door and flicked the switch and the white ceramic bowl burst into brightness above his head, pushing away the desperation he was feeling. It was a simple bedroom with a dresser and three windows, a rocking chair and a round hooked rug beside the bedstead.

Downstairs were the other children, and Will thought of Lowenstein, who had brought those others into the world, and wished he were here to consult with, a pair of experienced hands, another set of diagnostic eyes. To have somebody in the room other than this woman groaning. This woman—he forced himself to look and smile as she rolled her head against the pillow and closed her eyes—this woman who was Maggie, who used to be Maggie in his classroom. Maggie on the waterfront, her long legs tangling in the riggings of her father's boat above his head. Maggie who stared straight into his eyes when he examined her, his inquiring fingers sliding into her to see if all was in place, not like most who shut their eyes or looked up into the ceiling.

The old tenacious dread slid out into the shallows. It had always gone wrong for the Fitches. Why had he thought it could be any different? Why had he thought he could begin again in the same town, with the same name as his father's? He nearly laughed aloud, the bubble of fear rising in his chest as he listened to Maggie now. This deep dark grunting dread, this was what held on. He had married Emma. He had come back to town a doctor. He had thought he could plan a future and kiss his wife like anyone else. But the truth was, the old dark feeling swam just there. It would never go away. And here was proof.

Suddenly with terrific energy, Maggie bolted up and turned her back around, looked at Will wildly but didn't seem to see him, kneeling on the bed with her hands on the wall behind the headboard. She turned away from him and then back, groaning, *stop stop stop*, the word panting out as regular as a machine. *Stop stop stop stop*—her voice rose and then she arched her back away from the pain driving around and around inside her, and when it was over she groaned wordless, and slumped against the board. Will watched her, nervous. It was as though he'd seen a rag doll shaken in the mouth of a dog, her body flung this way and that, and then flung away, the doll left to lie flat and limp, pale and sweating.

The eerie sound of a child humming to itself came up from down below. It was a tuneless little sound and it came so purely up through the floorboards that Will realized the walls kept nothing out, that the children down below had heard their mother, that he and she might just as well be behind a curtain in the middle of a crowded public ward.

"Maggie?" he whispered, licking his lips.

She might have fallen suddenly asleep, though she lay pale and sweating with her eyes closed. The child's tune snaked around in the air with no apparent destination or pattern. Will sat and listened, his own brain stuck and tired, the light slowly departing from the attic, leaving the old white sails to glow where they had been piled. *Oh,* sang the child, *oh, oh, oh that opportunity rag.* Will tried to remember the children's names and ages. Who was the singer down there, and where were the rest? *Oh,* hummed the child again, his voice dipping lower. Maggie's hand fell open on the bed. Had she passed out, or was she only asleep? She was asleep, Will saw now, deep asleep, her mouth parted a little and a flush spread upon her cheeks. The series of waves that she had been borne upon, crashing once and once again and then once more, had receded and left her to sleep. Will rolled his wrist over to check the time. Four minutes had past. The little boy—it must be a boy, Will had decided, the tone was so pure—had moved toward the front of the house and the voice now came from there, sliding backward and up through the floorboards at his feet. Maggie's eyelids fluttered slightly. Did she hear the one child, he wondered, calling to the other? For that is how it seemed, this one sweet little bird down below humming in the middle of this terrible scene, the mother nothing but a string held in the fierce tiny grips of the unborn and the child already here and pulled on, mercilessly. He stood and pulled a washcloth out of the basin, wringing it damp.

"Maggie?" He placed the cloth on her brow.

"Oh," she sighed. "Where's Jim Tom?" She sounded like herself for the first time in three hours.

"Downstairs," Will said, so relieved he nearly gasped. She was rousable, after all. She was right here.

"But who's that?"

"One of your boys, I think. Jimmy, maybe?"

She smiled. "No. Jimmy can't sing." She opened her eyes and in the creeping dark, the whites had the same sort of dim glow as the sails. Will's heart stuck for an instant with some sense that he was looking at a ghost. "Henry?" she called.

The singing stopped and footsteps ran to the bottom of the stairs. "Yes, Ma?" Henry called up.

"Sing some more, sweetie," she called and fell back to sleep.

6.

SLIPPING INTO THE THEATER, Iris stood at the back letting her eyes adjust to the dark. The end of a newsreel was playing and lines of German soldiers marched toward her through frozen French fields. Their bodies moved like marionettes, the heads held stiffly and turning left to right as they came down the screen. Because she was standing up, they marched toward her at eye level and she had the sensation of being overtaken by a crowd.

"Goddamn Krauts!" someone yelled. The outlines of the seated people appeared against the wall of soldiers still marching, the ups and downs of their heads and shoulders like an old Greek pattern on the bottom of a vase. Iris took a step forward into the dark theater and chose a seat toward the back.

The newsreel ended and the lights stayed down as the credits introduced the picture. Iris leaned forward to slip her coat off her shoulders and then settled down into her seat. It was a movie from the thirties, one she had forgotten she had seen. But as the opening scene unfolded under the rich tones of the narrator, she remembered she had been here before. It was an old-fashioned love story broken by a war, and she felt herself slowly succumbing to the tug of the characters, into that bright English chatter of the actors as the love affair began. The movie played over her, and she didn't remember enough of it to feel impatient. In fact, she had the delicious sensation of returning to a place she had once loved but had forgotten, like a room in childhood. The lovers had married, and now there he was, brave man, sailing off to war.

Her heart started to beat a little faster, as though she were walking down a long corridor with many turns. She had remembered what lay at the end of this movie, but she could not remember clearly how it all arrived there. The man had been caught behind enemy lines. He was surrounded, and now he was being marched to the commander. Iris sat up straight. She remembered now. She remembered it all, and the anxiety of what was to come made her heart pound still harder. He was not going to make it, that's right. He was not going to make it, and the reason why he was not going to make it was because his signal—the flare he had shot up into the sky before capture—would not be seen. He had shot his flare, he had seen the bright white arc in the sky, and he had marched away, his head high, because of his faith that the signal would be seen. His men were only a mile away, he knew.

But what he didn't know, what he couldn't see: that was what Iris couldn't bear. She almost stood to leave. Almost. She had forgotten this horror at the center of this lovely unfolding flower of a movie. She had forgotten that the men, his men, were dead. "Run," she wanted to say to the screen. "Run," she wanted to say to him, marching smartly away without a backward glance. "You're on your own. There is no one left to save you. Run."

But the story wouldn't save him. The men were dead and only she and the other people watching knew. As they watched it all play out in front of them, it was the terror of that knowing and the fear he must have felt the moment he understood. He was alone, they felt it. And the sorrow. To watch helplessly, thought Iris, was the worst part. But also, to see the pattern, too. To see the terrible, inexorable pattern of it—the dead and the dying, and the knowledge that he could have run, but didn't. He took the wrong path. He made the wrong choice. And he died.

The lights came up with the music crashing loudly into the air. Iris stared straight ahead, not wanting to see the others move around her. She stayed where she was in her seat until the last of the movie flickered past and the reel clicked behind her. And then she turned her head and there, sitting six or seven seats over, sat Harry Vale.

She blushed. He might think she had followed him in here, that she had stayed on the porch steps and watched to see where he went. But she hadn't, she thought crossly. She had finished her work and then she had gone to the movies herself. Why did he have to be in here at all? Perhaps he hadn't seen her. She tried not to move or draw attention to herself. There was an aisle on his side and he could just stand up, anytime; there was no need to look over here. He could just stand up and leave. She decided to wait him out and leaned over as if she had to pick something up off the floor. When she leaned back he was standing up and looking straight at her.

"Did you lose something?"

"No, I—"

He nodded. She was sitting bolt upright in her chair, her coat half on and half off.

"I didn't think I'd see you here."

"Why's that?"

He shrugged and that grin came again, like the grin on a bear. "War movie."

"It's not about the war," she said too quickly.

"Could have fooled me."

She pulled her arm through the sleeve of her coat. "I mean, I don't think the war is what is important."

He watched as she reached inside the opposite sleeve and pulled out her scarf. "What is important, then?" He made his way across the intervening seats between them.

"The fact that there's nobody there in the end."

He didn't say anything, but now he was standing right next to her. She flushed. "I suppose you disagree."

He shook his head. "No. There is nobody there in the end."

"Except God," she corrected, more for herself than for him.

"God," he repeated, without inflection, as if he had said *bar stool* or *pin*.

"You sound as if you don't believe He's there."

"Oh, He's there, all right."

He smelled of Old Spice and axle grease and one of his hands rested on the back of the seat in front of her so casually, so easily, it made her unaccountably happy.

"I know He's there. Every time I catch a mistake at work, I know it's Him. Or else how would I have seen it?"

"Because you're good at what you do."

"But"—she smiled, almost flirting—"why am I good?" She pushed herself up from her seat and turned to make her way out of the theater. The low light from the sconces along the walls was as dim as candles. She could hear him behind her.

"Walk you home?"

"I've got my bike."

He didn't comment, and not knowing whether she'd said yes or no, Iris turned in the direction of the post office. He followed. Other people's voices and laughter ricocheted out of the dark, and the disconnected bursts of talk came and went like fire. She crossed her arms in front of her, her pocketbook hanging off one elbow.

"Nice night."

"Yes." She smiled to herself and agreed, again. Out here among all the others, the fact that the two of them were walking side by side made it clearer they were walking together.

"Hi, Joe."

"Lo," the other man said as he wobbled by on a bicycle.

"Where's he off to at this time of night?"

"Night fishing, I'd guess—never mind the Germans."

"The Germans," Iris said firmly, "are bombing the British."

He turned his head and looked at her, but she couldn't read the expression on his face. He looked at her and then he looked away, and for the briefest instant she felt again that she might have been measured and fallen short. The bicycle spokes clicked around and around between them.

"Anyway, they'll never allow them in this far."

"I'll say one thing about you," Harry said easily. "You've got a hell of a lot of faith in God and the government."

"I work for the government," Iris observed, relieved by his tone. Perhaps she hadn't disappointed.

"That's my point."

Iris looked over at him and caught his grin. She shook her head. "What's your point?"

"Government's just a bunch of human beings same as you and me."

"With a plan."

He whistled. "Who made up that plan?"

"People at the top," she answered swiftly, "who have an overview of the whole situation. People who pay attention, who know. It's their job."

"Like you." He stepped aside to let a group pass them by, but she kept on walking, wanting him to see what she meant, wanting him to get it.

"Not at all like me," she said briskly when she heard him again beside her. He had tipped his head to hear her and his arm was just under her elbow as she spoke. "I'm paid to watch out for accidents, for cracks in the machinery. My job is to prevent the system from derailing."

"How in the hell do you plan to do that?"

"I pay attention," she said firmly. "All the time. I watch out. That's my job."

He chuckled in the dark. "You're a little nuts, aren't you?"

"That depends," she smiled back, "on where you're standing."

"Hello, Frank, Marnie." Harry had stopped short.

Iris swallowed and nodded to the couple in front of them. Marnie

Niles was bundled in a long coat, next to her husband. Now she patted Frank's hand, which was resting easily on her hip. Harry and the postmaster, that hand said. Think of it. Iris's heart sputtered open.

"Hello, Harry." Frank Niles smiled. "Miss James."

Harry nodded. Iris stood beside him feeling like the lights had suddenly been switched on.

"Where are you two off to?"

"We're walking Iris home," Harry answered swiftly, and he turned to her, waiting. He was waiting for her. Iris nodded, afraid to trust herself to speak. Marnie's eyelids lowered slightly, as if she'd seen a sign.

"So long," Harry said.

"See you," Marnie called out. Iris stepped off the curb after Harry. They walked away from the bright splash of town in the opposite direction, where the arm of land curled into a fist, and began the slow climb up Yarrow Road to Iris's cottage. After a long patch of quiet, they heard footsteps up ahead on the tarmac, though Iris's bicycle lamp caught nothing but the dark hedge and the rosehips, black balls hanging. A man appeared in the light.

"Otto," Harry said.

Startled, the German man lifted his eyes off the road; he seemed not to have seen the two of them coming, or their light. He stepped around the beam of the lamp and moved toward them.

"Harry," he said, and nodded at Iris.

"You okay?"

"Yes, yes. I am just walking." He nodded again.

"Okay, Otto." Harry clapped the man on the shoulder. "Good night."

"Good night." His footsteps carried on behind them into the pitch black. She wondered how he made his way on the dark road like that.

"He walks up here most nights, I think." Harry started walking again.

Iris gave the bike a push. "Why?"

"He comes up to the bluff to stare at France."

"Dear God," Iris breathed.

Harry's hand found hers on top of the bicycle handle and closed over it. Just like that, she thought, amazed. They kept on walking without a word. She let her hand slide off the handle so they were walking hand in hand now; the farther they went, the more quiet and the clearer it grew that they had arrived. That's how these things started. So little.

And then, very gently, he slowed, turning toward her, resting one hand back on the bicycle so they were holding it upright together and he pulled her toward him and she had to shuffle a little to get close, maybe a hairsbreadth taller than he; when his lips found hers, she did have to tip slightly to meet him. His kiss was soft at first, his lips against hers gentle, an introduction. Then it seemed he had decided something, for he pulled her toward him harder and drew her in close, and in the dark, with her eyes shut, she had simply walked through a door into this soft, wet place encircled by a man, kissed and kissing, and she could have been any-where, she realized—anywhere at all, if this man kissed her in the post office, she'd walk into the circle gladly and lose herself over and over to find this spot in the dark, this damp wide opening.

They kissed for a long time, and when they pulled away, she real-ized they were still standing in the middle of Yarrow Road, and that her hand was stiff with cold on the bicycle handlebars. She thrust it into her pocket, letting the bicycle fall against her hip.

"Would you like some tea?"

"Yes," he said, and they started back up the road, as though nothing had happened, she marveled. There was all the time in the world now, because it would happen. This would happen. She had never felt so free. That's how these things started. So little. She turned and smiled at him in the dark. They started slowly off again.

Outside Jim Tom and Maggie Winthrop's fish house, someone sat on the stairs, the red ember of a cigarette a punched hole in the dark.

"Evening," a voice called out to them.

"Who's that? Jim Tom?"

"Aye."

"All right there?"

"Maggie's having the baby."

"Everything all right?"

"Aye. We've got Will Fitch inside."

"Good luck, there."

"Aye, thanks."

They walked in quiet the rest of the way up the hill, the lights of Franklin behind them like a low cluster of stars, the shingled sides of the houses they passed glowing violet in the half-moon. The porch light was on at the Fitch house, making even darker the row of summer cottages of which Iris's was the last, the only one the owner, Mr. Day, had insulated and put a stove in for himself.

"We used to break in here when we were kids, to smoke, in the off season," Harry said following Iris onto the tiny cottage porch and then through the door. She reached for the switch under the lamp shade and the light sprang on. Though the largest in the row, Iris's cottage had been fixed like all the others. Two rockers and a tiny sofa placed "in conversation" at the edges of a round hooked rug. Two tiny bedrooms on either side of the living room, and between them a kitchenette along the back wall. Everything fresh. Everything bright. Nothing important but the air and water flipping lazily back and forward outside the trim windows. On all of the porches, two wooden chairs sat facing the harbor. It had been just what Iris wanted when she arrived last year.

Without looking at him, she moved to pick up the teakettle and took it over to the sink to fill it. The water coughed in the pipe and then glugged out.

"Who's *we*?"

"Frank Niles and me—and Fitch. The doctor's father."

She set the kettle on the stove, lit the pilot, then turned on the flame. She pulled two mugs down from the shelf above the stove and set them on the counter. Pausing, leaning against the kitchen wall, she reached down into her skirt pocket and felt for her cigarettes and lighter, shaking out a cigarette and putting it in her mouth, glad of the distraction. "I hear he was a drunk."

"Yes," said Harry simply.

She looked up. He took the lighter gently from her fingers and then he reached and pulled the cigarette from her lips. He was going to kiss her again, she realized, and she felt more awkward in here, in the light, standing in the middle of her own kitchen, than she had in the wide open dark of the town road. He leaned forward against her, placing his hands on the wall behind her head, and drew her lips to his; without thinking, she put her hands on the loose waist of his coat and pulled it, pulled him to her. Beneath his mouth, she smiled.

"What?" he asked against her lips.

She shook her head. One thing would lead to another, she need not think at all. The whistle blew on the kettle and he reached a hand out and switched it off.

After a long time, he leaned back. "I ought to leave you," he said.

"Ought to?"

He kissed her again. "Ought," he smiled. "Not want."

Her hand bunched the cloth of his jacket and tugged at him, like a child. "Hold on."

"What is it?"

"I have something." She blushed and walked back along the hall into her bedroom, stopping at the bureau. Her heart was pounding so hard in her chest, it nearly hurt her. She had imagined handing the certificate to him, neat and clean, offering it with a small smile so he knew it was done gladly. But standing in front of her bureau, her face in the mirror looked terrified. Whatever would he think? She hesitated.

"Oh, for pity's sake," she whispered to herself. She bent and pulled open the drawer, thrust her hand in and closed it over the envelope in the middle of her sweaters.

"Here." She held it in front of her. "I wanted you to have this before—"

He looked at her, curious. "What is it?"

"Here," she said again.

He took the envelope from her. "You're giving me a letter?"

"Of a kind." She couldn't look at him. He turned the envelope over and slid the certificate out.

"Intact?"

She nodded, blushing furiously.

He put both hands around her waist. "I'm an old, broken-down man, you know, not a catch at all."

"Oh, I didn't mean that—I didn't mean that I was catching you."

He laughed. "*I'm* hardly intact."

"I mean, I just thought—"

"Shh." He touched her face. And she saw that it was all right.

OUTSIDE there were stars so thick you couldn't put a finger through a hole in the sky. Harry set off in the direction of town, his body electric with the fresh memory of the woman he had watched for so long simply stepping right into his arms. After a few minutes, he turned and counted the house lights shining in a row—from Bowtch's to Fitch's, to where the town ended with Iris. The image of her picking her way uprightly beside him in the crowd tonight flashed into his head. What had she been saying? He had thought he smelled lemons in her hair and had leaned closer as she spoke. He slipped his fingers inside his coat pocket where the certificate rested against his heart, and walked the rest of the way into town with his hand loose upon the paper.

Ahead of him a sound rose like an animal caught in a trap. He frowned and stood still, listening. The sound grew into a groan and the groan swelled, and even from where he stood, outside and twenty feet away, he knew it was Maggie. *Christ.* He paled, listening. *Holy Christ.* And he turned and headed as quietly as he could away from that noise and down the dark road into town.

7.

A S HER CRY died out of the room, Maggie lay sweating on the bed, growing clearly weaker. Worse, her contractions were slowing. Eleven minutes had passed between that one and the one before.

"Maggie," Will whispered. "I need to get you to Nauset."

She was shivering now; he couldn't tell if she had heard him.

"Maggie." He reached forward to help her onto her feet.

Suddenly Maggie grunted. "I need to get up," she cried. "Will, I need to stand up!" She looked up at him with wild, unseeing eyes, her chest heaving. Jesus, he needed another pair of hands. Her legs began a spastic tremble and she flung herself over to her side, but she was too weak to pull herself up and off the bed.

"Okay," he said. "Okay, Maggie." He sat behind her and thrust his arms under her armpits and heaved both of them forward to standing. They took two steps away from the bed and Will realized that she was too weak to stand by herself, that he was holding her up on her feet and as she leaned forward at the waist, her eyes closed and with one deep grunt the baby shot out from between her legs straight onto the floor. She gave another great groan, and went limp.

"Shit," Will cried. Maggie fell to her knees, forcing Will to hold on, lowering her gently to a spot beside the blood-covered baby, squirming on the floor. "Okay," he gasped. "Okay, Maggie, take it easy."

His training took over. Moving quickly, he wiped the baby's eyes and nose and cleared the airway with a bulb syringe. He pulled the baby close and her little chest heaved its first breath. "It's a girl, Maggie," he said, elated. "What do you think of that, Maggie. A little girl?" Quickly, he clamped and cut the cord, a sudden shock of happiness coursing through him as he wiped her whole body and wrapped the tiny new one in a clean blanket. It was all right. Light was beginning to streak the night, in glorious pink bursts. It was done. The baby let out another furious tiny wail and he chuckled down at her, tucking her into the length of his arm and turned to hand her to her mother.

He glanced over his shoulder. Maggie had fallen asleep where she lay on the floor, her eyes closed, dripping with sweat and panting, gone gray. She was sliding into shock; the smell and the fever had been warnings. He set the baby in the middle of the bed.

"Maggie," he said sharply, trying to rouse her.

As fast as he could manage, Will half lifted, half shoved Maggie back onto her feet and lay her on the bed beside her baby. Pulling back her nightgown, he felt the uterus to see if the afterbirth was ready to deliver, but when he put his hands on it, a clot of blood the size of a melon glutted out from between her legs, stinking like death. "Okay, Maggie," Will said, terrified. The odor was a dense thick paste in the room. "Okay, now."

There was too much blood. There was a tremendous lot of blood, and more still pulsing from between Maggie's legs. The baby opened her mouth and wailed a thin reedy sound and Will saw that Maggie didn't seem to hear. She seemed intent on racing backward out of life, the color draining out of her face, her breath coming in gasps. She was drenched with sweat, and the blood would not stop coming. She was going to hemorrhage to death.

"Maggie?" Will reached for the pulse at Maggie's neck. It was there, but it was desperately faint.

"Maggie, stop," Will heard himself pleading to the panting figure on the bed, just like any desperate man—not a doctor at all—calling down the tunnel along which Maggie seemed to be slipping. "Stop. You've got to stay right here."

He rifled through his bag for the ergot and drew the syringe, tapping his finger against the glass so the clear liquid rose to the end of the needle. But when he turned around to the silent, unrousable woman on the bed, Maggie had stopped panting. Maggie had simply stopped. He reached again for her pulse but this time there was nothing. Will straightened, the syringe pumping its juice out uselessly on the bedcovers. The time stretched impossibly, his brain trying to understand that there was no way back to the other side of this, just moments ago, when Maggie was alive and the baby in his arms. No way back to just half an hour ago.

How had he lost her? How did he—? (Did he? Or was it in her? *Was* it in her?) Nobody could have stopped that bleeding, he knew it with one part of his brain: the uterus had failed and shut the body down. Perhaps if they had been in a hospital, perhaps if there had been more doctors, a nurse. A sob rose up in his throat and Will shook his head savagely; there was no time for tears.

He could hear Jim Tom's step on the stairs, climbing toward them. He ought to cover Maggie, he ought to straighten the bed. What did one do? The baby girl punched a fist out of the blanket she was wrapped in, and Will saw forward into the life of this tiny little girl and of the boys downstairs, without their mother. He saw the eldest boy, that singing boy, looking up as his father came heavily into the room. He saw the suppers ahead, the boys and their father at the table. The empty spot nearest the stove. He saw all the way through to a day in summer two years ahead perhaps, the baby girl walking, the boys and her, all of them passing him, the doctor on the street. He saw them stare at him.

And he would know, despite the charity of the town—the whispers and the nods, *the doctor did his best*—he would always know: Maggie had died because he had not read the signs. There had been warnings and he had not seen them fast enough to save her.

Will stood, bloodstained and frozen to a spot on the floor in the middle of the room, understanding the scene with the perfect clarity of an exhausted mind. Maggie had died because he failed. He was a Fitch, after all. Here was his place in the lottery. Here was his war. The hand had dipped into the bowl and fished out this number. Everyone's life rested on a central fact, Emma insisted. And here was his.

"Will?" Jim Tom cried from the doorway.

8.

GOOD NIGHT, *people* called to Emma on the street. *Good night,* and then again *Good morning.* All through that month, after Maggie's funeral, after Will went back to work, day after day everyone in town was very kind, very kind; those were the words Emma kept cycling through her head, drawing around her like a muffler. One evening, Emma was bending down to reach the corn starch and the women in the next aisle over in the market hadn't seen her.

"I saw the new baby," Marnie Niles was saying to Florence Cripps. Emma turned around.

"She's beautiful, isn't she?" Florence answered.

"Jim Tom seems to be holding up."

"I'll bet Will blames himself," Mrs. Cripps sighed.

"Well, even good doctors have their little graveyards, God knows."

Without a word, Emma turned and pushed past the two women and through the market door, ignoring their calls to her. She walked the three blocks along the darkening street to find Will. But there was no light on in the infirmary and when she got there, she saw a sign with his tiny print on it, hanging on the door. BACK TOMORROW, it read. Only that. Her eyes filling, she turned and began the walk home.

On the morning Maggie died, he had come home and she had run to him so glad to see him, she hadn't thought his ashen face had anything in it that could hurt her. At first she had thought he was just exhausted from the long night at Maggie's, but then she realized he was clinging to her.

"What happened?" Emma asked, beginning to feel frightened and leaning away to see his face.

He shook his head.

"What? What is it?" She drew back, close to him. He started weeping into her hair, and she clung fast to him, letting his tears slide down through her hair onto her forehead, trying to figure out what had happened.

"The baby?" she whispered at last. "Did something happen to the baby?"

He held her tighter.

"Will?"

"No," he cried into her hair. "Maggie."

"Maggie?" She didn't understand what he said.

"I lost Maggie."

She pushed away from him. "I don't understand. What do you mean?" But her heart was pounding in her chest.

"Maggie is dead. I lost her."

"No you didn't," she said quickly. "No you didn't. Will. It wasn't you. There must have been something wrong. It wasn't you."

He didn't answer.

"Will?"

"I couldn't stop her bleeding."

He didn't seem to notice that she was holding on to him again. She stroked his face. "It's all right," she whispered. He closed his eyes. "It's all right," she soothed. He listened to her, and she nearly thought he had gone to sleep, when he roused himself and shook his head as though he'd made a decision.

"It doesn't matter."

Her hands paused on either side of his face. "What doesn't matter?"

He reached and took her hands in his and pulled her down to sit beside him.

"What doesn't matter?" she asked again.

"None of this."

"What do you mean?"

He was silent.

"Answer me, Will," she said fiercely. "Look at me."

The face he had raised to hers was full of such anguish, she nearly put her hands over his mouth to stop him from answering.

She let herself in the front door and unwrapped her scarf slowly, folded it slowly, and placed it on the bench. The radio was on, Will always had it on now, but it was hard to make out the words. She took off her hat and put it on top of the folded scarf. Last she shrugged her overcoat and hung it on the peg. When she came around the corner onto the threshold of the front room, Will held his hand up.

"I got my very first view of an underground shelter crowd," the man was saying, *"at the big Liverpool Street tube station. It was around eight o'clock on a raidless night, and somehow I must have thought that there'd be nobody down there that night, or that if they were, they'd be invisible or something, because I wasn't emotionally ready at all to see on benches on each side, as though sitting and lying on a long streetcar seat, the people, hundreds of them. And as we walked on they stretched into thousands. People looked up as we came along in our nice clothes and our obviously American hats. I had a terrible feeling of guilt as I walked through there—I felt ashamed to be there staring. A bombed building looks like something you have seen before—it looks as though a hurricane had struck. But the sight of thousands of poor, opportunityless people lying in weird positions against cold steel, with all their clothes on, hunched up in blankets, lights shining in their eyes, breathing fetid air—lying there far underground like rabbits, not fighting, not even mad, just helpless, scourged, weakly waiting—"*

"You hear?" Will said from the door.

"What?" Emma looked at him and then wearily at the radio.

"Thank you, Mr. Pyle," the radio said. *"That's all from London."*

"You hear him? You hear how it is? It's worse and worse. They need our help. Doctors are in short supply."

"And in Washington this morning—" A businesslike voice clipped into the room.

Will crossed and switched it off. "I have to go."

"Go?" she asked wildly. "Go where?"

"London," he said, as if it were the simplest thing in the world.

"Will," she said softly, afraid to speak any louder, afraid to give it any more voice. "You are the doctor. You can't go."

"There's Lowenstein."

"He's retired."

"He's a good doctor." Will stuck out his chin. "He never made mistakes."

"Oh." She saw what he was doing now, the dismal math. "You for Maggie."

He shook his head, excited. "You said it yourself last month. You said yourself, we ought to do something, remember, about the boy?"

"The boy?" She shut her eyes. His eagerness was bright as a fever. "What boy?"

"Who lost his mother. The boy the radio gal brought home. He was all alone. And you remember, you said it, darling. What's happening over there is happening, right now. Right now that boy could be wandering around—"

"Stop it!" she moaned, opening her eyes, heartsick. The danger had never come from the draft, it had come from Will. Will himself.

"Sweetheart, there are people over there who need help, who need another pair of hands, and I can bring them. That's the deal. That's what you were saying without saying it right out. When we know there are people in need, right now, in the same breath as what we are breathing, we cannot look away. It is not abstract. We have to go. That is humanity. The whole thing relies on it. Human beings do not look away."

She stared at him. How little she knew him, how little she had known him after all.

"No matter how you want to dress it up, Will, you don't need to go. You don't need to prove anything. What happened here was not your fault," she persisted. "What you're doing doesn't make any sense."

"Sense?" He sprang up. "It's the only goddamn thing that makes sense. What happened with Maggie *was* proof."

"Proof of what?"

He didn't answer.

"What proof, Will?" She could barely breathe. "Proof of what?"

The ghost of his father—no, not even the ghost—here was his father, all flesh, slumped in one of the kitchen chairs, his white hair carefully combed and oiled, stinking of gin. Perfectly harmless, except to his family.

Will didn't answer. And his father looked up at him and grinned the dull, familiar grin. Beaten.

"Dad owned the bank in town and lost it." He stopped and shook his head. "Worse than that. Dad owned the bank, but when he lost it—when all the banks crashed in 'thirty-two—he shut the doors and locked this town out for three days.

"For three days, he sat in there, saying nothing. Never even came to the window. And Mr. Cripps and Frank Niles, Lars Black—all of the men you've met—stood banging on the doors outside. Day after day after day. By the morning of the fourth day, Harry Vale and some of the others brought up a dory mast from the beach and rammed the door of the bank."

He had never told her this part.

"Dad was sitting in there, with a German bayonet from the Great War across his knees, bawling." Will snorted. "Like some kind of hero of the Alamo, or some damn idea he had about duty. About protecting—"

"What happened?" she whispered.

"Not a goddamned thing. He put down his gun and walked out of the bank and walked home to my mother."

Emma waited, so nervous she couldn't speak.

"He went on and on like some character in a book whose part is over—for years after that, looking like the hired man, hair carefully combed back from his forehead, in khaki trousers and shirt, and smelling ripe as a gin bottle. He should have died, snapped in the instant, that defying moment. Better for my mother and me waiting it out with him."

"Waiting what out?" Emma was incredulous.

"*Life,*" Will cried. "When it should have been over. It should have ended—" Will snapped his fingers.

Emma recoiled.

"You mean to die there," she said. "Is that it?"

"What a queer thing to say."

"I'm trying to understand what you mean to do," she said helplessly.

"I mean to help."

"You're running away," she leveled at him. "You are running."

He froze. "Is that what you think?"

"Yes."

He nodded and leaned against the kitchen door and went through it. Emma stood in the middle of the kitchen watching the door swing back and forth, back and forth, until it closed. Let them kill each other over there, let them tear each other's throats out—why should we help? Why should other people's lives mean more than theirs? Why should Europe take him and deprive his own town? Or her? Why should she, who had already given enough—had already suffered—give any more?

A flat cry cast out between the houses and she turned her head toward the window over the sink. Was it a child? She listened. Again it came. A child, protesting sleep perhaps in one of the nearby houses. She pulled her cardigan close. Now a second cry came. Much closer this time. And then she saw the white body cross the window, flying itself into the air, the sharp beak open now again and calling as it swaled into the spent sky. A gull. It had been the cry of a bird. She shuddered as the white dot disappeared into the gray, not liking having been fooled.

She walked straight through the kitchen door and down the hall. He was sitting in the dark in the front room, leaning against his mother's cushions.

"Will?"

"Six months," he whispered. "I'll be home in the summer."

She looked at him a long time before her lips parted in answer. What could she say? What would stop him? He was already gone. "Okay," she said slowly and quietly.

WITHIN THREE WEEKS he'd heard back from City Hospital in London. They were delighted to have his help on staff. Within six weeks he had passage and papers. In the end there was very little to pack. And when the last morning came, Will reached forward and put his hand on the front doorknob and opened it as though it were any other. The cold winter sun slashed into the hall. Emma clasped her purse to her chest and walked through it, past him.

"Wait," he said, and he pulled her back inside. "Give me a kiss inside, in here." She looked up at him. His attention was focused on the living room as though he wanted to gather it into a blanket and toss it over his shoulder, take it with him. She put her hands on his overcoat and closed her eyes as her hands reached the solid of his arms inside the sleeves. "Good-bye," he whispered. She held on to his arms and then she stepped even closer and slid her arms around his neck, holding him very hard against her. *God*—the word pealed in her head, her throat too tight to speak—*God. God. God. God. Look down.*

"Prove it to me, Will," she said into his coat.

"What's that?" he murmured.

"Prove to me that people stay alive."

"You'll see," he said into her hair, and let her go.

They emerged from the house. Above them the gulls dove in and out of the cold bright blue day. Emma tucked herself neatly beneath Will's arm. His one hand rested on the belt of her coat, and he reached for her with the other; they held hands and moved as if they were skating. He didn't look at her but she felt his hip against hers as he steered her down Yarrow Road.

She wanted to push it all back. No time, no town. Nothing but each other's hands and the tempo of their tread. The sky seemed to bowl up and away, curving like a cat. It was a mild morning, as can sometimes happen, as though May had slid in quietly for this January day. There was no wind at all. They walked along, and under the silent morning sky, she imagined she could pull Time like taffy, stretching it longer and longer between her hands until the finest point had been reached, the point just before breaking, and she could live there. A point at the center of time with no going forward, no looking back. Clasped in this way, without speaking, walking into no discernible ending, she could almost believe they tread on time.

The street remained empty all the way into town. There was no one to say good-bye. The bus idled on the curb in front of the post office. Flores was having some trouble with the door to the luggage hold, and there was a small delay as he and Will jimmied the catch, but then suddenly the last kiss came, and Will was gone.

Winter

1941

ONE DAY SOMEONE you saw every day was there and the next he was not. This was the only way Frankie had found to report the Blitz. The small policeman on the corner, the grocer with a bad eye, the people you walked to work with, in the shops, on the bus: the people you didn't know but who walked the same route as you, who wove the anonymous fabric of your life. Buildings, gardens, the roofline, one could describe their absence. But for the disappearance of a man, or a little boy, or the woman who used to wait for the bus at the same time as she did, Frankie had found few words: Once they were here. And I saw them.

Reporting had always meant the lining up of details—the heat of a day, the frayed hem of a woman's skirt—details like pebbles on a beach, cast up to be collected and arranged into a story. She had come to Europe, she had laid detail after detail down for Ed Murrow and for herself. The snow piles of glass, the bombs raining down, the sky black with bombers a city block wide, and the jumpy impatience of people in the funk holes waiting it out until they couldn't stand it, *couldn't stand it, do you hear?* And they'd get up and walk out into the street in the middle of it all—impatient for the night to be over, the bombs to be done—and were killed where they walked, mad for the end to come and find them.

And she had believed that the scraps of life pulled together into a shape. But there was no shape that morning after she had left the boy, Billy, at his house, and pushed through her own front door where the thick smell of gas and ashes found her immediately. And even as her mind saw the blue air where the back of the house had been sheared off from the front by the force of the bomb, neatly, as if an elevator had dropped straight down through all five floors, she had run up the stairs where the door to her flat still stood, though the sky stretched through the torn end of the hall. The back of the flat had simply vanished, while the front remained as usual, the lamp on the table, the hooks across from the door on which hung Harriet's coat, and Dowell's. It was unreal. No shape. In the first few seconds she stood in the door, looking at Harriet's coat, seeing that there was no bedroom anymore to the left, while to the right the morning light reached all the way through the glassless windows of the front room, and seeing that a letter waited from Harriet's cousin in Poland, waited patiently by the front door, standing perfectly normally against the wall, waiting for Harriet.

"Harriet?" she had called out, her scared voice choking in her throat.

There was no shape for details like that. Shape was the novelist's lie.

AND YET, AND YET—she thought, making her way toward Broadcasting House—the story that had possessed Harriet, the secondary story of the Jews, was quietly shaping into something clear and horrifying. In the room she had rented after Harriet was killed, Frankie had continued Harriet's habit of filing away stories devoted to the Jews in Europe. A crazy quilt of paper stretched on the wide wall above her makeshift desk: tacked up, in no particular order, were news reports, the letters from Harriet's Polish cousins, handwritten notices she had found in the parks and pasted on the sides of buildings: *Jens Steinbach, are you here?* (This one was handwritten in both German and English.)

By now, Alsatian Jews sent into the unoccupied zone had joined German Jews pushed over the border to join the floods of Jews sent from

Austria, Danzig, and the Sudetenland part of Czechoslovakia, where they were being pooled at the bottom of France, the men diverted to the camps at Le Vernet or Les Milles and the women and children to Gurs. The lack of food, clothing, shelter, and medical supplies meant that the race of these people to flee to other nations had become a race against death.

Last month, Vichy France had signaled it would release thousands from the holding camps provided they could prove that other countries would be willing to admit them. It asked the United States to grant refuge particularly for "Jews forced out of Luxembourg, Belgium, and Germany." But Secretary of State Cordell Hull declined, asserting that "the basic principles" of the Intergovernmental Committee on Refugees could not be seen to favor one race, nationality, or religion. The Jews were being interned because they were Jews, and were being denied refuge on the basis of being Jews.

These clerical errors, Harriet had written, are human beings caught by pieces of paper now stuck in camps like Gurs with sixty to a room. *Send food, clothes, underwear, and medicine*, the cables from the camp shot into the air following relatives who had gotten out. *Send food, clothes, underwear. Tell my sister. Tell my cousin.* Scraps of paper were thrust into visitors' hands as they left the place where ten thousand women waited for news. Ten thousand scraps of paper.

"The Immigration Department does not refuse visas," Frankie's friend Kirchway had written in *The Nation*, "it merely sets up a line of obstacles."

There had been a teacher at Farmington, where Frankie had gone to school, who chewed her food so slowly Frankie had thought she'd lose her mind in between bites, sitting there at the round table, the forks on the left and the knives on the right and the girls in a circle, stilled, all talk slowed to the pace of the presiding teacher who chewed and thought and chewed. And one night, Frankie had simply leaned back in her chair, opened her mouth, and screamed.

Du calme—Frankie heard her mother's voice in her head—*du calme*.

But it was nearly impossible now to look away from what was clearly happening in Europe. The Jews were in a permanent, ceaseless pogrom. And the patrician habit of deflecting strong passion or insight first into calmer waters, to reflect, to take stock, belonged to her mother's generation. Fine for Mrs. Dalloway, impossible for Mrs. Woolf. A writer, a real writer, in possession of a story headed straight for its rapids, eyes on the water, paddling fast for the middle in order to see as well, as closely as could be. In order to see like that, one had to entertain the fact of brutal, simple cruelty. The Germans were, in fact, gathering the Jews in camps and ghettos and simply *letting them die there.* If Frankie could tell that story, if she could tell it as well as Murrow was telling the Blitz, she could move the Jews and their plight onto the front pages—she could bring what was being buried now in details, what could be dismissed as random and unintentional, into full narrated sight.

"I don't like what's happened to your voice, Frankie darling," her mother had said through the telephone last week. "You sound—" There was a long whistle down the line, the vast silence of the sea between herself and her mother standing in the hallway of their house.

"What, Mother?"

"Desperate."

"It is."

"Come home, dear," her mother said, finally. "Come and rest."

The moon was red tonight, set off by the fires reflecting in the frozen Thames. Though by now she was so used to noting these details, description seemed hardly enough anymore. All I have been doing— Frankie nearly ran up the stairs to Murrow—is painting vivid word pictures. Pictures from the Blitz. While Harriet's story grows.

She paused in the open doorway of Murrow's office.

"Frankie." He rose and came around his desk toward her, motioning her into the chair. She smiled hello and sank down. A two-week-old *New York Times* lay triple-folded next to his sandwich on the desk. A cigarette burned in the ashtray in front of him. She pulled out a cigarette and he reached forward with his lighter. She bent into it and nodded, thanking him, exhaling.

"Send me into France, Mr. Murrow. Please."

He tapped the lighter closed and slipped it into his pocket.

She stayed on her feet, in the grip of a restless urgency, but, knowing how she must look to her boss, exhausted and excitable, she tipped her chin at the paper on his desk. "Any news in there?"

Murrow eyed her calmly. "What's doing, Frankie?"

"Okay." She looked at him and pointed at the *Times*. "There has been only one story about the situation of the Jewish refugees in France to hit the front page of that paper. And that was about Secretary Hull's response to the French. Everything Harriet filed got buried in the middle pages. Why aren't the stories landing? Why can't they see?"

"See what, Frankie?"

"Beginning in Spain," she fell into the pitch, "the years of war in Europe have burst the boundary between battlefield and home, crashing through villages, setting people in flight—people walking away from their homes, from Spain into France. Now add in the Jews sent off by the Nazis—and what you have is a tide of people swept across Europe, and now caught in the south of France, where they sit waiting, their backs to the sea."

"Go on."

"Refugees in war is a story we all know. But who is really in those camps and why? Why are they there? Have they done something? I've heard people here talking as though there were a real reason. Ordinary people balk at paying attention because it can't be true that people are simply rounded up and given twenty minutes to get ready to leave their lives, taking no money with them, only to face a bureaucracy that insists on papers and money and things in their place. It can't be true, the civilized world thinks, because that would be *mad*."

Her voice was shaking. She thrust her hands into her pockets and leaned forward.

"What if people back home could hear their voices? We could make the refugees real. We'd get the stories of the people stuck—" Her throat closed up. "Darn it." She smiled to ward off the tears springing into her eyes.

"It's okay," he said.

"Okay?" She pushed away the handkerchief he offered her and wiped her eyes with her fingertips. "Okay?" she repeated, almost laughing, and then she gave up and covered her face with her hands.

"It's tough," Murrow said again, more quietly.

"I just want to continue what Harriet had started, tell this story, tell it all."

He nodded. "So you can do what with it?"

Get us off our duffs, she didn't say. "What are we doing back home, Ed? What are people doing, for Christ's sake?"

"Living their lives."

"How *can* they be?"

He didn't answer and she knew she had just stepped on a boat that was leaving shore.

"In that first week, you remember, Ed—you remember all of those people, thousands of them in the East End with their suitcases, lining up, queuing for Christ's sake for the buses to come and take them from South Hallsville School, take them to other parts of the city, to safety."

Ed nodded.

"Bombed out of their houses, they were promised transport out of there and told to stay put until the buses came. And they did. And half of them were killed on the third night because the buses never came— the ones who had lived through the first night, dying on the third, because the buses never came—"

"Okay, Frankie."

She stood up. "My point, Ed, is that people here are bombed out of their homes. But it seems clear that the majority of people in the detention camps are there *because* they are Jewish. Even though the reports stress that there are many nationalities, the refugees are Jews. It's deliberate. They've been deported and gathered. What's the plan? Is there a plan? That's all. That's what Harriet was tracking. Don't we want to know? Shouldn't we find out?"

He didn't answer.

"I want to get the story that pricks a hole in the idea that the Jewish plight is simply the usual face of war—"

"Whatever the hell that is," Murrow snapped.

"Fair enough." Frankie nodded. "But this is not random casualty. It's abnormal. It's a pogrom."

"Go on," he said after a little.

"Let me go over there. Let me get their voices on disk—like the BBC's 'Children Calling Home.' We could call this 'Voices of Europe,' or something. A broadcast of ordinary people talking. Talking and real. Real as the people on the other side of the radio—the voice of war, people in the detention camps trying to leave the war, just as true as the bombs—and they're simply people. Hasn't that always been our story?"

"In English?" Murrow was skeptical. "How are you going to deal with the languages?"

"Whatever they're speaking in . . . they're speaking. *They* are alive. And real, perhaps *more* so if they are speaking another language. Their voices carry that to an audience. And every day fifteen to twenty-five more of them are dying at places like Gurs."

She waited. We do not create mood, Murrow had lectured her when she'd first arrived, we tell what there is to tell. Our job is not to persuade. Just provide the honest news. One person to another. And when there isn't any news, why, just say so. The news is not atmosphere (although there were shelves of disks at Broadcasting House that used to be used for just that—crickets and birdsongs, Big Ben sounding, and nearly sixty bands on one disk devoted to False Alarm: Cheerful Voices with Chink of Teacups). The war news now came live: the newsreaders' voices, the microphone on the roof recording the progress of the bombs, and the conversation between broadcasters in the very moment of the Blitz. The world could listen to the war as though we were all pulled up to the fire.

Murrow shook his head. "It's too diffuse, too unfocused. Especially if the voices aren't translated. They are just sound. Voices without a story. People need to know why they are listening and what they are being asked to hear."

"Or they won't understand?"

"They won't listen." He was impatient. "You have to point, Frankie. You have to focus people's attention on what you want them to hear."

"But—"

"It's not news." Murrow was finished. "And I need you here."

She stared at him blankly, then stood up. "Okay, Boss."

"You're on in five minutes," the engineer called after her as she emerged from Murrow's office.

"Don't I know it," she waved, holding on until she could push through the door into the woman's loo, where she gave way at last in great gulping sobs, her forehead leaning against the cool tile. And when she had heaved it all out, she pushed back from the wall and turned on the tap in the sink and leaned her face down into the cup of her hands and dunked in the water.

"*There are many positive reports*," she began a few minutes later, closing her eyes to the microphone, to the lamp overhead, to Tom, the soundman, sitting behind the glass in front of her, and imagined her mother as she always did, the open ear turned to her.

"*There are many positive reports from Europe making their way to us here. It has only been a few short weeks since Mr. Laveleye proposed the V for victory sign to unite the occupied people of Belgium, France, and Holland, and we have word that the symbol has appeared, it seems, everywhere. Chalked onto barn walls, on city pavements, on the sides of trucks gliding*" *through towns, the V stands. If washed off, it reappears hours later. Like a ghost finger, pointing. The sign, always the same, infinitely repeated, must remind a German soldier stationed there that he is surrounded. And the walls speak: we are watching, we are waiting for you to fall. All over Europe the silent, invisible V proclaims the voices that cannot speak, asserts the presence of the people underneath."* Frankie paused the infinitesimal moment, the beat of silence that carried the words all the better.

"Yesterday evening I found myself once again on my stomach, flattened to the sidewalk for protection after a close call. Nothing had been hit nearby but the sound had been deafening and there are always the three or four seconds right after a bomb when you are too shaky to stand. After a little while, I pushed myself up, first to my knees, and then slowly to my feet. Across the way on the other side of the street, two boys, about ten years old, had pulled themselves off the ground also and were busy trying to back their frightened horse into the stays of their delivery van. Come on, they cajoled, weeping, wiping their tears on their sleeves, Come on, the boys patted and murmured, though they could not stop their own sobs. And slowly, ever so slowly, the animal calmed and stood. Sniffling, the boys climbed up on the cart, clucked and jerked the reins, and went off again down the street.

IRIS HAD COME to a stop in front of the radio perched on the shelf in the sorting room of the post office above the hot plate and her teakettle.

"Waiting and watching. Weeping into your sleeves—those are not the traits of heroes, neither Ulysses, nor Aeneas, and not Joshua. Think, rather, of Penelope. Think of all the women down through the years who have watched and waited—but who, like the boys with their horse, wept and picked themselves up and went on—and you will have a small sense, then, of the heroes here. The occupied, the bombed, and the very, very brave. This is Frankie Bard in London. Good night."

Iris reached for the knob and slowly turned it to the right. She didn't, as a rule, like the sound of that gal's voice, didn't like the undercurrent that seemed always to run through it that she held the truth in her hand and everyone better damn well take a look. Nonetheless—Iris stood back from the radio and crossed her arms—she was fairly sure that the radio gal had just redefined the nature of a hero. She considered the black box. Yes, she was certain that that was what Miss Frankie Bard had done.

10.

HARRY VALE SAT at the top of the town hall looking for Germans. It was a bright, brisk evening. The high flagpole of the post office divided Franklin harbor in half, pointing like a compass needle due north, and still making him nervous as all hell. The attic windows commanded this unobstructed view of the harbor out one end, and out the other, a view across the wilderness of dunes to the sea. Straight on past the curl of Land's End, the black smudges of boats bobbed up and down on the blue.

He didn't give a damn what Roosevelt said about our boys not fighting in foreign wars. The fact that there stretched forty miles of unprotected coastline from here all the way down to Nauset made Harry feel naked as a girl. And the longer the Blitz had gone on over there, Harry couldn't knock a rising hunch that the Germans were drawing the world's attention to London while something else was coming in the dark. He had spent many nights walking up and down along the bluff above town after leaving Iris, standing and staring out to sea.

He figured that if the Germans were to attack, they'd land on the back shore, taking Franklin first, and then sweep up the Cape into Boston. And the Krauts would have showed them all up for sleepwalkers. Even

the boys who were going to be drafted—especially those, he corrected—
Johnny Cripps and all of them, sitting in rows upon the benches put up
on either side of the town hall steps, teasing. "Seen any Germans yet,
Mr. Vale?" their laughing questions light and persistent as midges.

"Not today." He'd grin for them and pass through the swarm. The
Coast Guard was no better. Boys, again. Not a one of them really
thought a Kraut could ever get close enough in to see, though they'd
made it here in 1918, a U-boat surfacing in the waters just off of Nauset.
But not this time, the boys boasted. Not in 1941.

"I can see it all so clearly," he'd said to Iris one night.

"Harry," she protested.

"They're coming," he'd sighed. "I just can't figure when."

In the end, Harry couldn't think of what to do other than climb the
stairs up here one lunch hour last month, to sit with his binoculars and
face out to sea. He didn't expect to see anything, but it sure as hell made
him feel better.

On the first day, he'd kept his binoculars leveled at the flat waters, his
sandwich unwrapped and clutched in his hand. He stayed for a couple of
hours, watching, then went back to the garage.

The following day he climbed the stairs to the town hall again. And
then again. Now he was up here every day from four o'clock on. Hell,
no one needed gas anyway. He watched the empty palate before him,
sure of two things: he was an idiot and he would be right. Sooner or later
the U-boats would strike over here. He waited, like the stern man jigs
for cod, the thick line loose in his hands, eyes off to the side, relaxed—
every muscle ready to strike.

Down below and across the green, Iris appeared on the porch of the
post office with a wet mop. She wrung the head dry over the railing, in
three swift twists. Her red hair swung forward and back as she did so,
shining and flashing above the plain navy of her blouse.

She gave a fierce shake to the mop at the end and disappeared back
into the dark of the porch and through the doors. There was a quiet like

an afterclap in the air around the door through which she had vanished. Harry found himself staring down there to see if she'd come back out. The putter of a Ford came slowly down Front Street. Someone shouted. But from the post office there was nothing.

Harry lowered the binoculars to his chest, suddenly aware he'd been holding his breath.

AT THE END of the day, Iris pulled down the metal shutter on the lobby window and snapped off the light in the back, crossing the worn wooden floor of the lobby by the light of the streetlamps out front. Every evening, she put her hand on the door, preparing herself for an empty porch, which surely must happen, mustn't it? Tonight, she put her hand on the door and pulled it open. But there was Harry as always, waiting outside.

"Hello." She drew in her breath, pleased.

He stood up.

"Say," she said, pulling the post office door shut behind her, "I have good news for you."

"Shoot." He smiled.

"You'll be happy to know," she arched her eyebrow, "the post office inspector is giving the matter of the flagpole serious consideration."

"That does make me happy." He was wry.

"Come on"—she chuffed him, following him down the stairs—"it's a start."

"Right you are. Let's go."

She stood where she was, halfway down. "Harry," she said, "I did ask for you."

Now he turned back. "Thank you, Iris."

She studied him to be sure, but there was no trace of the tease in his face. "Thank you," he repeated. "Maybe they'll see the sense in it."

He held his hand out.

They set off quickly down the empty street. It was Wednesday evening all along the way, their neighbors tucked around the table, or resting, their feet up. And though it was the end of February, still, there were canned peaches in a bowl holding the gold of last summer, the sweet syrup sliding down the globes. There was Count Basie coming on in half an hour. There was wood stacked up in the wood box. The pods rattled on the laurel trees in the doorway and the storm doors clicked in and out on their latches. Iris was glad she had decided on a scarf. They walked along silently together, their hands sunk deep in their overcoats.

As they climbed Yarrow Road out of town, Harry reached into his pocket for his flashlight and flicked it on, aiming it ahead. The eye of light caught the silvered frozen grasses and the sand stretched away from them in pillows and valleys all the way up the bluff to the Fitch house roof. From the east a low wind whipped in off the dark band of the sea. "Listen." Harry cleared his throat. She looked over.

"I'd like to come in tonight."

"Sure," she said, her heart thudding.

"And stay."

She stared at him a moment, and then she smiled. "Sure," she said again.

When they arrived at her cottage, Iris simply went through the door and stood in the middle of the room and Harry put his hands on either side of her arms and guided her to the chair, where he sat her down. Iris looked up at him.

He leaned forward and touched Iris on the cheek. Iris closed her eyes and felt Harry's lips brush hers and then pull away, and when Iris opened her eyes to see where that touch had gone, Harry stood above her, his face very close, studying her, and Iris smiled and closed her eyes again and felt those lips return, this time firmer, intending to stay. She leaned her head back against the wall and Harry pressed in, his warm mouth playing against Iris's lips, until Iris opened with a gasp, his lips moving from Iris's mouth, traveling and kissing the hollows and dives of her neck, then along the ridge of Iris's jaw and back up onto her mouth again. Iris never opened her eyes, following their trace with her pulse.

Harry pulled her from the chair. "Let's go lie down."

He rose and very gently led her into her own bedroom and, still holding her hand in his, keeping her close, he reached and turned on the lamp on the bureau. Then he sat down on the end of the bed and pulled her to sit beside him. They sat side by side for a minute. Then he leaned forward and untied his right boot and pulled it off. Then his left boot. Then his socks, which he lay on top of his boots. She sat right next to him. There he was, barefoot now, on the bed beside her. He turned and looked at her.

"What do I do?" she asked.

"I'd like to see you," he answered.

Slowly, she tugged the cardigan off, and then began unbuttoning her blouse, sitting straight beside him. He reached and put his hand on the bare triangle of flesh above her bra. Her heart leapt to meet his hand. They lay slowly down and he began to kiss her again, and his hands went roaming. Up under her skirt and down her legs and up slowly over her cotton-covered breasts, touching and stroking. And she reached to finish unbuttoning her blouse so that that mouth could find her. She wanted skin and the soft marshland of this man's body against her own, she wanted that mouth to climb and rove, she wanted that mouth everywhere on her. And that mouth moved on her, moved all over her as if it owned her, it took and stalked, as if it had known her and known where she hid, always. And she closed her eyes and felt what it meant to be held and touched, and after a while she pushed him gently up and she rose onto her feet at the end of the bed and unhooked her bra, and tossed it to the ground and unbuttoned her skirt and stepped out of it, and pulled her underpants straight down, rolling the stockings all the way to her ankles. He stood and unbuckled and dropped and slid out of his clothes and then they were back on the bed again and she could feel him nudging against her, nudging, and then he reached down so he could guide himself in.

"Oh," she said and he stopped. The tear had been quick and sharp, but now there was the thick heat of him pulsing inside.

"It's okay," she said to his face, and with a small moan he pushed in another bit. She closed her eyes, feeling it, him, coming in a little more, then a bit more, then all the way in. And the surprise of him inside, tight tight, all the way inside. She felt herself around him, holding him. And then, he started moving inside. Inside *her*.

Nearly asleep that night, Harry put his hand, heavy and warm, on the spot between Iris's breasts, on the bone. And she smiled. The heaviness, the himness there right in the middle of her chest, on her chest, rested there, keeping her in the bed, keeping her here. It had never occurred to her that she was looking for a tether. She had thought she was the one who sped things along, the one who sent things on their way, but there she was for the first time, delivered.

11.

A LOVELY, DREAMY SNOW had begun falling, as if the sky weren't certain itself whether to empty or hold back. One flake, then another. Then six or seven at a time until at last the snow poured down, straight and thick as rain onto the sand and into the water, sliding down the steep crevices of the roofs. In the snow, Emma thought, looking out at the afternoon disappearing in the gently falling white, nothing terrible could happen. Sudden things, violent swift motion, would be blurred and blotted. Will had been gone now forty-six days.

On such a day—she bent and tucked the blanket in tight on Will's side of the bed—the world might not bear to hurt a newly pregnant woman. Maybe there was a clause, not divine exactly, but primordial, in which harm would stop short at the gate—seeing the woman crossing, her hand resting on her belly—and neither lift the latch nor step across. She paused. Couldn't she trust that? Couldn't that be the way?

She reached over for the packet of cigarettes by the side of the bed, lit one, and exhaled. It was dinnertime in London, before the bombs. She pictured Will pulled up to some café table, his big, long body folded around his plate and eating with the steady, regular concentration men paid to food. She loved to watch him eat. The smoke drifted up and toward the window and she followed it out past the four walls of their room, outward onto the afternoon road frozen under the winter sun.

Outside, three more bombers appeared on the ridge of the horizon, traveling low and racing out to sea. And in the quiet they left on the horizon, she crossed his boyhood room, now theirs. Darling, she thought, darling—she moved to the desk pushed against the window facing away from the harbor, looking straight into the crazy jazz of the town's roofline—I am disappearing. She sank into the chair and reached for the pen given to Will when he graduated from Franklin High School, and pulled out a sheet of letter paper. The white page regarded her. She wrote two words, *Come Home.*

She folded the paper quickly, then again, so it slid easily into the narrow envelope. She raised it to her lips and licked, and smoothed it shut with her hand. There. That was all she would say today. She stared at the shut envelope. *Dr. William Fitch,* she wrote on the front, in the care of *Mrs. Peter Phillips, 28 Ladgrove Rd., London.* In the upper corner, she wrote *Mrs. William Fitch, Franklin, Massachusetts.* Her name looked across at his. She turned the envelope over. *Come Home,* she thought again, looking down at it. *Please,* she wrote quickly on the flap. But she covered the word with her hand.

She stood abruptly and walked downstairs with her teacup. She hadn't told Will she was pregnant. She hadn't told anyone. For now the secret was between her and the baby. Through the kitchen window above the sink, and way out, the long low hulls of the navy wavered on the water. In the months after the president had promised Churchill fifty destroyers, the horizon had been crenellated by these far-off ships. And now that he had promised even more, there seemed to be a distant wall of metal on the sea. Through the snow she couldn't tell whether they were coming or going, or if they moved at all. The navy hung there and she stared across the gray waves slamming against the iron hulls of destroyers.

That water, that single ocean, was all that stood between us and terror, Mr. Walter Lippmann had commented on the radio last night. *We must help the English hold the Atlantic, or all that we hold dear will drown. Your boys, your homes, the simple pleasures of your neighbor's talk, well-meaning, American, free—think of it going, think of it gone*—and she had snapped it off.

The snow had stopped. She grabbed for her yellow scarf and tied it over her head as she passed outside.

A powdery inch lay underfoot. Emma took the broom by the door and swept the porch clear and down the steps and then in a kind of frenzy all the way out to the gate. When she had finished, she looked back at the house and saw the tidy path like a child's drawing leading to the front door. She felt inordinately proud, as if she had offered something and the house had taken her up on it. She left the broom at the bottom of the garden and began the walk into town.

"Hello." Iris James came around the corner from the sorting room and smiled at Emma. "There's another letter for you today."

"That's good." Emma nodded shyly as she walked across the lobby to her box, pulling the key up on its chain from beneath her sweater. The key slid easily in and turned. She pulled the single envelope out, shut the box, and opened the letter where she stood. She could see at a glance that it was miserably short. *Dearest*, it began—*Nothing whatsoever to report except regular, even rounds.*

How was she to survive on this kind of talk? Without his arms around her, without his smile catching her eye across the table, without the smell of his hair and the taste of his mouth on hers—the words that mouth might say didn't add up to anything at all. The letter was nothing but a husk in her hand.

She was aware that Miss James had stopped whatever she was doing, and she looked up to find the postmaster standing in the window watching her. She slipped Will's letter back into the envelope.

"How are you holding up?"

"All right, thanks."

Behind the postmaster, the telegraph machine whirred into life, tapping out a sharp staccato message. Emma froze, her hand in the box. Iris kept her eyes on the doctor's wife, listening to the iron hammers, one two, one and two, pounding black letters onto the white sheet. She turned slightly backward, gauging the length of the message. Emma stared at the postmaster. The steel drum turned after the ping of the end of a line. The message continued, clattering across the two women's silence. The drum turned again.

"It's too long," Iris commented.

"Please"—Emma blew out her breath—"go and see."

Iris studied her a minute. Then she turned away from the window and walked to the back of the sorting room where the telegraph machine was set up against the wall. It was still going, going on far longer than *We regret to inform you*, and even though Iris was certain it was a telegraph for Mr. Lansing, or Mr. Pete in the town offices, the girl's worry was hard to shake and she hesitated an instant before leaning over the message. *Bona Fide Credit* it began. She turned and went back to the window.

"It's nothing."

"I'm being silly." Emma gave a weak smile.

"Perfectly understandable."

Emma nodded and slid her letter to Will across the counter along with the three pennies. Iris opened the drawer and pulled out a stamp, passing it over the sponge pot and sticking it firmly to the envelope. Emma watched.

"Will it be all right in the end, do you think, Miss James?"

Iris turned around, the confusion plain on her face.

"Oh, go on." Emma was only half joking. "You can lie to me."

"Yes," Iris answered. "It will be all right in the end."

Emma gave her the first real smile Iris had seen. "You sound so certain," she said gratefully.

"So long," Iris said quietly.

Emma waved backward over her shoulder. Iris watched her all the way out and down the stairs until she vanished at the level of the street. The doctor's wife came in and out of the post office every day at four o'clock after the mail had been sorted, her chin up, her back straight, walking like daffodils waving in spring. That was how Iris thought of her. Every day she approached the box with the same determined step, unlocking it and reaching in without looking, to pull the envelope out, allowing herself a little smile only when it was firmly in her hand. Each afternoon was a gauntlet thrown. Each day Iris watched Emma gamely pick it up and toss it back, her shoulders softening with relief as she slipped back out the post office door.

It took two weeks for letters to cross the Atlantic, and though there'd been a letter every day since the doctor left, Iris dreaded the afternoon when that box would be empty. Of course there would be a half-dozen reasons for a day without a letter, and Iris was ready to give them, but the truth of the matter was that the day before he'd left town, she had sat at her stool in the back and watched Dr. Fitch walking around and around the small lobby with his hands jammed deep in his pocket, and with nothing, apparently, to mail.

"Miss James?" he finally called.

She had come to the window. A white envelope lay faceup on the ledge, but he put his hand over the letter as if she might take it from him. She looked up at him.

"I—" He was looking at his hand and Iris could see there was nothing for her to say. He shook his head and barreled forward. "It's for my wife," he said, "if I'm dead."

Iris kept her eyes on him, waiting for the next bit. He still didn't look up at her, his eyes remaining fixed on that letter. "I want to make sure she gets it," he said, by way of explanation.

"All right," said Iris finally. And then he did look up, looked directly into her eyes, and smiled.

"You didn't contradict me," he said gratefully.

"How could I?"

He nodded. But he didn't seem to want to leave. "Let me ask you something."

She waited.

"If something happens to me, how will Emma get the news?"

The pale in his cheeks made him look like a sick boy, she thought. And he was asking questions like a sick boy in his bed, his feverish eyes above the smile, imagining the worst.

"You understand, I won't be over there in any official capacity," he went on, before she could answer, "I'm going over all on my own, which is why I'm just wondering about it. When someone is traveling, for instance, abroad—and something happens, how does the news arrive?"

"By telegram, I think," she answered. "If anything should happen."

Will nodded. This seemed to satisfy, even to comfort. "So it will be you."

"If it is anyone," she said softly. She had to say it.

"It's all right, you know." He shook his head, a little impatient with her kindness.

Iris drew in her breath sharply. "For you, maybe."

He looked at her. "So, you *do* watch. You do pay attention to every-one in here."

Ignoring the remark, she reached for her pack of cigarettes tucked at the inside corner of the counter. The doctor had his lighter ready, and when she leaned in for the light, she smelled ink on his hands.

He flipped shut the lid on the flame. "Emma doesn't believe anyone is watching her."

"What?"

"Watching over her, I guess I should say."

"What does that mean?"

"She believes that if you are in the world without parents or someone who loves you, you are invisible. That no one sees you, because no one needs to. No one needs to watch out for you."

"Well," Iris said, "that's true enough."

He shook his head. "But you just told me off on her behalf."

She exhaled, studying him. "Dr. Fitch, I didn't tell you off."

"You did, though." His likable face broke open into a grin. "And it makes me think you're not half so disinterested as you let on."

Iris merely raised her eyebrow.

The smile on his face faded slowly, but he put out his hand to Iris. "Keep an eye on her, will you?"

She nodded and took his hand in hers. "Good luck, Doctor."

"Thank you," the doctor said softly. "Thanks a lot."

And then she had taken his letter and put it in the drawer with the postal savings account ledgers. It had slid in and out of her gaze nearly every day for months, so often that she knew the curve of the doctor's hand perhaps as well as his wife did.

Now she looked down at the letter Emma had slid across the counter at her. On the back of the envelope, on the tip of the flap, Emma had written the word *Please*. And then she must have placed her hand down and traced it, so the handprint spread across the envelope's flap like a small ghost. It nearly broke Iris's heart—the hand was so slight and fit the envelope so neatly. And there was that "please." *Please*, what? Iris carried the letter over to the mail sacks, her heart thudding.

Never before had her faith in her own role in the system been so sorely shaken as in these months since the men had been drafted and sent off to Florida or Georgia, one of those states ending in *a* about which Iris had long ago formed a negative opinion. There was John Dimling to whom his wife wrote faithfully every day, and whose persistent silence in return had tempted Iris nearly to break her own code of conduct and write a message on the back of one of his wife's envelopes saying simply, *Shame*.

Please, the wife was asking her husband. For what? And though Iris would have liked to let Emma know that she had seen, Iris had to let the lines play out under her fingers, spinning down until the end slipped past, watching out in silence. To protect the words passing across time and distance, that was her special charge, especially now when the letter writers might come to harm. No matter how people behaved out on the streets and in their front parlors, or upstairs in their bedrooms, their mail came and went as silent witnesses. As the postmaster, she knew everybody's business and almost everybody's sins. Some postmasters fell in love with the secrets, and played them out as breathlessly as a bad novel. Some couldn't have borne simply standing by. But she'd give a quick glance at the person handing her their mail, a nice smile, and then she'd turn and toss what they gave her, passing it on. She watched it all. And she never said a word. The whole thing depended on her silence. She was aware that no one else in the town might think of her in this way. It beggared belief that an unmarried woman her age would not be convulsed by a desire to poke about in other people's secrets, never reading their postcards, never noting return addresses. Nonetheless, she promised the letters before her. Nonetheless, she thought fiercely, it had to be so. *Please,* Lord. She dropped the letter in, then noosed up this last mail sack and locked it. She shook her head. That was the job.

One thing after another, she reminded herself, and cut the string on the newly arrived Sears catalogs. There were two extra. Without thinking, she slotted one into Emma Fitch's empty box.

Spring

❦

1941

B Y NOW, death had long since lost its power to shock. Everyone had a story: there were thousands piled up in London's heart. But ever since the first of the year, Hitler had been playing with London's nerves. There were three nights of bombing in January, then nothing for a week. Then again, and heavier. Then nothing. One day, then another in March, then nothing long enough for daffodils to appear and grass to start sprouting on the banks along the Thames. The city slid into April on a month of quiet. Then came the bombings of the Wednesday and the Saturday—bombs so bad, Ed Murrow joked, you wore your best clothes to bed in case your closet wasn't standing in the morning. And since then, the memory of those nights had settled into everyone's crouch, everyone's quick steps, everyone's fixed attention on the sky. Would they come again tonight? Or was it over? You didn't know. You went to bed ready to run.

DARLING—Emma looked up. But the post office lobby was still empty. Miss James had gone into the back. *This morning the sky was yellow, thick and yellow with ash and smoke and through it the sun rose finally, red. There are clothes in the trees, Emma, blown from the houses the bombs obliterated. The fires are still burning tonight. If they come again, they land the knockout punch, I'd say.*

Last night I went into the heart of London where the docks are centered and the warehouses and the poor, where the bombs hit heaviest and the fires drew the Luftwaffe planes again and again, and the exhausted faces of the men and women in the underground shelters turned to me and I tell you, darling, I bent over them, talking as I took their pulse and held their hands, and though I am the doctor, it is as if they have something to give me. That's how this work feels right now. Tremendous, inspiring, complete—my love if

She crumpled the page and stuffed it in her purse.

"Everything all right?" Miss James had come around the corner.

Emma paused. "Yes." She recovered herself. "He sounds fine."

She did not, the postmaster considered, look like she was sleeping very well. There was a small bump where the baby was growing, yet Emma seemed to Iris as though she were slighter somehow, frailer.

"It's good news, Emma."

"I know," Emma said mutinously. "Of course it is." Because it meant he was alive, she knew Iris was trying to tell her. Alive and well. And fine. And that was good news, of course it was—but she was tired. Tired of pretending the whole thing was all right. Tired of cheeriness. Really she'd like to stay here in the post office, bring in a chair and sit, while Iris went about her business. She'd fall asleep maybe, and every so often Miss James could tiptoe in and check on her. And she could sleep here until the baby came and Will came home.

"He sounds so happy in his letters," she said wistfully, after a little.

"He believes in what he's doing."

"Yes, but what am *I* doing? What about sitting here and waiting for word? All I think about is getting the news, and I can't see straight sometimes. I wish there was a voice over my head, saying something like 'it's all right,' or better, 'it's not all right.' Then I could continue." She flushed and looked down. "I wish I knew that when the bad part comes, God will sit up straight in his chair and cry, *Watch out, Emma*—"

"Like the movies." Iris kept a hold of her voice.

"It's silly."

"Not so silly, really." Iris shook her head. "But you oughtn't to think like that."

Sometimes it was easier just to stay quiet. Emma regarded Iris. Most people had grown up with parents, with two pairs of eyes upon them. There was no way to make anyone who was used to that attention understand how swiftly you could disappear.

"Hello, Harry." The postmaster's voice dropped a note as the doors behind Emma shuddered open.

Emma straightened up and turned around.

"Iris," Harry answered. "Hello, Mrs. Fitch." He came to rest beside her at the counter.

Tears welled up at the sound of her name.

"Pretty tough," he said. Emma looked at him gratefully and nodded. He reached over and patted her hand. Then he turned all his attention on Iris.

"How's the day?" he asked her quietly.

There was dark in that tone and smiles in the dark, Emma realized. Iris reached down into her pocket and pulled up her cigarettes. Harry had his lighter out for her and she leaned forward into the flame. In the street outside, the first shoots of spring carried forward, there were cars nudging along the black tarmac and bicycle bells, there was a couple necking on the benches in the green. People laughed and passed by. A man yodeled. The sun crossed one inch more over the bright beautiful earth. But in here everything had stopped. A woman took her first long pull on the cigarette, and the man leaned away from her, having given her the light. They were divided by a foot and a half of marble—and her.

"Good-bye," Emma said hurriedly.

"So long, Emma."

Emma stopped and turned, her hand on the door. Miss James was leaning forward on her elbows watching her, and Mr. Vale, his hip against the counter, turned also to see her go. Emma nodded, and pushed through the door, tears sliding down her cheeks as she walked down the post office stairs and through the gate, starting blindly up the road.

The roof and chimney of the Bowtches appeared, and above that the roof and chimney of the Snows. After that, at the highest point rose her own roof. A sharp spring sun slapped hard on the water, and she had to turn her face away from the harbor glare and stare instead at the faces of the shingled house she passed on her way up the hill. She was tired. There were people back there in town, all over the world, lots of them, sweating and shouting and grabbing handfuls of life, handfuls to toss around, toss at each other, toss away. Her chest tightened. When she had come here, she had thought she could join them. She thought she *was* joining them when she put her right foot down on the carpet in the aisle of the little church—and hesitated a minute, looking up and seeing Will standing there at the end—and then running toward him. She had thought she was erasing the line in her heart that said she was alone in the world. She put her hand wearily on the gate. Other people believed they were tethered to the world and didn't imagine it could break. But she knew. The memory of her mother's voice was as light and vague as a veil sliding off the back of a chair. All that remained of her brother was the memory of their shared bed, his breath on her cheek finding her in the dark sometimes, just before sleep. Death was the lightest kiss, the coolest touch, a pinch on the thread and then you were gone.

Up ahead, Jim Tom Winthrop was coming toward her, the baby tied to his back in a makeshift rucksack. Emma stumbled and looked down, hoping not to draw his attention.

"Hello!" he called, and pulled his cap down over his ears. There was nothing to do but wave as he walked to where she waited on the pavement.

"Where are you off to?"

"Back home." Her eyes strayed up to the bundle on his shoulder.

"You want to see?" He swung around so she could peel away the blanket he had stuffed over the top of the knapsack and peek in. The baby was fast asleep with her mouth open.

"Beautiful, isn't she?"

Emma nodded and replaced the blanket.

"How's things?" Jim Tom was looking at her closely.

She tucked the blanket under the straps of the knapsack, not trusting herself to look at him. "Just fine," she answered, stepping up onto the sidewalk. She looked back down the street in the direction of town, hoping for some distraction, or someone to come along. But the street was as empty as daybreak. "How are you?"

"Oh, we're pulling through—"

"Good," Emma encouraged politely, taking a step away, trying to indicate that she was on her way home. "That's good to hear."

"I'll walk with you a little ways," he offered. "She sleeps as long as I'm moving."

"All right," Emma answered, and set off, a little desperately.

"Hang on," he teased.

She slowed down.

"The boys have been grand," he continued, and fell into step alongside her, "and little Maggie's giving us something to do so we don't think too much about"—his voice failed him suddenly. Emma didn't look at him. He pulled a handkerchief from his pocket and blew his nose.

"Aah," he said thickly into the handkerchief. He shook his head, wiped his eyes, and turned to her. "Sorry," he said, "it just comes over me."

Emma stiffened.

"Tough, isn't it?" Jim Tom slipped his handkerchief into his pocket. "For us left behind."

Us? A wild, unreasoning fury rose up in Emma's chest. "I beg your pardon"—she turned on him—"but Will hasn't *died*."

He quit walking and she simply kept going, her fury like jets pushing her forward and away. It had been horrible, *awful,* but she didn't care. There were wood fires burning in the houses along the way and the smell of someone's cooking, and the comfort they spoke of home fed her fury. It was wrong that Will had gone. There must have been something wrong with Maggie before she went into labor. It wasn't Will's fault. Will hadn't owed the world a good goddamn, but Maggie's death had made him think so. Home? There was no home.

She arrived without seeing at her gate, and stopped. On that first afternoon, she and Will had turned in here and she looked up the walk to this house. She tried to recall seeing the weathered shingles and gray sills, but all she remembered was Will's hand on her elbow, guiding her forward.

"You ought to paint."

She jumped.

The man in the overcoat she saw around town was standing next to her. The German man who worked for Mr. Vale. Standing quite close.

"Oh," she said. "Hello."

His eyes took her in and held her for a moment as if he might have something to give her, Emma thought irrationally. He was very close. He smelled like salt and something deep and dark like bread. Very near.

"You ought to paint it," he said again.

His voice curled around the English words slowly, as if he negotiated a dangerous turn.

She frowned. "What?"

He pointed to the windows where, it was true, the paint peeled from the shutters and off the sills, leaving bare wood. "It rots," he said more slowly.

She nodded. The two of them stared up at the house.

"I like the fresh white." He went on. "One could see it miles way."

"Miles away," she corrected reflexively.

"I could do it for you."

"Oh." She almost laughed, and turned to face him, understanding now. He needed work, that was all. He needed a job.

"But I can't do something like that. My husband's gone, and—I don't have any money," she fudged. There was plenty of money for house repairs. Will had even left instructions for how to get at it, in case of a leak.

The man in front of her had dark blue eyes, and a deep crease ran down from one of them as he smiled. "Some day."

She blushed. "I can't paint the house."

"So?" He bent toward her. "All right, then." And he kept going in the direction of the dunes past town. Before she pushed the gate open, she turned to watch him walking away. She wanted to call him back, almost, but let the impulse go.

"Hello?" she called into the empty house as she did every day on returning.

She walked straight back through to the kitchen. "Hello?" One of the dishes shifted in the drainer. The late trap boats were sliding back into the pier below, and she stared at them, leaning her belly on the lip of the sink.

The house ought to be painted. Emma reached for the kettle and walked it to the sink, letting the water run cold before filling it. She set it on the stove, pulled out cigarettes and her matches and turned around, understanding at last what the foreigner had meant by miles away. Like Hansel's breadcrumbs lighting a white path along the dark forest floor to find his way home, the German man meant the house ought to be seen from off shore. She inhaled against the match and drew the flame.

Will? She exhaled.

She wandered away from the window and down the hall where the magic eye on the radio cabinet against the living room wall glowed with the dull green of a strong signal.

More than anything right then, she wanted to turn the knob to tune in Will speaking—hear his voice calling, *Emma Emma*. She sniffed. She turned the shortwave knob until the crackle gave way to a voice, brought her a voice to fill the empty house. She wanted someone to speak to her, right then, any human body. *Do be sensible, my mother writes me. Do take care,* the woman said quite slowly. *But what is sensible anymore? In the mornings waking first to the quiet, a city thrown over with quiet, like the blanket on a parakeet's cage. Fear has long since been domesticated.* KEEP CALM AND CARRY ON, *the signs have gone up all over the city, roller-pasted on the still-standing brick sides of buildings.*

KEEP CALM AND CARRY ON.

Emma reached and switched on the light without breathing, and then stood directly in front of the radio, her arms crossed over her chest, her heart pounding.

In the great big novels of the last century, there was time, Frankie Bard continued, *time to survey the vast expanse, here a figure approaching across the heath, there a girl sitting at her window teaching a boy to read in the factory's shadow. There was time and there was quiet for page after page. What can be written now to tell of the smashing bombs, the noise and rage at the skies? How we are yanked out of bed, no time to think—perhaps you cannot hear a story like the old ones anymore. The quickest thing to cure a person of omniscience—a belief in some orderly overseeing eye—is war. Chaotic and unaligned, people die or are saved without an orchestrating arm. The orchestra plays chords but the notes take off, willy-nilly.*

"Shut up," Emma whispered to the eye. "Shut up, why can't you?"

13.

O N MAY THE TENTH, one hundred bombs a minute rained down
on London for five straight hours in what was the most devastating
single night of the Blitz. Fires exploded everywhere and at once, and
where there had been, even on the other nights, pockets of calm, dips
of peace, that night the din in the skies could drive you mad. Hit were
Parliament, Big Ben, and Westminster Abbey, and countless houses
smashed to pieces.

Now, a week later, more than anything, Will needed sleep. He had
worked steadily since the tenth, and had been wandering in the direction of bed when the air-raid siren wailed up into the night somewhere
to the west. Will rubbed his eyes and looked down at the letter he was
writing to Emma. He needed sleep. He needed one night in his own bed.
Antiaircraft guns battered at the sky. Perhaps the bombs tonight would
stay in one place and he could stay home, he thought, glancing at his bed
just as the nearer siren three blocks over began its banshee wailing. He
groaned and stretched. He'd have to get himself down into a shelter if
he wanted any sleep at all tonight.

He looked back down at the letter. "*Emma, darling,*" it said. He had
wanted to tell her about the strange image he had had tonight when he
was walking home. *Darling*, he wrote. But he had lost the thread of what

would come next. *Good night, my sweet. I'll write more tomorrow, I promise.* He finished hurriedly and folded it into the envelope, licking the flap. *Emma Fitch*, he wrote out on the front, *Box 329, Franklin, Massachusetts, USA*, and shoved it into his jacket pocket. A third siren went off, this one to the north. He slid his lighter and cigarettes into his jacket, stood, and reached for his hat.

"Dr. Fitch." His landlady knocked at the door. "The siren's gone off."

"I'm awake, Mrs. Phillips, thank you for checking." He opened the door and called after his landlady, who was already hurrying down the stairs. He turned and pulled the blanket off his bed, considered the pillow, but left them both behind.

Out on the street, people hurried toward the brick shelter at the end of the block. The fires set to the north roared up into the sky. There was a whistle and a swish and the bomb hit so close that Will felt as though his lungs were sucked from his chest. He staggered back against the boardinghouse. The air released him and he started to run, heading at a jog for the Kensington High Street tube station, judging there'd still be space there. Just as there had been on the tenth, the consistent drone of the planes above was a blanket in the head. He reached the stairs down into the tunnel and slowed as he descended.

There were interlocking rooms within the station, their tiled caverns inconsistently lit. Will picked his way through the first two, already full, and found a spot in the corner of the third where he could sink down and rest. Relatively comfortable, he thought, stretching his long legs out along the floor. Room enough for sleep.

But he had not been prepared for the stink down here, and how easily the restive, impatient fear passed around in a room. A second run of bombs went off one after the other; it sounded like it was right on top of their heads, the noise so deafening that Will ducked instinctively, even though he was fifty feet underground. The bombs lasted fifteen seconds and then stopped. He half-stood to go help up above, but he was so tired, he realized his legs had fallen asleep, even if the rest of him hadn't. A steady stream of people creeping in to find place in the shelter began, and families shushed the crying children, and the men and women wrapped themselves in blankets and leaned one against the other. A latecomer, a tall blonde, picked her way shakily across the outstretched legs of the others and sank down into an open spot across the way. For a long while she leaned her head against the wall and closed her eyes. Then, rousing, she pulled her sweater off and shoved it under her bottom.

She was the type of girl men say they would die for. The kind who could stop a room with her smile, though Will was fairly sure this one might not try. He appraised the one long leg crossed over the other, gracefully at the slim ankle. Blond, brainy, too old for games. She looked more like the kind who's got something and knows it, but didn't need to advertise. Like Emma.

Her name sent a flush of warmth across his chest. He closed his eyes and rested his head on the wall. *Emma*, he invoked her again, *Emma, Emma*—like a bellows—but all that came were the teasing, incongruous pieces: her head against his shoulder, the flip of her hair carefully curled under and resting against her thin little neck, or the narrow leather belt she wore at her waist. Lately, he could not quite call her face fully to mind. He had a photograph of the two of them taken on their wedding day, but the longer he was away, the more that girl standing next to him didn't seem to be Emma. She was a pretty girl tucked under the arm of a good-enough-looking guy. He had the absurd but persistent fear that the girl in the photograph—with her brown hair, brown eyes, soft little chin tipped up as if someone had just told her to be brave—had erased Emma. So that now, when someone asked about her, he found himself only able to say "brown hair, brown eyes"—he lit the match to the end of his cigarette and shook it out with an exasperated snap of his wrist—for Christ's sake. She sounded like a fairy-tale girl. And she was no girl. They had made love. There. He remembered her blushing up at him, asking whether Tolstoy meant it. Making love. In those two words she was there. She was true blue—but in the dark she was also so soft, moving under his hand, he could almost feel her now. And the image that continually came to mind now was not her face, but her figure from behind. The dress, the belt, the sweet line of her calves down to the leather flats. The way he had first come upon her from behind at the party, and then a year later when he'd asked her to marry him and, without turning around, without saying a thing, she had simply leaned back against him, trusting him to remain where he stood.

He opened his eyes. Where he stood. Three thousand miles across the ocean from her in an air-raid shelter while the Krauts rained bombs on his head. With every passing day, every hour gone, he risked losing her and he knew it. And though he tended to the wounded and the dying, lately he set out in the night searching for Emma's face among the women on the street—Emma or someone like her—to fix again her image in his mind. A woman's glance backward over her shoulder, the wisp of hair falling across a chin. Not hers, but calling her just for a fleeting moment into being. He was looking for the shadow of his love. And in some crazy way, he believed that as he walked in search of her, she protected him. Her face, the face he could not conjure on his own without these others, had come to be a charm against the bombs.

"Do you mean to die there?" she had asked him calmly the night before he'd sailed, her chin firm, her dark, serious eyes raised to his.

"What a queer thing to say." He'd pulled her to him, spreading his hands across the small of her back and feeling her body beneath the blouse. The kitchen tap dripped into the copper basin of the sink behind them.

"Because if you do," she said against his shirt, "die, I mean, it will have been for nothing."

"You don't mean that." He'd stood back and tipped her face up to his.

She wouldn't answer. He squeezed her arms. She looked at him.

"I do." She stepped out from between his hands. "To hell with them. Let the English take care of themselves."

"Em—"

"And what you're doing won't add up. It's not right. Or good. It won't square, Will." She was savage in her calm. "What happened here was not your fault," she said, "and that's all."

He shifted in the dark. *Right. Good.* The old words sounded in his ears like capes for kings. What he had stumbled on here among the bombs was new as an alternate sky. He'd come over to play out what he now saw had been some simple equation: himself for Maggie. As if one and one made two. As simple and childish as the idea of redemption. But he'd come to understand that each one of us was alive, intensely alive, right until the instant of death. And then each of us was gone. There could be no substitutions. He had held so many dying hands over here, he understood it at last. And what he wanted to say in the letter he just wrote Emma was that he was happy here, beyond all measure—but he couldn't. Not to the people whose faces he bent over, and especially not to Emma, who was slipping away.

Though he wrote her every night after supper, he found he couldn't write anything but the news. The news and that he loved her. He loved her. But then this larger thought, the reason he stayed on, and would stay past the six months he had set himself, hung beside him wordless. The life he had lived, at home, was over. How could he tell her that without scaring her? If he returned, nothing up until now mattered— which was to say, nothing need be proved anymore. And tonight, walking home from the hospital in the dark, not paying attention to where he was going, he had suddenly realized he was guiding his way forward by the single small lights of cigarettes, the sign of other people moving, disembodied, through the dark toward him: people whose faces he couldn't see, but whose voices he heard, whose footsteps passed by.

And he had nearly burst out crying on the street. Those tiny red lights in the dark going forward and moving away, those single Lucky Strikes, that's what it was to be human. We lived and died, all of us—lucky strikes. Single lights and voices in the dark. He slipped his hand under his jacket to feel for his letter to Emma. It was there. He'd mail it first thing. And maybe tomorrow what he wanted to say would be clearer than *we are all lucky strikes.*

"Have you got a light?"

"Christ!" He jumped.

The leggy blonde from across the way stood in front of him. He hadn't seen her move.

"You're American." She was looking down at him, amused.

"That's right." He got smoothly up onto his feet, and she realized he was quite tall and rangy with an open, easy face. Good bones—her mother would have approved. A bankable man. He fished his lighter out and leaned toward her. She cupped his hand and drew on the flame. His seersucker jacket glowed slightly in the underground light. She cast another glance upward and saw he was staring at her, as if he thought he might find something in the thicket of her hair or in the severe cliff of her chin.

"Do I remind you of someone?"

He smiled and flipped the lighter closed. "Not at all."

There was room against the wall next to him, and she nodded at it. "Mind if I sit here?"

"Not at all."

"You're very well brought up." She lowered herself down. It was darker over here away from the windows, and she had the sensation of having pushed farther backward into a cave. The floor shook as she sat. Some shells hit close, though they were muffled by the building above their heads. There was a break and then a burst of guns again, and then the unmistakable shriek of another descending shell. The walls shook and the air seemed to be sucked up and blown back down, exhaling the cellar damp.

"Bad as the tenth, do you think?"

"No." She shook her head. "Nor the Wednesday bombing, either."

"They won't break," Will commented quietly to the ceiling, as though he told a secret to the Krauts.

"Course not," she affirmed.

"It's remarkable."

"Well, what else are they going to do?" she asked drily, speaking in the direction of his cigarette. "Give up?"

"Yes." He looked down at her. "It's always a possibility."

She frowned. "Funny, I would have figured you more for the gung ho type."

"What's that?" She heard the grin in his voice.

"You know, charge the hill, never say die, that sort of thing."

He did laugh. "You got the wrong guy."

"Yeah?" she smiled into the dark. You started with what you saw—good-looking man in a good suit—and then you poked to see what was behind it; you never knew what you'd find, that was the thrill of it. That was the game. She kept her voice cool, a reporter's voice. "Who's the right guy?"

The end of his cigarette flared up and dimmed. He stayed on his feet. She watched him stretch with the languor of a big man, comfortable taking up room, his hands grazing the ceiling above them, and saw he wouldn't answer. He lowered his arms slowly and held out his right hand. "Will Fitch."

"Frankie Bard." She gave him hers.

He whistled, keeping her hand. "The radio gal?"

"That's right." His hand was warm and broad.

He let her go and sank down beside her, folding himself into the dark nook.

"Never thought I'd see you down in one of these," he remarked. "You're usually up on the roof."

"Usually am," she answered. "I nearly fell down here, got blown in really, by that last one—" She shrugged. "I figure I've made it this long without a scratch, better stay put. I hate the funk holes, though."

"I'm with you," he agreed. "How long have you been over here?"

"Just over a year."

"And what brought you?"

She looked over at him, conspiratorially. "Why?"

"Just a question." He pulled his knees up and shook his head. "Killing time. Wondering what a girl like you is doing in a hole like this."

"I came over here to save the world, brother," she drawled.

He chuckled. "How will you manage that?"

She shifted her position, moving off her knees, and briefly put her hand on his shoulder to steady herself, her hair swinging toward him. "Telling the truth." Her voice was as light as her touch had been. But there was no smile in it.

"You think so?"

"'Course I do," Frankie said squarely.

To her satisfaction, he whistled. "Well, you're good. Your stories made Emma cry."

"Your girl?"

"My wife."

Frankie raised her eyebrows. "What are you doing over here when you've got a wife back home?"

He crossed his arms over his chest and leaned sideways, slightly away from her.

"Same as you, I bet," he said beside her. "Aside from saving the world."

"Yeah?" She sat up a little, sending the notepad forward on her lap. "What's that?"

"Help out if I can. Make some sense out of things."

It had been a long time since she'd heard this easy American surety. "That's very noble." She poked at the conviction. "I just wanted to be where the action was."

He shot a look at her. She returned his gaze.

"Hell," he said. "I don't believe that for a minute."

She raised an eyebrow. "Why not?"

"A girl like you?"

"Whatever that means."

"Come on," he teased. "You don't fool me. You're from some swell house somewhere with elms on the lawn."

She chuckled. "I'm from New York."

"But it's a brownstone," he guessed.

She flashed a quick grin, conceding. "Yes, all right."

Someone cried out in his sleep, and with a start Frankie realized she'd forgotten the others around her. She pulled her notebook out of her satchel and flipped it open.

The perfect line of her forehead and long even nose made him think improbably of a virgin warrior. A Diana who wore her red lips like a sword. And the page on her lap—he watched as she pulled out a pencil from the dark as though she were going to write something down—a shield.

"What kind of work are you doing over here, if you don't mind my asking?"

He nodded at the notebook. "You going to interview me?"

"Maybe."

He shook his head. "I'm not a story."

"Fair enough." She put the pencil down flat.

"I'm a doctor."

"What sort?"

He paused. "Family doctor. I've got my own practice back home."

"Where's that?"

"Franklin, Massachusetts." He leaned toward her as if in confidence. "Where the *Mayflower* first landed."

"In what history book?"

"Small-print history." He grinned. "They landed, took one look at the trees bent sideways by the wind off the back shore, and turned right around."

"You sound pleased as punch."

"It's the best way to describe the kind of people who live there."

"Not Puritans, I take it."

He shook his head.

"Your parents still live there?"

"No." But his voice had tightened.

"Hey," she answered lightly. "Just killing time."

A fire engine screamed by and disappeared.

"What's it like there?"

"Why?"

"Why not keep talking?" She had picked the pencil back up and written the words *what happened back home?* and then circled them, and kept going in a circle around and around them, slightly wider and wider on the page. He could hear the scratch of the lead, long loops and short jabs that couldn't add up to anything. He wondered briefly how much sleep she'd had. She seemed incapable of being still, a restive, roaming spirit, like a message boy in a hotel lobby, he thought, and somehow this called Emma back so forcefully in the dark that he nearly moaned. There she was, suddenly, in front of him, looking at him with that peculiar capacity to wait and listen and call him forward just by her quiet. Not restless. Still. Christ. He shifted slightly away from Frankie in the dark. "It's a town like most, I guess. The last town on Cape Cod. The outermost town."

"How many people?"

"Five hundred or so. Twice that in the summer."

He was getting away, retreating up her simple questions rung by rung. She caught herself, and smiled. She *was* interviewing him, though she hadn't any idea where they were heading. He had got hold of her. Not the other way around. It was never the other way around. You simply caught hold of the rope and climbed blindly along, following it until it arrived at the end.

"And you left all that, to come over here," she observed quietly.

He didn't answer. When she looked up, he was staring at her.

"She really isn't anything like you," he mused. "Her nose is smaller, a little round at the end there," he pointed, "and her—"

Frankie cleared her throat. He lifted his eyes to hers.

"Sorry," he said quickly. "It's become a habit of mine."

"Staring at women?"

"Studying," he corrected, a little sheepish.

She nodded and glanced away. He had wide hands. They lay like good dogs, flat and restrained upon his legs.

"I guess you miss her."

"I'm afraid I've lost her, coming over here."

"Nuts," Frankie answered. She'd bank on his wife being one of those child-women who wore kneesocks and pearls like most of the girls she'd gone to school with. "She'll be right there when you get home, wondering why you didn't bring her cashmere instead of wool."

She was so far off the mark that it made Will smile. "Emma wouldn't care about cashmere," he said.

From the deepest corner of the shelter, across its width and to the left of them, unfurled a small unmistakable moan. Frankie stiffened. A second, long and low, belled out, more deeply into the dark, the wave of the woman's pleasure opening around them all, until it vanished back into her throat where it began, followed by the man's chuckle and an abrupt quiet as though he had shut the door. Then nothing. The silence left behind in the shelter was full of their sex, and everyone else suddenly found themselves silent, too, listening at the open keyhole, wanting together in the dark. Wanting more. "Christ," the doctor sighed, pulling out the cigarettes again.

"No, thanks." Frankie shook her head.

He slid one out, pocketing the rest. Then he tapped it against his long first finger and, sticking it in his mouth, he reached toward her and she felt his hand wrap around her upper arm just above the elbow.

"This part on her," he said very quietly, "makes you want to put your hand around it."

Frankie looked at him and then looked down where his big hand held her, his fingers nearly able to wrap around. She shivered. And the hand that held her let go, sliding into his pocket and pulling out his lighter.

"It's funny meeting you," he said, taking a drag in on the flame.

"How's that?"

He pocketed his lighter. "There was one story of yours. A few months ago. About a boy." He cleared his throat.

She nodded, her eyes on the spark of his cigarette moving in the dark.

"A boy after one of the bombings," he went on. "You were bringing him home."

"Yes," she said. "Billy. That was mine."

"It was a good story," Will Fitch said.

"A good story." She sighed. "That story got me into hot water."

"Why's that?"

"Too grim," Frankie exhaled, "and my voice shook."

"So what?"

"Too emotional. The news can't be emotional."

"Well, I don't know about that," Will answered, "but it hit both of us pretty damn hard. You left us sitting there wondering what happened next—" He stopped short. What happened next had been Maggie, Will remembered. The boy in the Blitz had been a story from before he lost Maggie. He shuddered slightly. "Any idea what's happened to him?"

"No," she answered. "I don't know. I moved."

"Must be tough not to know what happened, not to know whether he's all right."

She didn't answer. The truth was she had passed by Billy's house several times in the past six months, half-hoping he might be there. But he had vanished into the war. Uneasily, she stretched her legs out along the floor. Her foot touched something soft and it slid away.

"It gets you thinking about *all* the parts in a story we never see"—he cleared his throat—"the parts around the edges. You bring someone like that boy so alive before us and there he is set loose in our world so that we can't stop thinking of him. But then the report is over, the boy disappears. He was just a boy in a story and we never know the ending, we never get to close the book. It makes you wonder what happens to the people in them after the story stops—all the stories you've reported, for instance. Where are they all now?"

Her heart began to thud slowly. She didn't like where he was going with this, and she imagined getting up, but his voice—with its familiar tints of Harvard and supper parties and the assurance of old money with which she had been raised herself—worked on her like hands on her hands and would not release her until done. He would not stop and she could not stop him.

"You must be pretty tough," he went on beside her. "I couldn't bear it—I guess I just like to know how things turn out."

"Well, I don't have to *bear* it." Frankie glanced over at him, provoked. "I tell what I see. I watch and I listen, and I tell all about it. That's the job," she said impatiently. "Telling it. Passing it along. That's the point."

" 'Course it is." He sounded doubtful.

She looked at him. "Listen, the only way out of this is to tell it all. Tell what happens. All the time. And the only way to tell it all is to keep moving. Keep moving and keep telling."

He watched her with his head to the side, as if listening through a stethoscope. "Only way out of what?"

In the slight pause, she felt something slip from her grasp, gone so quickly she wasn't sure what it was. She shrugged. "Out of this mess."

"Why would you want to get out of it?" he asked very gently.

"*I* don't want to get out of anything," she said testily in the direction of his shoulder. "I'm the one over here, aren't I? I'm the one trying to catch what's happening over here so we can—oh, for Christ's sake," she broke off, "it doesn't matter."

"So we can what?" he pursued.

She didn't answer.

He let it go, leaning his head back against the wall. "Sometimes I'm out in the middle of the hell up there, even in the middle of people crying out and that retching smell of gas and fire, and I have to turn my face away to hide my smile." There was no mistaking the joy in his voice. "Everything matters here," he said quietly. "Everything adds up."

She glanced over at him. "Nothing about this adds up."

"It does," he said to her. "It's all there is."

"That's nuts," she retorted angrily. "It's random as hell out there—that *is* hell—random, incomprehensible accidents happening night after night. A man calling to his son to run toward him for safety and in the moment that the boy runs, in the twenty steps between them, is hit, is killed—"

"And you saw it."

She frowned.

"That's all there is. That's what I'm saying. You saw it."

"Nuts." She shook her head.

"Listen, I came over here because I had some crackpot idea of order—because a woman died in my care, I thought I ought to go where I could do the most good, help, stand in the way of more death. But you don't."

"Don't what?"

"Don't stand in the way of anything." He was so sure, it was almost electric in the dark. "You can only stand alongside."

"Oh, for Christ's sake." She pulled away. It was embarrassing, this naked excitement. She'd heard it in her father's voice at the end of too much drink. Flushed and possessed by the wine and the fervor, he would denounce some politician, or make some sweeping absurd gesture and the fire in him would blaze up, too hotly she'd feel, looking at her mother, ashamed. Too bright. Like some great beautiful boy. She looked away into the shadows. That was it. The memory of her father was coming toward her, pale and urgent, through the dark. Gliding forward on the low begotten currents of Will Fitch's voice. Her father. Ruined sorrow.

"For the first few weeks after I got here," he went on, "I walked into the hospital ward every day, desperate to heal, to soothe, to save. I worked hour after hour, steady, more like a miner than a man. Inching forward along the beds, taking pulses, temperatures, stitching and binding wounds. Keeping careful records. How many. Who. After a month I had worked more hours, seen more patients than any other doctor on the hall. And they would keep coming. Day after day. No matter what I did, they would keep on dying. Or living.

"And one day, I got it. I lifted my head from the child's chest I was listening to and realized, with a shock of relief: whatever is coming, comes. That's what holds it all together. We are all of us here in the mess. There's no way around it. And all I am in the face of it is a single voice and a pair of hands. Not anyone's son anymore. Not anyone's husband. Anonymous but necessary. Vital. A Lucky Strike."

"Listen," Frankie snapped. His happiness was maddening. "Whatever is coming does *not* just come, as you say. It's helped by people willfully looking away. People who develop the habit of swallowing lies rather than the truth. The minute you start thinking something else, then you've stopped paying attention—and paying attention is all we've got."

"I'm looking straight at it, Miss Bard," Will replied calmly. "You can't stop the mess. You can't change what's coming"—he looked across at her—"and you shouldn't try."

With an impatient sigh, Frankie pushed off the floor and stood all the way up, needing to move. Needing some air, some light. She reached to refasten her skirt, which had come unbuttoned in the back, and bending to grab her crumpled sweater, she saw that the doctor hadn't moved. Unnerved, she reached for her satchel beside him.

"If the world had paid more attention in 1939," she thrust, "maybe we wouldn't be sitting here in the dark, dodging bombs."

"We'd be sitting somewhere else."

"With your wife, for instance."

"Yes, all right," he agreed sadly. "With my wife."

The door to the shelter was thrown open and the long, high whine of the all clear sounded as first light stretched through the opening. Something like a sob was rising inside her, and she pulled her satchel over her head, settling it across her breast.

"You've just got to get home," she said carefully, "that's all."

He stood up and held out his hand. "I don't know."

Frankie hesitated with her hand in his just briefly, before dropping it and slipping through the knot of waking Londoners and out the shelter door into the soft blue morning. She stood a minute on the pavement above the shelter, back up in the spring air. It was a little after five o'clock. The light shifted on the street, suddenly plunging dark and then immediately bright again upon the pavement. No matter what happened, spring behaved as it always had. It was still just one morning in late May in London.

Late May in London. On her bed under the eaves at school, these would have been the words that called to mind tea parties and strawberries and Henry James, when all civilization could be contained within the blue borders of an English sky. Except for the smoking buildings and the stink of burning rubber and metal, one might almost imagine Dorian Gray, flushed and gorgeous behind one of those windows, and Mrs. Dalloway coming out onto the square. Almost, Frankie thought, noticing the hunk of mortar missing from the side of a house across the square. As if it had been bitten.

"So long," Will Fitch said behind her. "I'll be listening for you."

"So long." She nodded at him again and watched him walk briskly, singly away down the long block of Wilmot toward the busy hustle of Oxford Circus. She watched him set his hat back on his head with one hand, and watched his suit jacket narrow smartly as he buttoned it at the waist. And she could feel herself unclench as he walked away. Christ, he had gotten under her skin. What had happened to her down there? She tugged at the strap across her chest, embarrassed in the upstairs world by the force of her reaction to the doctor below. She shivered. It had just been too damn dark, too close. And his voice beside her, probing, prodding, insistent as a ghost. That American voice. Out here, aboveground, in the familiar ruin, she felt more like herself.

The doctor had gotten nearly to the end of the street. She stifled a momentary urge to call out to him, and stood a minute longer to watch him move out of sight. In the distance, at the far corner, men and women crossed the street. It looked like it would rain. A woman walked toward him from the opposite direction, carrying a baby in her arms.

Afterward, Frankie couldn't remember, but something the woman did made the doctor turn and look at her, as though he had recognized her, and didn't see the London taxi coming from the direction no American thinks to look, didn't see the black, efficient machine, and stepped off the curb. Frankie took one step forward with a scream and the other people emerging from the shelter turned and all of them saw the large man flipped up off his feet and tossed into the air—where, even still, though they all saw it happen, he might live, he might not have to fall back down—until he did fall, hit the road flat on his back heavy and hard, with a sick, unmistakable thud, his body a punctured sack.

She heard a low hissing from the front of the cab. The taxi driver sat frozen inside, his hands on the wheel, the taxi inching forward toward the spot where Will had been flung.

"Stop!" Frankie ran along the street. "Pull your brake, God *damn* it." She scrambled to Will and sank down beside him. His nose was broken and the bone had shot through the skin, naked and off-kilter, bleeding a steady stream down his cheek. He stared up past her shoulder at the sky. Frankie tried to wipe the blood away with her hand, but there was too much, and the mark of her fingers crossed his face. She tried to gather a part of her skirt to wipe it off, but the blood was streaking past now, covering the marks. His eyes opened and shut, and he moaned.

Frankie couldn't see anything broken other than his nose, though beneath his breathing she heard a low persistent sigh, as if air was escaping somewhere.

"What do I do? What should I do?" The cabbie had gotten himself out of his taxi.

Above Frankie, all around her, a crowd of people stood and stared down at Will lying flat on his back, the breath wheezing in and out of him, his eyes open. Behind them, ambulance bells rang and the daytime traffic of the city honked and whirred. Even now, in a city where the number of dead had climbed into the thousands, where the rotten smell of burnt flesh and rubber hung in the air and where the exhausted grimy faces of men and women in the mornings on the streets were unremarkable, this was not. The man had simply not paid attention. It had nothing to do with the war. They couldn't help it, they had to talk, and their voices above Frankie sounded like the wild clucking of birds.

"Get an ambulance," Frankie cried. "Get an ambulance, someone!"

Will made a sound as though he were clearing his throat. There was blood coming from his mouth now. Frankie felt faint.

"Dear God," the cabbie whispered.

Frankie jammed her hands under Will's arms. "Help me," she called to the driver. He bent and the two of them half-dragged, half-shoved Will onto her lap. She cradled his head in her elbow and looked down into a face that someone had already pulled the shade on. A warm pool spread in her lap, though she couldn't see the source of the bleeding. She wrapped her arms around Will to keep him warm, and the frantic clanging of ambulance bells came on, then passed down Oxford Street. Had someone gone for an ambulance?

The cabbie was trying to give her something. An envelope. She stared at him. "It was on the street, there," he pointed. "His, I think." She looked at the address and shoved it in her jacket pocket, and caught Will's eyes on her.

"It's okay," she said to him quietly, though she knew he could not hear or answer. "I've got you." And she rested one hand on his head and the other on his heart, until she felt it stop.

14.

ALONG WHILE after the ambulance had driven away with the doctor's body, Frankie sat on the curb, her mind scrambling backward to the earlier minutes when he was there beside her in the dark, before the air and the light and the cab. The London dawn clattered and called its way into a full morning, and the crowd that had gathered around her slowly melted back into it. Taxicabs continued up and down the street. She sat there for ten minutes, twenty, another half hour. In the tiny garden across the way the dew-heavy crown of a daffodil slipped sideways onto the grass. Someone's baby wailed from one of the open windows. A footstep struck hard along the pavement. One of the house doors thunked shut upon the street. The blood on her skirt had dried. Finally, she stood up and made her way home.

By four o'clock, the spring day had soured and a quiet drizzle begun. Frankie woke up, her heart racing. The tired-looking pot of geraniums on the fortress-deep windowsill in her single room faced her. She shivered and sat up on her elbow. But for the geraniums, it still looked like the room of someone living elsewhere. Her heart slowed and she swung herself out of bed and sat down in front of the typewriter.

Perhaps by now the doctor had been identified, and the word had begun its journey out along the cable, through the telegraph wires, to someone in Massachusetts who would type it up and send it on. From Boston down the Cape, out to the end to Franklin, where someone else would hold the telegram, and know what it meant, and have to deliver it. And Frankie tried to imagine who would hand the doctor's wife that piece of paper. But she couldn't see the town, or the person in her mind's eye, or even the wife. Just a hand holding the piece of paper, with the fact, but not what happened. She took a piece of paper from the drawer below the typewriter and slid it into the roller, then flicked the carriage lever several times until the page rolled up on the other side. *May 18*, she began, *London.*

We think we know the story, she typed slowly. *We think we know the story because there's a man and a woman sitting together in a funk hole in the dark. There are bombs. It's a war. There was a war before, and we've read the stories.* She stopped, reading the two lines on the page. *We've read Hemingway. We've read Miss Thompson and Martha Gellhorn. We think we know who will die and who will live, who is a hero, who will fall in love with whom; but every story—love or war—is a story about looking left when we should have been looking right. That's the*—Frankie flicked the carriage lever three more times, rolling the paper free of the typewriter. It wasn't going to fly, she knew it wouldn't. Not for Murrow, certainly. But neither for Max Prescott or the *Trib*. What, for starters, did she think she was writing about? The Death of an Idealist? Death of a Good Old Boy? She stood up, rereading the lead. There was nothing to say. On a night when many may have died, she wanted to write about one. A man had died by accident this morning. A man who believed that despite the mess, everything added up. A happy man in the middle of the Blitz. She rubbed her eyes, thinking of Max on the other end of the line, *Hell, Frankie, where's the story?*

A clot of blood released into her underpants. Then another. Christ. She shimmied the three steps over to her bureau, holding her hand between her legs so nothing dripped onto the landlady's carpet. She reached and found a Kotex and a pair of clean underwear and fastened the one to the sanitary belt around her waist, pulled the other up, and tossed the soiled underwear on top of the blouse already soaking in the tiny sink by the door. The tap sputtered as she filled the sink higher, and then she filled a water glass and poured it around the roots of the geranium, and the chalky green smell rose from the leaves and reminded her sharply of her mother's garden and of summer at home. Her mother would have liked Dr. Will Fitch. She put down the glass, gently. The slant view out the window gave her back slate rooftops, slick and blackened by the soft English drizzle. It was nearly five o'clock.

She changed quickly into her clothes and closed the shutters on the window. Outside, the mist clung to her hair and the wool of her sweater, making her feel safer, as though bombs couldn't do their full damage in soft weather, which was absurd, but there it was. After two or three blocks, she realized she was getting soaked and put up her umbrella at the same time as someone across the street, the umbrellas opening like black blooms. She pushed down the handle at the cleaner's and shook her umbrella slightly, not sure of what to say about the doctor's blood.

"Never mind that," said tiny Mrs. Dill, forcefully gathering the skirt and rinsed blouse into a pile. "We'll get it out in a jiff. Hold on."

Frankie turned around, nearly out the door.

"Yes?"

Mrs. Dill was holding up Will Fitch's letter, which she'd taken from the pocket of the skirt.

"Thanks." Frankie slid it into her skirt without looking at it.

The rain and the green spring had crept forward across the soaking opened husks of buildings along Portland Place. Broadcasting House always appeared to Frankie to rise up out of its surrounds like a fortress, ringed by a moat of canvas sandbags, now sprouting, Frankie saw, what looked to be grass. She pushed through the swinging doors into the lobby where the smell of cabbage seeped up from the two sublevel floors on which the studios and the shelter shared space with the kitchen. Aboveground spread the archives and offices. And the people. Frankie made her way to the linoleum staircase rising through the middle of the building. People and their voices, the short waves of laughter and hot, high speech echoed all around her. And gossip. Hello, Frankie. Hello, hello. She rose through her compatriots as though she were swimming back up for air.

"You look like hell," Ed observed as she slipped into the office where he stood at his desk.

"Thank you, Mr. Murrow." Frankie tried to be light, hanging her coat on top of his on the back of the door.

"What happened?"

She turned around and didn't meet his eye. "A man was killed this morning."

Murrow studied her. "Someone you knew?"

Frankie shook her head. "I met him in the funk hole last night."

He frowned.

"Hell, Ed." She blushed. "It wasn't like that. He was American, that's all. And he was hit by a cab because he was looking the wrong way."

"That's tough."

Frankie looked up. "Yeah," she said. "And he's got a wife back home."

"That's tough," Murrow said again, more quietly. He pointed to the chair in front of him. She sank down in it.

"Okay?" He was watching her.

She nodded.

"Look at this." He handed her a teletype from the New York office, the excitement in his voice making her look at him quickly before reading the page in her hand. J. Edgar Hoover had just come out in print damning what he called the Fifth Column Hysteria overtaking the nation. Suddenly, there seemed to be spies under every bed, illegals hiding in every corner, saboteurs skulking in every garage. The FBI received nearly three hundred calls a day reporting suspected foreign-born spies and Hoover wanted to inject some sense into the population. This was a reversal. A year ago he'd been warning the country about being careful.

"There you go, Frankie."

She looked at him, uncertain.

"There's the frame. Now it's American news," Murrow said. "Now there's a reason to tell the story—who is fleeing Germany, who's really on those refugee trains."

The familiar rush of getting an assignment coursed through her, her excitement surging up and subsuming the doctor's death. "When do I go?" Frankie sat forward in her chair.

He grinned the smile that inspired all of them to try anything he asked. "Soon as you can pack."

"Done."

"Good girl," he said. "Here you go."

She stood up and took the press pass, gaining her safe transit through Germany and France. PRESSE ETRANGÈRE was stamped across the page. *Valable du 19 Mai au 9 Juin, 1941. Nom et prénoms: Mlle. Bard Frances. Nationalité: Americaine. Profession: Collaboratrice au "Columbia Broadcasting System."*

"Here's the deal, Frankie. I've got you three weeks to get in, go around, and get out. It'll take you two or three days to get into Berlin, depending on the trains, and I'm slotting you in for three broadcasts along the route to Lisbon, starting in five days from Strasbourg just over the German border in France. Choose a family for each leg of the journey, all the way from Berlin to Lisbon—that's how this story has legs. It won't matter what language they're speaking because you're bringing us along with you, you're the eyes, the ears, and the translator, too. They're story is alive because you're in the train car with them."

"Okay," she said, hardly believing her luck.

"And I'm giving you one of these." He pointed to the square wooden case about the size of a Victrola sitting on his desk.

"That's what they're calling portable?" Frankie frowned.

"What's the trouble?"

"It looks heavy as hell."

"It's about thirty pounds," he conceded. "They put it in a wooden case for you to lighten it up. The others come in steel."

"How's it go?"

"It's a snap." Murrow flipped the top of the case. The turntable took up most of the top of the recorder; the arm of the cutter needle lay across the back. A set of headphones, and the microphone with its cord, rested on top of the turntable.

"You've got storage here in the lid for sixteen disks, double-sided— each side can record up to three minutes of whatever you put in front of it."

She nodded. That gave her about an hour and a half of recording. She watched Murrow plug the microphone into the side of the machine.

"This knob"—Murrow pointed the knurled knob set into the front of the machine—"switches on the amp, takes the brake off the motor, and"—he turned it—"lowers the recording head onto the disk. Say something."

She raised her eyebrow. "Anything?"

He switched the knob off. Then he turned the knob counterclockwise. *Say something*, his voice emerged from the box. *Anything?*

She grinned. Immediate playback. She could replay material instantly without any processing. No one had done anything like this yet.

"Record anything you can. Record the train. Get the talk. Get it all. If you can use any of what you record right away, go ahead. If not, just broadcast whatever you're seeing, whatever you're hearing, and we'll use this material when you get back. After Strasbourg, aim for Lyon at the end of the month. Jim Holland is there. Then Lisbon on the fifth of June. That'll give you plenty of time to make it home."

She nodded and got up from the chair.

"And Frankie?"

"Yes."

"When you get to the transmitters, keep the story tight," he went right on. "The censors are trigger-happy. Get in. Get out—we're not at war with them yet, but they'll black you out any chance they can."

"Right," she said, sliding the disk recorder off the desk by its wooden handle. Christ, she grimaced. It *was* heavy as hell. "So long."

There was no one to say good-bye to, no one here to leave. She left a note for the landlady, packed a nightgown and the other two skirts she owned with their three blouses into the blue leather overnight bag her mother had given her years ago, covered them with her underwear and enough Kotex to get her through, and made the night train to Dover with twenty minutes to spare. She hurled the suitcase and then the recorder after it up onto the rack above her head and sank down into her seat. The sharp corner of an envelope poked from her pocket and she pulled it out and turned it over. *Emma Fitch*, the envelope said. *Box 329, Franklin, Massachusetts, USA.* She had forgotten all about the doctor's letter. Frankie stared at the name of the woman to whom the news had not yet happened. For these few hours until the cable came, the doctor was still alive, and his wife had not yet crossed over to the next part.

Where Frankie was. She shivered and thrust the envelope back down in her pocket. She would mail it from France, so it arrived after word of his death. The doctor would have liked the ends sewn up, she thought, looking into the night outside the glass. His voice beside her, his hope and his joy, flared up like firelight now. Christ, that had made her mad. The whistle blew, the compartment lights snapped off, and the train nosed its way slowly out of the station into the blacked-out city. Frankie slid the letter back into her pocket and watched the blank dark gather the train in its fold, hiding it from the Luftwaffe as it hurried to the coast where the boats to France were waiting.

15.

ONE OF THE impossible absurdities of war was that the trains between countries still ran. Like mechanized ants, the trains continued, and a person could get from Dover across the Channel to Calais in a morning, and on into Paris by the end of that day. That and the fact that the northern French countryside bloomed a light fairy green could drive a person mad. *Not at war, not at war,* the train clacked over the rails the following morning. The Norman fields had been turned and planted, and the poplars spiked against the pale sky. Men, loosely wrapped, worked in the fields, paying no attention to the passing train.

The train reached Paris at a little after six. Montmartre's dome rounded above the sharp roofs in the near distance. Frankie had pulled the window down all the way, and spring crept into the compartment, even as the train slid slowly past the outlying market towns. A woman on a bicycle kept pace with the train, and Frankie watched her ride past the swastika flapping from the flagpole in the village square, so upright on her seat, her head covered in a scarf, so *French.*

She didn't have much time to find the train for Berlin, but there was little trouble getting on. She climbed onto the second to last compartment and settled herself into a seat as the train started up and Paris fell slowly away.

When the train passed out of France into occupied Belgium, the engine was uncoupled and changed, and the travelers sat in the dark for hours, making it feel like another bloody funk hole, Frankie thought. The sun had set long ago and the blackout curtains pulled in the windows of the tiny station, clear evidence that the British bombers had penetrated this far.

The train crossed into Germany, pushing forward into the dark, the telegraph wires glinting like needles in the night. Sometime before dawn, they stopped at what looked like a crossing and an order was given just below Frankie's compartment window, and then repeated farther down the line. She lifted her shade and saw what looked like a ghost army in the night, the dim moon glinting off chin straps and gun barrels. There must have been a hundred men down there, all of them silent, waiting to move. The locomotive shuddered and sighed.

As they drew nearer to Berlin, the train emptied of ordinary people. Few were traveling so far east. By the time they reached the city the following morning, Frankie was alone in her compartment. She sat a minute before getting off. The air was lovely outside and, as in Paris, she could just see the broad flank of the avenues stretched away from the train station and the slight green against the marble buildings, all of which dislocated the present. She stood and pulled her bag down from the rack above her head, grabbed the recorder, and emerged onto the platform where what looked like hundreds of people were waiting. She turned around. The only train she could see was the one she had just left. It wasn't so much a line of people as a wave, held in check by the shut doors of the cars. In these exhausted, fearful groupings the present returned. Some faces stared at her as she passed, and she nodded hello. They dropped their eyes as though she were dangerous.

The few other passengers had gotten off as well, and at the end of the platform the line for passport control began to thicken. She'd be glad of a bath and a drink, she thought, getting into the line that snaked toward her. A bath, a drink, and then a long, long walk into the city. The safe-transit pass had been read and refolded at each of the border check-points, and her passport stamped. She set down her bag and the recorder and kept them between her legs, handing over the letter.

"How long?"

"Overnight." Frankie smiled at the officer. He was tidy and round. He looked up at her with startlingly black eyes.

He took her papers, looked at them, and spread them out on the table. His fingernails were bitten to the quick. "No, Fräulein." He shook his head.

She frowned and leaned over the table. "What do you mean?"

He looked up at her, pleasantly. "If you plan to leave Berlin tomor-row, you must stay here and take the next train."

"Why is that?"

"There is no room," he answered blandly, handing her papers back to her.

"I'm a reporter," she said as evenly as she could.

"Ah?" He looked her up and down, his eyes without light and letting none in.

"And what is it you are reporting?"

"On the trains out of Berlin."

"For what purpose?"

"To give my country a feel for the wartime conditions."

"Conditions have never been better."

"Exactly." She looked at him.

"No, Fräulein." And he gestured to the man in uniform behind him.

"I'm American."

"We have plenty of Americans already." He shrugged. The second man came to stand beside her.

"May I cable my office?"

His lip curled. "Your office? Fräulein, if you wish to ride the trains, this will be the last one out for a very long time."

"Why's that?"

He shrugged and waved her papers. She took them. His raisin eyes swung slowly up to hers. "Good journey, Fräulein."

She bent and picked up her two cases, and turned back into the crowd.

The heavy smell of fear hung in the close air of the waiting room. Several people looked up when Frankie entered, but their attention was on the officer beside her. He might make an announcement. With every hour stalled, not moving, the exit visas—clearly stamped with the date by which they had to leave the country—went closer to expiring and they had not yet even begun the journey. Each person held hard-won transit papers as well, allowing them to pass through on their way to the boats. A problem with either meant that at any point they could be turned away, refused entry, sent back. So they had to get on the train. The train Frankie had just left stood idle on the track behind her. Through the glass right in front of them stood the voyage out. It sat there, guarded by two soldiers, guns slung over their shoulders.

The washroom door was surrounded by women; Frankie went to join them.

"How long have you been waiting here?" Frankie asked in German.

One of the women turned around. "Since morning. The train was supposed to leave at ten."

It was nearly two o'clock. The journey had begun, Frankie realized, half-writing the script. *The journey begins on an empty platform with no train in sight.* The door of the washroom opened in front of her, and a tiny curly blond-headed woman clutching a child by the hand emerged. Her blouse strained over her pregnant belly; she had the scattered, wide-eyed look of someone waiting for the next blow. She kept tight hold of her boy, though, and steered him through the women. Frankie turned and followed her to see what the husband looked like. But the woman sank down into a spot on one of the benches, evidently held for her by a matronly older woman in a black cotton dress. No husband. Frankie turned back. Hers might be the story to follow. A military band had begun to play in the cavernous center of the station, and Frankie felt the drums in her bones.

Suddenly, the scene through the window burst into life. Several soldiers ran down the platform, signaling the two already there to move to the front. A fuel car backed down the parallel track, its engineer a great blond man calling jokes down to his comrades; everyone burst into laughter. The drums stopped and the steady thrum of the diesel filled the station with life. The mood around Frankie lightened, too; perhaps *now* they were leaving. People began to stand up, holding their possessions to their chest, watching the one train couple with the other, giving it fuel.

From down the avenue came the sound of whistles and the motors of several engines. Frankie counted six trucks, pulling right into the station alongside the tracks. Out of them jumped men in uniform, boys mostly. Within minutes, the platform in front of her was crowded with them, standing awkwardly around waiting, as were the people in flight, watching through the glass. Despite, or perhaps because of, the audience in the waiting room, the young men seemed to Frankie to play at being soldiers, in the manner of schoolboys, strutting and smoking, clearly anxious to set off, to be sent into the thick of things. The opinion in the room where Frankie waited was that the soldiers were headed for the Russian border. There had been three call-ups in the last two weeks from central Berlin. Soldiers and tea and all the tinned meat left in the city, a woman with a thick lip and quiet watchful eyes commented to Frankie. Everything to Russia, she said regretfully. And the trains, a man put in beside her. All the trains, too.

Frankie glanced back at the bench where the mother and her little boy still sat, the boy asleep against his mother's arm. The woman was clearly on her own.

A sleek Daimler crept along the platform, leaving order behind as it passed. The boys became real soldiers, their shoulders back and their legs snapped together. An officer stepped out of the car and shouted some kind of encouragement, and then the line slackened and the boys stepped on the train. Within an hour, the waiting room stared again at an empty track. Frankie went to find some dinner and sat herself in the station café, watching the same blank track as those in the waiting room who would not leave their spots by the door. The boy was up on his feet in front of his mother now, slapping his hands together, trying for her gaze. Every so often, she'd look down at him, away from the train track. Sometimes she'd smile. Frankie decided against approaching her now, all of her attention strained toward the hoped-for train.

Around three a.m., a siren went off and a new train pulled into the station, much smaller than the one Frankie had ridden from Paris, this one only six cars, and everyone in the waiting room rose up and surged forward. There was no hanging back, no chance to let others take spots before her. The crowd moved in one panic-stricken wave toward the door of the waiting room, which someone had opened, and then gushed through onto the platform to halt at the gun-metal exterior of the cars. The doors were pulled shut and none of the lights were lit; it seemed unmanned at first to Frankie, and eerie in the dark. A man shouted something from the front of the train, and the family beside Frankie looked at her. Did you hear? She shook her head.

Then suddenly, like Aladdin's cave, the doors were thrown open. Again, the human wave gathered and Frankie felt herself lifted off her feet briefly. Someone cried out behind her, and over her shoulder she glimpsed the tiny mother and her toddler pressed against a man's back. Frankie shoved her overnight bag under her arm, freeing her to reach back and grab the boy's hand, pulling him up and against her out of the crush. *All right*, she said to him, *it's all right. Franz!* His mother shrieked. *I've got him! Je le tiens!* Frankie cried back. The mother grabbed Frankie's waist from behind, and all three of them were pushed forward and up the stairs into the train.

Frankie opened the first compartment, saw that there was a half-spot, and pushed her way in, putting the boy down between two men. *Here*, she pointed to the mother, who was panting, her breath coming in fast panicky claps, and the younger of the two men leapt up to give her his seat. She sank down onto the compartment seat; her little boy stood frozen, his eyes fixed on his mother's face. Her breathing was rapid and ragged. Frankie wished desperately she had water. "Put your head down," the older man suggested softly in German. He was heavyset but shaven. He was used to giving directions. Perhaps a teacher, thought Frankie. Why was he traveling alone? The mother didn't hear. "Head down." He stood up to grab her by the shoulders and force her head down. The train gave a lurch, knocking everyone in the compartment off balance. The man stumbled against Frankie, but then righted himself and spoke more gently to the young mother who looked up at him finally, nodded, and bent over.

Someone banged on the train window and Frankie looked up and saw the frantic face of a woman outside pressed against the glass, shouting at her. The train shifted and sighed and crept forward. The woman on the platform dropped her arm, but there was a relentless banging still on the car below the window. It became clear that the train was going to leave everyone on the platform behind and Frankie stared down into all those faces upturned to hers and knew she was looking at ghosts. They were not going to get out. A different train, on a different night perhaps. But this one was full, though everyone out there held a ticket, and a large enough train had been promised. They were drowning there right in front of her, within sight of the lifeboats, within sight of shore, and here she was, taking up a spot.

She whirled around to get out of the compartment, to get out of the train, to give someone, anyone else, her place.

"Let me pass," she cried to the older man sitting next to the compartment door, but as she reached for the handle, he closed his hand over hers.

She frowned. "Let me go."

He pointed at the door, and through it she looked into the backs of a handful of people pressed against the glass, and against them, in another row, stood more. The corridor outside was jammed with men and women. There was no getting out of the carriage. Oh God, she thought, turning around to face those outside, a sob rising in her chest. And the train started off, gathered speed, and pulled faster away from the people on the platform below, and its whistle blew.

Frankie sank down onto the case of the disk recorder, her suitcase on her lap in the dirty spot of open carpet between the two benches, and she leaned her head against the door. There were seven of them and the child jammed into the compartment. And none of them spoke. The mother's breathing had quieted and slowed. Her little boy pressed against her and watched the others. There was no room for him on her lap, but he would not squeeze onto the bench beside her. For a while the train's motion and patches of moonlight along the blackened city outskirts held everyone quiet, the journey started at last.

Get on a refugee train, Murrow had instructed; and though it was obscene, absurd of her at this point in time, having seen so much, she had harbored the impossible illusion that "refugee train" meant people who were saved. These people might as well have leapt. No one was safe, none was saved. Until they got to the end, they were simply on the run.

"Fräulein?" The younger of the two men was the first to break the silence in the car. Frankie looked up. He was pointing to her and then to his seat. He wore an ill-fitting hand-knit sweater pulled over a knotted tie, and the hand he held out was smudged with ink. "No, thanks," she said, shaking her head. He lifted his hand and smiled at her, as if to say, well perhaps later then, and she smiled back at him. He nodded and crossed his arms over his chest, leaning back against the compartment wall, evidently satisfied. He had offered. The knot in Frankie's stomach relaxed just slightly in the wake of that familiar gesture. All of them, there in the dark, heading away from Berlin, traveling out, could offer each other a seat, could still offer something, and still refuse.

Across from him, nearest the window, a round-faced woman

somewhere in her middle age released her attention on the rest of them and pressed into the corner. She rested her head against the window frame and closed her eyes, her chin settling in her several collars. A blue jersey strained across the pointed tips of a brown wool suit jacket, and on top of that a darker blue, also wool, shirt and sweater. Even with her eyes closed, she gripped the handles of the battered leather case on her lap. Beside her sat a very pretty young woman, whom Frankie at first took to be the older woman's daughter, but it was clear soon enough that she was traveling with the boy beside her. They were both dark-eyed and fair-skinned, and the sister's curls flashed out from her tight cap, dancing with the motion of the train. No more than twelve, he had watched Frankie refuse the man's seat with curious attention.

"American?" He looked down at her eagerly.

She nodded.

"We are going there," he pronounced.

His sister put her hand on his knee to stop it jiggling.

He turned to her, frowning. She put her fingers to her lips. Frankie smiled at him and caught the imperceptible shift of the older woman in the corner, drawing herself farther away from the girl. The moonlight caught her full in the face and her eyes blinked open once, then firmly shut. The sister took her brother's hand quietly in hers and leaned her head back against the compartment wall. In the frightened, exhausted silence, the tiny boy across from them had fallen asleep on his feet, clamped between his mother's legs and resting his head on the enormous swell of her pregnant belly. This close, Frankie saw how dirty his hair was and matted, the backs of his legs grayed with soot. The mother was no more than a child herself, and Frankie watched as she turned to look into the blank black of the night train windows, the sleeping face of her boy turned up to her like a little skyless moon.

For the fourth night in a row, Frankie settled herself in the thick dark between sleepers and, like her companions, tried to doze. But as soon as she shut her eyes, the doctor's big body flipped effortlessly off his feet into the air before her. She shuddered and opened her eyes. The old woman in the corner was crying without sound, tears streaking down her cheeks. Her hands still held on to the bag in her lap, resting like a stone. The boy and girl beside her had fallen asleep on each other. The young man who had offered his seat slept with his arms across his chest, his head down as though he was considering a question.

She fingered the clasp on the black case beneath her. She ought to take it out and start asking questions in her simple German: *Where are you going? Where have you come from? What happened?* She ought to focus her attention on the mother, get the beginnings of the story, get her voice on the disk at the outset of the journey. Although the brother and sister might be equally good to concentrate the story on. Frankie watched the older man watching out the window. She wondered whom he had left behind. And for the first time in her career, she wondered whether she had the guts to ask him. *Seek Truth and Report It,* the journalist's code instructed. *Seek Truth. Report It.* And *Minimize Harm.* Every one of the sleepers around her must have left someone behind. And she thought of the desperate faces of the people who hadn't made it onto this train. Minimize Harm? She shuddered. Let the sleepers sleep. Tomorrow would be soon enough to begin.

Two hours later, the train slowed and then pulled into a tiny blacked-out village, whose station was no more than a wooden sign pounded into a short field of flattened grass and a bench facing the tracks. Frankie saw the single light of a watchman's lantern glowing from the bench like a yellow eye. Everyone in the compartment sat up and pulled their papers out, readying for the scrutiny. Their compartment was in the middle of the train, and it took over an hour for the inspector to reach it. The fear was infectious, heavy as a blanket. The progress was agonizing. Why was it so slow? In the car next door, they could hear raised voices followed by abrupt silence. Their door swung open and an old man with a torch stood in the opening, his jaw slack. Just an old man doing a job, thought Frankie, handing her papers up to him without any visible interest or ire.

"American?" He squinted. She nodded. He didn't look at Murrow's letter; he took her passport, turned it over to see the insignia, then handed it back. He lifted his torch and looked at the boy whose eyes flared enormous in the light, then at the mother, and the old man snapped his fingers for papers, though once in his hands he hardly looked at them. The door closed after him and left them all in an uncertain silence. That was it? They sat together in the dark listening to the opening and closing of the rest of the compartments in their carriage.

"You are good luck," the older man said slowly in the quiet after the train resumed. The dawn was breaking in the near fields and a low spring morning arose, the slanted red coloring the stubble outside. They had crossed the first hurdle, but they were still in Germany.

"I beg your pardon?" Frankie was aware that the old woman in the corner had opened her eyes and was listening to them.

But the man only shrugged. The brother and sister had fallen back asleep, and the boy's lips had fallen open in a soft round.

"Where are you heading?" she asked the man in German.

"Lisbon." He nodded. He had been lucky, he said. He had not made it onto the previous two trains. His exit visa expired in one week. The fingers on the hand he held up were stubby and well-worn. Not a teacher— Frankie changed her mind—a shopkeeper, a butcher. Someone with a trade.

She smiled. "What is your name?"

"Werner Buchman," he replied. The woman across from him closed her eyes, as though releasing hold.

By the afternoon, the train had slowed and stopped in three isolated towns. Each time, the police boarded the train and made their way through the thick clot of people, one by one. No one could leave the stations, and during one stop, Frankie made her way along the platform, all the way to the barrier, and looked through it into a village market day. Out here, far from the city, there were potatoes and new onions. A woman held three potatoes in her gloved hand and looked up at Frankie across the way. The May sun glinted off the metal buttons of her coat. Behind her, the poplars were greened on the top, a light girlish green.

By the third stop at Leipzig, the group in Frankie's car had noticeably relaxed, and Frankie suspected that Werner had been right, that because she was in the car, the others were passed over lightly. The tiny mother was smiling at her boy who had crawled over to the young man in the sweater, now on the floor in Frankie's spot, and taken the piece of string he had tied to a sweet, pulling it back and forward as though teasing a kitten. The boy sucked on the sweet and leaned against his mother. The brother and sister played cards, and the sister hummed to herself as she held hers. The little boy had wet himself, but the window was pulled down and the smell of mown grass from outside made it unexpectedly barnlike in the car. They crossed into the Black Forest as the sun set. With luck they'd make it to Strasbourg and the French border by ten or eleven. Then Lyon, Toulouse, and the day after tomorrow, to the Spanish border at Bayonne. From there one could count on two solid days across Spain and into Portugal to arrive at the sea and the boats at Lisbon. Four days from here, if all went as hoped.

Frankie reached down and opened the lid on the recorder. The two boys stared at her. She'd start with the mother and the little boy, she decided. And she'd start slow.

"*Wie heißt du?*" Frankie smiled over at the toddler, turning the switch. "What is your name?"

He stared back at her. His mother poked him idly with her finger. He took the sweet from his mouth. "Franz." He was very solemn.

"Franz Hofmann," his mother whispered.

He started off after the name. "Franz Hof . . ."

The brother put down his cards. "Franz Hofmann," he said to the little boy. "Go on."

But Franz shook his head.

"And you?" Frankie asked the sister, in her rudimentary German. "Speak into here," she motioned. "Say your name."

"Inga?" said the sister, shyly. "Inga Borg?" The brother laughed and took his turn, pronouncing the English words slowly, as though he beat them on a drum. "I am Litman."

"Where are you from?" Frankie asked.

The boy turned to his sister. Watching, Frankie wasn't sure whether he didn't understand or if he was frightened by the question.

"We have papers," his sister said to Frankie in German.

"Of course." Frankie nodded to assure her. Then she leaned forward and said to the recorder in English, "This is Frankie Bard, traveling south from Berlin on the Deutsche Reichsbahn. The sound you hear is the train making good time on the tracks." Inga watched her. "I have with me a brother and sister, Inga and Litman Borg. They look to be about seventeen and twelve years old, traveling alone. Tell me, where are you two traveling to?" She repeated the question softly in German.

"Lisbon," Inga answered.

"And where to, after that?"

"America."

"And where have you come from?"

The disk recorded the silence as Inga put her hand on Litman's arm to stop him. He looked up at her, and Frankie saw him see something in his sister's expression—his mother, maybe, his aunt?—that was enough to shut the light off on his smile. Frankie turned the recorder off, frowning. The thing was heavy and in the way. How was she to reach them with it sitting there like a small animal on her lap?

The mother slipped a piece of bread from her bag and handed it to her little boy. Everyone watched him eat. The woman in the corner stared fixedly out of the window. Frankie wondered whether she was deaf.

The young man in the sweater pulled a string from his pocket and wove the string between his fingers in a game of cat's cradle and held it up to the brother, who shook his head stiffly, clearly too old for such childishness. The young man laughed at him and Frankie saw a row of broken teeth between his lips. When he turned to her, holding his two hands woven together by the child's game, she smiled back at him and slipped her thumbs and forefingers under his, drawing the string onto her own hand.

"And you, Fräulein, where are you heading?" The man spoke in heavily accented but precise English, repeating Frankie's phrase.

"With all of you," Frankie answered as he looped his fingers in the string and pulled. He frowned.

"I'm riding this train to tell America who is on it."

He studied her. "Why?"

"So people know."

"What are you?"

"A reporter."

"So?" He let his fingers drop and the string went slack upon them. "And what is that box?"

"It records you, your voices." She sat back. "Sound."

"And what does America think?"

"America doesn't know what to think."

He nodded and crossed his arms, then his light, appraising gaze flicked off. The stubble on his chin was blond and sparse. "Shall I tell America what to think?"

"Shoot." She smiled at him.

He paused.

"Hold on." Frankie put her hand up. "Hold on." She pointed to the machine. He nodded. "Start," she said, switching the knob on the top, "slowly."

"I am Thomas Kleinmann—"

She looked up and saw he was holding out his hand to her and she reached across the spinning disk and shook it. "Frankie Bard."

He let go her hand and leaned back. "I come from Austria, in the mountains around Kitzbühel, where I live with my mother and father." He stopped. She nodded, go on. The disk whirled around.

"In the months after the Anschluss, after Austria fell to the Nazis and the Jewish laws were put into place there, my mother worried more and more about my brother, who was studying in Munich. Finally one day, she sent me to bring him back home."

Litman had slid his hand under Inga's beside him, quieting to listen to a story in words they did not understand.

"I travel all night on the train, arriving in the city early in the morning. I make my way to my brother's address, but my brother has left that same morning, according to the neighbor, to return home. We have crossed paths.

"I sit down at my brother's desk to write our mother and father and tell them what happened, but before I begin, there is a knock on the door. I shove the letter into my pocket and I go to answer. The police. They have come for Reinhart. Why? I ask. They do not answer. He is not here, I say. They take me instead. It does not matter to them"—Thomas shrugged—"which Jew they have."

The woman in the corner sucked in her breath. Frankie glanced up, realizing that the woman understood very well what was being said.

"I walk through the streets with a group of twenty others. We go to the police station, I am put into a room. Wait, they say. So, I am waiting, I pull out of my pocket the piece of stationery for my letter to Mother. It has on it the name of my brother's professor and the letterhead of the electrical engineering college. So, I write myself a letter of recommendation and take it to the policeman at the head of the room."

"Ah, says the guard, looking at it, go through there. I follow where he points and go into a tiny room where a large man, a friendly man, sits behind a pile of papers. This man looks at my letter, looks at me, and tears it in half. Go, he says, and points through another door. It is the door into the police yard. Out there, sixty or seventy men sit. No one looks at me. I walk all the way to the fence. I can see the river and the gardens behind houses.

"By this time it is afternoon, and the sun is very hot in the square. I walk along the fence and I stand in the little shade of the roof. For two hours I stand there and then there comes the instruction to go into the center of the square for new orders. Hsst, I hear at my shoulder. I turn around and see the guard I had spoken with earlier that morning, the guard to whom I had shown the letter. Hsst, the guard says and points me along the fence to a door. I look around. Is this is a trick? Is anyone watching? But there are just many men tired getting to their feet, and I go along the fence and out the door, a miracle. The guard is holding it open.

" 'Elektrotechnik?' The guard grins. 'Professor Peter Schmidt?' I nod, dumbly, I don't understand. He points me to walk through the door and points to a second door, ten meters away, where another guard sits. I look at him, but the guard nods, go on, and pushes.

"I walk forward. I am not breathing. I reach the second guard. I can see the walk by the river beyond the police station and people returning from market. I stop and look at the guard. He doesn't look up. He reaches over and unlocks the gate.

"For twenty meters I walk straight ahead. Will I be shot, or shouted at, seen? Thirty meters. Now I am walking in the street. After forty meters, I know that I am free. I turn the corner at last. I am hurrying toward my brother's apartment, and I understand—it hits me, yes—I am out because the guard studied Elektrotechnik also."

He looked at Frankie and shook his head, his disbelief palpable in the dark.

"Then you are the lucky one here," the old woman in the corner broke in.

It was as if a shadow had spoken. "It is you," she repeated, in English. "There was God," she insisted. "Looking out for you, at every turn."

"People looked out"—he cleared his throat—"not God."

"The same."

He shook his head. "There is no God." He turned to Frankie, his voice urgent and low. "There is only us, Fräulein."

The train shuddered, slowing for another stop. Frankie turned the knob and the recording arm lifted off the disk. They had reached the German border at Kehl. On the other side lay Vichy France: Strasbourg, Lyon, Toulouse. And then on past France to Portugal, to the ships at Lisbon.

The lights of this station were blinding and numerous, and everyone was ordered off the train. Frankie stood.

"Except Americans."

Frankie looked up in surprise, but the German officer had passed down the compartment.

"Auf Wiedersehen." Litman waved to Frankie. She nodded, confused. Were they going to get back on this same train? What was happening? Litman and Inga were the first out of the compartment, followed by Werner Buchman, the tradesman who carried the young mother's bag, while she carried the sleeping Franz. Slowly, the old woman, whose name Frankie had never gotten, got to her feet, stiff after so many hours of sitting. She turned around and looked at Thomas as if to take his image to heart. He bobbed his head at her, and reached up for his case on the rack as though he were following shortly after. The compartment door slid shut after the old woman, and Frankie stood to take the seat she had left by the window. It was slightly warm and Frankie reached and opened the window, letting the night air into the compartment.

"Now I must ask you to hide me," Thomas said, very low.

Frankie didn't move.

"I have the transit papers," he went on quickly, "but no exit visa."

She stared back.

"You understand?"

She nodded. Her heart was banging against her ribs. He looked at her briefly once more, and then he swung himself up onto the luggage rack and slid himself behind the suitcase. Frankie forced herself to look away from him and out the window at the people below, suddenly anonymous again, her companions from the compartment dispersed into the crowd. After a few minutes, she caught sight of the curly head of the mother and her little boy, and was comforted.

Frankie kept her eye on them, loosely following their progress in the dim light. It was too early to know whether to be afraid. The stop might be, even now, even after all that had happened, just routine. Some of the people had turned expectantly toward the station, facing it as though some kind of answer might come from it, some promise of order; but the mess of people on the platform below didn't move, and some simply sat down in place to wait. Above her on the luggage rack, Thomas lay still. Frankie closed her eyes and dozed a little and when she woke from time to time, she'd look down into the crowd to mark the progress of the woman and the little boy. After an hour or so, three black cars pulled up alongside the train and the border guards on the platform began shouting for people to get up and move down toward the end. Frankie saw the mother struggling up to her feet, then drop as though she had tripped or been pushed. When she rose again at the height of the crowd, she was looking frantically around, and Frankie saw that little Franz was gone. The crowd surged forward, shoving toward a gap at the end of the platform. Frankie scrambled to her feet and onto her seat, trying to see down into the crowd and catch sight of the child, but all she could see was the mother trying to stand against the push of the crowd. The man behind her shouted, *MOVE, we're moving!* and there were whistles, and two guards shouted at the mother and one grabbed her arm to come away. And then Frankie saw the boy—twenty impossible, unreachable feet from his mother.

"There!" Frankie cried out. "There he is!"

At the same time as Frankie shouted, his mother had caught the sound of his crying and started pushing against the human tide to get at him.

People roared at her and shoved back and the boy, hearing her cries, cried back, *Mama! Mama!*

"There!" Frankie shouted again, frantic. The mother could not get at her child. "There he is!"

Mama, Franz was wailing. *Mama, Mama!*

"Shut up, Fräulein," Thomas hissed at her. "They're going to shoot. For God's sake, shut up!"

"There!" Frankie pounded against the window. And one of the German officers, disgusted by the commotion, turned around and shot.

The crowd went silent. Hands that had been waving dropped. Truly frightened people did not scream, Frankie saw—they went quiet, they went watchful. Had he shot into the crowd? Had someone been hit? It was too hard to tell. There were too many. Where was the mother? Frankie stood at the open window, her mouth still in the shape of her cry. And then the officer who was a few feet from her window looked up at where the sound of her banging had come from and slowly leveled his revolver on her. She stared back at him, both hands on the glass, unable to breathe. And then she was yanked down off the seat by Thomas and pulled away from the window onto the floor. Outside the train, the quiet continued and the two of them lay there, Frankie sobbing into her hands, too frightened to look up. She couldn't bear the quiet. What had she done? Her heart was pounding so fast, she thought she was going to be sick. Someone shouted. Frankie looked over at Thomas who was sitting up, his ear against the compartment wall. Perhaps the soldier hadn't seen Thomas, perhaps from the outside it had merely looked like she had fallen backward off her seat.

The floor beneath them shuddered and bucked, and very slowly the train began to move again with the two of them inside. Frankie caught Thomas's eye, but he shook his head. What had happened? The roof of the station slid past in the window above her head. The train was going to leave the boy and his mother behind. *Halt! Halt!* Shouting broke out along the platform, but Frankie couldn't tell if it came from the people or from one of the soldiers. The train kept going, moving along almost to the end of the station. Where it stopped.

Frankie's heart heaved and dropped and she looked at Thomas sitting across from her on the floor in the dark compartment. For a moment there wasn't a sound, and she thought they might start off again, but then a whistle blew nearby and the carriage door was thrown open. Someone came up the steps and along the corridor; the compartment door slid back. She looked up at an officer of the Gestapo. Behind him, another man waited.

The officer bowed to her and asked her to get up on her feet. Very politely, she and Thomas were asked to come down off the train. Polite, and their guns were not drawn. There was something wrong with the engine. There was a bus waiting. Could they come, please. Numbly, Frankie reached for her suitcase and the disk recorder and passed down the corridor, aware of the three men behind her. The train had evidently been halted in the field just past the station. She climbed down the steps of the train onto the grass by the side of the train tracks. There was, in fact, a bus waiting; inside it, Frankie made out the heads of three others. First, there was the issue of papers.

"Is something wrong?" She faced the Germans.

"No, no," the first officer answered mildly, "nothing." But Frankie saw him change his grip on the gun in his hand, and a sick dread rose up in her chest. She turned to Thomas, beside her. He had closed his eyes. "No," she whispered, and put her hand on Thomas's arm and felt how thin he was beneath the cloth.

"Step away, Fräulein." The officer was genial.

Frankie turned her back on the officer and spoke into Thomas's closed eyes. "Thomas"—her grip tightened on his arm—"Thomas?"

"Go on." He shook his head.

"Thomas," she whispered, "please. Let me—"

"Fräulein!"

Thomas opened his eyes and looked at her at the same time as Frankie felt herself roughly pushed aside and the officer took his shot. Thomas fell at Frankie's feet with a sigh.

Frankie blinked. The officer behind her stepped away. She stared ahead at the empty spot in the air where Thomas had just stood. Slowly she turned around.

The officer's eyes slid from him to Frankie. She stared back at him.

"I could detain you."

Distantly, as if from another lifetime, from inside the station, the telephone rang.

Across the field it rang twice, three times, four. Someone answered it. The officer looked up and, with an expression of disgust, he waved Frankie toward the bus. Shaking, she bent to pick up her suitcase and the recorder, looking one last time at Thomas. Blood streamed from his ear and across his neck into the ground. She whimpered.

"Go."

She turned around, and she walked away from Thomas, from the boy and from his mother somewhere back there on the station platform. She walked ten feet down the tracks away from the police before she started weeping. She walked a few more feet, waiting to hear a shot, waiting to hear a shout, anything at all. She lifted her arm and wiped the tears off on her sleeve. Between the train behind her and the bus ahead on the country lane there was nothing but the sound of her own breathing and her feet clipping stones and then the cool metal of the rail that she grabbed as she climbed on.

16.

T*HIS IS FRANKIE BARD, CBS news, from Mulhouse, France, just
west of the Franco/German border.*

Emma turned around from her mailbox, a letter in her hand. The
clipped female tones emerged into the post office from the green Bakelite
box behind Miss James's head. *There is a great deal of speculation about
who is trying to leave Germany where—we are told—conditions have never
been better, where the war is being won on all fronts, and where peace and
bread are plentiful.* The voice paused. *There are, it is true, plenty of crack-
ers to be had here.* Emma looked at Iris. That last was a joke, wasn't it?
The woman on the radio sounded like she was smiling, though she also
sounded exhausted. *Still, people are leaving, are trying to leave, by the doz-
ens. You have to imagine walking out of your house or apartment and closing
the door and never going back. In your hands are a suitcase and maybe a
shopping bag filled with a piece of sausage, some cheese perhaps, whatever
you were allotted in the store, something to tide you over, you hope, until you
reach the border. In the suitcase, if you are a Jew, are two changes of clothes
and your papers*—her voice snapped off, and then came back on—*You
have a window of escape you are shooting for. If you are one of the very lucky
few, you have an American visa. More likely, you have a visa for Cuba, or
Argentina, or Brazil. You have ninety days to reach your destination or the*

visas expire. But you have to get on a train. And cross Europe to get to the boats at Lisbon or Bordeaux. You have ninety days, and the trains are few and full. Everywhere. So the windows from here look to be closing. Now the voice was shaking. Emma closed her box and locked it and walked closer to the voice. *You must imagine a Europe no longer made up of houses in villages where generations remain. Imagine people without houses, without the frame and mortar and brick around them, floating out here, trying to swim as hard as they can to get away. You have to imagine that there is right now, in Europe, a sea of people moving. If one of you were to write them a letter, you have to understand, there is nowhere a letter would find them*—Iris turned around and switched it off.

"We don't have to imagine a goddamned thing," she said evenly to Emma. "It's a mess over there, and that gal should get control of herself."

Emma was staring at the wireless as though it might spring back into voice.

"He's okay," Miss James said to her gently. "It's okay. You know where he is. You have a letter in your hand."

Emma looked down at it. "Yes."

"So. There you are."

There you are. That's what Will always said. Lord.

THE EYE of the evening train moved slowly forward into Mulhouse station and stopped. Some of the faces on board turned to look down on Frankie standing there on the platform waiting. Some of the faces stared, and she couldn't look at them too closely and bent to pick up her baggage and walked, under their gaze, to the single open door. She was the only passenger, and the train jolted forward and started sliding away from Mulhouse even before she had found her way down the corridor to a seat. It followed the main railway corridor west, through Belfort into Besançon, where she stopped for her first sleep in a bed in five nights.

Too tired to do anything but point at a bottle and a loaf of bread and some cheese, she carried everything up to her room and sat down on the cot to undo her laces, and woke up the next morning lying across the bed, her feet on the floor, still in her shoes. Only half-awake, she slid out of her shoes, got under the covers, and fell back asleep staring up at the plaster ceiling.

Frankie woke again far into the afternoon to the sound of church bells. She lay in the middle of a bed, in the tiny upstairs room of the Burghorst Pension, at the edge of a French provincial town and listened to the world going on outside her door, outside the window without her. *Clap.* A man shouted at schoolchildren running by, and their fast footsteps and laughter carried up through the open window. *Clap.* She frowned, trying to make sense of this steady clap, the sound of wood on wood and then, when it came again, she understood that someone's shutter was banging. Someone's window needed to be pulled closed. She lay there, floating like a child. No one knew her. No one called for her. She felt relieved of duty. There had been a change in plan.

She snorted. Change of goddamned plan. Try to get all the way to Lisbon, Murrow had said. Stop and broadcast in Strasbourg, Lyons, and Lisbon. She was pretty sure it was the twenty-third of May, and by now the patched-in report from Mulhouse would make it clear she was going to miss Strasbourg. She wondered if it had even gone out on the air, let alone made it to the States. She ought to cable Murrow.

She sat up at last and stood to step out of her skirt. The rim of an envelope poked out of the pocket when the skirt fell to the floor. Frankie looked at the envelope, uneasily. The doctor's letter was beginning to hold the faint power of a relic. She ought to mail it, oughtn't she? Get it on its way. Kicking the skirt to the side, she went to run the water in the sink and put the plug in, watching the sink fill. She tried to put the days in order. When had he died? Five days ago? Six? Frankie sniffed and turned off the water, reaching for the sponge and some hand soap. She pulled off her blouse and brassiere, and stood naked on the rug, giving herself a baby's sponge bath. In the mirror, her hand guided the sponge across her breasts and down the long shine of her stomach, where it disappeared from the glass. For a moment she stared at the torso in the glass, the sponge dripping soapy water down her leg, and she crossed her arms over her breasts.

You must be pretty tough, the doctor had said down there in the dark. She shuddered, remembering how nervous and cross he'd made her when he was asking about Billy. She unfolded the towel left by the sink and rubbed herself dry.

What happens to the people after their story is told?

I don't know.

You must be pretty tough to bear not knowing.

Sinking down on the bed with the towel around her shoulders, she pulled out a cigarette. The smoke shot deep into her lungs and she closed her eyes, exhaling it. She lay back and smoked the cigarette all the way down to where its fire crept close to her fingers. Then she stood and fastened her skirt around her waist and buttoned her blouse at the neck and cuffs, then pulled her jacket on. The doctor's letter lay on the floor. She picked it up and pocketed it again, and closed the clasps on the suitcase.

Around the square the stores had reopened, and old women and housewives passed in and out, and old men sat on the benches at the center under a linden tree. There looked to be meat in the butcher shop and bread in the bakery. In every window hung a picture of the Führer, though Frankie saw no sign of the German police. At the edge of the square one shop was shuttered, and in block letters a notice had been written on the metal: *Qui achète des Juifs est un traître.* She stood in front of the store and wondered if the family inside had made it out of this town, had gotten onto a train and somewhere they'd be safe. She wanted to think of them arriving. Not stopped. The tiny boy's face on the platform below her in the crowd at the station in Kehl turned toward her. Where were Inga and Litman now? The old woman? Werner Buchman? Frankie shut her eyes. Thomas appeared, and sank to his knees, shot in front of her. Shaking, she turned away from the blank shuttered shop window and made her way back to her room.

Get in, get the story, get out, Murrow had said. Follow a family, he'd said. Christ. You couldn't follow anyone over here. There was no way to know for certain whether anyone would make it from start to finish.

The bottle of wine and yesterday's cheese stood on the table. She pulled the cork and poured a glass and drank it standing up, staring at the portable recorder in its case. She poured another glass of wine, popped open the case, and turned the knob.

The disk moved slowly around, and there came the faint susurrus of the needle on the metal record. She set the glass down, flicked the button that stopped the turntable, and set it going backward, watching it hum. Then she flicked it and Thomas's voice sprang out of the machine. She listened to him all the way through until the record went silent again, around and around with nothing on it. There. There they were. In his voice lay the train and the night, his eyes on her as he told her his story, the narrow ridge of his shoulders stretching the wool of his sweater. The brother and the sister listening. Thomas was dead. But here was his voice. Here he was, alive.

Out the open window a long range of snow-topped mountains zig-zagged sharply against the morning blue. The bell in the churchyard behind her rang the quarter hour, and the sound thudded with her heart. She stood for a long while staring at those bright tops and imagined herself north. North and east into the mountains, north across several peaks, from white point to white point, through the Jurals, into Switzerland, across the wide shoulders of the Swiss Alps into Austria, to Thomas's house—where his mother and father were waking and waiting for news. Where was he? Where was their son? They would never know. If she were a bird, she could cross the silence to tell his mother—he almost made it. But what she knew had neither tongue nor voice to carry it. Surely God ought to look down and see that one part of the story had been separated from the other, and find a way, somehow, to put them side by side. How could He stand these gaps, these enormous valleys of silence? And Europe was full of people vanishing into this quiet.

The memory of Harriet Mendelsohn standing in the kitchen on Argyll Road shaking a fork at Dowell, playfully, hit Frankie with such force, she had to grab the windowsill. *Jens Steinbach, are you here?* The pitiful scraps of paper Harriet had collected and brought home to stick above her bed testified to the windy silence sweeping across European towns.

And what had Frankie thought? That she'd get over here and find the single story that would make the world sit up and listen? These are the Jews of Europe. Here is what is happening. *Pay attention.* But there was no story. Or rather, she turned from the window and considered the portable recorder. There was no story over here that she could tell from beginning until the end. The story of the Jews lay in the edges around what could be told. She sucked in her breath, the doctor's words ghosting her thoughts. The parts that whisper off into the dark, the boy and the girl listening, the woman in the corner, the mother's distracted face looking up into the moonlight, her hand in her boy's curls as he slept. The sound of that little boy's laughter caught for one impossible second, caught and held. There, in the wisps, was the truth of what was happening.

The following morning, Frankie got on the first train south from Besançon and negotiated her way into the corner seat in a third-class compartment. She had sixteen days left on her *permis de séjour* and ninety minutes of blank disks and no plan other than to record as many people talking as she could. She was not going to travel forward in a straight line to Lisbon—one thing after the other, stations on a journey with a beginning, a middle, and an end—she was riding trains with people. And she would get those people down until she ran out of time. She opened the case of the disk recorder and plugged in the microphone. A young couple traveling with their baby watched her preparations closely. When she was ready, she looked up. *"S'il vous plaît?"* The woman looked at her husband and nodded. Frankie turned the knob.

"Comment vous appélez-vous?"

"Eleanor." The woman smiled.

"Où allez-vous?" Frankie held the microphone toward her.

"À Toulouse," the woman answered, pulling the tiny sweater snug over the baby's stomach.

"Juifs?" Frankie asked.

"Oui."

The husband frowned at the machine on Frankie's lap and shook his head when she turned to him. Frankie turned the knob and the arm lifted from the disk. France passed by through the train window. Poligny, Bours—towns picked up like stitches on a needle, the names looped over and held. And Frankie rode through them, asking as many people as would answer, *What is your name? Where are you going? Where have you come from?*

When Frankie walked off the train in Lyon five days later, she pushed through the doors and climbed the four flights up to the studio. A man about her age, dressed in a tan linen suit, took one look at her and dropped his chair back to upright.

"Hello, Beauty," he said.

After days of riding the trains, speaking only in French or her cribbed German, the broad, wise-cracking son of the Midwest made her nearly want to weep. "Hello," she said uncertainly.

"Jim Holland." He stood up and held out his hand. "I've been on the lookout for you. Big boys are worried as all hell."

"Frankie Bard." She shook it.

"Looks like you could do with a hot bath and a drink."

"I could do with a place to change, if that's what you mean."

He reached for his hat and his coat and piloted her back to his rooms, where he sat outside the single bathroom of the boardinghouse, in a chair tipped against the door, his long Nebraska legs stretched across the hall while she bathed. Then he shepherded her back to the studio into the familiar business of setting up for a broadcast, typing out her script for the censor, waiting to get London on the line, sitting at the mark in front of the mike.

"Jesus, Frankie." Murrow came through the line.

"Hello." She nodded, smiling at the taut, familiar voice.

"What the hell happened at Strasbourg?"

"Never made it."

"You okay?"

"Yeah," she said, her eyes on the German censor who had come in and sat down in the chair by the door. "Doing fine."

"Getting anything?"

She paused. "The whole deal, Boss."

"Good girl," he said. "What's the story going to be?"

The hands on the clock said eight-twenty. The technician held up one finger, and Frankie nodded at him. "So long," she said quietly. "I'm on."

"Good luck." Murrow signed off.

The censor placed both hands on either side of her script on the table. The three of them waited in silence as the hands of the clock clicked past. When the technician looked at her, Frankie leaned forward and pulled the mike close. *"This is Frankie Bard of the Columbia Broadcast System coming to you from Lyon, France. Good evening."*

Frankie composed her face amiably for the censor, but he was reading the script. He wasn't paying attention to her lips or the tone she had injected into her voice.

"Many years ago, the noted reporter Miss Martha Gellhorn came to speak at my alma mater, Smith College. She was speaking then about the condition some people lived in during the first terrible years of the Depression. She gave as heart-wrenching, as riveting, and as specific an account of the pain and the suffering of these people as anything I ever heard. After she finished, one of the head girls raised her hand and asked, 'What are we to do about all that, Miss Gellhorn?' There was a little quiet around the answer as Miss Gellhorn took her time. And it made some of the girls nervous. 'Pay attention,' Miss Gellhorn retorted at last. 'For God's sake, pay attention.' "

In Franklin, in the post office, despite herself, Iris James turned around. *"For nearly three weeks, I've been traveling the trains, with the scores of mainly Jewish men, women, and children standing in lines to get out, get away. I've shoved into compartments, I've asked countless questions, I've heard story after simple story of flight. In station after station, I've seen lines of people waiting for too few seats on too few trains, and I'd like to get those haunted faces out of my head, but I can't.*

"All the half-finished stories over here, the people one sees and then loses without a word, call to mind a man I met last month, an American doctor—"

Iris stared at the wireless.

"And he said something I dismissed at the time as being just the sort of mash of American spirit and cockeyed optimism we all seem to have been raised on. He said to me: Everything adds up."

What American doctor? Iris had turned all the way around from the window and was standing in front of the radio with her hands on either side of it as if it could be shaken into an answer.

"Yesterday afternoon, in an ordinary market in Bayonne, I began to believe it myself. I had gone into the market because it is the start of summer and I was hungry, and I had seen a man carrying a tiny carton of strawberries in his hands. I went into the market in search of strawberries. It was very hot, and the market was beginning to close. Besides myself, there were a handful of German officers, also, it seemed, in search of fruit. They moved quietly through the crowd, in the direction of the strawberry vendor.

"I heard what sounded like music coming from somewhere high up, as though someone in the shuttered apartments above the market was practicing his violin. The music repeated and grew louder, and I realized it was more than one someone, it was five or six violins, and they were playing the opening movement of Beethoven's Fifth, played it out over our heads into the air. And it was the same four notes, repeating. Then somewhere close by me, a man began to whistle, joining the fiddlers above, though you'd never have seen who it was.

"Little by little, the market hushed, and I saw the woman selling strawberries straighten up and look at the German soldier choosing fruit. The violins sent the notes again into the air coming from one of the windows. Gradually, the six or seven soldiers in the squad looked at each other, looked for each other around the square, because it had now gone eerily quiet, completely quiet. Save for that music."

Frankie glanced at the censor sitting in front of her, one long finger resting easily on the switch of the microphone, like a pianist waiting for the downbeat of the conductor's arm. He looked up. She smiled at him and switched gears.

"If you have Beethoven's Fifth—surely a triumph of German passion and heart—go and put it on. Go and listen and you will hear the Europe—under Germany"—she kept speaking into the microphone, her eyes on the man across from her, whose fingers had closed on the button. And she started to hum—*Da da da Dum—"*

He pulled the microphone away and switched her off. She sat back, exhausted, giddy with skating the edge like that, and looked straight at him, daring him. She had just sung out the Morse code for the letter V.

Jim Holland pushed through the studio door.

"What are you doing, Fräulein?" The censor was studying her.

She smiled back at him, guileless. "I love Beethoven. I wanted to hum a little of it."

The man before her was graying and precise. He may have been a professor at one time, a linguist. She couldn't tell whether he knew where she had been headed in the broadcast, or because with an instinct for trouble, the minute she had strayed from what she had promised to say, he'd shut her down. She could see him considering. Was she a greater danger? Ought she to be questioned?

"How about that drink?" Jim Holland broke in.

She raised her eyebrows at the censor, like a schoolgirl asking permission.

The man paused for another moment and then finally, with an expression of disgust, waved them both out of the studio.

Jim shepherded her down the stairs and out onto the street, one hand on her elbow. She held on to the recorder and let herself be taken along the street, around the corner, and into the tiny bar where he found them a table and two drinks and an ashtray. She sank down.

"Jesus, you cut that close."

"Humming the Fifth?"

He nodded. "It spooked him."

"Good," she chuckled. "Those people were humming resistance, *humming* it." She smiled and sipped her drink, then leaned back against the wall with a satisfied smile.

"How long you been over here?" She shook out a cigarette.

"Couple of months."

"Here in France?" She leaned into his lighter.

He nodded.

"Seen much?"

"Seen enough." He looked over at her, his eyes lingering on the neck of her blouse. It didn't matter that she was one of Ed Murrow's, nor that that broadcast had been brave, even well-written; he didn't give a damn. She had as fine a pair of legs below the sweetest narrow hips he'd seen in a long while. And she'd come from London, where the big boys were. He asked her questions he didn't care about the answers to and nodded while she answered, though after a while she didn't answer much, and thought about the moment that would come at the end when he'd pull her toward him, his hands on those hips. Pull her against him. He smiled at her.

The hairs on her arms lifted under his gaze and she crossed them over her chest. He slid his attention back onto the crowd in the bar.

"Listen," she said, "let me play you something."

"What is it?"

She was woozy from the drink. "I want you to hear someone." And she reached down for the recorder she had put by her feet, looking around the bar for a quiet spot. Jim stood and carried their drinks over to a table in the corner by the telephones, under the stairs and out of the chatter of the crowd, and Frankie followed him there. He sat down and lit a cigarette, watching her open the case again, slide the disk from the sleeve in the lid, and then, looking at him, switch it on.

He had to lean toward the disks turning to catch Thomas's voice, and he stayed that way all the way through until the silence turning at the end. He looked back up at her.

"He was dead within an hour of this," Frankie said.

Jim raised his eyebrow.

"I'm starting to think that none of it matters," she said, and snapped the machine off, "except this. Nothing we can report can do better than that. A man speaking. Just his voice. Just him talking before he is killed." She snapped the lid of the case back down around the recorder.

Holland shook his head. "That's not reporting. You need a frame. People need to know where to look. They need us to point."

"We get in the way, don't you see?"

"You can't just go around and wave your wand and expect people to talk and then to expect that's enough. You've got to have a story around them. Otherwise it's just sound."

"But what if the sounds you record are enough?"

"You're a reporter, Miss Bard"—Holland pushed back—"not a collector. You report."

"I don't know." Frankie was exhausted. "Maybe people talking, just being there, alive for the minutes you can hear them, is the only way to tell something true about what's happening over here. Maybe that's the story," she finished, "because there's no way to put a frame around this one, no plot."

He seemed to think about it for a minute.

"Listen"—he leaned over the few feet between them—"what's the point in having such a nice body if you're not going to use it?"

She blinked.

"I *am* using it," she answered, and closed the lid on the recorder, stood, and pulled it off the table. She walked out of the bar without another look and found the street that led back to the station. Within an hour, she was back on a train, this time traveling west.

17.

FOR THE NEXT ten days, Frankie got on and off trains, headed west
as far as one train would go, and then turned around and headed in
the opposite direction, toward the boats at Lisbon, toward the ports in
Bordeaux, the microphone held out to catch the answers to her questions: *What is your name? Where are you going? Where have you come
from? How long have you traveled? How much do you have? Will anyone
meet you?* Through the bulge of France, across the central plain, heading
south and west, there were men and women crossing who spoke every
language Frankie had ever heard—*Jmenuji se Peter Kryczk. À nevem
Magyar Susannah. Je m'appelle Charlotte Maret. Regina Hannemann. Ich
heiße Hans Jakobsohn. Je viens de Brancis. Je vais à Lisbon. Mein Name ist
Josef. À Lisbon. In Lisbon. Oui, juif. Oui, je suis juive. Und das ist meine
Frau, Rachel.*

In her notebook, for each voice, she wrote a paragraph. How the man
answered, saying each word so slowly it was as if he pulled the language
down from air. *Und.* She copied his intonation into her book. *Das. Ist.
Meine. Frau.* When he was done he looked at her, smiling, looked away.
There. How a piece of wood in a child's hands was worn smooth on
one side to show a penciled face. How one mother's rings slid down the
long line of her fourth finger, and how she'd push them together again,

staring out the window. *Merci, Mademoiselle,* a man had said quietly, after she'd asked the questions, after he'd said his name into the microphone, carefully and slowly. *De rien,* she'd mutter, her throat closing over. Jim Holland had been right. She was collecting them; she knew it. She was gathering their voices without any clear idea yet of what she thought she was bringing back to Murrow, but she had to stuff something in the mouth of that quiet. She wanted to get as many voices as she could, and send them soaring, somehow outward, upward, free. The days and the nights slipped past like beads on a wire. One day there was suddenly a burst of women, all of them set loose from the detention camp at Gurs. *Gurs,* Frankie had asked to be sure. *Gurs?* The name of the camp that had stood for so long in her head as the center of the story she meant to get to sounded a clear sharp note, like a bell struck from a time she could hardly recall.

She had been riding trains that stopped and started in the middle of nights so often that she had lost the ordinary markers of nights spent in specific beds, in particular places. Some nights she'd close her eyes and the train and the whistles and the sleepers all around would cast her backward, and when she'd wake, for a minute it was Thomas sitting there, still alive, in front of her. Sometimes she lost track of which direction she was facing, she lost track of everything except the faces and the voices and the start and stop of the knobs in her hand; and she kept asking, kept recording as if she'd lose them all if she didn't get them down.

She knew she was running out of time. And yesterday, she had run out of disks. At the end of the second side of the last empty disk, the woman sitting in the corner of the train had waited as Frankie lifted the arm of the recorder, waited, watching as Frankie stared down at the disk. There was no more room. *Mademoiselle?* The woman asked. And Frankie heard the woman's question, heard the sighing of the man asleep at last in the opposite corner, heard the summer rain dashing against the side of the car, the scores of people left on the platform, wet, waiting—and couldn't stop recording. She flipped the disk over, set the recording

needle down, and simply started recording over again on top of what
was already there. *Vas-y,* she nodded at the woman, holding the microphone toward her. *Je suis seule,* the woman answered Frankie's earlier
question. Frankie could be ruining the disk, erasing the earlier voices, or
not recording anything at all. But it didn't matter to Frankie now. If it
worked, there would be voices on top of voices. Chords of people.

"Mademoiselle?" The hand shook her.

"Mademoiselle?" The hand shook her awake. Frankie pulled herself
up against the hard bench, trying to crawl back up from the well of sleep.
She focused on the man in front of her. *"Oui?"*

"Le train." He pointed. Frankie stood up. The platform writhed with
people under the glaring station lights suddenly turned back on. She
reached for the recorder and her suitcase. *"Merci, monsieur."* She smiled
tiredly. *"Et le train, où va-t'il?"*

"À Toulouse, madame."

The crowd had already massed around the shut doors of the several
compartments and stood waiting, looking up at the metal sides of the
train with the mix of resignation and worry that Frankie had seen over
and over in the last two weeks. Babies in baskets. Women looking over
their shoulders at the stationmasters, wanting to be first to see motion,
first to see the sign that the train was leaving, that the doors would
open.

She judged the crowd. Many of them must be bound for the boats
moored along the coast west of Bordeaux. Some might be traveling as
far as Périgueux and then would turn south to Bayonne and through the
Pyrenees toward Lisbon. A calendar hanging beside the cash register in
the station tearoom said June the fifth. Summer. She stared at the date,
trying to call up Broadway in Manhattan and the sound of motorcars
and street barkers selling bottles of Coca-Cola and double-or-nothing
Jujubes to bet on along the way. If it was June the fifth, she had four days
left on her *permis de séjour.*

The doors slapped open. She found an empty compartment and

settled herself in the corner seat, placing the recorder on the banquette beside her. The sixteen disks rested snug in their sleeves, holding close to seventy people, she guessed. And inside her suitcase lay the notebooks, with paragraphs of all the extra details on the people whose voices she had. The day before yesterday, her German failing in the wake of an old man's torrent of words, she had simply handed him the pen and the notebook and pointed for him to write down what he was saying. Fuck Jim Holland, she thought. It wasn't nothing, what she had done.

The short, harsh blast of a whistle nearby made her jump. A man shouted. She looked up and saw the single spire of a village church in the near distance. The train bunched forward and then stopped at a tiny station. Below her on the platform stood a mother and her son. She held his hand though he looked to be about ten.

The train door slammed open and the conductor put out the step stool. Mother and son stepped up into the train. There was a whispered discussion out in the corridor, and then the compartment door slid open. Frankie glanced up at them as they pushed inside, the mother carrying one suitcase, which she placed on the rack above their heads. They sat. He looked out the window, excited.

The train hissed up and started away. The mother closed her eyes briefly, as though she were praying. After a minute she opened them, looked sharply across at Frankie, and then, turning away, rested her attention on the boy. Out the window the sunbaked fields ran backward under the blue stretched sky. *Maman!* he shouted, pointing, when a man on horseback galloped alongside the train. She looked where her boy pointed, but the smile she had hung on her lips dropped as soon as he looked away from her, back outside. He slipped his hand out of hers to pull closer to the window and, emptied of his hand, the mother rested hers on the boy's knee.

"Where are you going?" Frankie asked companionably after a while.

"*En Espagne,*" the boy answered, glancing at his mother who nodded, not looking at Frankie. There was something in the quiet between them that prevented Frankie from asking them any more.

They traveled for over two hours in silence. The mother's hand never lifted from her son. It was the local train and made many stops at stations like the one where the mother and son had boarded. The air was balmy outside the window, and the sun winked in and out through the day.

As it approached Toulouse, the train slowed. Everyone was to get off and either board trains for the north or the south, or stay on this train and carry on across the border into Spain. The boy's hand crept back into his mother's. The outlying houses of the city pulled slowly enough past now, that one could see the curtains in the windows and crockery on the shelves. The mother pulled her boy around to look at her, her hands holding each of his arms. He stared into her face.

And then Frankie understood that the boy was going on alone. Perhaps there had been only one set of papers issued. Perhaps there was only one sponsor in another country for the child. There were many perhaps. But it was clear now that the mother was sending her son onward. Her despair spread through the compartment, thick and silent as a fog. She checked inside his jacket for his papers. She stood and pulled his bag down from above and checked again that he had the food she had packed. He sat very still, watching her hands in among the things she had packed when they left home. Then she sat again next to him and pulled his hands onto her chest, turning him to face her. He was trembling. She drew him to her and kissed him on one cheek and then on the other cheek, so slowly, looking at every bit of his face, and then she reached and folded him to her. The train stopped with a jerk and went quiet.

Up and down the corridor the compartment doors slammed open. Outside a whistle blew. There was shouting back and forth along the station platform below the window. Finally, the mother let go of her boy and stood. The boy grabbed her hand. She gently pried his fingers loose. Neither of them said a word. She turned to open the compartment door and he followed right behind her, his hand touching her back. But she turned to him with such a smile on her face, with such calm, wide love, that the boy stopped and dropped his hand.

She pulled open the door and stepped through. He stood in the middle of the compartment. In the passageway, she turned and held her finger to her mouth, as if to say *shh*, and then kissed her fingers to him and was gone. For a single, long moment, the boy stood where his mother had left him, stood staring at the compartment door through which his mother had vanished.

The recording needle would have cut this silent line of heartbreak into the disk. And what it had cost the mother, that last smile she gave, that last comfort so that her boy could pass through the final moment, no one would ever know. Frankie looked down at her hands, away from the boy who was now pressed against the window glass, watching his mother disappearing into the coats and dresses of the others, plunging into and then lost in the thicket of the crowd.

He sank back into the seat, not looking anymore out the window. There were no tears in his eyes. There was nothing. He didn't speak and Frankie didn't move. They sat together in the car as the train refueled and took on more passengers. Two women and a man pushed into the compartment. They sat in silence as the engine charged to life and slowly, very slowly, started sliding away, foot by foot. The boy shut his eyes and Frankie watched his lips moving, and realized he was counting.

When he opened his eyes, nothing had changed. He turned his head and stared out the window.

"*T'inquiètes pas.*" Frankie swallowed.

He looked at her, then back out the window. But then, he stood up, swaying, and crossed the few feet to slide down next to Frankie on the seat. Her eyes met those of the woman sitting across the way. The woman stared back at her and then down at her hands. Frankie glanced over at the boy and saw he had closed his eyes again. After a little while the boy sighed, and Frankie realized he'd fallen asleep, his head at an awful angle, hanging forward. She reached and pulled his head against her shoulder, crumpling him toward her. Then she leaned her own head back against the seat, but found it impossible to sleep.

They reached Bayonne at the Spanish border at first light. Frankie opened her eyes and turned her head. The compartment doors slapped open up and down the train as people got off with their baggage, heading toward the end of the platform where the Vichy police sat waiting.

"Where are you going, you and your mother?" The woman across from Frankie addressed the boy in French.

"She is not my mother."

The woman frowned at Frankie.

"Where are you going?" she asked the boy again.

"Lisbon," he answered.

She nodded. "Good luck, little one," she whispered, and stood up.

"Come on," Frankie said to him, "off we go."

The lines snaked all the way down the platform nearly to the end of the train. Frankie and the boy joined them and began the shuffle forward. Where are you going? Eh? How long have you got? Angoulême, Madrid, Lisbon. The names of the line toward the ships at anchor. Ahead of them, a woman wailed sharply. The boy looked at Frankie, worried. *Non!* They could hear her cry. *Non. Je n'ai qu'une semaine. Monsieur! Non!* Frankie stepped out of line to see if she could get a better glimpse of the woman, and was shoved roughly back in place.

It took nearly three hours to reach the head of the line. The boy sat on his suitcase quietly, as if sitting at his desk in school, moving forward with her when the line moved, but he would not talk to her. Neither would he leave her side. When they reached the officer on the other side of the desk, she handed over her transit papers first. The man glanced at them and thrust them back at her.

"The next train to Paris doesn't come again for three days after tonight."

She frowned. "But I'm not going to Paris. I'm going through to Spain."

He pointed at her letter of transit. Clearly marked in blue ink were the words: *De 18 May à 9 June 1941.*

"But what is the date today?" she asked.

"It is the seventh. So, mademoiselle, you have run out of time," he answered, motioning to one of the guards behind him, who pulled Frankie out of the line and off to the side. "You must get on tonight's train to Paris. Return here in eight hours."

He motioned for the boy's papers. Confused, the boy looked at Frankie standing there, out of the line.

She shook her head.

"*Viens!*" the officer snapped.

The boy unbuttoned his coat and pulled his papers out, his hand shaking, but the officer hardly looked at them. He stamped them and signaled the boy through the open gate. "*Vas-y.*"

The boy stared at Frankie where she stood at the edge of the table. Then he looked quickly in the other direction at the open gate. He looked back again at Frankie, stricken.

"Eh!" One of the guards pointed at him to move.

"Go on," she said thickly.

"*Vous ne venez pas?*"

She shook her head.

He frowned and looked down, picked up his suitcase, and walked slowly past the officers toward the gate. Frankie's eyes filled, watching the small set of shoulders moving forward, utterly alone. *Where am I going?* she imagined him saying. *Where am I going? When will I get there? Who will I know?* At the door to the waiting room on the other side of the gate, he turned around and looked at her. She nodded at him, still nameless, and lifted her hand and waved.

He was shoved forward by the man behind him.

She stood there, to the side of the table, in the company of the others who were not to be let forward onto the next train, trying to catch sight of him again, long after he had vanished. And when the door closed, she imagined him getting on that train on the other side of the door, then getting off it again. She imagined him all the way up to the Spanish border, into Bilbao where the tracks ran south into Madrid, then out the other side to Portugal, into Lisbon, off the train and right up the gangway of the boat. This boy, this solitary boy, she tried to carry in her mind's eye all the way out of here, as though she could take up for his mother, as though she could take him, like an aunt, or a godmother, and put him directly on the boat. She willed the ending, a happy ending, standing there.

"Mademoiselle!" The officer motioned her toward the station. She could see through the open doors all the way out into the square, dizzy with light at this hour. It was market day, and several stalls were pulled up and draped with canopies. Men and women bent and straightened, turned and talked. A woman tossed her head at someone Frankie couldn't see. There were melons piled in caskets on the tops of barrels. There were radishes. There was a man selling potatoes.

She looked back over her shoulder at the door that had shut on the boy whose ending she would never know. She grabbed a bag in each hand and walked across the cool marble of the train station out into the summer day.

A telephone sign hung from the corner of the post office building at the opposite end of the square, and Frankie walked in. The woman at the window had hair that curled around the nape of her neck like thick fingers. She tapped her nails on the counter while Frankie counted out the centimes and pushed them forward to pay for the call.

"You would like stamps as well?" She raised her brows, impatient.

"Stamps?" Frankie stared.

"You are in a post office, madame."

Frankie was too tired, she knew that, but the woman before her, staring at her like that with the faint, French curl of derision in her voice, made her throat close.

Behind the woman, the telephone rang, and she pointed Frankie toward the telephone closet set at the end of the counter.

"Where in the hell are you?"

"Hello, Ed." She smiled. "Bayonne. I'll be on tonight's train to Paris."

"Thank God," he sighed. "What the hell are you doing?"

"What you asked," she replied in return. "I'm getting it on disk."

"What, exactly?"

She shrugged. "I don't know—them."

There was quiet down the line.

"You need to get back here."

"I will."

"I mean now, Frankie."

"I will." She nodded. Someone behind him said something she couldn't make out.

"Say, Frankie." He was back on.

"Yes."

"Bayonne has a fairly decent transmitter. What do you say you get over there later on for one last broadcast from France."

She nodded, but didn't speak.

"I'm clearing the six-eighteen spot for you."

"Okay," she said, very low. "Ed?"

"Yeah, Frankie?"

"Is anyone listening?"

"How do you mean?"

"Is anyone listening to us? To all this, I mean?"

"Frankie." Murrow's worry made it through the telephone wire.

"And if they are listening," she went on, "then why aren't they here?"

There was quiet on the line.

"You need to get back here."

"I will."

"I mean now, Frankie."

"I will." She nodded. "So long," she said, and carefully put the receiver back down in its cradle. Then she sat there in the narrow wooden booth as one tear slipped over after another.

"Mademoiselle?"

Christ. She shook her head and wiped her cheeks with her hands. She stood up and pushed against the hinge of the door, stepping out into the post office lobby. Out the window, a farm wagon slid past, the back of it piled high with strawberries.

Get in, get the story, get out. Well, she was getting out. She could get out. She could get out and go home. And she would broadcast, she had told them she would. But it would be this story—this market, and that farmer driving past, and the woman in the post office, the boy on his way into Spain, his mother returning to her house empty of her son, all the people with whom she had ridden and recorded, the people whose lives she had cupped and held for a moment—she'd send out onto the air.

When the town's censor, a beefy man who tipped his brim up when she entered the studio, held out his hand for the script, she smiled, shook her head, placed the recorder on the table in the studio, and pointed to the seat in front of the mike. *"Puis-je?"*

He frowned but waved her in.

Smiling all the while at the man, she opened the lid, selected one of the disks, and slid it onto the metal pin. When the soundman behind the censor pointed at her, she took a deep breath and plunged in. *"This is Frankie Bard for the Columbia Broadcasting System in Bayonne, France.*

"What you are about to hear are the voices of several people on one of the French trains—a man, three women, and a child. They are all of them refugees, all of them traveling toward the west, hoping upon hope to get there, to get toward where you sit right now."

The man sitting across from her hardly blinked. He watched as she stood and gently lowered the arm down into the metal groove of the recorded disk. *Je m'appelle Maurice*—a man's voice swam up into the air—*Maurice Denis. Je vais à Lisbon, et puis aux États-Unis.* The voice stepped lightly over the *m*'s, lithe and expectant, though the man had slumped in the corner of the railway carriage after he'd finished speaking, and Frankie had written in her notebook that he carried only a soft satchel, that he wore a wedding ring, but that he traveled alone. Frankie kept her eye on the censor who watched the spinning disk intently. Now the voices of the girls rushed in, one of them speaking her name urgent and low, as though she was telling America her secret. *Oui, Madame,* she had said to Frankie, *je m'appelle Laura.* The voice was thrilling heard through the hiss and scratch of the record as she went on to say where she had been born and where she was going and yes, like the others, yes, I am Jewish—we are Jewish, the voice pronounced, my sister and I. And Frankie, like a shepherd followed after in the gaps, translating the girls' French into English, so they were understood. But the girls soared into the air. Like the single strand of color lifted free and shining out of a mess of yarn, the fullness of the voices, the round girl tones, spoke lives. And this was radio's soul, Frankie thought, this human sound sent into the air to make a dome of the sky, a whispering gallery.

Frankie watched the clock and, after a full sixty seconds, lifted the arm off the disk. *"Those were the voices of the Jews of Europe. They are on the trains tonight. They are traveling even now. Alive for now. Right now—"*

"Arrête!" The censor snapped her off.

Frankie stood straight up from the table, her heart pounding. He remained seated and motionless. Either she would make it to the door, or he would arrest her. He stood up and came around the table, slowly, stopping in front of her. There was no more than a foot between them, and she could smell the sweat on his uniform under the cologne. He stared at her and for a long second she wasn't sure whether he knew which way he was going with her. She kept her eye on the silver button of his collar, waiting. When at last she looked up at him, his gaze slid off her and away.

He put his hands on her hips and drew her toward him. She gasped out loud, as his thick hands went down into the pockets of her skirt and slid out again easily, his fingers raking her stomach through the silk lining. *"Danke."* He flicked a smile at her and looked down at the papers he had pulled out. He opened her letter of clearance, looked at it, and then folded it back up. He looked at her passport, fingering the pages, one by one. Then he slid the letter of passage into the passport. Last, he looked at the doctor's letter. He seemed to take a long while. She blew out her breath, but it came as a kind of strangled sigh.

"What is this?"

"Nothing," she shrugged. "A letter."

"To whom?" His eyes were flat.

"My sister," she said softly.

He shook his head and looked over at the radio operator, smirking. Frankie didn't see whether the other man paid any attention; she kept her eyes on this one. He swung his gaze back down, and she saw that he would let her go in the end.

"So?" He bent toward her.

Frankie kept her eyes on him and nodded. When he held the letter out, she reached for it. He gave it a little yank, and she held fast. He burst out laughing and stepped out of the way of the door, and she jammed the letter back into her pocket, bent to pick up her suitcase and the recorder, then walked through the door of the studio as carefully as she could. She kept her eye on the next door at the end of the hall, making it all the way and through that door, and down the first turn of the stairs before she started shaking. Around the second turn of the stairs, a dim triangle of light shone over the door to the street, and she pushed through it, into the wide, inconsolable blue.

Summer

❦

1941

WAR WAS COMING, everyone said it, though it was hard to believe what they said. Outside the windows here, gulls and swallows divided an undivided sky; the clear blue draped over a flat green sea, day after hot summer day. June had opened her throat wide and wider, and it was honky-tonk all the time. Tourists poured off the Boston boats into the throng along Front Street, mixing with sailors on shore leave walking in packs. The sunstruck beaches popped with parti-colored umbrellas while the turrets of navy boats crenellated the horizon far off in the bay.

"Anyone back there?" a man called from the lobby. Iris jumped and looked at the clock.

"Coming," she answered.

If there was a psychology of summer people it was this: though they were out here on vacation, way out on the tip of the American world—sunstruck, hungover, or stupid with lying in—they responded to the morning as dogs to the sound of their master's voice. Alert and bright, they trooped into the post office with letters and cards, wanting to get the work of their vacation out of the way in the morning. Then the rest of the day could go to the dogs. The rest of the day could slip easily as the evening sun into the surrounding ocean.

Iris stood in the window dispensing stamps and postal orders, direct-
ing newcomers to the town hall, nodding and counting and looking up
for the next person in line to step forward. Yes, one could reach the back
beach by way of the dunes. But one ought to carry some water. About a
mile and a half. Yes, it looks like it's going to be a scorcher. The summer
people came and went like froth at the tip of the wave, and she listened
as one half-listens to the symphonics of chickadees and a crow. Out the
back window, she heard the deep grumble of engines.

"Will it rain again, do you think?"

"Your guess is as good as mine."

"Come now, Miss"—the old man's eyes glanced past her shoulder to
her name printed next to the Post Office Department mandate stuck to
the bulletin board—"James. You ought to know the weather."

"Sorry, sir."

Emma did not look at the old man as she passed. Neither did she look
at Iris. She concentrated on getting to the box, reaching for the key in
her bag and inserting it carefully in the lock. She could have risen on her
toes to see whether there was the angle of a letter inside, but she always
used the key. Iris watched her turn it and open the door and put her hand
in, though by now she'd know that her hand would come out empty. She
closed the door back upon the box and turned the key quietly again, and
now she would know it was another day—the fourteenth day—without
a letter.

"Hang on," Iris called out quietly.

Reluctantly, Emma stopped where she was, a few feet away, and
turned around.

"How are you doing?" Iris followed up.

"Fine." Emma nodded. "I'm fine." She dropped her gaze, a little nervous in the older woman's stare.

"There'll be something tomorrow."

"Please don't," Emma said in a stiff little voice. "Please."

The lobby doors split open upon the sound of men's laughter. "Well,

well, get a load of this joint!" One of the men sang out with a great smile.

"Miss James." Johnny Cripps singled out Iris. "Nice to see you again, as always."

Iris nodded in the general direction of the men but kept her eyes on Emma.

"Hello, Mrs. Fitch," Johnny breezed.

"Hello," Emma said, feeling everyone was a little too close.

"There it is." Tom pointed to the wall beside Emma's head, and the three of them looked up at the poster Iris had put up the day before yesterday and went silent. There was a girl dressed in a sailor blouse and cap, her thumbs hooked around blue suspenders, her hips thrust forward. *Gee!! I wish I were a Man*, the lettering read—*I'd join the Navy*.

"Christ, *I'd* join the navy," muttered Johnny Cripps, "if she were in it."

Emma turned around. She needed to get home and sit down. She needed to get home and lie down. She needed to get out of her dress and her stockings and this kind of chatter.

"So long, Miss James." She looked up at Iris and turned, nodding at Johnny on her way out.

"So long," Iris called.

The men watched her out the door, and in the silence the telegraph machine pecked away like a bird in the back.

"Hell," Iris said under her breath and pushed through the partition door and out to the post office porch, keeping her eye on Will's wife walking slowly down the sidewalk, past the shops, holding her brown pocketbook firmly in her fist as though it might get away. It banged slightly against her knees and made the small woman smaller, carrying it like that, like a little girl. At the corner, she paused and looked carefully in both directions. Something caught in Iris's throat and she had to look down, look away from the woman taking such care. *God almighty*, she whispered, clearing her throat of the tears. When she looked back up,

Emma was halfway along the next block, her head and shoulders thrown back as though someone had told her to stand up straight.

"It's sissy to cut it down."

Johnny Cripps and the Jakeses had emerged behind her and were staring up at the flag.

"I beg your pardon?"

"Cut down the flagpole, the way Mr. Vale wants."

"He doesn't want to cut it down," Iris said carefully. "He wants to lower it."

"Is he right, do you think, or just nuts?" asked Tom Jakes.

"Nuts," Johnny said without a pause. "The Germans can't get all the way over here to get us."

"You going to the meeting tonight?"

"What meeting?"

"Defense. Mr. Vale's asking around for all available bodies."

"I don't think he means someone like me," Johnny answered with a laugh. "He means people without skills, I think. No offense, Warren."

"None taken," Warren said easily.

"Oh, for pity's sake." Miss James yanked wide the post office doors. "Go on, all of you. Don't stand out here spouting."

She crossed the lobby and pushed through the door into the back part of the post office, shutting it firmly behind her. Grabbing the kettle and walking it over to the sink, she tugged the cold water faucet open, letting it run over her hand until she felt the chill from the deeper well water, the water pumped up past the stuff sitting in the pipes all night long, and the cold on her skin, the deeper cold, recalled her to herself. The topic of the flagpole had gone back and forth between Harry and her so often, she had almost thought it was private. And though of course that was silly of her, there was no reason to get so cross. The flag was hers, but it wasn't *her*, after all. The Post Office Department had yet to give an answer on the issue of the flagpole. It was out of her hands. She filled the kettle and put it on the electric hot plate snug up against the sink, pressing the knob on high. Still, it made her uneasy, the talk like that on the lips of young men.

Was war something in a man's blood at conception, then? The father knocking into the mother exploding the boy seed inside her? With every passing week Harry seemed to grow more urgent, bird-dogging the war. He'd given up all of the garage work to Otto, so convinced was he that a U-boat had set out for this coast. There were the men like Johnny Cripps in the lobby who bunched and bragged and scoffed, their yearning and their fear in equal parts. And there were the mothers, when they were sure they were alone in the post office, sighing in relief when one of the boys had failed his physical. "I never thought," said Biddy Green, "I'd wish for something wrong with him, flat feet, a crooked limb— something not quite right to save him." Impossible wish. Harry Green was the big boy of the lot and effortless in his young body, diving off the edge of the pier at the highest arc of summer—Iris had watched him out the post office window—his arms cleaving the slack water, like a god cracking open the mortal surface of the world.

She stalled at the back windows of the post office sorting room, which framed the pier and the harbor beyond. It was low tide, and the trap boats pushed slowly out, one by one. She watched them, following them around Land's End, out into the open water of the sea, as if she could look into the broad heart of whatever was coming.

Though there was nothing there to see, she told herself impatiently.

EMMA KEPT HER EYES on the road out of town. The boys in the post office made her tired. The boys and their talk made her feel still more invisible, like a balloon at the end of a longer and longer string, held by no one. Floating off. There was nobody. No breath in her ear at night, no length of his leg along hers under the covers, no body. She felt like she had begun to disappear. Back into the gray, unaccented time when one day flipped over into the next without distinction, as in her life before Will, when she hadn't a soul in the world.

Look at you, she conjured his voice saying it. Before bed, after making love, on the street, across the table. Look at you. There you are. And there, she had found, she was. For the first time in her life, with Will, she had come to see herself because she'd look down and *see herself*—her waist, her arms, the bone on her wrist—in his hands. Because he'd been watching her. Like a fairy kissed into being, or the mermaid suddenly walking, or any damn story about someone who had been invisible, suddenly, fantastically, appearing.

Someone was hanging in the air ahead of Emma as she pushed up the last bit of the hill on Yarrow Road, the sun behind the figure in the sky, turning it black, a black letter. But it was Otto, she realized. Otto Schelling's body carved the letter *I* bending into the air. His waist leaned against the rung of the ladder set up against the second-floor window, the loose fabric of his trousers blowing backward slightly in the small breeze. He was thin and reedy and careful, his outstretched hand holding the paintbrush like a pen, running it along the bottom sill. He dabbed and then pulled back. Reedy but strong. His legs spread across the ladder were planted. He would not fall.

When she finally had decided to paint the house, it felt like an answer dropped through the mist in her brain. The clarity, the surety with which one day she had simply understood it was the answer, had stopped her where she stood at the kitchen window. She would not run. She would not turn away from the water between Will and her, she would paint the house a bright hard white, a charm to bring him home. To her. He could be on the boat right now, meaning to surprise her.

She went to sit on the porch steps, her back against the column, her legs stretched out before her. The sun had crawled up to the top of the sky and hung heavy above them. Otto was the letter *I*. The boats on the bay hardly moved, their triangles pasted on the hot sky. Otto made a sound through his teeth somewhere between a whistle and a sigh, running the paintbrush smoothly along. When he reached the side rim of the window, he stopped and looked over his shoulder at her.

"No," she answered. "Nothing."

He nodded.

She watched him. He had a wife, she knew, over there. And she knew he sent money to her, she had been behind him in line at the post office. She knew he had one shirt and one pair of trousers, because he appeared every morning for the past five, just exactly the same.

"Otto, where are you from?" She squinted up at him.

"Here."

She cocked an eyebrow.

He shot her a brief, amused glance. "Even you."

She flushed. "What do you mean?"

"Everyone thinks they're going to get themselves a Kraut." He paused lightly over the word.

"What are you talking about?" she asked, faintly.

He shook his head and jabbed gently at the corner with the brush.

"They follow me," he said.

She frowned. "Who does?"

He tipped his head toward town. "The men in the café," he said. "The boys."

"What do you mean?"

His hand descended evenly down the middle pane along the narrow band of wood, then across on the horizontal. He didn't answer.

"Well, the Germans are out *there*"—she tipped her head at the ocean in front of them—"according to Mr. Vale."

"What do you think?"

"It's phony baloney," Emma said stoutly.

He chuckled, and she saw his teeth and the pink curl of his tongue. She frowned, but he smiled even wider. "What is it?" She couldn't help smiling back.

"So reizend und doch so naiv."

She squinted up at him. He was still smiling at her.

"Sometimes," she said lightly, so as not to make it matter, "I think you might be following *me*."

"Yes."

"Why?"

He pointed to her belly with the paintbrush.

She flushed. The truth was, she had forgotten the baby, would forget for long stretches of the day, forget the whole thing until she lay down at night and her stomach flopped over like a dog beside her.

He climbed down two rungs and began the boards beneath the sill. The ladder crosshatched the sky above his head. He was, she watched him, profoundly alone, a long lean line, a body painting wood.

"Where is your wife, Otto?" she said to his back, very softly.

He glanced down at her. She looked back up at him. He picked up the brush and dipped it in the can. The white paint glowed in a long line out from under his brush. He drew the line as far as he could and then returned to the ladder and dipped again.

"My mother paints her house green," he said. "This annoys her neighbors."

"In Germany?"

"Austria." He stopped and looked at her. "In Salzburg."

"Oh," she said. He turned back around and paused for a minute, his hand holding loosely on to the ladder.

"I do not know where is Anna," he said. And shook his head, and said again, correcting himself, "I do not know where Anna is."

"Perhaps she is in London." Emma squinted at the harbor, not looking at him, knowing it was impossible but wanting the words in the air. "Perhaps she is with my husband."

He didn't answer. Nor did he pick up the paintbrush again. Neither moved. At last, Emma stood without a word. She walked back down the path and straight out the gate because she couldn't bear his stiff, sad body etched up there in the sky, and she couldn't bear her own. And she kept walking, straight out into the dunes, until she had to stop because of the cramp in her side. She stood there between the sea and her house and held her hand to her side and felt her heart bang and bang and bang. When she looked back toward the house, she saw him still up on the ladder, his body arching out, an overlooking angel.

19.

HARRY SAT WITH his binoculars leveled out the back windows of the town hall, across the wilderness of dunes to the sea, breaking the great swath of water into quadrants and staring fixedly at each one in turn, then randomly, so as to keep his attention agile. For a solid hour he stared, his sandwich lying unwrapped in his lap; then, without thinking about anything, he ate, his eyes trained on the empty palette before him. He waited as the stern man jigs for cod, the thick line loose in his hands, eyes off to the side, relaxed—every muscle ready to strike.

He had been staring at the water for so long that the scene in front of him no longer meant anything. In the automatic way a man crosses a street or reaches down to unlatch the hood of a car, Harry stared at the sea. Water and light and the boats bobbed back. Some days he was certain the sea would part, and up would rise the U-boat he was waiting for. Other days he was pretty sure he was a goddamned fool. But by now, coming up here and watching had become a habit.

Harry put down the binoculars and the lobster boats on the water reverted to shapes, a thick child's smudge for the hull run under the squat trapezoid of its wheelhouse, glass glinting in the bow. Beyond them the navy edged far off in the broad flat blue. Just yesterday, a marine brigade landed in Iceland to garrison it and begin protecting the shipping lanes.

Transport ships from Admiral Breton's TF-19 included two battleships, two cruisers, and twelve destroyers. And now there was word that the U.S. Navy was to provide escort for ships of any nationality sailing to and from Iceland. It was clear we were trawling for war.

How do you know where the ball has been hit? an admiring reporter had asked Red Barber, the great baseball announcer. *How do you know where to call the ball?*

I don't watch the ball, Barber answered, *I watch the fielders. I watch how they move. If the right fielder starts running, I know it's a knock into right field.*

Harry picked up the binoculars again. He didn't expect to see anything, but he sure as hell wanted to be ahead of the game.

FLORENCE CRIPPS STOOD on the open part of the green, nearest the post office, working her way around a great heap of shining metal, tossing pots and pans back up that had slid down from the top, pruning the edge into a tidy circle. It rose nearly three feet high—an aluminum pledge in the center of the town. Dishpans, coffeepots, waffle irons, kettles, roasting pans, double boilers climbed one on top of the next in a firm line toward becoming a bomber. Florence's hair stuck straight out in the heat, and she was flushed from bending over.

From where she sat in Adam's Pharmacy, Emma watched Mrs. Cripps across the green holding a teakettle up by two fingers as though it were a mouse. The pharmacy was empty at this hour and she had come in for a cup of somebody else's coffee while she wrote Will. The fan above her head flicked the page of the magazine in front of her idly open again. *Pregnancy is not a disease,* the bold black type cautioned. *A woman's body must be exercised and toned to prepare for the child . . . and the man after the child,* the subtitle teased. Emma slapped the copy of *Ladies' Home Journal* closed and slid it back into the wire rack beside the soda fountain.

The page under Emma's hand was getting sweaty, and she pulled her palm off it and looked at the words—*Mr. Schelling thinks we should paint more than just the trim on the house, or else it will rot*. It had been thirty-eight days without a letter. Over a month of silence, into which she had written day after day, sending him letters as though repeating a charm.

Maggie's boys trooped by, the eldest one carrying the baby girl in the blanket sling. Every afternoon they went down to the pier to meet Jim Tom's boat. She'd seen the family there, the boys helping wash the boat down, cleaning the catch, the baby set up on top of the bait box. It didn't hurt so much to look at them now, without their mother, as it had once, but she still couldn't talk to Jim Tom. When she saw him coming, she'd nod and wave, as though there was much she ought to do.

She ought to finish her letter. But it was simply too damn hot to write, she thought now, listlessly. She looked at the page. *Will? Where are you?* She leaned down and put her lips on the spot at the end of the sentence, leaving the faint red trace of her mouth. There. She folded the page and slipped it into the envelope and slid off the pharmacy stool and out the door, crossing silently to the pair before the pile of junk growing on the green.

"Hello," she said.

Mrs. Cripps turned around. Without anyone saying a word, the town had begun to treat Emma, now six months pregnant and showing, carefully. Talk stopped at her approach and sprang up afterward like grass. The doctor's wife oughtn't to be out in this heat, Florence thought. She was pale and panting.

"Well, hello," Mrs. Cripps replied.

"How much have you got?"

Mrs. Cripps stared back down at the pile. Nearly three quarters of the Franklin households had brought something down for the aluminum pledge drive. "Five thousand dishpans, ten thousand percolators, two thousand roasting pans, and twenty-five hundred double boilers will make one plane. If everybody contributes even one of these, we can proudly say that we have built"—she stalled gamely, doing some rapid calculation—"a wing?"

"Tip of a wing, more likely." Harry came up behind them.

Florence stared down, ruefully. "Perhaps no more than a helmet."

They were silent. "Imagine going to war in Mrs. Gilson's double boiler," Florence put in, then immediately wished she hadn't spoken. Harry had been to war and back and never married, which said it all about war. She glanced sideways at him, but he was rapt in studying some hidden piece. He flicked his cigarette off to the side of the aluminum heap and toed a pie plate off the hubcaps below.

"These aren't aluminum, Florence."

She stared at the hub cabs offered her so proudly by the Taraval boys.

"And they're stolen," he continued mildly.

"Stolen!"

"From my shop."

Emma stifled a smile.

"They *look* aluminum," Mrs. Cripps protested.

Harry allowed as how they did.

Mrs. Cripps bent and retrieved three stainless teaspoons that had been knocked off onto the grass at her feet. She wondered what else was on the pile, other things that looked like the real thing but weren't. Scraps that might not stand up under fire. She tossed the spoons hard at the top again. "Saw you had that German man over, Emma." She straightened. "You ought to be careful."

Emma flushed. "Otto?"

Mrs. Cripps nodded.

Emma turned on her. "Otto Schelling is Austrian, Mrs. Cripps. Not German."

"Never mind that. He's not American, and he's too damn quiet."

Emma frowned. "Lots of people are quiet," she said. "I am quiet, for example."

"You are all alone up there." Mrs. Cripps tipped her chin in the direction of Emma's house. "That's all I'm saying."

"Yes, thanks, Mrs. Cripps. I know that." Emma flushed up again, angrily, and made her way past without saying good-bye.

"He's up there most afternoons, Harry," Mrs. Cripps declared, as much to Emma's retreating back as to the man still standing beside her.

"How do you know?"

"You're not the only one keeping an eye out on the town," she retorted.

"I believe he is practicing his English," Harry said mildly, his eyes following Emma marching away toward the fish houses.

Otto was not a spy, Emma thought. Of course he wasn't. He was a housepainter. Hadn't he proven as much the last couple of weeks, every morning up on that ladder? But where was Will? All she wanted was to look up and see him walking toward her. All she wanted was Will.

Manny and Jo Alvarez were still out on the water, but Manny's cousin's boat had come in early, it looked like, so she made for his fish house at the near side of the harbor. She didn't know his name, but when she knocked on the fish house door, he motioned her in. The boy stood beside him wearing red overalls, a size too small, she thought, paying attention to the codfish laid out on chunks of ice in front of her, their eyes the color of metal.

"How much you want?"

"One," she answered, and then thought she'd like extra for chowder. "No"—she nodded at him—"two." The fisherman pulled two of the limp bodies off the ice and onto the porcelain scale, causing it to bounce up and down in front of her. Then he turned and threw them onto a length of paper laid out on the shelf behind him.

"Sweet?" The boy asked Emma, his voice catching over the hard stop of the English word. He was a dark child, with great big hands that hung awkwardly from the narrow sleeves of his shirt.

"No, thank you." She looked at him. Tall for his age, and maybe not altogether there. The overalls had two steamboats embroidered into the top pocket, and the red corduroy was frayed along the bib. Her heart hammered, suddenly.

"Where did you get those?" She couldn't stop herself.

The boy looked back at her, uncomprehending.

"The overalls," she pointed at him, impatiently. "Where are they from?"

The boy froze. The father stopped wrapping the fish and turned around, his face careful and flat. She took a step forward and bent over the fish, ignoring the father and making an effort to smile. She could see Will almost the more sharply for how the overalls fit this boy so badly, this not-boy conjuring him. It was one of the pictures she had kept on the mantel. Her five-year-old husband, squinting into the camera and the sun. Will's mother must have given them to the Church Thrift. They must have been passed from hand to hand for years.

"You want your fish?" The fisherman put a hand on his son's shoulder.

She stepped back and nodded, taking the fish. They watched her put it in her basket and count out the coins into the father's hand. She had to say something more. "Listen," she said softly to the boy. And something in her voice must have made him lean forward. "Those overalls once belonged to my husband," she whispered. "Tell your mother."

The boy's eyes darkened and he stepped backward. *"Muerta."*

Emma heard the word before she understood what it meant, because she said again, "Tell your mother—"

"Go away." The man swatted at the air in front of her, shooing her off, as if to protect his boy from her.

"Mama e muerta," the boy said.

Emma turned, stricken, and made her way out the fish house door and down the pier, the fish piled in crates around her, aware of the man's and the boy's eyes trained on her. Now, appearing like this so suddenly on the shoulders of a Portuguese boy, the overalls had the force of a message. She walked without thinking to the end of the pier onto Front Street and across, straight into the post office.

The wooden shutters were drawn against the steep slant of the summer sun, like the bedroom of a child who has been put down to nap, the light creeping around the shade, the room absolutely still save for the tiny chest of the sleeper, raising and lowering, while the wooden slat at the bottom of the shade lifted in the slight breeze and tapped against the sill. *Tap, tap.* And Emma remembered, violently, the face of the nurse bending over her to check whether she breathed in the fever tent, the white face of the nurse whose own mouth was covered with gauze. The sweetness of the order in here, the reliable calm, made her want to cry. In here someone was taking care of things. The cool and the quiet swept over her. Perhaps she would just stand here and then turn around in a minute and walk out. The sound of envelopes being slotted, the *pock* as the edge of the letters hit the end of each wooden box, was regular and soothing. *Pock* and then the *swish. Pock. Pock.* Emma closed her eyes and listened. *Pock.* Someone was watching over. Someone was in charge. *Pock. Pock.* Perhaps the room itself was all she needed.

"Emma?"

She shook herself. Her heart was banging.

"Are you all right?"

She nodded. Miss James stood in the window.

"Would you like a glass of water?"

Emma nodded. "Yes, please."

Miss James turned and went into the back room. Emma heard the tap opened and the sound of water rushing. She felt heavy and flat, as though she'd run into a wall and stuck. But when the postmaster returned with the glass of water, Emma walked toward it and drank gratefully. Miss James stood waiting. When she was done, she put the glass down.

"Something has happened," she said. "To Will."

"No," Miss James answered quickly.

Emma lifted her eyes up to the postmaster and studied her face. "You're certain."

"Emma"—Iris flushed—"there's been no news."

"To hell with the news," Emma whispered, and turned around and walked out.

The doors *chung chunged* behind her. Iris stayed very quietly where she was. She listened to Emma's feet clatter down the post office stairs, and she heard the whine as the gate opened and shut at the bottom. She waited a full minute before she reached down into her skirt pocket and felt for her cigarettes and lighter. The flame curled around the end of the Lucky Strike and she inhaled deeply. Then, at last, she retreated to the comforting order of the back room.

20.

AT FIVE-THIRTY, the doors banged open into the post office lobby and Mr. Flores walked in carrying the last mail of the day on his shoulders.

"Not a damn thing interesting in here," the bus driver announced.

Iris raised her eyebrows.

"What've you got for me?" he grunted.

She pointed toward two sacks in the back, and he pushed through the door in the partition, lowering the one sack he carried onto the sorting table. Iris turned to help him hoist the outgoing mail back up onto his shoulders and went to hold the door open for him on his way out.

"Midge Jacobs in the middle office down in Nauset says there's something for you on top," Flores commented, "something needing your attention."

Iris pressed her lips together. She ought to report Midge Jacobs. Mr. Flores had no business knowing what there was or wasn't for her to do.

"Thank you," she said, and closed the partition door firmly behind him, locking herself in on this side. She leaned against the door for a moment, listening for Flores's footsteps to die away outside, then she reached up and brought down the pebbled glass window in the oak partition with a shove. She bent and unlocked the pouch with the key she kept around her neck, and reached in to pull out the mail.

At the top of the sack there was the special envoy used by postmasters to convey messages, official notices, and bulletins from the postmaster general between stops along the route. She pulled this open and lifted up the flap. Besides the usual business there was also included an envelope wrapped in a letter from Midge Jacobs up the Cape. She read it and then stared at the envelope in her hand. *Mark Boggs*, it said, *Fort Benning*—

She put the envelope down on the table and read Midge's note again. *Please cancel the enclosed as I cannot send it on with no date.*

Without a date, Iris corrected reflexively. The canceling mark was too faint to allow and that mistake—she had been so tired last night, she remembered, she must have missed how faint it was—had been caught and now sat there before her. The system had not buckled, the system held. A mistake had been made. A mistake would be corrected.

She dumped the contents of the rest of the sack out onto the table, the topmost letter skating out across its old beat surface. *John Frothingham*. She placed it at the top of the table in the sixth position, replicating the alphabet. Very likely from his sister judging from the postmark. *Beth Alden*. She put that one in the first position. *Jane Dugan*. Another for Beth Alden. Iris flipped the envelope. Both from Private Mark Boggs. How nice, she smiled. Beth Alden, the grocer's daughter, was sturdy and clear-eyed and not particularly pretty. Nice for her to have this boy.

Iris stared down at the letter in her hand. *Mrs. Fitch, General Delivery, Franklin, Massachusetts.*

It wasn't in Will's handwriting. The salt breeze came in and lifted her hair lazily.

"No," said Iris. The letter was from England.

"Hello? Anybody back there? Hello?"

She thrust the envelope into the pocket of her skirt and turned around, her heart pounding.

"All right," she snapped, "I'm coming."

A man needed stamps, and she nodded and opened the stamp drawer, her hand already over the section where she knew she would find what she sought. Her fingers closed over the blue printed sheet. How many? She raised her head, and then counted the ten off the sheet, the words of the letter pressed against the fabric of her skirt, catching in her mind's eye. Eight, nine, ten. She looked up and handed the man his stamps, and swept his change into the palm of her hand, even as she closed the drawer. The man in front of her nodded and turned to go. She slipped her hand in her pocket. The man turned around. "Say," he said. "It's thirty cents for ten, am I right?"

"That's right," she said.

He walked back to the window. "Then you owe me another nickel."

"I'm so sorry," Iris said hurriedly and found the coin. Sand was dribbling out of the bag of her attention, faster and faster. She handed the man the coin, her face deliberate, but the beginnings of an alarm, the intimations of news, started tugging at her. She had a letter in her pocket. Emma's letter. Three more people pushed through the door. What could they want? Iris frowned, glancing at the clock. It was four minutes to closing.

"Yes, all right," a young woman with terribly sunburned shoulders complained as Iris followed her right to the door. "What's the big rush?"

She snapped the door shut on the girl and clicked the bolt. Then she turned and pushed straight through the partition and hauled the metal shutter down on the lobby window. She regarded the row of boxes. Nothing fluttered, nothing stuck out.

At last, she pulled the letter from her pocket and looked at it. All her years in the post office she had watched out for accident and mistakes—correcting a mismarked envelope, catching insufficient postage on a letter—making sure that the mail passed through, that the mail passed effortlessly through from beginning to end. In Boston, she prided

herself on the fact that no one else watched as closely as she, a benefi-
cent spider protecting the threads. Like the glass chutes down which the
letters poured in the greater post offices, Iris imagined herself the kind
of perfect vessel through which people's thoughts and feelings could
pass and upon which nothing snagged or got stuck. But the whole thing
relied on never once looking inside an envelope; Iris had never even held
a letter up to the light to read the writing there. The whole beauty of the
system, the godliness, lay in making sure the trains ran smoothly on the
tracks, that letters sent out arrived, no matter what was inside.

She ought to get on her bicycle and ride up the hill to Emma's house.
She ought to go to the door and knock and when the woman came to
answer, she ought to hold out her hand and give the letter over. She
ought to do all this, but even as she ought, Iris filled the kettle and set
it on the burner and waited. When the whistle blew, she opened the
spout, holding the envelope in the current of steam. The envelope came
unstuck easily and she slid out the single sheet of paper.

18 June 1941

Dear Mrs. Fitch,

I'm sorry to say that I may have bad news. I have not seen your
husband since the night of May the 18th when we had a bad night
of the bombings. As that was over a month ago, and your letters
keep coming, I thought you ought to know.

But my dear, when I went up to his room just now, I found his
wallet with all his papers in it, just sitting there in the top drawer of
his desk. I cannot think why he didn't take it with him on that last
night, but it is very unfortunate—if something has happened—

I'm sorry, dear. I fear the worst. Perhaps you ought to make
enquiries to hospital?

He was a good man and he spoke of you often.

Yours very truly,
Edwina Phillips

Iris put the letter down and walked back out through the partition. She straightened the single table in the lobby in short order, the postal forms and savings account applications arranged from left to right against the wall, then filled the sponge pot for the envelopes and wiped the lip on the pot of mucilage. She moved the wastepaper basket closer to the boxes. She came back through the partition, then reached and ripped Tuesday, July 8, down, so the calendar read Wednesday, July 9. She spun the wheel carefully on the franking machine, flipping the iron 8 over to the 9, and pulled the stamp drawer out to check on the numbers. And the doctor's letter, stuck under the iron change tray, stared back at her. Iris shoved the drawer shut and looked up, guiltily. She opened the drawer farther and pulled the letter out from under the tray. *Mrs. William Fitch*, it said. *PO Box 29, Franklin, Massachusetts.* Iris stared at the handwriting, and the memory of the man, standing before her with this letter in his hand, came back so forcefully, she had to look up. The lobby was empty. *Give it to Emma, when I am dead.* Those were his words. She stared at it. *It will be you*, the doctor had said, relieved. *It will be you who tells Emma.*

But he wasn't dead. He was missing. She shut the drawer.

And nameless. She reached for the landlady's letter again. That was what she meant, wasn't it? Will might be hurt somewhere in a hospital bed, hurt so badly he couldn't speak and there was nothing to identify him. Iris frowned. Could that be? There had been nothing in his pockets, nothing on him at all?

She thought of the tidy pile of Emma's letters the landlady had stacked just inside the doctor's room—there must be forty of them silting against the door. Every one of them stamped and put through the machine and into the sack by Iris. Emma's letters and then all the letters sent to the boys and men who had gone from town—Mark Boggs, the Winstons, Jake Alvarez. All of them written to, all of them writing, and knowing, too, as did everyone in town, that the closer we drifted toward war, the greater the odds for at least one of them, that a man would get

out of his car and walk up the pathway to the door and knock. And anyone walking past would know the news before the father on the other
side, before the door opened.

When her brother had died, the man had come just as they were lighting the lamps, and the lamp on the table flared up behind her, its whis-
ker of light flicking off the window, causing her to look up. And so she
saw the greengrocer standing there in the hallway, for one split second
before her mother caught sight of him, too. Those days, if he stayed in
his shop, he was fine, but when he walked anywhere in town, it meant he
carried news, and everyone watched where he was going.

"Bonnie." He stepped forward into the room, his hat in his hand.

"No." Iris's mother had snapped at him.

No. Iris thrust Emma's letter back into her skirt. Not yet. Not
half-news, no-news, like this. Not when Emma had a baby on the way.
If he had died, the news would come, but where was the harm in hope
until then? Time would catch up. If something had happened. But not
until after the baby. Not until after the poor girl was strong enough, and
ready. She flicked off the lights in the back room, unlocked the partition, stepped into the lobby, and went back out the post office doors into
the heat and mayhem of the summer evening racketing on just outside,
where Harry waited.

"Hello." She faltered.

"Any good news for me in there?"

"What?"

He put his hand on the flagpole.

"Oh," she swallowed. "No, I haven't heard anything yet."

"Iris," he said quietly. "Please. Ask again."

She nodded. She ought to say something. Her heart thudded and
turned quietly over in its cage. He had already started down the stairs,
expecting her to follow.

"Are you all right?" He stopped and looked back at her. "You've an
odd expression on."

She felt the letter in her pocket. If she left the building with it, she was stealing, wasn't she? She was a thief.

"If you had a chance to spare someone from hurt, Harry, would you do it?"

He considered her. "What sort of hurt?"

"Would you do it?" she repeated, tense.

He frowned. "*Can* you keep someone from hurt?"

"Of course."

"How's that?"

"Keeping mum. Keeping them in the dark."

He didn't answer. She stood above him on the porch, lost in some private reckoning. He shook out a cigarette, lit it, and looked back up. She was watching him. Harry held out his hand. "Iris?"

She went slowly down the stairs to him. It was wrong what she was doing. Never in her life had she done something like this. He pulled her closer and took her hand and set off down the crowded street. They walked along silently, and the evening sang out golden. After a little, Iris withdrew her hand from his, shoving it deep in her pocket.

Harry glanced over at her. Her long legs took great strides along the road.

"The thing is," Iris said quite quickly, afraid to look at Harry beside her, returning to the spot on her mind, "all kinds of things can grow in that dark. Calm, for instance. And hope."

"So?"

She swallowed. "Would it be wrong, that calm?"

"Why?"

"Because it was false."

"False?"

"Groundless."

He was quiet.

"That's what calm is, isn't it?" he answered after a while. "A little break from knowing what's on its way."

Iris stopped walking. "What's on its way, Harry?"

She sounded so miserable. Harry turned around and looked at her. She stared back. Here, he realized, here it was. It was so little, so unannounced, but a door had suddenly, irrevocably, opened in his heart. Love had found him here in the middle of his life, at the edge of the world in the shape of a redheaded woman with some trouble on her mind. He reached and gently pulled her hand out from her pocket. "I don't know what's on its way," he said gruffly.

She felt how warm his hand was around hers. *It will be you*, the doctor had said. Iris thought of Emma coming into the post office, her tiny shoulders thrown back, daring anyone, daring the world to hurt her. *It will be you*. And Will Fitch had been relieved. That was it, she realized. The doctor had entrusted Iris with the letter, so that Emma was not alone.

"Whatever it is, Iris," Harry went on quietly, "you can't stop it."

But until that baby was born, Iris could push back Time on either side of the small woman, hold it off, and then ease her gently through the opening into what was to come. That's what she was meant to do this one time. That's what the doctor meant. That was the point, someone was watching. Iris was.

Iris brought Harry's hand to her cheek, smiling. It would be all right then. It would be all right in the end. The face she turned to him was so grateful, so wide with her love, his heart bolted toward her.

"All right," she said.

"Right you are," he grinned back. "Let's go."

The sea appeared in bigger and bigger patches at the end of town as the houses dwindled away on their walk out to the breakwater, until finally the two of them stood facing the Atlantic. The last crooked finger of Cape Cod curved away ahead of them, and a mile or so out the simple white lighthouse at Land's End blinked. Beneath that sky, with nothing moving on the water, it appeared like a chess piece or a child's wooden block forgotten and set down.

"I want to get married," he said suddenly, beside her.

"As well you should," she answered primly.

He laughed out loud. "To you."

She blushed and turned toward him, chuckling. They had come to the end of the land and begun.

"Well," she said, smiling foolishly at him.

"Yes?"

"Yes," she answered. "Yes."

When they turned from the sea and set foot again on the pavement, Iris slid her hand into Harry's pocket and his fingers closed over hers. They drew back toward the hot throngs of the summer town, the lights appearing in the houses, blinking like low-lying stars. Bicycles spun past in the creeping dark.

There seemed to be a crowd of people outside the post office. It was one of those nights when everyone had found themselves out in the late light, walking into town. Someone facing their way waved and then more of the faces turned and Iris made out Frank and Marnie Niles, and Florence Cripps. Iris could imagine what they saw. The postmaster and the mechanic joined in his jacket. Harry's grip was firm on hers, and she smiled. This was how it was now. This was who they were. They were going to be married. They were, in the eyes of the town, already joined. Clearly, cleanly walking just like that down Front Street. Years after, she would remember the warmth of his hand on hers and the last of the sun on her cheeks, and she would remember that moment, in the silence before someone broke it, the single moment of highest summer, brimful, with no room for more, and not time yet for the tipping, the pouring out and away.

21.

IN THE BAR at Grand Central Station, the *whoosh* of the revolving doors let couple after couple into the busy crowded room full of smoke and chatter. Max Prescott of the *New York Trib* watched them in the long mirror stretching above the length of the bar. The men in suits raised their fingers to the maître d', signaling how many; the women turned aside and studied the room. Some men, like himself, were alone and made directly for the bar, where they shrugged off their jackets and folded them across their laps. Every time the doors moved, the distant hammer of trains in the station outside *chug-chugged* and moaned, the mechanical beams of industry crossing and recrossing the luncheon hour. It was the end of summer and hot as hell. The fans overhead moved the damp shirts of the men from right to left, cooling against their skin as it moved.

"Hello, Boss." Frankie dropped onto the stool beside him.

She had appeared without warning—though he had been sitting here waiting for her—as though she'd stepped through the veils dividing one moment from the next.

"Yes." She nodded at the bartender. "Whatever he's having." She turned to the old man, conspiratorially. "What *are* you having?"

"Bourbon and water."

"One should never drink bourbon before six o'clock," she observed.

"Scotch?"

"Scotch"—she tipped her glass gently against his—"is for the servants."

He shot her a look. She was thinner. And though her tone was light, she seemed exhausted and wary, like a cat who has narrowly escaped a bath. He had caught her last broadcast, two months ago from France, and she had sounded odd then, snapped off somehow. But he hadn't given it much thought until her mother had rung, frantic for news—she hadn't heard anything from Frankie in over two weeks. Had he? He'd put in a call to Murrow, even Mr. Paley was concerned, but after Jim Holland in Lyon, no one had seen her or heard from her and Europe was full of eyes and ears. Hell, they were the press corps. But there wasn't a word from Frankie, and there was nothing to think but that she had been caught in some lonely room where the world did not pay attention. She had been in the wrong place in front of the wrong person. Max had been so certain this had happened, when he heard her voice on the telephone yesterday he had turned his head to look out the window to make sure it was still New York outside. I'm back, Max, she had said without a greeting. But I'm through.

They drank in silence. Their long habit was to be quiet until there was something to say. And often, there was nothing at all to say other than the four or five sentences that had brought them together. Most people he knew, his wife included, wouldn't make it through an hour on the promise of four sentences. But Frankie Bard was like a camel. She could hold her words for days—as long as she could watch the goings-on.

"I had forgotten what all this looks like."

He looked up into the mirror and saw she was staring at the people in the restaurant behind them.

"All what?"

"This." She pointed. "No one here thinks they're in any danger."

"They've left it outside," he suggested.

"No, they haven't." She tipped her chin at the scene behind them, played out in the glass. "They don't believe it's there."

He watched one of the men behind him lean over to his companion and say something in her ear. She turned her cheek toward his whispering mouth, though her attention remained on the menu in front of her. The clatter above and around them was as protective as a bower. "Human nature," he ventured.

"No, Max." She crossed her arms in front of the drink. "American nature."

He chuckled, uneasily. "Sounds like you want them to pay."

"That's right." She nodded.

"For what?"

She shrugged. "For this." She nodded again at the ordinary lunch behind them. One of the waiters crossed through the smoke with a tray held high on his way to the kitchen, and the people leaned away from him as he passed. The talk in the room was a low, insistent murmur against which glasses clinked and silver clattered upon the china.

"People can't imagine what they haven't seen," he answered. "That's why they need you."

"Beg your pardon, Max, but that's horseshit."

"You signed up to see what they haven't," he observed. "You can't blame people for it."

"Why in hell you think I'm quitting?" she asked coolly.

"Hell of a year to quit," he fired back.

She finished her drink. The bartender sidled inquisitively down the length of the bar. The old man nodded without looking at him. He knew Frankie well enough to know she never explained. Whatever had happened over there was going to stay over there. She turned and looked at him, then gave him one of her old smiles.

He took the drink the bartender placed in front of him and pulled it near.

"Take a break," he suggested.

She shook her head. "I want to get off the bus."

"It's the only story there is, Frankie."

"Hell it is," she answered.

"I don't get it."

She shrugged and kept her eyes on the mirror. "Maybe I'm not up to telling it."

"Bull." The old man thrust out his chin.

Frankie didn't answer.

"I used to think you wrote a story like a hunter threw a spear," she said after a while. "You aimed. You drew back your arm, hurled, and it landed. It was a straight shot. Beginning, middle, and end."

He glanced at her.

"The harder a story was to file over there, the better. Can you do it, Frankie? You bet, it's already done." She looked at him. "It was easy. Hell, it was grand. There was no choice to pull back or look away, you dove in with your eyes and ears open, and you reported what you saw. That was your job. To see and to tell. There was a purpose. There was a plot."

"Frankie—" He had turned all the way around on his stool. She pulled out a cigarette and he reached forward with his lighter. She bent into it and nodded at him, exhaling.

"But there I was one night, Max, standing on a velveteen seat on a train leaving a station, desperate to correct, desperate to right a wrong, gone horribly, finally wrong. I had stood up on that seat as though I were God and I could save those below. As though I could change the story"—she turned to look at him, hearing Thomas's cry, *They're shooting, Fräulein! Shut up! Shut up!*—"and I got a man killed."

"Frankie—"

"What the hell, Max. It never mattered. It was never a straight shot. The war is still going on whether I tell it or not, and now I'm the one holding it."

Max studied her, waiting her out.

"All that time over there"—her finger slid along the rim of the glass—"getting it down, getting it right. But it can't be gotten—the story just whispers off in the dark. What happens next? What happened? I can't bear it." She stopped, remembering her own voice snapping impatiently to Will Fitch, *I don't have to bear it.* "Christ, Max—listen to me." She smiled, tears springing into her eyes. "Don't pay any attention."

He turned toward her. "Okay," he said, seeing she had begun to cry.

"Okay?" She pushed away the handkerchief he offered her and wiped her eyes with her fingertips. "Okay?" she repeated, almost laughing, and then she gave up and covered her face with her hands.

Someone's joke rose in the background and hit its mark, and the sudden burst of laughter fell down around the room like rain. Frankie turned around on her stool and caught sight of a woman entering the bar on the crest of that laughter. She was lithe and bare-armed and her skirt skimmed above her tanned calves as she moved. Max turned around also, and the two of them watched the woman sit down and lean her elbows on the table—languorous, hot—and rest her chin on her hands, her long, bare arms folding into two soft hooks.

As long as there were people to watch, this was where they'd look, Frankie thought. At a beautiful woman in a bar. How easily the face of the world turns away. She glanced at Max in the mirror and bent to pull the bundle wrapped in a tea cloth from her satchel, unwrapping the disks from the train and setting them down on the bar.

"What the hell are these?" Max asked her.

"What I recorded."

"France?"

She nodded.

"Does Murrow know you've got them?"

She had come off the train from Paris, gone straight to her flat, and packed her bags. She had grabbed Harriet's stories, the random pieces of paper above her desk, and stuffed them between the pages of her notebook. She had closed the door of the room behind her and slid the key under the landlady's door. She had done it all so fast, it was as though she were leaving the scene of a crime. On her way to the boat, she had left the portable recorder at the front desk of Broadcasting House without a word to anyone upstairs. She had run. She had gone straight down to the docks and bought a ticket and waited the several hours until setting sail, sitting in a dockyard pub, staring as the great hoses strafed the sides of the boat, the water streaming down, cleaning off the salt.

"He does by now," she answered sadly.

"What's your plan?"

She shook her head and shrugged.

"Frankie," he began.

"None of it matters, Max"—she looked up at him—"but this—these." She pushed the edges of the disks in line, making a perfect black tower of acetate.

He watched her. "What's on them?"

She smiled, sadly. "Nobody. People. People who are alive."

"What's the story?"

She traced a line down the cool glass in front of her. "There isn't a story, Max."

"There's always a story."

She took a long time to answer. "Well, then I've lost whatever it is."

He pushed back on the stool. "You're simply going to shut up?"

"I don't know."

"You can't shut up," Max said. "It'll kill you."

"You know something," she blurted out, not caring how crazy this sounded, but needing to push the words forward, the worst things forward. "No matter how much we all want some old man up there, there sure as hell isn't anyone watching over it all. It's just an empty sky, Max."

"Course it is, Frankie."

Frankie stared at the perfect patrician line of his profile, the line that caused the girls in the secretary pool to call him the Yankee Clipper behind his back, and tried to smile.

"But that's just it. Then no one is listening. No one hears the gaps. So what I've got here is nothing but seventy-odd lost voices traveling the distance but landing nowhere, sliding off the inner dome of the sky. And yet still, somehow, I think these are the whole deal." She stopped and rubbed her eyes. "Oh, Max," she asked, tired as a child, "what's the next part?"

"We're going to get into the war."

She nodded and finished her drink.

"Seek Truth. Report It. Minimize Harm. Ha." Frankie slid off the stool and stood up. She tugged at her jacket and caught his eye in the mirror.

"Do me a favor," he said, "take your mother, take a break, and go out to the Island, or the Jersey Shore, somewhere nearby where I can pester you."

That brought a little smile. "I'm headed up to the Cape this afternoon."

"Hell of a long way to go for a break."

"It's only Massachusetts."

He grunted.

"I've got to deliver a letter." She leaned over and kissed him on the cheek. "It's the one goddamned thing I'm going to get right in months."

He raised his hand but didn't look at her. But then he wanted her back as soon as she was gone, and swiveled to call after her. She had taken off as swiftly as a bird and was making her way here and there through the tables, tall and electric. He let her go. She had been the one who had seen it over there. And she had broadcast it back to them sitting at their desks, and she had made them look it directly in the eye. Whatever the hell that meant. He signaled the bartender for the tab. Nothing could be looked at directly in the eye, and he knew it. He looked up at the mirror over

the bar and the dress whites scattered among the tables had the effect
of a field of cotton lit up by the weird wild light that always precedes
a storm.

FRANKIE WALKED as fast as she could away from her old boss into
the heat of Grand Central Station—into the middle of the American
travelers, into the hurl and worry of getting on the right train, the right
track, kissing good-bye, good-bye—and stopped at last under the dome,
the tears streaming down her face. On the timetable in front of her, the
white letters staggered out across the black board. People jostled around
her, also stopping, looking up, before moving on. What she saw in the
station was merely what she saw. Boxes and slants. The green shunts
of summer lilies stuck in a pot by the ticket booth. Nothing to look at,
nothing to see. And nothing to report. It was a nearly unbearable pleasure. She sniffed and wiped her face with her hand. She gazed up at the
clock where the hand stitched second to second toward the top. After
another minute or two, the white numbers and letters combined to mean
something, and she made her way to where the Boston train waited.

A month ago, Frankie had walked down the gangplank of the SS
Norway and into her mother's arms. She had let herself be taken home
and put to bed. Downstairs, the voices of her mother and the house-
keeper bowled across the hours, stretching in the summer heat through
shuttered rooms. She had stared up into the ceiling with her arms crossed
over the cotton blanket, while New York racketed outside. In the second
week, she asked for a gramophone and lay there in the bedroom she had
grown up in, her dressing gown hung up on the bedpost, her slippers
lined neatly beneath, listening to the voices from the train.

When her mother came in to sit beside her, she closed her eyes and
crept her way backward to where she had been. Backward to Harriet
and their apartment. Billy's mum. Back to the doctor in the shelter on
the last night of the Blitz, and his eyes on her as he died. Back through to

the trains—to Thomas. To the children. To that last boy she could not follow. So many. There had been too many.

Forward and backward, she crept in her mind's eye, until slowly, like a river bluing, in the last week, she had come to a picture of the doctor's wife at a door and herself on the other side. She imagined handing her her husband's letter at last; and then, she imagined her smiling, as though she had something to give Frankie in return.

At Nauset, Frankie made the bus for Franklin with plenty of time. She sank down into a seat and yanked open the window.

She woke when the bus grumbled to a stop, bumping her head off the window where it had rested. There were people in the streets walking just below where she sat. People in the evening air, laughing. Frankie put her hand out on the seat in front of her and pulled herself to standing. The bright evening light glowed off the windshield and Frankie stepped off the bus and onto the sidewalk; she went to stand in the shade of one of the two trees in front of the post office, waiting for the driver to hand down the bags.

It was the second weekend in August and the town seemed to have gone slightly mad for fun. Vacationers, emerging in their linens and poplins, bathed and glistening from the day on the beach, were out in the early-evening light. They strolled and chattered, looking in shop windows, like loose twigs nudging slowly down an easy stream, their voices lighting along the lanes. Though it was just six o'clock, signs were up in some of the café windows. NO MORE LOBSTER. NO MORE PIE. As she stood there, she heard a shout and a crash, a clang of metal on metal, and then right away the swooning warble of a trumpet as the guesthouses along the rim of the harbor swung into sound, and a tea dance orchestra started to play.

Perhaps she had made a mistake coming here, she thought uneasily for the first time, leaning over to grab the handle on her bag. Perhaps there was no quiet to be had. Though Europe was falling apart, splintering and exploding, at least she understood the direction. But all this—she gazed down the street—motion without purpose, where was it going? There was a movie house, and a dance hall, but the whoops and hollers seemed to come from all over town. She picked up her suitcase and the portable Victrola, swung her satchel over her shoulder, and walked to the end of the sidewalk, waiting for the line of Chevys and Plymouths to thin.

Across the street, a tall red-haired woman emerged from the post office and uncleated the flag at the top of the stairs, her post office blues sitting nicely on her hips. A Dorothea Brooke, decided Frankie, for a snappier fiction. Her lips were painted a shade of red that did nothing for her, as if to say, never mind, Frankie thought. Never mind these lips.

She watched the postmistress loosen the line on the pole and as the flag swam down in the evening light, several young men raced down Winthrop Street for the harbor, brimming at high tide. The damp heat of the day still hung in the evening. Ahead of her they reached the sand and, shedding hats and shirts, ran straight to the water, their khakis sliding down to their hips and hanging there by the grace of their belts. They threw themselves in and then, shouting and blowing, threw themselves on each other. White as winter, their chests and arms flailed beneath the water like fish in a barrel. The draft board must have all of their lottery numbers up Cape. Frankie passed them and walked up Front Street to where it met Yarrow Road, heading single-mindedly up the hill and out of town.

To her right, a ragged hedge of beach roses and slash grew up out of the sand. The late afternoon sang, and on the other side of the hedge and down the bluff, the flats shivered as the tide drew out farther and farther. Salt and roses mixed in the offshore breeze under the warning calls of the gulls.

Up ahead of her, six white cottages the size of playhouses lined up like girls regarding the gentleman caller come at last to the dance. Frankie's cottage was the fourth to last; as she passed the others she heard the showers running; tired children complained, and the cool extended voices of mothers shook out like towels in the breeze. A woman sat on the porch next door, smoking a cigarette, her feet propped up on the railing so her dress slid down her tanned legs. She looked across at Frankie and waved lazily.

Frankie waved back and pushed open the screen door. The two rooms inside were painted a bright white with filmy curtains hung to lift and lower in the sea breeze. Everything fresh. Everything bright. A small sofa in the front room. Two chairs placed on either side of a side table proudly sporting a gramophone. Music and light, drinks in the evening. Summer—the suggestion was clear—could be found in these three things. The air and water flipped lazily back and forward outside the trim windows. The window above the sink faced directly into the high dunes, motionless and baking in the evening quiet, the silvery-green compass grasses sticking up from the sand like quills.

Through the windows the blue sky arched effortlessly away. Frankie dropped her bags and filled a glass with water from the sink, then went back outside to sit in the slow slide to evening. She was high enough up and out of town that she could see it all before her, uninterrupted. The fishermen threw tackle and gear on the decks of their trap boats and up through the general quiet came the burst of their end-of-day shouts. Her eyes filled suddenly at the sounds of ordinary life. She knew she'd been rambling this afternoon with Max, and she could imagine how it sounded. She wished she'd never brought up God. She wasn't even sure what she was trying to say.

She turned her head. To her left an old man, napping on one of his porch chairs in the evening sun, had moaned aloud. Neatly dressed in light-colored trousers and a white shirt and dark sweater, his arms rested on the curve of the chair, given utterly to sleep. Sleep? She rose out of her chair, disgusted. The months of reporting, the pages of script she had written over the past four years. What good had they done? She gave one last look at the two strict rows of houses leading into the center of this town. She might as well have broadcast directly into the wind.

22.

THE FOLLOWING MORNING, a half-dozen young men sat upon the stools inside the town café, three of them in their waders, hands pressed around the hot coffee. Through the quiet that had descended, Frankie made her way to a stool along the counter, nodded to the woman pouring coffee, and took her place. "Thanks," Frankie said, accepting the full cup pushed before her.

"Morning." The man beside her grinned. It was the leader of yesterday evening's swimmers.

"Morning." She nodded back.

The door pushed open and a man silhouetted by the brightness outside stood for a minute on the threshold, nodding hellos, before moving forward to the stool beside her. He put one foot up on the step and climbed up lightly, as if into a saddle. He was neat as a barrel, small and compact, his gray-blond hair cut very short along the ridge of his skull. He set his hat down on the counter beside the plate as carefully as a judge.

"Harry," greeted the young fisherman beside Frankie.

"Hello, Johnny," Harry said.

The chime for the top of the hour rang out on the radio and the room fell silent as if in front of a fire. *British and Soviet forces have invaded Iran,* the radio announcer's voice came on, followed by the three chimes signaling the news. *Worried by reports of German "tourists," Britain and Russia today decided that Iran must accept their protection of oil supplies. British land forces advanced in two areas to secure oil near Ābādān and northeast of Baghdad to take similar sites around Kermānshāh. Meanwhile the Russians marched on Tabriz. There was little Iranian opposition to either the British or Russian forces.*

Johnny grunted, "Damn right."

Frankie sipped her coffee, wrapping her two hands around the cup, and listened to the war coming in through the wire like anyone else.

The announcer's voice went on, cataloging the fronts around the world. In Occupied France, twenty thousand German troops were searching Paris for suspects after a weekend of stealthy attacks on the occupying forces. German authorities threatened to shoot hostages if attacks continued. The citizens of Leningrad fought on. And then, Betty Bonney's cool lilt came dancing out of the radio, the light tone bolting into the room, singing "Joltin' Joe DiMaggio," high above the laughing trumpet's screech. Johnny Cripps stood and leaned across the counter to turn the radio off in disgust. "When are they going to send for us?" he muttered, sitting back down.

The man beside him shook his head. "They won't."

"Oh, we're going, all right," another declared.

"Well, I'm not," said his neighbor.

Around the thick boasts, the older men sat and stared into their mugs. The war? thought Frankie. The war was right here in the old men's silence. She felt the man named Harry listening beside her, one palm laid flat on the counter while he smoked.

"And what in the hell are we supposed to do anyhow about a couple thousand Jews rounded up in Poland?" the man on the other side of Harry erupted. "DeVoris won't even take them into his hotel down in Sudbury."

"DeVoris or Jameson. Neither of them will."

Frankie turned her head away and concentrated on her coffee.

"How do they get away with it?"

"No vacancy. That's all. There's never a vacancy for 'em."

"Anyway. It's their trouble. And the Krauts just killed those ones to make a point. Jews aren't the issue, it's all about territory. And there's been one kind of war or another in Europe since—"

"That's why we've got the advantage," someone broke in. "We haven't had our own war for eighty years."

"Sure we have. We just don't call it war. But there's always an enemy, you bet. Indians. Darkies. Polacks. Always someone to knock off the lip of the pot."

"You going communistic on us?"

"This time the Krauts'll bring the war here," Harry remarked quietly, looking straight ahead.

The group of older men looked up at him seated at the counter. He turned his head slowly toward them. A couple of them nodded, Frankie noticed. The others stared into their cups.

"I don't know, Harry. What about the Japs?"

"What about them?"

"Shouldn't we worry about them?"

"Hell, let President Roosevelt worry about them," Harry shot back. "The Japs are way the hell over on the other side of the world. I can't worry about the Japs. The Krauts are already in the Atlantic. I'd say we'll be headed into their guns long before the Japs get around to reading Roosevelt's papers. I'm worried about what I can see is a clear danger to us, here."

Frankie caught the glance thrown between Johnny and one of the other younger men.

"But Harry, don't you think it'd be better to just wait until we know what the real news is?"

"When the Germans come they will simply come, and there won't be an announcement."

He was the kind of man men listen to, but Frankie could see that they didn't want to listen to this. It defied reason. It defied imagination.

"How can you be so damn sure?"

"I can't," Harry answered.

One of the men who had been shaking his head during Harry's point about the Japanese snorted.

Harry shrugged.

"You'd be better off paying attention to what's happening over *there*," Frankie said, as evenly as she could, "where Jews are being rounded up, moved out of their homes—not in thousands"—she tipped her head toward the man who had spoken—"in tens of thousands. Floods of people walking. A sea of bodies, moving, waiting in lines, pushing up against the doors of consulates and embassies—everywhere. Masses moving and nowhere to go."

"But, plenty of them are getting out—hell, I read a story just the other day about a group of 'em making it all the way to—"

"It's too late." Frankie cut him off. The man beside her shut up. "It's too late for most of them. And now they're trapped and it's going to get worse and worse. There are SS killing squads walking into Russian towns and gathering Jews—murdering them all." She got up off her stool. "And over here, you've been sitting on your hands."

"Horseshit," Johnny muttered.

Shaking, Frankie glanced at Harry. She hadn't meant to speak. She opened her pocketbook to find some change for the coffee.

"You were over there?" Harry asked.

She nodded.

"Where?"

"All over. London mostly." Frankie slid some coins in front of her coffee cup, aware of the men watching her, the room stilled.

"Doing what?"

"Reporting." Frankie stuck out her hand. "I'm Frankie Bard."

Harry whistled. "Harry Vale." He took her hand and shook it.

"You that girl on the radio?" Johnny pushed in.

She nodded.

"Here for a stay?"

"Few days," Frankie said.

"Going to do a radio piece on us?"

"Got anything to tell?" Frankie asked coolly.

The men around Johnny chuckled. Frankie turned back around on her stool. The café talk began again. She sipped her coffee. It was one thing she hadn't banked on—in fact, could have had no way of knowing. She had never heard her own voice come across on a radio, had no idea what she sounded like, or the impression she had made. Last week, she had heard Murrow coming straight through the wires into a store in New York and out the open doors into the street where she was passing, and it stopped her dead in her tracks. She knew the studio he sat in at that moment, knew exactly how he cupped the base of the microphone with two hands like a child, knew that he spoke with his eyes closed so he could hear his own beat, and there he was on a sunny August afternoon, blaring into the crowd. But she wasn't prepared for people listening to her that way, knowing her voice.

"So, what would you put the odds at a U-boat landing over here?" Harry asked.

"Is that a real question?"

He rested his eyes on her face. "Suit yourself."

She shook her head. "I don't buy it. Now that they're in Russia, they'd be fighting too many fronts."

If she had disappointed him, Harry didn't show it.

"Do you have cards?" A man too old for service stood in the doorway, thick blond hair snaking beneath his cap in loose long curls. He moved easily into the café, the floorboards creaking under his shoes;

he stopped in front of the cash register, resting his hands lightly on the counter, looking into the rows of coffee mugs on the shelf behind Betty's head.

"What kind of cards you looking for?" she asked.

"To play."

He spoke with a German accent. In a bowl below the cash register there were boxes of matches and playing cards. Betty Boggs reached down and pulled out a deck of the new spotter cards, marked with the silhouettes of German bombers, placing it on the counter for the man to see. He picked the box up. "These?" He frowned.

"That's what I've got."

Frankie and the men watched as he turned the box over and examined the back. Messerschmitt Me-110 German Bomber, it said under the black curve of the warplane's underbelly. Next to the seven of diamonds stretched the silhouette of the same plane from head on, as if it were flying low and about to drop a bomb. He took his time looking, but Frankie sensed he knew every eye in the place rested on his back.

"Do you want the cards, then?" Betty asked him quietly.

The man looked at her. "Yes," he said. "I want the cards," and he put a quarter on the counter.

"Thank you." She nodded and walked away from him to the cash register down the counter. Then she stood there, her hands on either side of the register, waiting for him to leave. He didn't linger, and Frankie watched him step off the curb in front of the café and cross the street.

"Who's that?" Frankie asked.

"Some kind of Kraut." Johnny winked at Frankie. "So you watch yourself."

"What do you mean?" Frankie said tightly. The sly excitement in Johnny Cripps's voice was hateful, a bully's know-it-all.

"He's not from here," the man beside Johnny explained. "He's named Schelling. And he's been here since spring."

"Now he's painting Doc Fitch's house, bright as the sun. You worried about that, Mr. Vale?" Johnny frowned. "It sticks out now, awful bright."

If she could just close her eyes, Frankie thought wildly, and steady herself, she could ignore what felt like a flock of birds suddenly lifting in her chest. Just like that, the doctor's name had been tossed out into the air. She wasn't ready.

Harry shook his head.

"Why would you be worried?" Frankie asked, tightly.

"Krauts'll have a marker on the shoreline," Johnny tossed off. "A big white mark on the bluff overlooking town."

"You hear what Fitch's wife said about that in the market to Beth the other day?"

Harry looked around at Tom Jakes, standing at Johnny's elbow.

"Said she wants to make sure the doctor could find his way home."

"What?" Frankie said sharply, and leaned over to see the man talking.

"You hush up." Betty Boggs was fierce, setting the coffeepot on the counter. "You shut right up, Tom Jakes."

"What do you mean?" Frankie swallowed. "Where is Dr. Fitch?"

"London," Johnny offered.

"He went to help out during the Blitz," Betty Boggs said stoutly. "He took it awfully hard after Maggie died," she went on, almost to herself.

"How's Jim Tom holding up?" the man behind Harry asked.

"Better than any of you lot would be," Betty retorted. "He carries that little girl everywhere with him. But it's hard on his own like that with five little ones all in a row, even with his mother down the road."

Frankie slid off her stool and stood abruptly.

"Anyway," Betty nodded at Frankie, "Doctor Fitch ought to be back soon."

"Okay." Frankie concentrated on fastening the snap on her purse. "Okay, thanks."

"So long," Betty added, sweeping the coins Frankie left into her apron, but she smiled at Harry, pulling the circle closed.

Frankie pushed through the screen door and emerged back out on Front Street where the summer crowds ambled in and out of shops in the bright morning air, her blood pounding in her ears. The doctor was dead. The Blitz had been over for weeks. A man across the way caught her eye and lifted his hat. Frankie nodded and forced a slight smile. It was August. The doctor had been killed in May. He had *died*. She had seen him die. She lifted her head from the white patch of sun on the pavement and saw the German man who'd come in for the cards walking slowly in the direction of the post office and she followed after him, not really thinking what she was doing; she stopped at the post office stairs long after the man had disappeared into the gas station up the street. She'd never imagined she'd be the one walking into town with the news of the doctor's death.

For a long while Frankie stood where she was, looking up into the shadowy porch of the post office. She was here because she had a letter. It was as simple as that. There was a letter and she was meant to deliver it. She had carried it with her from London to Berlin and back again. She had moved it from the pocket of one skirt to another, across the European continent, across the ocean, up the East Coast, to here. It lay, as it had, against her cigarettes in the satin of her pocket. All she had to do was take it out and hand it over. Though, of course, she could simply mail it. She didn't need to tell Emma Fitch what had happened, did she? "Oh, for pity's sake," Frankie said angrily under her breath, and took the stairs two at a time.

There was a line in the post office and Frankie waited off to the side, by the mailboxes. It was peaceful in here, regular and calm, and the woman in charge stood in her window, proud as a figurehead on the prow of a ship.

"Good morning," Iris said. She brought the canceling stamp down on three letters in a row with a satisfying thump, then turned and tossed what she stamped behind her in quick impatient flicks of her wrist. Frankie followed the envelopes winging silently over Iris's shoulder into the sacks, not wanting the order to stop.

"Hello," Frankie answered.

Iris nodded and went on with her work. When, after a little while, Frankie had neither come forward nor turned around and walked out, Iris looked up.

"Can I help you with anything?"

"Does everyone in town have one of these?" Frankie began, looking at the mailboxes in front of her and still not moving from where she stood in the middle of the lobby.

"Yes," Iris frowned. "Why do you ask?"

"Just wanted to know if that's how people here get their mail."

"Yes."

"And you are the postmistress?"

"Postmaster," Iris corrected her. "There's no such thing as a postmistress. Man or woman. It's *postmaster*."

"In England you'd be called a postmistress."

"You've been in England?"

"Yes." Frankie advanced slowly on the window. "I'm just back."

"Are you here for a while?"

"For a rest," Frankie answered.

Iris nodded, warily. The woman didn't seem capable of rest.

I have a letter, Frankie wanted to say. *Take my letter.* "Let me just make sure I've got this right—"

Miss James waited.

"Every single piece of mail goes through your hands?"

"Why?"

"All the news, all the word in town goes through here?"

"Just what exactly are you asking?" Iris asked, a little sharp.

Frankie shook her head. "I'm trying to understand something."

"Everything that has to do with this town comes through here, yes. That's how the Post Office Department works. That's how the whole bailiwick runs. Someone mails a letter and it goes through the system, gets sorted and sent and sorted again, and then is delivered where it ought to be."

"I see," Frankie said, exhausted. "So if a piece of news were to come here, you would see it? You're the first beach?"

"What beach?" Iris swallowed. "What news?"

"Anything. That someone had died, for instance."

"Who are you?"

"No one," Frankie answered. "A reporter."

"Are you writing a story?"

Frankie shook her head.

"No one has died," the postmistress said evenly.

The clock buzzed as it passed ten-thirty.

"All right," Frankie answered. "All right, so long."

A Plymouth rumbled past Frankie where she had halted at the bottom of the post office stairs. A blue Plymouth driven by a man in a hat. She watched it maneuver slowly along the hot street. Across the way a couple of the men from the café were sitting on the two benches. She stared at them. How *can* this be going on at the same time as that? Before her the town bunched and unraveled in the heat. She felt as dislocated as she had that morning Harriet had died, waiting for Billy, the little boy she had walked home, to turn around on his front step and look at her. *Home?* She remembered erasing those words in her head as she watched him understand that his mother was dead. She wasn't inside the house. She wasn't anywhere. *Home* was a word from another world, another language, where people woke and stretched and saw a clear sky out a bedroom window hung around with birds.

It was nearly eleven by the time she returned to her own cottage. Some of the bathers had come back already from the beach and were sitting out on the neighboring porches before lunch. She pushed open the door into the shaded interior and reached for the bottle of whiskey she had brought and a glass and drank it neat at the sink, still standing.

The doctor flipped into the air, and then the little boy smashed down into the crowd, and Thomas looked at her just before he was shot. Like a series of cards ready to fall, what had happened began toppling down the long passageway in front of her, the one falling and silently, surely, pushing the next over, then the next—tumbling in a line before her standing there at the sink, her legs trembling. She followed the images all the way to the nameless boy on the last train turning to find her before he disappeared on his way and clapped her hands over her mouth, leaning against the edge of the bureau with the final image in her head.

Behind her, the black bulk of the gramophone sat. She turned around and stared at it a minute. The disks from the trains lay wrapped in her satchel. She pulled one out and set it down gently on the turntable. Then she flicked the knob and the disk jerked and began to turn forward slowly. She hooked her pinky under the arm of the needle and nudged it carefully over and set it down. *Speak into here,* came her voice, *Say your name.* She sat down, and the faint drumbeat of train wheels, *ratata, ratata, ratata,* came through on the disk beside her. *Speak,* her voice came more softly. *Inga? Inga Borg,* the girl answered again, shyly. And her nervous, narrow face swum straight up before Frankie again. *I am Litman,* her brother's voice shot forward. Frankie closed her eyes, listening to the familiar pattern, through the girl, her brother, the man, to Thomas.

The needle skittered to the end of the disk and the *sh, sh, sh* spun around the little room. She sat up and pulled the arm off, flipped it over, and set the needle down on the other side.

There was the old man speaking in broken, halting English, *I looked and saw my wife there on the stairs. She was so—*he coughed, and Frankie heard herself murmur something to him—*wanted.* Frankie remembered the man had been sitting alone at the station. *They woke us up,* a woman explained in French, and *I had no time to get food for my boys. Your name? My name is Hannah Moser—*

The voices were old and young, soft and round, and rasping, brittle, thirsty. *Just like that,* her voice instructed somebody. They spoke languages Frankie didn't know, hadn't heard ever spoken, mountain Hungarian, Serb, Croat, thick tongues and slivering syllables peeling off into the air as Frankie listened through disk after disk. Three minutes to a side. Most said their names. There was a child who couldn't say it—every time she asked, he started and burst into fits of laughter, and Frankie's laugh was on there, too, go on, she'd giggle, try again, *Pet*— and then he was off.

She set the needle down on the last disk, the one she had recorded on top of what was already there, and the first seconds of sound—*Jaspar, I am, Greta, went looking for him, what is? The smallest house at the end of the block was marked but I, Ruth, Sebastian, am*—sprang out at her like some mad creature.

She sat there listening to the weird chaos of that last disk—*Hannah, I am, non, non j'ai dit, C'est quoi, ça? Ein Kartoffel. No!*—voice replacing voice, high and low and insisting one on top of the other. Human voices chasing each other into the air, only to be followed finally by the *shh shh* of the machine, as she listened to the silence overtaking the men and the women, the giggling children. She had ridden with them, she had stood in lines, she had watched them pass through doors and climb back on trains. *Merci, Mademoiselle,* they had said. *De rien,* she'd said. Just the month before last.

2 3.

THERE! THERE HE IS! THERE!

Frankie woke up, her heart slamming against her chest. Someone had been screaming, and after a minute she realized it was her. Her throat was sore and dry. She pulled her knees up under the covers, staring into the mirror over the bureau at the foot of the bed. A woman stared back at her whose white face seemed to have no eyes. Frankie blinked slowly twice and the woman's scattered face crept back into place. She slid her cigarettes and her lighter off the night table and pulled the pillow up higher behind her back, her heart still pounding.

She had the sense of having to climb a long way back up to the world. The shade hung still. The light in the room was softer. She looked over at the clock and saw she had slept far into the afternoon. She heard women's voices out on one of the porches and she lay there a little, with her eyes closed, listening without hearing what they said. She opened her eyes. All right. She swung her legs off the bed and stretched.

From the end of her bed she could see straight through the living room to the door onto the front porch, where someone was sitting in one of her chairs. She stood up quietly and went to the window, but the high back of the white slat chair kept whoever it was completely hidden. She pushed open the screen door.

The German man from the café rose from the chair. He pulled off his hat and nodded at her. He smelled faintly of turpentine.

"Hello." She was wary.

"Are you all right?"

"What do you mean?" She frowned.

"You were screaming."

She didn't answer.

"I heard you screaming." He looked at a spot on the door behind her head, as though to give her privacy. "From my ladder." He turned and pointed to the big house past the cottages.

"Come in, why don't you?" she said quietly.

"No." He dropped his gaze back down to her.

"All right," she said, and sank into one of the chairs, leaving him standing above her.

"You were frightened." He meant it as a question, she realized. And nodded. And pointed him into the other chair.

"It was a dream. A nightmare."

"From Germany?"

"What?"

"You were in Europe," he said. "That's what they are saying in town."

She nodded.

He sat down abruptly in the chair beside her.

"Did you just get out of Germany?" Frankie said quietly, her eyes on him.

"Austria," he nodded. "In April."

The worn fabric of his coat caught the afternoon sun in its sheen. His hands shoved in his pockets, bent forward, he might have been any one of the men who had leaned in to her microphone and said his name. He was so familiar, just then; he seemed more real than anyone she'd met since coming home.

She reached to touch the sleeve of his coat. "Come," she said to him. "I want you to hear something."

Without waiting to see if he followed, Frankie stood up and went inside, took the last disk off the gramophone, and searched through the pile to find the one with Thomas on it. Then she flicked the knob and the disk jerked and began to turn, slowly, forward. She hooked her pinky under the arm of the needle and nudged it carefully over and set it down toward the middle of the side.

Her voice came across first. *"Speak here,"* she said, *"speak into the machine."*

"Begin?"

There was a space on the recording where Frankie had nodded in answer. His voice came through a little stronger, as though he'd moved closer. *"I am Thomas Kleinmann. I come from Austria,"* and he cleared his throat, *"in the mountains a—"*

Otto had come inside and stood in the doorway. The two of them listened to Thomas's voice all the way to the end, Otto still standing, and when the disk ran out, Otto came all the way in, dropping his hat on the chair. He went over to Frankie, where he stopped, looking at the gramophone.

"There are more?"

She nodded. He sat down. Carefully, she flipped the disk to the other side and set the needle down. Then she brought the bottle and two glasses and sank down onto the sofa, and they listened past the second disk into the third and then the fourth. When the second side of that one finished, Otto stood, polite as a parson, lifting the arm off the disk, and replaced it with the next. And then the next.

I am not making these people up, Frankie thought, as voice after voice filled the room. Here we are. Here. *I am Marta,* a woman was saying. *I have just left Gurs.*

Otto bolted out of his chair, lifted the needle, and set it gently down again, and the woman's voice slurred out and caught itself, speeding forward in nearly flawless English—*I am Marta. I have just left Gurs.*

They opened the gates the day before yesterday, without any warning. One of the women in the nearest building ran to our block and said hurry, hurry, and four of us stood up and followed her. It was as though they had gotten sick of the whole thing—these women and children waiting, dying—they were sick of us and simply left the gate open. Let the Jews out. Cluck, cluck. Let the chickens go.

And then we were on the other side. In France. With a bundle of clothes and old papers. But I had long since stopped thinking that papers meant any-thing at all anymore, papers, train schedules, the promises from another life. Now it was food and sleep and clothing. That was all there was to pay atten-tion to—

There were so many women walking with me through the trees.

Her voice stopped.

Thank you, Frankie's voice slid out.

Otto didn't move. He stared at the disk going around and around, his head bowed, his hands hanging loose from the ends of his sleeves.

Frankie switched the knob on the machine to stop the disk, her heart pounding.

"My wife," he said finally. "She is there. At Gurs."

ACROSS THE TWO short lawns, where she stood in her kitchen win-dow, Emma dropped her hand. She had been about to knock. She had watched the two of them in the chairs, staring at the water in front of them, talking. She had watched long enough to want to break in, and she had lifted her hand when the woman had reached out and touched Otto, and now he looked as though he might break down. And the woman had not taken her hand from his arm. Emma felt a knock inside her, so strong and so sudden, it was like a visitation, like an angel come to say *Now*. She caught her breath. The woman filled her with a vague uneasy dread, sitting over there with her long legs and her scarf and sunglasses; now the two of them, their heads tipped toward each other, not speaking, seemed to her like the pictures of angels weeping, one in an overcoat, the other in a blouse, overlooking, understanding what was coming. What was coming to her.

Her eye rested on the framed photograph on the windowsill of her father standing behind her mother who was sitting in a chair, holding her. She reached toward it and picked it up. There *had* been someone who held her, someone who watched over her—here was the proof. She looked at the faces of her parents, turned away from the camera—and from her now—staring instead at their baby. She took a long breath. Beside the photograph of Will, taken at his graduation from medical school, she set her own down again. She turned the frames slightly toward each other, as though to introduce them. She looked back up. But the angels had left the porch.

For an hour, Emma watched out her window facing the cottage into which Otto had disappeared, as though whatever they did inside had somehow to do with her. As though, when they came out at last, they would come out with something for her.

But when the two of them did indeed emerge onto the little porch and Otto pointed out Emma's own house to the woman, Emma was suddenly frightened. She turned from the window and hurried down the hall to the front of the house, meaning to close the door, meaning to lock it, to go upstairs and sit on the bed and let them pass her by.

They were already coming through the gate at the bottom of the garden and, seeing her frozen behind the screen door, Otto waved.

"Emma!" he cried.

Go away! She wanted to shout back. *Go away.* Instead, she pushed open the screen door and stood watching the two of them come up the path toward her.

"Emma!" She had never seen Otto excited. "Emma, here is someone from over there. Here is someone who has been in France."

"France?" Emma looked at Otto blankly and then shifted to the woman who seemed stalled there at the bottom of her stairs. She looked ill.

"She has been there. She has records."

"Yes," Frankie said, her mouth gone dry. "Well."

"Tell Emma what you told me," Otto said to her.

Emma looked down at him swiftly. "About what?"

"There was a release of refugees out of Gurs." Frankie forced one word after the next. "Sometime last month."

Otto nodded up at Emma, urgent. "Hear?"

Emma frowned. "I don't understand."

"My Anna is not at Gurs, perhaps." Otto's excitement made Frankie look away. "That is why she is not writing letters. She is not there. And Miss Bard says she has recorded some of these women. There may be Anna in her machine," he pressed.

"Miss Bard?"

"Hello." The woman at the bottom of Emma's steps took a step closer. Her face was very white. "I am Frankie Bard."

Emma halted. She had been about to take a step forward. Frankie Bard was the voice on the radio. Not a living body in a white blouse and narrow skirt, appearing like this, out of the blue.

"How can that be?"

"How can what be?"

"You're over there."

"I'm over here, now."

Emma shivered.

All these months, when Frankie had pictured the doctor's wife, had imagined bringing her his letter, she had seen herself standing before her and giving comfort to someone terribly in need. Instead, here she was standing at the bottom of the doctor's stairs, facing a slight pregnant woman, whose stomach mounded from her small frame, like a matchgirl with a ball.

"When is your baby due?"

"Next month," Emma answered, cautiously.

"I ought to go," Frankie said quickly to no one in particular. "I am making you uncomfortable."

"Not at all." Emma flushed. "It's just you have always been on the radio. My husband and I used to listen to you together. We used to talk about your stories," she offered.

Frankie couldn't move. All she had to do was open her mouth and look at Emma and say the words—*I know. I know you did. I met him. I spoke to him*—and she couldn't. She could hardly breathe.

"The machine has people's voices on it," Otto broke in. "Emma, she can tell you what it's like there. She can tell us—"

"Okay"—Emma reached down and put her hand on Otto's sleeve—"okay, Otto. That's enough." She glanced down at the reporter who had crossed her arms tightly over her chest.

"Thank you, Miss Bard, I don't intend to be rude, but you see, I don't want to hear about it." Her voice skated rapidly, high and light. "It doesn't do me any good to hear about the attacks and the counterattacks, which Douglas bomber was lost where. I don't want to know what he may be going through. I mean I do, but I don't want—" She stopped. "I don't want any more news, Miss Bard," she finished quietly.

"Mrs. Fitch—"

"No." Emma stopped the reporter. "My husband is gone. And for weeks, I've had nothing from him, no word about him."

Frankie swallowed.

"So these days, I am concentrating," Emma said softly, "very hard. Every day, I am concentrating on keeping him alive. I close my eyes, Miss Bard, and I imagine where he is, and I imagine the harm that might be coming toward him, and I imagine it backward, the wall rising up off of him where he is buried, the glass that may have found him, put back whole. And I imagine him safe"—her voice trembled—"and sound."

She put her hand on the side of her belly, wincing as she walked slowly down the stairs past Frankie and Otto. Wordless, Frankie turned around and followed. At the end of the garden, Emma had stopped and was waiting with her hand on the opened gate, clearly waiting, Frankie realized, for her to go.

24.

IF FRANKIE WAS proud on any score, it was that she had always been
first up to tell the truth. She thought of herself as fearless—some kind
of Joan—brave, fiery, impassioned. Everyone had. All her life she had
pitched herself headfirst into the race. But she had traveled all this way
up here, walked right up to the doctor's door, opened her mouth, and
said nothing. She nearly laughed. The joke had been on her the whole
time. All the while Frankie was recording voices, looking into faces of
people whose endings she worried she'd never know, *she* was the ending. She was the ending coming for that small fierce woman next door.
She was the scissors. And she had thought she was the thread.

What had she imagined? If she handed Emma the letter and told her
the whole of what happened, the part leading up to the moment when
Will hadn't looked the right way (because that was the story, that was the
bit that stuck in the throat), somehow it would help? If. That was the heart
of it. If Will Fitch had not looked at the woman crossing, if he had not
been searching every face for Emma's, he might have looked the right
way and seen the taxi coming. *There! There he is! There!* If Frankie had
not shouted, Thomas might never have been found.

If.

She kicked off the blanket, too hot to sleep, and went into the front room of the cottage, pushing the windows up to catch the night breeze. The light in what must have been Emma's bedroom was on, a small yellow square high up in the dark night. Frankie turned from the window and switched the gramophone on. It didn't matter which disk she played; she set the arm down onto the record and turned off her own light.

We belong to a Federation of Cassandras, Martha Gellhorn had confided bitterly one night at the Savoy. And Frankie had looked at the older woman's face and thought, *not me.* The picture of the beautiful mad Cassandra, winding through the streets of Troy, calling *Listen! Listen,* banging her gong, was a caution, not a sign. But now her own words had flown, the proud brave words she thought she owned. Here she was, on a porch at the edge of the country—incapable of speaking, incapable of doing anything other than playing disks with someone else's voices on them, again and again.

Emma's light had gone off next door. Frankie nodded at the dark house. Incapable even of delivering the news.

For the next few days, Frankie's habits fined themselves down to single lines. She found herself in the old familiar state of restless dread, like the feeling before giving a broadcast, the hours of the day growing heavier and heavier until she could speak. She spoke to no one. She slept. She woke. She walked down into town to the café, and then, returning, hesitated at the gate of Emma's house. Most mornings Otto was up on the ladder, painting the north side of the house. In the afternoons she walked, heading out of town on the black tarmac and then cutting left and into the deep billows and tuffets. And Frankie fell into the deep silence of the hours and the dunes, like a bird fallen to the currents of the sky.

Now Time held its breath. The world was pushed back. As if nothing could happen and nothing had happened, Time tumbled on past the moment when Will had died and Thomas disappeared and the little boy walked away from Frankie through the gates; and somehow, in the silence, Frankie couldn't see her way backward—or forward.

The screen doors in the other cottages slapped open and shut, announcement and conversation all in one so that Frankie knew when she was alone and when she had the company of these familiar strangers. And the late light smudged the golds of sand and sun, so that that spit of earth, that ear curled into the harbor, floated in perpetual indecision between land and sea. The tide emptied and filled beneath the broad crisscross of clouds; the post office flag rose every morning exactly at seven-thirty above the roofline of the town, and fell every evening exactly at six. Leaning against the mirror on the bureau, the doctor's letter was the first thing she saw in the morning and the last thing as she turned her light off at night.

On the fourth day, Frankie crossed out of the dunes just as Emma was coming up the street on her way back home.

"Hello," Frankie waved, though it felt like her blood had turned to sand in her veins.

Emma waved back halfheartedly.

"I've decided to stay in town," Frankie offered, crossing the road between them and coming to a halt, her heart in her throat.

Emma nodded. "I can see that."

"I hope that's all right."

"Why wouldn't it be?"

Frankie didn't answer.

The doctor's wife leaned her hip against her closed gate and was studying her. "You're not as grand as I imagined."

"No?" Frankie reached for her cigarettes and shook the pack toward Emma, following with her lighter. There was the brief sizzle as the flame caught, and then the grateful intake of Emma's breath.

"On the radio, you come across as someone very tall. Taller than you are, anyway, and kind of "—Emma pushed her lip out—"impatient."

Frankie smiled.

"Were you scared over there?"

Frankie paused.

"I'm sorry," Emma said quickly. "I don't mean to pry."

"Christ," Frankie answered weakly. "Please—pry the lid right off."

"You never sounded scared," Emma mused.

"How did I sound?"

"I don't know. Indignant. And clear." Emma looked away. "And sometimes, happy," she went on softly, "like my husband."

All the breath rushed out of Frankie's body and she had to concentrate on Emma's face. "Happy." She swallowed.

"I'm sorry," Emma flushed, and pushed open her gate. "Sorry I've kept you. I said too much."

"No." Frankie cleared her throat. "Mrs. Fitch."

Emma turned, expectantly.

I don't want any more news, she had said. And now, again, looking straight at her, Frankie lost her nerve. "Not at all." She managed a smile. "You aren't keeping me at all."

Emma let her eyes rest on Frankie's smile and, after a minute, nodded. Then she turned and went slowly up the stairs into her house.

Her heart pounding, Frankie opened her own screen door, walking straight back to the bedroom, and stared at the letter. Her mind stalled, her mind spun and stalled. Every limb of her body had gone impossibly heavy. She couldn't pick up the letter. She could not kill him. She turned and left it there and went into the front room.

She had bet her career on a piece of advice Max gave her when she started: You told a story by letting the small things speak. You looked straight at it in order to *get* the picture, and then you had to keep looking straight to *give* it. The minute you looked away—into description, into metaphor of any kind—the thing collapsed, silently and completely, before you. But she was lost, every which way, on this one. She had blinked. She had looked away. And now she had no idea how to say what she had come to say. If there had been any good, there wasn't any now.

There might have been a time when she could have simply told Emma what happened, when she could have looked at her and given her the letter and snapped shut the gap in time. Will died, this is how, and where and when. Instead here she was, like an archer, pulling back the string, pulling it wide, and wider.

An archer? Frankie sniffed. She was a liar.

She sat like that, immobile as her heart slowed and the day crept forward.

In the cottage next door, someone flicked on the radio and the unmistakable thrill in the radio announcer's voice charged the air—"*has been captured. That's right! U-Boat 570 has been taken. On a routine mission south of Iceland, the German sub surfaced immediately below a Coastal Command Hudson bomber. We have word that the German commander has surrendered, and the submarine today is on its way to Iceland.*"

It was switched off. The door slammed open and a man in bathing trunks skipped down the steps into the sand, carrying an umbrella. The heat buzzed. A shaft of sun lazed through the window and lay along the table like a cat. It was a glorious, hot afternoon on August the twenty-eighth.

Frankie stared through the window as if she could see something, anything other than the sky. The sea. The white prows of boats. It was a three- or four-day journey by boat from Iceland here. For the first time, she wondered whether Harry Vale, sitting up in the town hall, might have the right idea. Were there U-boats in the ocean sliding toward them? The U.S. press corps was not under the government thumb, but she knew how easy it was to cushion the truth, and it had been so long since she had been entirely on the receiving end of the news that Frankie had forgotten what it was like to be outside the rumors, the buzz, the word passed from one correspondent to the next. Rumor and gossip, the steady talk of other reporters, people collecting the bits and pieces and handing them on somehow kept at bay this feeling that something could come from anywhere, any direction. Without the tiny scraps of word, without the others also watching, talking, parsing war, there was the feeling that anything could happen. Anything could come.

It was naptime along the road. Naptime at the end of summer. She could see the bodies lying in the sun far below on the harbor beach, and the still deep quiet made her hurry forward.

By the time she reached town, she knew who she wanted to see, and as she passed into the shade of the green, and out from under the trees into the open eye at the center, not looking up at the window, she suddenly wanted Harry Vale to be up there. Wanted him up there watching.

She pushed open the heavy door of the town hall and into the linoleum quiet. On the right, the door to the town office stood open; from inside there came a faint sound, like someone scratching or rubbing two boards together, and when she rounded the corner, the woman filing her nails looked up at her without missing a beat, the tiny sawing sound never pausing.

"Hello," Frankie began, "I wonder if you can help me find the way up to the watchmen?"

The woman had a round face, unfortunate for someone built so small. She put down her nail file. "What's that?"

"The men who run the Civilian Defense Unit, upstairs."

"You mean Harry?"

Frankie nodded. "Harry Vale."

The woman tipped her chin in the direction of the hall behind Frankie. "Up the stairs," she pronounced.

"Thank you," said Frankie, turning to go. "Is he up there now?"

The woman regarded Frankie and gave an elaborate shrug, as if she sat behind a desk upon a stage. "If I knew that," she smirked, "it'd ruin the secret."

"What secret?"

"You could be a Kraut," the woman suggested, picking her nail file up

again. "And I don't want to give anything away, one way or the other."
She gave Frankie a broad smile.

"If I were a Kraut," Frankie observed, "you'd be dead."

"Hey," said the woman, the dull thick red pulsing into her round
cheeks. "No need to be nasty."

Nasty, thought Frankie, as she proceeded out the door and across the
round hallway to the stairs. You don't know the half of it. The silence
from the office behind her followed her out. By the time she had reached
the bottom of the stairs, the filing of nails had begun again, and she
heard the light tapping of feet resume. She took the stairs lightly, two
at a time, around and around and up. When she pushed open the door at
the very top, she was out of breath.

"Oh, it's you, Miss Bard," Harry Vale said, turning from his chair.

Frankie paused in the doorway. Harry Vale sat in a straight-back chair
at the center of the row of three windows at the near end of the attic.
The afternoon sun poured in, his figure silhouetted against the light. He
held a pair of binoculars in his hand, which he had lowered when she
appeared; turning slowly back to the window, he lifted them once again
to his eyes. He didn't rest his back against the chair, but sat slightly forward as if he were on drill. She observed a Bunsen burner tucked away,
and beside it a cot with its top sheet tightly tucked beneath a blanket.
And though it was the top of town hall, Frankie was under the strong
impression that Mr. Vale was prepared to live here. It had the spare vital-
ity of a tent—everything necessary, everything handy, though the wide
room stretched around them and the empty floorboards smelled like
the sea.

"May I?" she asked, crossing to sit on the chair beside his.

"Please," said Harry.

Frankie arrived at the windows and took in the wide-angle view of
the top story. The whole of the harbor, not just the center, was spread
before her, as well as the road into town. She could even see the ridge of

Emma's roof. From up here, Harry Vale could watch over them all with the unimpeded eye of a god.

"Well," she commented. "That's quite a view."

He nodded, staring straight out.

She pulled her cigarettes out of her pocket. The post office flag billowed wide above the roofs. Frankie lit her cigarette. "Is it true you want that pole down?"

"Where'd you hear that?"

"Café." Frankie exhaled.

"No one's got his eye on this water," Harry said slowly, "and this is how they'll come in."

"That what Civilian Defense says?"

"What I say."

"What does Civilian Defense say?"

"Horseshit, as far as I'm concerned."

"What does it say?" Frankie persisted.

"Says look up into the skies. Defense wants spotters in place, with their binoculars aimed straight up."

"You're pretty sure."

"You tell me, Miss Bard," he said, so gently it caught her off guard. "What did we fight the First War for?"

She turned to look at him. He returned her gaze easily. "Fair enough," she said to him.

"Hell," he said, "here we are all over again."

"Well—not exactly."

"You ever consider coming to speak to Civilian Defense?"

"Why?" She turned on him. "People would just as soon hear a lie as the truth. We should have been in there years ago, but no one gave a goddamn, though reports were clear."

He grunted agreement and walked to the other set of windows where he stood, binoculars raised, and stared out. He was on a schedule,

Frankie realized. It made her want to cry. This single-minded brave idea of order. This man, raising his arm with the same precise angle to the sea each time he stopped to look. This hand and that head working singly and without distraction, bent on getting on.

"Let me ask you something. What were you hoping for, being over there?"

"An end." Frankie was relieved to divert the conversation.

"To war?"

"Yes," Frankie answered, nettled. "Well, no. I wanted it to begin, actually."

"How the hell did you think you could do that?"

"The more people knew, the more they could see—see what had to be done."

"Bull." He shook his head without turning around. "No one here can see around the edges of the photos, or whatever story you try to tell about it, into a war—into what lies there."

"What does lie there?" she asked softly.

"Accident."

She waited.

"*Chance's strange arithmetic*," he recited quietly. "Wilfred Owen."

She drew in her breath sharply.

Harry picked up his binoculars.

"Jesus." Frankie stared.

He shrugged. "We can't change what's coming. Something is always coming."

"Is that supposed to be a comfort?"

He grunted and sat down in the chair. "It's all there is."

His stomach mounded over his lap, and his sweater was taut around it. She watched him watching, and then she turned in her chair and looked at the water, which spread like a picture away from the town. And she was oddly comforted. This man brought back Will Fitch, sitting beside her—*All you are is a voice and a pair of hands*. She had turned on the doctor in the dark, turned to stop the flood of his relief coming at her, his relief and his joy. Now, in his town, she sat there, quietly. Was he right? The first of the bands started up, calling evening on. Schoolboys gathered and lounged against the post office gate, one of them throwing a stone against the wood. And throwing it again. And again.

Now the boys had arranged themselves in a casual firing squad, pretending to take shots at something she couldn't see at first, until she pulled forward in her chair. And then she stood straight up without a word to Harry Vale and ran for the stairs, taking them two at a time, her hand sliding down the banister for balance. Past the second floor, down onto the first floor where the clack of the typewriter paused and then resumed as she burst past and pushed through the heavy door. Two of them ambled after him, following Otto up the street. Frankie ran across the green toward the rest of the boys who were still standing with their arms raised, aiming at his back with their fingers.

"Goddamn it!" she shouted at them. "What do you think you're doing?"

They went dumb. Their arms slack.

Her heart was pounding so hard, she could hardly speak. "You little *shits*," she spat. "You goddamned *little shits*." She looked up the street toward Otto who had stopped at the sound of her voice and turned around, seeing for the first time the boys who had been tailing him.

"Get out of here"—she turned back to the boys—"and if I see that again, I'm going straight to the police."

One of the boys grinned and looked down.

"What's funny?" Frankie was aware of Otto coming back toward her.

Another boy looked up.

"What the hell's so funny?"

"My dad's the policeman," the first boy hooted, and they all took to their heels, laughing, leaving Frankie where she stood, struck dumb by rage. Otto stopped in front of her.

Frankie looked up. "You all right?"

He shrugged.

Beth Alden, the grocer's daughter, had come out of the market and stood in the open doorway watching them.

"Otto," Frankie whispered, "why won't you tell them?"

"What should I tell them?" he commented quietly.

"That you're Jewish." Frankie kept her voice as even as she could. "That your wife is over there."

He raised his head and looked back at the market.

"Otto," she prodded.

He shook his head. "I won't tell anybody anything anymore."

"But people don't understand. They don't understand who you are."

Otto raised his eyes and met Frankie's. Her heart was beating very fast. He looked at her a long time.

"So?" He raised his voice only slightly, but the fury pealed out. "Tell? Who should I tell? How? I should stand up in the park there?" He jabbed a finger at the town green. "Stand up on a platform? Tell everyone—*Ich bin Jude!*"

"All right!" she said, but he stepped away from the hand she reached out. He turned away and started walking fast, without running, out of town. She stood and watched him up the street, where he stopped at last and turned around. He stopped and stared at her and then he went on walking.

Frankie blinked, as if coming out of a trance.

"Miss Bard"—the postmistress had come out from the shade of the porch—"there's mail in here for you."

"Did you see that?" Frankie turned to her.

"What?"

Frankie was so angry she couldn't speak. She walked over to the bottom of the post office stairs. "Those boys," she spat. "There were boys pretending to shoot Mr. Schilling in the back."

"No"—Iris shook her head—"I didn't." The heavy doors thudded shut behind Iris as she vanished back inside.

"Christ." Frankie put her hand on the railing just to hold on for a minute. She made out Otto turning the corner at the end of the next block, then turning into the garage. "Christ almighty," Frankie breathed.

25.

WHEN SHE PULLED open the doors and walked through into the empty lobby, the postmistress was in the window. From the door, Frankie watched as she brought the canceling stamp down on three letters in a row with a satisfying thump, then turned and tossed what she stamped behind her in quick impatient flicks of her wrist. Easy, efficient, absorbed in her work, the postmistress was completely in charge. Frankie followed the envelopes winging silently over Iris's shoulder into the sacks. "Have you ever missed?"

"Never." Iris didn't look up.

"Never once? That's not possible."

"Sure it is. Look at Joe DiMaggio."

She glanced up then and grinned. Frankie walked in.

"There are moments, though," the postmistress conceded, "when I do think about the letters that miss. I wonder whether they ought to— whether I ought to leave them where they fall."

"You're joking."

"I'm not," Iris replied calmly, opening the stamp drawer.

"Have you ever," Frankie probed, "acted on that? Just let a letter be—"

"Never." Iris snapped the drawer shut, but Frankie saw that the thought had crossed her mind, if fleetingly.

"How did you come to be postmistress, if you don't mind my asking?"

"I passed the test."

"What sort of test is it?"

"The postmaster's test?"

Frankie nodded.

"Sums and differences," Iris answered. It was a block. One did not, Frankie felt sure, become postmistress by being merely good at math.

"You like being in charge?"

"Are you interviewing me?" Miss James returned.

Frankie shook her head. "Just curious."

"Yes." Iris regarded her. "I like making sure everything stays on track. I like things in their place."

"But it's more than keeping everything on track, isn't it? The whole town moves through here. You hold all the strings on your fingers, like a giant game of cat's cradle."

"That's what they think," Iris replied mildly.

"Who does?"

Iris tipped her chin in the direction of the town. "They want to believe that I'm in here keeping tabs on them—that because I see what comes to them, I'm somehow able to change things. Make things happen."

"Maybe it's only that they hope you're watching."

"Watching what?"

"Watching over them." Frankie shrugged. "Watching their lives."

Miss James raised her eyebrow and walked back into the sorting room. Frankie waited for her to come back.

"*Are* you watching?" Frankie asked.

"I beg your pardon?"

Frankie changed tacks, slightly embarrassed by the wistfulness she had heard in her own voice. "Well, think of all of the secrets you hold in your hands."

"I don't hold a goddamned thing in my hand but the mail," Iris replied, setting down a thick stack of newspapers and a letter in front of Frankie.

"But think of it. Something could be diverted, or stopped, and it would be your hand that fixed it, your hand that set the story going again. You're like a good narrator." Frankie paused, noting the flush rise in Iris's face. "Or even, the author. You could choose who gets their mail and who—"

"Even if I could, I wouldn't, Miss Bard." Iris cut her off. What did the reporter want? Why was she in here with her probing and her questions? "It goes against every single thing I hold dear."

Frankie held her gaze. "Like what?"

"Order," Iris answered. "Calm. Each thing in its place."

"Sounds nice." Frankie leaned on the counter. "Sounds sweet."

"Nothing sweet about it." Miss James lifted her head swiftly and stared at Frankie. "And you can take that high-and-mighty right out of your voice."

The postmistress stared down at Frankie, impassive and watchful as a Madonna on a wall. Without warning, Frankie felt tears starting in her chest. "Miss James—"

"When a person writes a letter, they take a pen in their hand and write down what they need to onto a page. They put it in an envelope. They stamp it. And they bring it in to me." Frankie raised her eyebrows, but Iris continued, paying no attention. "They hand it to me and I forward it. I put it in the mailbag. Mr. Flores takes it to Boston. From there it's sorted and sent all over the country, or the world. That letter. That letter is what the whole thing is based on."

"What whole thing?"

"All of it." Iris slowed, the effort of saying it aloud making it hard to breathe. "There is an order running beneath us, an order and a reason, and every letter sent, every goddamned letter sent and received, proves it. Something begins, something finishes. Something is sent, something arrives. Every day. Every hour. As long as there are letters—"

"Horseshit." Frankie broke in swiftly. "It's you, Miss James, not some high-flying order, not some reason. It's just us down here, doing our jobs."

"You don't believe that." Iris was terse. "I don't think you really believe that."

"You don't know the first thing about what I believe."

Iris turned around and pointed to the black radio humped on the shelf above the mail sacks. "I listened to you last month on that thing, telling me to pay attention. I stood right here and heard your voice through there and it told us what we ought to do, in the face of it all, was *pay attention*."

"Okay." Frankie swallowed.

"What the hell are we paying attention for? Why else would we be watching?"

Frankie held her breath.

"It's nothing different in here. Watching out. Paying attention all the time, and then sounding the horn."

"Paying attention to what?"

"Mistakes." Iris answered swiftly. "Cracks. In the machinery."

"Machinery?"

Iris studied the reporter. "Do you remember the story of Theseus?"

"Theseus?" This caught Frankie by surprise. "The Greek hero?"

Iris nodded. She wanted to quash the woman before her some-how, make her see. Make her take her tiresome, provoking questions elsewhere.

"Go on." Frankie exhaled.

"When Theseus sailed off to war, he promised his father he'd return under white sails if he was alive. And every day, all the years his son was gone, the king climbed the cliff to watch for the sails and saw nothing. Every damn day for years."

She stopped, not looking at Frankie. She had been told this story, long ago in school, and it had been the worst thing she'd ever heard.

"And then, one day, there were sails. Coming over the horizon. There were the sails indeed, after years of waiting. After years."

Frankie waited.

"But the sails were black. Black as grief. So the father, the king, walked off the cliff to his death in the rocks below, while his son sailed forward, triumphantly, his promise forgotten." Iris flushed. "Why didn't someone on the ship look up and notice the mistake? Theseus could have fixed it. If only he had known."

Frankie stared back at the postmistress, an idea creeping dimly forward.

"I've never gotten over the waste of that accident," Iris said quietly.

"But the story knew."

"I beg your pardon?"

"The story"—Frankie nodded, still not quite sure what she was saying—"*it* knew. The story wouldn't have mattered without the mistake. If Theseus had remembered to change the sails, the thing wouldn't have been told. The story would have ended, as they all do, with the hero's triumphant return. But that mistake made the story. That mistake *is* the story. That's why it's told."

Iris stared. "You can't really be so coldhearted."

"It's a myth, Miss James," Frankie went on, exhausted. "Mistakes happen all the time."

"Do you think I don't know that?" Iris turned, her voice shaking, and pointed to the sorting room. "Every minute—every second of every minute," she corrected, "there is the chance in there for something to go wrong."

"But it doesn't because of you, is that it?"

"It does. Things go wrong all the time, but I catch them. And when I do"—Iris leaned forward on the counter—"when I do, Miss Bard, I realize that I have been *allowed* to catch them. Every mistake, every accident, every bit of chance caught—is a look at God. It is God looking at us."

"Sure it is," said Frankie, gathering the newspapers in front of her, the blood high in her cheeks. She almost made it to the door. Something loose that had been flapping in the back of her mind caught hold. The talk was fine. The talk was cheap, wasn't it—here, a million miles from where Will Fitch had been hit by a taxi, where Thomas had been shot in front of her, where every day people were dying—real people ripped out of their lives, their bodies blown to bits, shot up and left to cry. She turned around.

"Listen to me," Frankie began. "A few months ago, I was sitting on a bench with a mother and her baby. It was a lovely spring day. There was a dog. *Dog*, said the baby to his mother—"

"Miss Bard—" Iris interrupted.

But Frankie kept right on going, staring at Iris, daring her to stop. "*That's right,* the mother said. *Dog*, he said again. She nodded. *Let's go then, shall we? Go*, said the baby. *Right*, said the mother. *Go*, smiled the baby and then the sirens went off and we all looked up into the sky. It was daylight. It was noon. They were bombing at noon—there must be some mistake, I thought."

"Miss Bard!" It was intolerable. Did the reporter think Iris didn't know about horror? About anguish?

"There was that one last moment," Frankie went right on, "and then I began to run in the direction I was facing, I don't even recall that I saw anything, for all I remember I could have run with my eyes closed, like a mole nosing toward some dim memory of an opening I had passed coming to the park—a cellar? the tube? And I threw myself down into that hole just as the building on the side of the park where we had all been sitting split apart with a tremendous noise. The noise and then the afternoise—the mortar and brick and glass hurled high up, landing back down on the earth all over, with a thud and a shatter. Then came the screams. I climbed back up the basement stairs and the white dust from the building cascaded down like snow. I could hear people crying out. Someone opened a door. Someone called. I heard the steady raining down of dust.

"And through it, toward me, someone was walking steadily, as though she had walked from Scotland and walked through the bomb and was going to walk out the other side. That's what I remember thinking, the way she was walking, she seemed immortal. Then I saw that it was the mother from the park, her baby in her arms tucked up tight. She was whispering in his ear as she walked through the others slowly picking themselves up, whispering over and over, the baby's face turned up to her, his blood running down the mother's skirt and blouse. *Darling darling darling* she was saying into the baby's ear."

The postmistress slapped both hands down on the counter so hard that Frankie felt the wood jump. "Stop it," cried Iris swiftly. "Stop it! Damn it all. Why can't you stop?"

Frankie blinked, her mouth closing over the end. Her round eyes roved and seemed to rest on the calendar behind Miss James's head as though she were picking her way carefully, slowly back, rock by rock across a stream.

"Because it happened," she said, and quietly, quickly as she could, made it across the lobby and through the doors.

The door thunked after the woman, and Iris stood where she was for several minutes. She stood stock-still and closed her eyes. Bit by bit, sounds reemerged and she smelled the salt in the breeze as it shifted. She stood there, very quietly, to let her heart sink back to normal, to let the picture that that other woman had held and shaken in front of her fade.

For Iris had seen it, she had seen the mother's face, the eyes frantically searching for help even as she walked straight ahead, whispering into the small dying ear. *Darling, darling, darling.* Iris covered her mouth. She had seen them so clearly on the waves of that woman's voice. That same voice she'd listened to on the radio and turned off when it got to be too much. The clock ticked again. The *tap tap* of someone's heels. The wind again. Iris turned around to the sorting room. Two sacks of mail waited where Flores had dropped them. There was the kettle on the hot plate. There was the shade pulled before the blinding slant of afternoon light.

But there she was also, her own hand slipping a letter into her pocket. There she had stood at the table in the back room and cheated Time. *Pay attention.* Every single word she had just fired at the reporter she believed to the core of her soul. And yet she had slipped a letter out of the machinery she so proudly tended. *The story knew.* Iris looked down at the stamp drawer. "Why did none of Theseus's sailors notice the mistake and call out to their captain?" she had asked her teacher, bewildered.

"That's the sorrow of the story," the teacher had gently answered. "They simply didn't. And Fate would have it that the father would see."

"But, who is Fate?" the child Iris had persisted, but her teacher never answered.

26.

LIKE A PENCIL line drawn between the beginning and the end of the beginning, on the eleventh of September, Roosevelt announced that the U.S. Navy would escort convoys of American merchant vessels across the Atlantic, shooting on sight any German raiders. Now the U-boats, who ran in wolf packs, would run head-on into the navy. And Russia, God bless her, refused to fall. *When you see a rattlesnake poised to strike, you do not wait until he has struck before you crush him*, Roosevelt warned.

The summer people climbed into their cars and snaked in a long line back to Boston and New York. Children pulled their kneesocks on and went to school. The tea dance players, knickknack shopkeepers, and café owners walked to the beach and lay there, falling asleep in the last of the sun. The holiday was over though the sky overhead still shone. Tourists gone, pockets fuller, the winter ahead could rock on the runners of one of the best summers Franklin had had since the Depression. And the post office inspector had denied Harry Vale's request, so the post office flag flying high above the town seemed to thumb her nose at the Germans, waving at those ships as gaily as a girl. The town was cast back to itself like a bare bone on the sand, and the reporter stayed.

"What *is* she doing here, do you think?"

"Who?"

"The radio gal." Iris pointed her cigarette in the direction of Frankie's cottage, where Frankie's bicycle leaned against the back. Harry turned around in his chair and looked across the three cottage lawns that separated them.

"Resting. That's what she's said."

Iris nodded, unconvinced. "Tough to be a war correspondent without a war."

"I think she may have quit."

Iris shook her head. "Not that one."

Harry raised his eyebrow. "How do you know so much about her?"

"I don't. I don't know anything, that's what worries me."

"She's shell-shocked," Harry said.

Iris frowned over at him.

"Iris." Harry reached across and took her hand. "What could she possibly have come here for other than what she says?"

Iris pushed up out of the chair, down the steps, and to the end of the tiny patch of lawn halted by the scraggy beach roses before the sea. Frankie Bard was a messenger. With something hidden away. She was sure of it.

SEEN FROM ABOVE, Frankie thought, letting the door slam after her, it would be impossible to tell whether this woman walking out every day, hesitating at the gate of the Fitch house, and continuing on into the dunes, had any stake at all in the world other than in holding this pattern, sleeping, eating, waking, walking out.

Late afternoon had climbed up the rod of the sky and hung there, the air clear and sharp, the blues of the water and the sky playing against each other, reflecting and resisting like sisters. She had set on the path that led through a grove of beech trees into the dunes behind town, and the sun bore down through Frankie's blouse as though curious. Someone was ahead of her in the curved hollow the bent trees made; she saw that it was Emma, walking without any interest in what she passed, as though someone had told her it would be good for her, and she obliged.

After a bit, Emma turned. "Oh," she said, putting some enthusiasm into her voice. "Hello."

"Hello," Frankie answered and caught up. "How're things?"

"Well enough," Emma said, her eyes ahead of her.

"That doesn't sound too good."

Emma didn't reply.

"May I walk with you a little?"

The tawny flank of the dunes appeared at the end of the tunnel of trees. It looked hot through there, and they walked slowly in single file for about twenty minutes, Frankie behind Emma, through the sand hills to the sea. When they reached the edge of the dune, Emma slid herself heavily down the dune cliff to the beach below, sliding and skidding all the way down to the beach, where she lowered herself onto the sand. Frankie followed and came to a rest standing above Emma who lay with her arms spread out on either side.

"Go on," she said, peering up at Frankie standing above her. "Lie down."

"In the sand?"

"Yes." Emma smiled for the first time. "Stretch out. You can't hear the waves any other way."

"I hear them just fine."

"Lie down," coaxed Emma and closed her eyes.

Frankie stood awhile longer and then, not looking down at the pregnant woman stretched on the sand, she squatted and dropped to her knees, lowering her bottom slowly. Then she stretched her legs out, keeping them together, and lay back. She closed her eyes. Immediately, she felt the wind shift above her, flowing over her rather than at her shoulders and back. It made her feel welcome somehow.

The sea still rolled and burst. The wind washed along her skin, the cool sand pricking the backs of her knees, Emma's breath rising and falling beside her. Frankie lay there, the surf lazing in and out. The little breeze shifted and touched.

"Can I ask you something?" Emma said, finally.

"Shoot."

"That little boy you walked home after the bombs one night—"

"Billy." Frankie looked over at her.

"The boy who lost his mother. You said he fell to his knees when he realized she had died."

"He did."

"And then what?" Emma waited. "What happened?"

"I don't know."

Emma was quiet. "Weren't you worried? Didn't you want to know if he was all right?"

"Sure I did. Of course I did," Frankie sighed. "But I never saw him after."

Emma didn't answer right away.

"So you could only see what's going on in pieces."

"As compared to what?"

"How it all goes together." And now she started to talk almost to herself, as if Frankie weren't there. "There are signs all the time. Things that repeat, things that overlap. Things you can't explain, but refer to each other." Emma was sitting. "Maggie Winthrop dying like she did, for instance, and Will taking it to mean that he ought to go to England, as though it were a sign. When she was sick already, she must have been—" Emma stopped, remembering Frankie across from her. "And now you see, they're both gone and it's me who's pregnant. There's a line between them, and it has occurred to me lately that I ought to understand that, see? They're both gone. The one led to the other, and something else leads out of this. Oh God, I'm tired," she sighed. She hadn't said aloud the real sign, the clear signal that had come through last month in the shape of a pair of overalls.

"Listen." Frankie reached over and touched Emma's hand. "It all happens very fast over there—you're in a bar and then you're outside and then you're inside and there's the boy and you walk him home and then you're home and—there isn't a line between them at all."

"But there is, there must be." Emma shook her head. "What about all those people?"

"What people?"

"I hear their voices sometimes at night, coming from your cottage. Otto says they are the people from France."

"Yes."

"You brought them back and played them—for Otto."

Frankie looked at her, helpless in the face of Emma's logic.

"Who else in this town needed to hear those voices more than Otto?" Emma asked softly. "Tell me that."

Frankie shook her head.

"What are you going to do with all those records?" Emma asked.

Frankie turned her head.

"All those people."

"I don't know," Frankie answered quietly.

"You ought to let them go," Emma told her. "You ought to let everyone hear them."

"Yeah?" Frankie challenged. "Why? Who around here wants to hear?"

Emma took a long time to answer. Frankie waited, her eyes fixed on Will's widow.

"Listen." Emma glanced at her, and looked away. "I don't know anything about what you do, Miss Bard. But I do know you told me a story about a boy I couldn't shake."

"Okay." Frankie watched Emma.

"You made the war come alive."

Frankie lay down in the sand.

"He was alive, because you were so"—Emma searched—"broken. Your voice was so sad."

Frankie looked straight up into the soaring blue cap of the sky.

"Those people on the trains talked to you." Emma stopped. "They must have told you their names and answered your questions because they wanted you to do something—pass them on, somehow."

Frankie stood up without a word and walked straight down to the water, coming to a stop with the tips of her shoes in the lip of the surf, and for a crazy half-minute Emma thought she was going to start swimming; instead, Frankie opened her mouth and what came out of her body was a wordless cry. Of pain or rage, it was impossible to tell.

Emma lay down again and closed her eyes, her heart pounding, that sound echoing in her ears. Keening. That's what that was. *And the little boy dropped to his knees.* There was a country of mourners, a country like sickness, unimaginable to the healthy, and Emma knew she was going there. Her heart banged against her ribs, and then it wasn't her heart, it was her baby pounding hard inside her.

She rolled onto her side to cushion the baby's kicks and the sand on her cheek and the salt brought back Will the second-to-last morning when they'd come out here *so they could make some noise*, he'd whispered; and his lips on hers were warm and his touch opened her lips under his and she could feel the opening all throughout her body. She had smiled against his mouth and cast off into the tide, letting herself be pulled down into the sand, feeling it shift and mold around her, her duffel coat buffering the cold. Behind the horizon of Will's head, the morning sky arched over her and its blue unblinking stare held hers. And as he sank into her with a groan, she had imagined God looking down and smiling on the bird they made, beating frantic rhythms rising into air.

When she sat up, Frankie wasn't in sight. The sky was tipping at the top of the afternoon and the sandpipers had grown bold again and skittered on the widening beach right next to her. The surf rolled forward and the wave coming in recalled a giant's hand, the white knuckles of surf drumming, the fingers tapping, tapping and pulling back.

Just beyond the edge of the breakwater, the gray outline of a battleship overlapped with the smaller, sleeker point of a cruiser alongside. Somewhere, far beyond these two, she knew several more wheeled and turned, practicing maneuvers. The cruiser pulled free of the hull of the battleship and the white plume of its wake appeared to her stark as a knifecut on the blue water. She turned and saw Frankie sitting on the top of the dune path, watching over her. There was the bowl of light and sky arching overhead; a peeper crossed by. Frankie stood up, and the up and down of her body stood like a signpost at a crossroads in the middle of a desert. Here, the reporter's body said to the sky, the sea, the woman below her on the sand, here.

"Come on," Frankie waved.

Climbing up from the bottom to the top of the dune was like climbing up a waterfall, having to dig into the sand even as it fell away under her weight. Just below the lip, Emma looked up, and it was as though she climbed out of a hole into the sky.

They took a few steps into the duneland and the sound of the surf fell immediately away, giving over to the hum of trucks and the train arriving on its harbor tracks. When they reached the middle ridge of the dunes, they could see both bodies of water ahead and behind, the sea lying blue there beyond the triangle of houses and here running into the plat of sand.

Emma might have liked to say something to Frankie, something large to show that she understood the cry Frankie had let loose on the water. Something, anything at all. She might have liked to touch her, gently, too, though she did not. She walked beside her, side by side, in quiet.

They emerged onto the town road from the dune path at the edge of the evening, and the windows and glass doors shot back the sinking light. Her eyes picked out the row of cottages at the very end of the road and then, by relation, her own roof. "Hang on," she said.

Frankie straightened and turned around. Emma was staring down the road to her house where Harry and Iris sat on the porch, clearly waiting.

If she didn't walk any closer, Emma thought, if she turned around and slipped back into the dunes, if she made her way all the way back across the sand and to the edge of the water, and started swimming, she could swim to him and find him and make what they had to say not true.

"I've got you," Frankie promised, and she took Emma's hand in hers.

27.

THEY HAD ALL been so gentle with her. Frankie, Miss James, and Harry. When she had risen the three steps to the porch where they waited with the news, she had stumbled, and Harry had walked to her. Come on, he had whispered, come on, put your arms around me. And she had looked up into his face and seen it. She had been so tired. But he smelled of axle grease and Old Spice and leather, and she raised her arms and let herself be carried into the house like a child. He laid her down on the sofa, calling her dear, and tucked the blanket around her, watchful as any mother.

A telegram had come. There had been a mix-up. Dr. Fitch had been hit by a taxi on May 18 and buried in Brompton Cemetery on the twenty-eighth. Deepest Regrets. And then Miss James had put the letter in Emma's hand.

"Dr. Fitch wanted me to give it to you, if he . . ."—Iris flushed— "when he died."

Emma sat there on the sofa between Harry and Iris and looked down at the envelope. *Emma*, it said. As though he were in the next room, calling. *Emma*.

Frankie wanted to stand up, but she was afraid to in case Iris stood up also and left. Emma slit open the envelope and pulled the letter out.

All the breath rushed out of Frankie's body, and she rose and made her way blindly down the hall where the breakwater lights blinked at her through the kitchen window a long way across the scuffed water. She walked to the window and stood, her mind stalled, her mind spun and stalled. Frankie leaned over to the counter and pulled the cord on the kitchen lamp. She filled the kettle and put it on to boil. There were no cigarettes, and Emma was low on tea. She shook the last of it into the bottom of the china pot. The light from the Frigidaire slivered on the linoleum, and she pulled the bottle of milk out and poured it into the pitcher, holding the door open with her hip, then she slid it back in and slammed the handle shut. When the kettle blew, she poured the water and walked back into the front room with the tea things. The three of them hadn't moved from the sofa, though Emma had Harry's handkerchief in her hand.

Iris reached for the lamp and switched it on. Frankie sank down beside the table and poured the milk into the bottom of the mug and then rested the silver strainer over the rim and lifted the teapot and poured. The steam hit her chin, dampening it. She could feel Emma watching her.

Emma held out her letter to Frankie. "Read it."

"I can't read your letter." Frankie's voice shook.

"Please." Emma handed it up to her and Frankie took it.

Sweetheart, it began, *If you hold this in your hand, I will never hold that hand again.*

Frankie closed her eyes and lowered the letter.

"Did you finish?"

"I can't."

"Please, Miss Bard." Emma's voice caught. "That's him, there—on that page. I want you to see him."

January 3, 1941

Sweetheart,

If you hold this in your hand, I will never hold that hand again. And the thought of that is unimaginable—impossible, because you are so real. And because I am. Here is my hand holding down the page, here is the other hand, writing.

I could say that one foot put in front of the other has led me here, but that would be a lie. If there is a plan, it is one we set in motion—we put our hands out, reach for something, and that sets the ball silently rolling down its track toward what will happen. My father put down his sword and shield, Emma, simply gave up, and I cannot answer why. I picked it up. I carried it forward. I left Franklin, went to college, became a doctor, and then one winter afternoon, I walked into a room where you were. Oh my love, nothing has been sweeter in my life than loving you, but I am leaving. And I cannot answer why.

In fairy tales, my darling, the dead watch over the living. But right now, you are reading what I am writing and so we are together, here. It is no tale. I am right here, my pen on the paper scratching out your name, Emma Emma Emma. And oh, how I loved you, Emma. You were my home.

But this is what I want to say—look up, right now. Take your eyes off this page, and look up. Miss James, I think, will be right near you. She will give you this letter and, from what I know, will wait for you to read it. She will wait. She will keep watch. And others, too. You are not alone. We are all around you, dead and living.

Look up—.
Will.

Frankie shivered.

I'm not going home, he'd said, just after he'd looked at Frankie and said, *it all adds up.*

When she looked up, Emma was watching her and smiled. And it was with a shock of relief that Frankie realized she was never going to tell. She was never going to hand the letter she had brought to Emma. She had carried it up here, and she would carry it away. The news had come. Will Fitch was dead. Iris had given Emma this last letter, the letter he had meant her to read when he died. Frankie had nothing to add but Will's happiness that night beside her in the dark, and she would not pass that on. She crossed the room, sank down beside the slight woman in the chair, put her arms around her, and held her.

And the seed that had lain curled in Frankie's heart all this while unfurled. Petal after white petal opened slowly from her heart and started reaching up and out. Some stories don't get told. Some stories you hold on to. To stand and watch and hold it in your arms was not cowardice. To look straight at the beast and feel its breath on your flanks and not to turn—one could carry the world that way.

They sat together, the four of them, a little longer, before Harry rose slowly to his feet. It was Thursday. It was the end of the afternoon. It was time to pick up and carry on to the other side of the day.

AND THOUGH SHE KNEW Harry was going to go back down the hill and to his watch, and that she'd see him later, Iris didn't want him to leave; she wanted him to stay a little longer here and then to come and sit in the back room of the post office, and then when it was time to close, to take down the flag and walk her home. She wanted him near and followed him out onto Emma's porch.

He had turned around at the bottom of the stairs and looked up at her, and she smiled down at him and nodded very slightly, made shy by the women in the quiet room behind her.

All that he loved in this world stood there above him. And as he looked at her, the word *Always* came into his head and stopped there. "See you tonight," he called as he opened the door of his truck and climbed inside.

It was five-thirty on a Thursday afternoon. Across the green, the lights were on in Alden's store and along the shuttered street the yellow bands glowed through the slats. Harry climbed up the town hall stairs quickly, without thinking, urging his body upward as though he were going to meet someone. At the top, he paused, winded. The bells above his head struck the half hour, and as the clamor died away Harry closed his eyes.

He thought of Will Fitch gone. He thought of Emma. And he watched the grocer's daughter come down the post office steps—annoyed to see it closed—stop and tuck her hair inside her scarf before she started away swiftly along Front Street. He followed her all the way to the break in the fish houses where the harbor appeared. The waves in the window's old glass shivered her form so she seemed like water walking on water. Her red scarf appeared and disappeared between the dark green of the beeches. He followed her, like a lighthouse keeper, to the end of Front Street and all the way out of sight.

He skimmed his gaze back across the roofs of town and toward the center and the harbor beyond and paused. Then Harry stood up and marked the thirty feet down the town hall attic to the window facing out to sea.

He raised the binoculars and anchored his elbows on the window ledge before him. The sun bounced off the chop in the near stretch, the tips of the waves like white kerchiefs waving. There was a record run on horse mackerel, and the trap boats were returning to the pier with fish so big caught in their weirs, the tail ends had to be sawed off and tucked inside the gutted bodies to fit the four-foot boxes stacked and stapled and bound up Cape. He slid his gaze off ten degrees to the east. Nothing. He leaned forward.

Far to the east, beyond the fishing boats, what looked like the gray shadow of a whale broke the surface of the water, waves pouring off its sides. It nosed forward slowly, the high wide turret of the U-boat climbing up into the empty air. Long and low along the water, the dark gray menace showed only its top half.

"Holy God," he breathed.

The U-boat stopped forward propellers and the gray shoulders of the sub rocked, holding steady, its metal sail fifteen feet above the waves. The Germans inside must have no idea how far in they had come; any farther and they would beach. Harry lowered his binoculars, barely breathing.

He raised them again and watched as the head and shoulders of a man climbed onto the bridge at the top of the sail, followed by what looked like an officer.

Come on. His heart raced, nearly laughing at the joke—they had come and here he was. Far away and up here behind glass. *Come on, you fuckers,* his eyes on the German sailor who had swung himself onto the rim of the bridge and was lightly pulling himself to standing, settling his body against the roll of the submarine beneath him. The officer raised a pair of binoculars and started to scan the shore.

"Come on, come a little closer," Harry whispered. "Come on in, you fuckers. You're going to run out of water."

A massive knock inside his chest made him drop his binoculars and grab for the windowsill to catch his breath.

Another knock came inside, and this one dropped him to his knees. He opened his mouth to shout—It is coming. They are coming. And a sound he'd never heard came from down inside him, came up through his throat, somewhere between a groan and a laugh, and the knock inside had spread sideways, and he closed his eyes to shut it away. He picked himself up from the ground, stumbling down the length of the attic where the rope to the tower bell hung. He could see it. He groaned again, the pain knocking his breath away, and grabbed hold of the line and pulled, grunting, not breathing. A feeble iron tap sounded. Another knock came at his heart, this time shutting out the light in the room. He pulled. Pulled with all his last life. Far away, there was a great clash. Again, one last time. Another crash. He had always known it. They had come.

28.

T HE FUNERAL for Harry spilled out of the church—some came from as far away as Bourne. He had been a private man, and he left no one behind, but the people sitting in the pews for Reverend Vine's eulogy felt the going all the more for the little said. He had been sitting up there in that tower so long, people couldn't get used to the idea that he wasn't still watching out for Germans.

Or that he had been right all along. When Harry had pulled the bell rope before he collapsed, several people had looked up toward the town hall tower but dismissed it as birds, the wind. But when Tom and Will Jakes, hauling far down the leeside of the back shore, caught sight of the U-boat surfacing, they'd tucked in their gear and sped home. And it was the two of them who stumbled on Harry's body beneath the bell rope. They'd looked at him and grabbed the rope and pulled, and pulled, and pulled again—Harry Harry Harry. And the bells kept on ringing all afternoon. And when the winds changed in the late afternoon, the sound of bells from up Cape kept coming, right across the harbor.

Reverend Vine finished and Jigg Boggs and Johnny Cripps, Frank Niles, Lars Black, and the Jakes came forward and hoisted the coffin onto their shoulders, leading the mourners out of the church. Frankie followed Emma and the congregation out, and stood at the top of the stairs watching the coffin being slid into the hearse. Drawn along by the silent line of people, the two of them walked behind the car. The fog had come in and settled a pale, misting curtain gleaming on their shoulders and hair. Halfway to the cemetery, Frankie turned and retraced her steps.

In the middle of the perfect fog-heavy green, Iris had come out of the church and was standing alone. The town was pushed back. The postmistress stood at its center and tipped her head back to let the wet fall on her face. If Harry were looking, Frankie thought, he would see this dark figure at the center of the swirling damp commotion, the moving air, full of silence and her grief. Through the webbing of the bare trees, there was no light shining in the window at the top of town hall. The eye had shut.

The casual way that one thing led to another, slick as a rope uncoiling and dropping silent into the sea, was proof positive that Death—if you could catch him—wore a smile. After all, it wasn't *why?* It was *that's it?*

That's it? That was how Harry Vale died? That was the ending?

There was an odd, regular sound coming from the direction of the post office. Iris had left the spot where she'd been standing on the green. At first Frankie thought what she heard was a tennis ball being hit against the side of the wall. *Pock. Pock.* She stood still, listening. *Pock* and then a pause. *Pock. Pock.* Iris was standing in the post office yard with an ax, leveling it at the flagpole. She raised and swung again.

"What are you doing?" Frankie cried.

If Iris heard her, she paid no attention.

"Stop!" Frankie started running toward the woman bent around the ax. The postmistress set the blade of the ax on the whitewashed flagpole again and swung. The wood began to split as the iron went past the midpoint and the sound of splintering ran up and down in warning.

"Stop!" Frankie cried from the bottom of the post office stairs.

Iris lifted the ax over her shoulder and swung it down again. The far rim of the pole was thinning under the blade. Soon it would topple.

The job was nearly done, and she gave the ax a violent yank toward her. The wood groaned, just as the top of the pole wavered an instant in the autumn air before giving over. It was then that Iris saw that the flag was still flying—she'd never thought to pull it down before setting at the pole. The great cloth sailed behind the falling spindle, and seemed to Frankie like a maiden plummeting, followed by her streaming hair.

The flagpole cracked like a bone, the flag cascading across the post office steps as the top of the pole wedged itself in the iron railing. Iris was leaning on the butt of the ax catching her breath when she looked up and saw Frankie standing there. Without a word, Iris went to the spot on the pole where the halyards were cleated and began to untangle the lines. Frankie pushed open the gate to the yard and climbed to help, but Iris pushed her hand away roughly. Frankie didn't have the courage to move away. Iris unhitched the flag and gathered it up in a bundle in her arms, passed Frankie on the stairs, and went with it into the post office. The door closed behind her.

Without the flag the fallen pole, cracked across the post office yard, looked obscenely bare.

The postmistress came back out and stood in the doorway, stood there staring at the toppled pole.

"Iris?"

Iris stepped across the fallen pole and walked down to the spot where she'd dropped the ax. Then without warning, she raised the ax and swung it down again.

Frankie jumped. Iris swung again, aiming for the same spot. Her strong arms swung and hit steady as a piston. Tears were streaming down her cheeks, but she didn't show any signs of stopping. After five blows, the fallen pole had been severed in two. Iris shoved the top piece down the stairs with her foot, so that the two halves rested at the bottom. Then she came after them and began to chop the near one into halves again. Half and half again, half and half again, splitting the flagpole into kindling without looking up. The ax swung over her head and down, over her head and down again, in atonement.

Heartsick, Frankie turned away and began the walk out of town and up Yarrow Road. The lights of the houses strung her along until she reached the empty stretch of dunes at the edge where the three lights ahead were Emma's, her own, and the outside light of the postmistress's cottage up there at the very end. She stopped walking and turned around.

Through the gathering darkness behind her, the squares and pockets of home lamps shone. She pulled her sweater tightly around her as a truck engine grumbled behind her, climbing slowly up the hill, and Frankie moved into the grasses to get out of the way. Slowly it gained on her, and she stopped to let it pass. It climbed the hill on the road out of town, passed the Fitch house, where it shuddered and went quiet and then caught itself at the top. The gears shifted as it crested, gathered speed, and fled off and away out of town, the grumble growing higher and more distant until it had gone.

There in the quiet, in the dark, Frankie stopped.

Behind her in the town, the postmistress pulled open the door and passed through into the post office and snapped off the lobby lights. Ahead of her, the three roofs were commas on the line out of town.

Hssss. Hsss. Speak, speak into the tape, Frankie heard herself broadcast into the night through the open windows of the cottage.

My name is Thomas. I live in a village in Austria, in the mountains—

"Otto," Frankie whispered.

He had walked out onto the porch, his arms crossed over his chest, as Thomas's voice carried out into the wind replaced by the little boy saying *Franz. Franz Hofmann,* his mother whispered. *Go on,* Frankie's voice sang out. *Speak into here. Say your name. Inga?* said the sister, shyly. *Inga Borg?* The brother laughed and took his turn. *I am Litman. We have papers.* The voices peeled in the sky, the surf behind them. *Tell them,* the man in the café at Mulhouse demanded, jabbing his finger toward her. *Tell them what?* Frankie heard herself asking. *Tell America what? De moi,* his voice raged into the air. *Dites-le de moi.* Frankie listened to the people she had listened to for months—*Qu'est-ce qu'elle fait, cette madame? Elle entends, Papa. My name is Susanna, and this is my father. He is Lucien. Lucien Bergolas.* There was the lower sound of the father speaking to his daughter. *Oui, oui Papa. He wants to say he is Lucien Alexandre Bergolas de Maille*—their voices catching in the wind, her cottage like a mouth, her cottage speaking, and Otto in front of them, daring anyone to interrupt.

Here—she turned and looked across the lawns to Emma's house. Here we are. Here we all are.

W*HAT HAPPENS TO a story around its edges?* Will had asked. *What happens after the part you gave us?* If there is a question that falls at our feet, an unanswerable question, the one that we do not know we have picked up to carry forward through the years, then this was mine. A story like a snapshot is caught, held for a moment, then delivered. But the people in them go on and on. And what happens next? What happens?

The story knew. Didn't I say that, long ago? Didn't I hurl that at the postmistress as proof that her faith in order was amiss? An eyelid shutters open and shut, separating this moment from the next, inside from outside. What is remembered from what is seen. And some moments we are allowed to see it all, all at once. Our lives moving backward and forward—so we are one in a million—that phrase that annihilates or transcends, depending.

Did Will love Emma? I'm certain he did. The memory of his hand wrapped around my arm, and his whisper, *this part of her makes you want to hold on*, still made me shiver sometimes when others touched me there, because I remember the longing in his voice to touch his wife there where he was touching me. He loved her with all his heart. But he could not stay. His fight with the world meant he had to turn his face away from his home and his heart and walk into battle. Why? It's the mystery at the core, the thing that kept me walking up and down streets, in and out of people's houses and their lives, asking questions. All around me, all my life, the glorious spectacle of human beings being.

And this vast, contradictory show I've reported, I'm leaving soon.

But not before I tell you the last part. I carried the doctor's letter from London, across Europe, back home, and up to the door of the woman to whom it was addressed. I knocked and she answered and I looked at her and did not speak. I carried it but I never let it go. It lies unopened here in my desk. That's all I have written, that's all I have to tell. That's what the story knew.

Note

Though there is no evidence of a German U-boat beaching in Cape Cod, there were numerous close calls. As early as February 1941, Germany's Admiral Dönitz ordered a feasibility study of a surprise U-boat assault on the East Coast, and by January 1942, the first U-boat rose successfully, undetected, in the channel of New York Harbor. Throughout most of 1942, German U-boats ran so close to the Eastern Seaboard that they watched the dark silhouettes of people walking up and back along the beachside promenades against the lights of hotels, cars, and houses. The high hulls of the tankers steaming toward Europe with food and supplies were lit up as well, making them fantastic, easy marks. Of 397 ships sunk by U-boats in the first six months of 1942, 171 were sunk off the Atlantic Coast from Maine to Florida, some within view of people onshore.

Though she could not have had access to the portable disk recorder in 1941, what Frankie uses is a prototype of what came into common usage in 1944, ultimately enabling reporters to make live recordings from the battlefield. I took liberty with the date because World War II was the first war that was brought into people's living rooms by radio, and I wanted to highlight the power of the voice to convey the untellable, the refugees speaking into an air into which they will vanish.

Edward R. Murrow's broadcast in chapter one; his broadcast and Sevareid's comments in chapter two; and the broadcast attributed to Ernie Pyle in chapter eight are quoted from *World War II on the Air: Edward R. Murrow and the Broadcasts That Riveted a Nation* by Mark Bernstein and Alex Lubertozzi (Sourcebooks, 2003).

Martha Gellhorn's comment to Frankie in chapter twenty-four is a reconfiguration of what she wrote in her introduction to *The Face of War* (Simon and Schuster, 1959). "I belonged to a Federation of Cassandras, my colleagues the foreign correspondents, whom I met at every disaster."

Walter Lippmann's remarks about war in chapter eleven are quoted from "The Atlantic and America: The Why and When of Intervention," *Life*, April 7, 1941.

Acknowledgments

Many people steered me straight in the course of researching this book—from the operations of a rural post office, to the mechanics of a submarine, to the physics of childbirth, to the world of radio broadcasting—and I'd like to thank Bob Smith, Bill Matzelevich, Whitney Pinger, Justin Webb of the BBC, Kevin Klose of NPR, and Bill Godwin and Brian Belanger at the Radio & Television Museum in Bowie, Maryland, for their generous answers to all my questions.

Maud Casey, Sean Enright, Linda Kulman, Susannah Moore, Rebecca Nicolson, Howard Norman, Linda Parshall, Claudia Rankine, and Joshua Weiner kept me on course during the writing of this book, not only reading drafts but asking essential questions of it and of me. There are hardly words enough to give them for what they gave me throughout these past years.

I am so grateful to the Virginia Center for the Creative Arts for time and space granted to me at a crucial time.

And last, without Stephanie Cabot's persistence and great good humor and Amy Einhorn's uncanny ability to see through into the heart of the matter, time and time again, this book quite simply would never have come to be.

And I am indebted to the following works for helping me to imagine the times: Mark Bernstein and Alex Lubertozzi's *World War II on the Air*; Penny Colman's *Where the Action Was: Women War Correspondents in World War II*; Stanley Cloud and Lynne Olson's *The Murrow Boys: Pioneers on the Front Lines of Broadcast Journalism*; Michael Gannon's *Operation Drumbeat: The Dramatic True Story of Germany's First U-Boat Attacks Along the American Coast in World War II*; Martha Gellhorn's *The Face of War*; Doris Kearns Goodwin's *No Ordinary Time: Franklin & Eleanor Roosevelt: The Home Front in World War II*; Gavin Mortimer's *The Longest Night: The Bombing of London on May 10, 1941*; Laurel Leff's *Buried by the Times: The Holocaust and America's Most Important Newspaper Reporting World War II: Part One: American Journalism 1938–1944* (Library of America, 1995); Nancy Caldwell Sorel's *The Women Who Wrote the War*; and Mary Heaton Vorse's *Time and the Town: A Provincetown Chronicle*.

The Story Behind the Story

When I lived in a small town at the tip of Cape Cod, I used to watch the woman who delivered the mail walking up and down the street carrying her mailbag. I wondered if she ever read the postcards she was carrying, since she could. And I wondered if she kept the secrets, which she must have, about all of us. One afternoon, I had a vivid image of this woman standing in front of the sorting boxes in the back room of the post office with an envelope in her hand. I saw her standing there looking down at what she held, deciding, and then simply sliding the letter into her pocket. So Iris James, the postmistress, was born.

At the time, I remember thinking—great, there's my next novel.

But whose letter was she holding, and why? I realized that in order for the novel to have any suspense, it had to be set during a time when an undelivered letter might actually matter—when the delay might create all sorts of mayhem. Because I had a whole stash of letters between my grandparents, written during the time my grandfather was serving in the Navy in the Pacific during World War II, I decided to set it then, plumbing their letters for atmosphere; and the letter the postmistress chose not to deliver would be from a man writing back to his wife on the home front.

So I had the outlines of a story, but still no idea what the story was about. In search of details that might trigger the novel's direction, I

spent months trolling through *Life* magazines from the war years, bon-
ing up on every aspect of the war—stumbling upon Edward R. Murrow's broadcast of the Blitz in London, reading news reports of the
refugees fleeing Europe in the summer of 1941, and discovering the
firsthand report of a German U-boat captain who surfaced undetected
in New York Harbor in January of 1942 and watched the lights of cars
hum up and down the West Side Highway, unbeknownst to the city's
inhabitants.

As my dim sense of the time period grew brighter, I began to write the
story of Emma and Will, how Iris James stood at the center of the town,
and of her unexpected love for Harry Vale, a man who was convinced
that the Germans were coming. One hundred pages into this town and
this time, Frankie Bard stepped off the bus from Boston, arriving—
completely unexpectedly—into the story.

But how did these characters combine to make a novel? How did their
three stories lead to the moment at the sorting boxes when Iris decides
not to deliver a letter? I still hadn't a clue.

The one morning in the spring of 2001, I opened the newspaper to
the now iconic photograph of a Palestinian father and his son crouched
behind a bunker, caught in the crossfire between Israeli and Palestinian fighters, the son burrowed into his father's lap as the father tries to
protect him from bullets. The photograph captures the moment just
before the boy is, in fact, shot and killed. And the fact that I—sitting at
breakfast in Chicago, my own son reading the comics beside me—could
see the last second of this boy's life was unbearable. I wanted to write
about this somehow—this aspect of war and its terrifying accidents and
how we come to terms with the fact that wars are being waged *right now*,
even as I write (and you read) these words. How do we *imagine* that
simultaneity?

A few months later, I moved with my family to Washington, D.C.,
and so I was there on September 11. The city's reaction to the attacks—
the F16s flying overhead for weeks afterward, the tanks in the street, the

signs that went up along major streets labeled EVACUATION ROUTE, the articles in *The Washington Post* detailing which of our neighborhoods would be affected by a dirty bomb, based on prevailing wind patterns—crystallized for me what it must have felt like in the United States immediately after Pearl Harbor. The question of how we know when we are really in danger as a nation became suddenly central. How do you come to understand that the moment you may be in is historic, and what do you do about it? What must it have been like for Americans trying to make sense of the news they were receiving from abroad?

I realized I wanted to write a war story that did not take place on the battlefield, but showed us around the edges of a war photograph or news report into the moments just after or just before what we read or see or hear.

By this time, I had read so much war reporting by the great journalists of the era—Martha Gellhorn, William Shirer, Ernie Pyle, Wes Gallagher—that the figure of the war correspondent had become compelling. But when I read that Bill Paley, the head of CBS, had decided—in a bid for radio's dominance over print journalism—that the war was to be carried live, I realized that the story of the person who records the war, who narrates the war, who then goes on into war's dailiness after making a broadcast, was one I wanted to tell.

As I began to haunt the Radio & Television Museum in Bowie, Maryland, listening to as many old broadcasts as I could, I realized that the immediacy of live reporting proved to be a double-edged sword: On the one hand, it brought a listener directly to the war. However, the rules of objectivity demanded that broadcasters had to walk a tight line, keeping emotion out of their voices, trying to prevent their voices from cracking. What would it be like, I wondered, for that voice carrying the war to be a woman's?

With a handful of notable exceptions, war reporting remained largely an all-male club. This was even more true in radio, where there was a distinct prejudice against the sound of women's voices. Betty Wason and Mary Marvin Breckinridge were two women who broadcast from Europe in the early years of the war; Breckinridge, in fact, worked for Murrow for the first six months of the Blitz. They served as Frankie Bard's inspiration.

The deeper my research took me, the more I thought about the position of those who can see what is going on, or see parts of what is going on, and are powerless to do anything but try to turn people's heads in that direction. Frankie Bard's epiphany at the center of the novel—when she realizes that she has seen someone die and knows the ending of a story his parents will never hear—carries the great sorrow implicit in the responsibility of knowledge. And I realized that what happened to Frankie in Europe was that the responsibility of carrying the voices of all the people she meets, whose endings she cannot know, grows unbearable. The portable disc recorder (which was not, in fact, put into wide use by the BBC and CBS until a little later in the war) became a vehicle for her to save them somehow.

And this became for me the central question of the novel: How do you bear (in both senses of the word) the news?

How Iris and Frankie come to betray everything they stand for—that mail must be delivered, that truth must be reported—is the war story I hoped to tell. It is the story that lies around the edges of the photographs, or at the end of the newspaper account. It's about the lies we tell others to protect them, and about the lies we tell ourselves in order not to acknowledge what we can't bear: that we are alive, for instance, and eating lunch, while bombs are falling, and refugees are crammed into camps, and the news comes toward us every hour of the day. And what, in the end, do we do?